The Last One

ALEXANDRA OLIVA

MICHAEL JOSEPH
an imprint of
PENGUIN BOOKS

MICHAEL JOSEPH

UK | USA | Canada | Ireland | Australia
India | New Zealand | South Africa

Michael Joseph is part of the Penguin Random House group of companies
whose addresses can be found at global.penguinrandomhouse.com.

First published in the USA by Ballantine Books, an imprint of Penguin Random House LLC 2016
First published in Great Britain by Michael Joseph 2016

001

Set in 13.5/15.75 pt Bembo Book MT Std
Typeset by Jouve (UK), Milton Keynes
Printed in Great Britain by Clays Ltd, St Ives plc

A CIP catalogue record for this book is available from the British Library

HARDBACK ISBN: 978–0–718–18250–2
TPB ISBN: 978–1–405–92317–0

www.greenpenguin.co.uk

The Last One

0.

The first one on the production team to die will be the editor. He doesn't yet feel ill, and he's no longer out in the field. He went out only once, before filming started, to see the woods and to shake the hands of the men whose footage he'd be shaping; asymptomatic transmission. He's been back for more than a week now and is sitting alone in the editing studio, feeling perfectly well. His T-shirt reads: COFFEE IN, GENIUS OUT. He taps a key and images flicker across the thirty-two-inch screen dominating his cluttered workstation.

The opening credits. A flash of leaves, oak and maple, followed immediately by an image of a woman who described her complexion as 'mocha' on her application, and aptly so. She has dark eyes and large breasts barely contained in an orange sport top. Her hair is a mass of tight black spirals, each placed with perfection.

Next, panoramic mountains, one of the nation's northeastern glories, green and vibrant at the peak of summer. Then, a rabbit poised to bolt and, limping through a field, a young white man with buzzed-off hair that glints like mica in the sun. A close-up of this same man, looking stern and young with sharp blue eyes. Next, a petite woman of Korean descent wearing a blue plaid shirt and kneeling on one leg. She's holding a knife and looking at the ground. Behind her, a tall bald man with panther-dark skin and a week's worth of stubble. The camera zooms in. The woman is skinning a rabbit. This is followed by another still, the man with the dark skin, but this time without the stubble.

I

His brown-black eyes meet the camera calmly and with confidence, a look that says *I mean to win*.

A river. A gray cliff face dotted with lichen – and another white man, this one with wild red hair. He clings to the cliff, the focus of the shot manipulated so that the rope holding him fades into the rock, like a salmon-colored slick.

The next still is of a light-skinned, light-haired woman, her green eyes shining through brown-rimmed square glasses. The editor pauses on this image. There's something about this woman's smile and the way she's looking off to the side of the camera that he likes. She seems more genuine than the others. Maybe she's just better at pretending, but still, he likes it, he likes her, because he can pretend too. The production team is ten days into filming, and this woman is the one he's pegged as Fan Favorite. The animal-loving blonde, the eager student. The quick study with the easy laugh. So many angles from which to choose – if only it were his choice alone.

The studio door opens and a tall white man strides in. The editor stiffens in his chair as the off-site producer comes to lean over his shoulder.

'Where do you have Zoo now?' asks the producer.

'After Tracker,' says the editor. 'Before Rancher.'

The producer nods thoughtfully and takes a step away. He's wearing a crisp blue shirt, a dotted yellow tie, and jeans. The editor is as light-skinned as the producer but would darken in the sun. His ancestry is complicated. Growing up, he never knew which ethnicity box to check; in the last census he selected white.

'What about Air Force? Did you add the flag?' asks the producer.

The editor swivels in his chair. Backlit by the computer monitor, his dark hair shimmers like a jagged halo. 'You were serious about that?' he asks.

'Absolutely,' says the producer. 'And who do you have last?'

'Still Carpenter Chick, but –'

'You can't end with her now.'

But that's what I'm working on is what the editor had been about to say. He's been putting off rearranging the opening credits since yesterday, and he still has to finish the week's finale. He has a long day ahead. A long night too. Annoyed, he turns back to his screen. 'I was thinking either Banker or Black Doctor,' he says.

'Banker,' says the producer. 'Trust me.' He pauses, then asks, 'Have you seen yesterday's clips?'

Three episodes a week, no lead time to speak of. They might as well be broadcasting live. It's unsustainable, thinks the editor. 'Just the first half hour.'

The producer laughs. In the glow of the monitor his straight teeth reflect yellow. 'We struck gold,' he says. 'Waitress, Zoo, and, uh . . .' He snaps his fingers, trying to remember. 'Rancher. They don't finish in time and Waitress flips her shit when they see the' – air quotes – ' "body." She's crying and hyperventilating – and Zoo snaps.'

The editor shifts nervously in his seat. 'Did she quit?' he asks. Disappointment warms his face. He was looking forward to editing her victory, or, more likely, her graceful defeat in the endgame. Because he doesn't know how she could possibly overcome Tracker; Air Force has his tweaked ankle working against him, but Tracker is so steady, so knowledgeable, so strong, that he seems destined to win. It is the editor's job to make Tracker's victory seem a little less inevitable, and he was planning to use Zoo as his primary tool in this. He enjoys editing the two of them together, creating art from contrast.

'No, she didn't quit,' says the producer. He claps the shoulder of the editor. 'But she was *mean*.'

The editor looks at Zoo's soft image, the kindness in those green eyes. He doesn't like this turn of events. This doesn't fit at all.

'She yells at Waitress,' the producer continues, 'tells her she's the reason they lost. All this shit. It's fantastic. I mean, she apologizes like a minute later, but whatever. You'll see.'

Even the best among us can break, thinks the editor. That's the whole idea behind the show, after all – to break the contestants. Though the twelve who entered the ring were told that it's about survival. That it's a race. All true, but. Even the title they were told was a deception. Subject to change, as the fine print read. The title in its textbox does not read *The Woods,* but *In the Dark.*

'Anyway, we need the updated credits by noon,' says the producer.

'I know,' says the editor.

'Cool. Just making sure.' The producer purses his fingers into a pistol and pops a shot at the editor, then turns to leave. He pauses, nodding toward the monitor. The screen has dimmed into energy-saving mode, but Zoo's face is still visible, though faint. 'Look at her, smiling,' he says. 'Poor thing had no idea what she was in for.' He laughs, the soft sound somewhere between pity and glee, then exits to the hall.

The editor turns to his computer. He shakes his mouse, brightening Zoo's smiling face, then gets back to work. By the time he finishes the opening credits, lethargy will be settling into his bones. The first cough will come as he completes the week's finale early tomorrow morning. By the following evening he will become an early data point, a standout before the explosion. Specialists will strive to understand, but they won't have time. Whatever this is, it lingers before it strikes. Just along for the ride, then suddenly behind the wheel and gunning for a cliff. Many of the specialists are already infected.

The producer too will die, five days from today. He will be alone in his 4,100-square-foot home, weak and abandoned, when it happens. In his final moments of life he will unconsciously lap at the blood leaking from his nose, because his tongue will be just that dry. By then, all three episodes of the premiere week will have aired, the last a delightfully mindless break from breaking news. But they're still filming, mired in the region hit first and hardest. The production team tries to get everyone out, but they're on Solo Challenges and widespread. There were contingency plans in place, but not for this. It's a spiral like that child's toy: a pen on paper, guided by plastic. A pattern, then something slips and — madness. Incompetency and panic collide. Good intentions give way to self-preservation. No one knows for sure what happened, small scale or large. No one knows precisely what went wrong. But before he dies, the producer will know this much: *Something went wrong.*

I.

The door of the small market hangs cracked and crooked in the frame. I step through warily, knowing I'm not the first to seek sustenance here. Just inside the entrance, a carton of eggs is overturned. The sulfurous innards of a dozen Humpty Dumptys cake the floor, long since past possible reassembly. The rest of the shop has not fared much better than the eggs. The shelves are mostly empty and several displays have been toppled. I note the camera mounted in the corner of the ceiling without making eye contact with the lens, and when I step forward a ghastly stench rushes me. I smell the rotten produce, the spoiled dairy in the open, unpowered coolers. I notice another smell too, one I do my best to ignore as I begin my search.

Between two aisles, a bag of corn chips has spilled onto the floor. A footprint has reduced much of the pile to crumbs. A large footprint with a pronounced heel. A work boot, I think. It belongs to one of the men – not Cooper, who claims not to have worn boots in years. Julio, perhaps. I crouch and pick up one of the corn chips. If it's fresh, I'll know he was here recently. I crush the chip between my fingers. It's stale. It tells me nothing.

I consider eating the chip. I haven't eaten since the cabin, since before I was sick, and that was days ago, maybe a week, I don't know. I'm so hungry I can't feel it anymore. I'm so hungry I can't fully control my legs. I keep surprising myself by tripping over rocks and roots. I *see* them and I try to step over them, I think I am stepping over them, but then my toe catches and I stumble.

I think of the camera, of my husband watching me scavenge corn chips off a country market floor. It's not worth it. They must have left me something else. I drop the chip and heave myself upright. The motion makes my head swim. I pause, regaining equilibrium, then walk by the produce stand. Dozens of rotted bananas and deflated brown orbs – apples? – watch me pass. I know hunger now, and it angers me that they've allowed so much to go to waste for the sake of atmosphere.

Finally, a glint under a bottom shelf. I ease to my hands and knees; the compass hanging from a string around my neck falls down and taps the floor. I tuck the compass between my shirt and sports bra, noticing as I do that the dot of sky-blue paint at its bottom edge has been rubbed nearly to nonexistence. I'm so tired I have to remind myself that this isn't significant; all it means is that the intern assigned the job was given cheap paint. I lean down farther. Under the shelf is a jar of peanut butter. A small crack trickles from beneath the lid to disappear behind the label, just above the O in ORGANIC. I run my finger over the mark in the glass but can't feel the break. Of course they left me peanut butter; I hate peanut butter. I slip the jar into my pack.

The shop's standing coolers are empty, save for a few cans of beer, which I don't take. I'd hoped for water. One of my Nalgenes is empty and the second sloshes at my side only a quarter full. Maybe some of the others got here before me; they remembered to boil *all* their water and didn't lose days vomiting alone in the woods. Whoever left that footprint – Julio or Elliot or the geeky Asian kid whose name I can't remember – got the quality goods, and this is what it means to be last: a cracked jar of peanut butter.

The only area of the shop I haven't searched is behind the register. I know what's waiting for me there. The smell I

8

don't admit smelling: spoiled meat and animal excrement, a hint of formaldehyde. The smell they want me to think is human death.

I pull my shirt over my nose and approach the cash register. Their prop is where I expect it to be, faceup on the floor behind the counter. They've dressed this one in a flannel shirt and cargo pants. Breathing through my shirt, I step behind the counter and over the prop. The motion disturbs a collection of flies that buzz up toward me. I feel their feet, their wings, their antennae twitching against my skin. My pulse quickens and my breath seeps upward, fogging the bottom edges of my glasses.

Just another Challenge. That's all this is.

I see a bag of trail mix on the floor. I grab it and retreat, through the flies, over the prop. Out the cracked and crooked door, which mocks my exit with applause.

'Fuck you,' I whisper, hands on knees, eyes closed. They will have to censor this, but fuck them too. Cursing isn't against the rules.

I feel the wind but can't smell the woods. All I smell is the prop's stench. The first one didn't smell so bad, but it was fresh. This one and the one I found in the cabin, they're supposed to seem older, I think. I blow my nose roughly into the breeze, but I know it will be hours before the odor leaves me. I can't eat until it does, no matter how badly my body needs calories. I need to move on, to get some distance between me and here. Find water. I tell myself this, but it's a different thought that's sticking – the cabin and their second prop. The doll swathed in blue. This phase's first true Challenge has become a gelatinous memory that stains my awareness, always.

Don't think about it, I tell myself. The command is futile. For several more minutes I hear the doll's cries in the wind. And then – *enough* – I unfurl and add the bag of trail mix to my black backpack. I shoulder the pack and clean my glasses with the hem of the microfiber long-sleeved tee I wear under my jacket.

Then I do what I've done nearly every day since Wallaby left: I walk and I watch for Clues. *Wallaby,* because none of the cameramen would tell us their names and his early-morning appearances reminded me of a camping trip I took in Australia years ago. My second day out, I woke in a national park by Jervis Bay to find a gray-brown swamp wallaby sitting in the grass, staring at me. No more than five feet between us. I'd slept with my contact lenses in; my eyes itched, but I could see the light stripe of fur across the wallaby's cheek clearly. He was beautiful. The look I received in return for my awe felt appraising and imposing, but also entirely impersonal: a camera's lens.

The analogy is imperfect, of course. The human Wallaby isn't nearly as handsome as the marsupial, and a nearby camper waking up and shouting 'Kangaroo!' wouldn't send him hopping away. But Wallaby was always the first to arrive, the first to aim his camera at my face and not say good morning. And when they left us at the group camp it was he who reappeared just long enough to extract each desired confessional. Dependable as the sunrise until the third day of this Solo Challenge, when the sun rose without him, traversed the sky without him, set without him — and I thought, *It was bound to happen eventually.* The contract said we'd be on our own for long stretches, monitored remotely. I was prepared for this, looking forward to it, even — being watched and judged discreetly instead of overtly. Now I'd be thrilled to hear Wallaby come tromping through the woods.

I'm so tired of being alone.

The late-summer afternoon trickles by. The sounds around me are layers: the shuffle of my footsteps, the drumroll of a nearby woodpecker, the rustle of wind teasing leaves. Sporadically, another bird joins in, its call a sweet-sounding *chip chip chip chippy chip*. The woodpecker was easy, but I don't know this second bird. I distract myself from my thirst by imagining the kind of bird that would belong to that call. Tiny, I think. Brightly colored. I imagine a bird that doesn't exist: smaller than my fist, bright yellow wings, blue head and tail, a pattern of smoldering embers on its belly. This would be the male, of course. The female would be dull brown, as is so often the way of birds.

The ember bird's song sounds one final time, distantly, and then the ensemble is weaker for its absence. My thirst returns, so strong. I can feel the pinch of dehydration behind my temples. I grasp my nearly empty Nalgene, feel its lightness and the fabric of the crusty blue bandana tied around its lid loop. I know my body can last several days without water, but I can't bear the dryness of my mouth. I take a careful sip, then run my tongue over my lips to catch lingering moisture. I taste blood. I raise my hand; the base of my thumb comes back smeared with red. Seeing this, I feel the crack in my chapped upper lip. I don't know how long it's been there.

Water is my priority. I've been walking for hours, I think. My shadow is much longer now than when I left the shop. I've passed a few houses, but no more stores and nothing marked with blue. I can still smell the prop.

As I walk I try to step on my shadow knees. It's impossible but also a distraction. Such a distraction that I don't notice the mailbox until I've nearly passed it. It's shaped like a trout, the house number fashioned with wooden scales of all colors. Beside the mailbox is the mouth of a long driveway, which twists away through white oaks and the occasional birch tree. I can't see the house that must exist at the driveway's end.

I don't want to go. I haven't entered a house since a hand-ful of sky-blue balloons led me to a cabin that was blue inside, so much blue. Dusky light and a teddy bear, watching.

I can't do it.

You need water. They won't use the same trick twice.

I start up the driveway. Each step comes heavy and my foot keeps catching. My shadow is at my right, scaling and leaping from wooded trunks as I pass, as nimble as I am awkward.

Soon I see a monstrous Tudor in dire need of a new coat of its off-white paint. The house slumps into an overgrown lawn, the kind of building that as a child I would have play-believed was haunted. A red SUV is parked outside, blocking my view of the front door. After so long on my feet the SUV seems an otherworldly entity. They said no driv-ing and it's not blue, but it's here and maybe that means something. I walk slowly toward the SUV, and by extension the house. Maybe they've placed a case of water in the back of the vehicle. Then I won't have to go inside. The SUV is splattered with dried mud, the splashed pattern insisting on the substance's former liquidity. Even dry, it's not dirt but mud. It looks like an inkblot test, but I can't see any images.

Chip chip chip, I hear. *Chippy chip.*

My ember bird is back. I cock my head to judge the bird's direction and in doing so notice another sound: the gentle burble of running water. Relief engulfs me; I don't have to go inside. The mailbox was meant only to lead me to the stream. I should have heard it on my own, but I'm so tired, so thirsty. I needed the bird to bring my focus back from sight to sound. I turn around and follow the sound of flow-ing water. The bird calls again and I mouth *Thank you.* My split lip stings.

As I backtrack to find the brook, I think of my mother. She too would think I was meant to find the mailbox, but to her the guiding hand wouldn't be a producer's. I imagine her sitting in her living room, enfolded in a haze of cigarette smoke. I imagine her watching, interpreting my every success as affirmation and my every disappointment as a lesson. Co-opting my experiences as her own, as she has always done. Because I wouldn't exist without her, and for her that's always been enough.

I think too of my father, next door at the bakery, charming tourists with free samples and country wit while he tries to forget his tobacco-scented wife of thirty-one years. I wonder if he too watches me.

Then I see the brook, a measly, exquisite thing just east of the driveway. My attention snaps to and my insides rock with relief. I long to cup my hands and bring the cold wet to my lips. Instead, I finish the warm liquid in my Nalgene — half a cup, maybe. I probably should have drunk it earlier; people have died of dehydration while conserving water. But that's in hotter climates, the kinds of places where the sun strips a person's skin. Not here.

After drinking I follow the brook downstream, so I'll spot any troubling debris, dead animals or the like. I don't want to get sick again. I shuffle along for about ten minutes, putting more and more distance between myself and the house. Soon I find a clearing with a huge fallen tree at its edge, about twenty feet from the water, and I release myself to habit, clearing a circle of ground and collecting wood. What I gather, I sort into four piles. The leftmost contains anything thinner than a pencil, the rightmost anything thicker than my wrist. When I have enough to last a few hours, I pick up some dried curls of birch bark, shred them into tinder, and place them on a solid piece of bark.

I unclip a carabiner from a belt loop on my left hip. My fire starter slides along the silver metal and into my hand, which is sunburnt and crusted with dirt. The fire starter looks a bit like a key and a USB drive threaded together onto an orange cord; that's what I thought when it fell into my possession through a combination of skill and chance after the first Challenge. This was back on Day One, when I could always spot the camera and it was all exciting, even the boring parts.

After a few quick strikes, the tinder begins to smoke. Gently, I scoop it into my hand and blow, eliciting first more smoke and finally tiny flames. I quickly clip the fire starter back onto my belt loop, then, using both hands, place the tinder in the center of my clearing. As I add more tinder the flames grow and smoke saturates my nostrils. I feed the flames the smallest branches, then larger. Within minutes the fire is full, strong, though it probably doesn't look very impressive on camera. The flames are only about a foot high, but that is all I need – not a signal fire, just heat.

I pull my stainless-steel cup from my pack. It's dented and slightly charred, but still solid. After filling it with water, I place it close to the fire. While I wait for the water to heat I force myself to eat a fingerful of peanut butter. After not eating for so long, I'd have thought even my least favorite food would be ambrosial, but it's disgusting, thick and salty, and it sticks to the roof of my mouth. I prod the gummy mass with my dry tongue, thinking I must look as ridiculous as a dog. I should have pretended an allergy on the application; then they would have needed to leave me something else. Or maybe I wouldn't have been selected at all. My brain is too tight to consider the implications of not being chosen, where I would be right now.

Finally, the water boils. I give any microbes a few minutes to die, then use my ragged jacket sleeve as a potholder and pull the cup from the flame. Once the bubbles die down, I pour the boiled water into one of my Nalgenes, filling it about a third of the way.

The second batch heats more quickly. Into the Nalgene the water goes, and after a third round of boiling the bottle is full. I tighten its cap, then jam it into the muddy bottom of the stream, so that the cold water flows over the plastic almost to the rim. The blue bandana drifts with the current. By the time I've filled the second bottle, the first is nearly cold. I fill the cup and place it to boil yet again, then drink four ounces from the cooled bottle, washing peanut-butter residue down my throat. I wait a few minutes, drink four more ounces. In these short, spaced bursts I finish the bottle. The cup is boiling again and I can feel the membranes of my brain rehydrating. My headache retreats. All this work is probably unnecessary; the stream is clear and quick. Odds are the water's safe, but I took that bet once before and lost.

As I pour the latest batch of water into my bottle, I realize that I haven't built my shelter yet, and the sky is clouded as though for rain. Fading light tells me I don't have long. I push myself to my feet, wincing against the tightness in my hips. I collect five heavy branches from the woods and brace these against the leeward side of the fallen tree, longest to shortest, creating a triangular frame just wide enough to slip into. I pull a black garbage bag from my pack – a parting gift from Tyler, unexpected but appreciated – and spread it over the frame. As I scoop up armfuls of dead leaves and pile them atop the plastic bag, I think of the priorities of survival.

The rules of three. A bad attitude can kill you in three seconds; asphyxiation can kill you in three minutes; exposure in three hours; dehydration in three days; and starvation in three weeks – or is it three months? Regardless, starvation is the least of my concerns. As weak as I feel, it hasn't been that long since I ate. Six or seven days at most, and that's generous. As for exposure, even if it rains tonight it won't be cold enough to kill me. Even without a shelter, I'd be wet and miserable but probably not in danger.

But I don't want to be wet and miserable, and no matter the extravagance of their budget they can't have placed cameras in a shelter that didn't exist before I built it. I keep scooping armfuls of leaves, and when a wolf spider the size of a quarter skitters up my sleeve I flinch. The sharp movement makes my head feel too light, partially detached. The spider clings to my biceps. I flick it away with my opposite hand and watch it bounce into the leaf litter beside the debris hut. It skitters inside and I find it hard to care; they're only mildly venomous. I keep collecting duff and soon have a foot-deep layer atop my debris hut, and even more inside as padding.

I lay a few fallen branches with splayed fingers of leaves atop the structure to hold it all in place and then turn around to see the fire is barely more than coals. I'm all out of sync tonight. It's the house, I think. I'm still spooked. As I crack off small sticks and feed them to the coals, I glance back at my shelter. It's a low, rambleshack-looking mess with twigs sprouting up from all sides at every angle. I remember how carefully, how slowly, I used to construct my shelters. I wanted them to be as pretty as Cooper's and Amy's. Now all I care about is functionality, though, truth be told, the debris huts all look about the same – except for the big one we built together before Amy left. That was a beauty, topped with branches interwoven like thatch and large enough for all of us, though Randy slept off on his own.

I drink a few more ounces of water and sit beside my resuscitated fire. The sun has departed and the moon is shy. The flames flicker, a smudge on my right lens lending them a starburst sheen.

Time for another night alone.

2.

The premiere's opening shot will be of Tracker beside a river. He is dressed in black and his skin is dark, the tone of tilled earth. He has spent years cultivating the aura of a great cat, and he now exudes without effort a feline sense of power and grace. His face is relaxed, but his eyes watch the water intensely, as though hunting something in the current. There is a slight curl to Tracker's posture that will cause viewers to think he's about to pounce – on what? – and then Tracker blinks toward the sky and it suddenly seems equally likely that he will find a patch of sunlight in which to nap.

Tracker is considering his options: attempt to cross here or search for a better spot farther upstream. He's confident in his ability to leap stone to stone across the twenty-foot-wide river, which is swift but not deep, but there is one rock that troubles him. He thinks he can see it shifting in the current's force. Tracker does not like to get wet, but he admires the transformative powers of water, and it is with admiration that he smiles.

Viewers will project their own justification onto this smile. Those who do not like Tracker for reasons of race or bearing – they've seen nothing of him yet other than his standing here, so their dislike can be only bias – will think cockiness. A particularly strident off-site producer will see this shot and think with glee: *He looks evil.*

Tracker is not evil, and his confidence is well deserved. He has overcome challenges far more ominous than a quick, shallow river, and much more natural than what waits for him on the far side of the river: the first constructed Challenge.

Across the river is also where Tracker will meet his eleven competitors for the first time. He knows there will be teamwork required, but he doesn't want to think of the others as anything but competitors. He said as much in a pre-competition confessional, along with much else, but as the strongest contestant he will not be allowed a sympathetic motive. Tracker's *because* does not make the cut, and the clip inserted into this shot will be of him steely eyed before a white wall, saying only, 'I'm not here for the experience. I'm here to win.'

His strategy is simple: Be better than the others.

Tracker lingers; the shot travels over the rushing current and through thickly leafed branches to where Waitress stares at a compass. She is dressed in black yoga pants and a neon-green sports bra that sets off the red hair falling in loose curls past her shoulders. A violet bandana is tied around her neck like a scarf. She's nearly six feet tall and slender. Her waist is miniscule – 'It's remarkable her guts fit inside,' a troll will scoff online. Her face is long and pale, her complexion smoothed by a thick layer of SPF-20 foundation. Her eye shadow matches her bra, and glitters.

Waitress does not have to cross the river, she only has to use the compass to find her way through the woods. For her, this is a challenge, and the shot conveys as much: Waitress stands, her curls framing her face as she turns in a circle and studies the unfamiliar tool. She bites her bottom lip, partly because she's confused and partly because she thinks that doing so makes her look sexy.

'Is the red or the white end north?' she asks. She's been told to narrate her thoughts, and she will do this. Often.

Waitress's secret, one viewers will not be told, is that she never submitted an application. She was recruited. The men in charge wanted an attractive but essentially useless woman, a redhead if possible, since they had already chosen two brunettes and a blonde – not platinum blonde, but blonde enough, the kind of hair that would lighten in the sun. Yes, they thought; a beautiful redhead would round out the cast.

'Okay,' says Waitress. 'The red end is pointier. That has to be north.' She turns in a circle, biting her lip again. The needle settles at *N*. 'And I need to go . . . southeast.' And though the points of the compass are clearly labeled before her, she says in a singsong voice, 'Never eat shredded wheat.'

She begins walking due south, then mutters the mnemonic again and angles herself to the right. After a few steps, she stops. 'Wait,' she says. She looks at the compass, lets the needle settle, then turns left. Finally, she walks in the correct direction. She laughs a little and says, 'This isn't so hard.'

Waitress knows she is unlikely to win, but she's not here to win. She's here to make an impression – on the producers, on the viewers, on anyone. Yes, she's a full-time server at a tapas restaurant, but she starred in a candy commercial when she was six and considers herself an actress first, a model second, and a waitress third. Walking among the trees, she has a thought she will not speak: This is bound to be her big break.

Back at the river, Tracker decides the rock is a relatively minor hazard, and that the known obstacle is better than the unknown. He springs. The editor will slow the footage, as though this were a nature documentary and Tracker the great cat he secretly thinks he inhabited in a previous life. Viewers will see the length and power of his stride. They will see – a few would have noticed already, but a close-up will demand the attention of the rest – his odd but recognizable footwear, their yellow logo a tiny mid-foot scream of color on the otherwise dark expanse of him. They will see his individually sheathed toes gripping stone. They will note his balance and speed, the control Tracker has over his movement, and some of them will think, *I should get a pair of those.* But Tracker's footwear is only an accent on his control, which is beautifully expressed as he leaps from stone to stone, passing above churning water. His body seems longer in motion than it did while still, and in this too he is catlike.

The ball of his right foot lands upon the unsteady stone, which rocks forward. This is an important moment. If Tracker falls, he will become one character. If he flows onward untroubled, he will become another. The casting process has finished, but only officially.

Tracker splays his arms for balance – revealing a red bandana worn braceletlike around his right wrist – and experiences a rare moment of less than total grace; he wobbles. Then he follows the motion of the rock, and he's gone, onto the next foothold, which is steady. Seconds later, he's across, breathing with moderate exertion, dry from his clean-shaven scalp to his individualized toes, dry everywhere save for a slight dampness in his armpits, which viewers cannot see. He adjusts the straps of his sleek, nearly empty black backpack and then continues into the forest, toward the Challenge.

The wobble will be edited out. Tracker has been cast as impervious, unstoppable.

Meanwhile, Waitress stumbles over a protruding root and drops her compass. She bends from the waist to retrieve it, and gravity grants her cleavage – just as Waitress intended.

Two ends of a spectrum converge.

Between these extremes, Rancher wears a cowboy hat that looks nearly as weathered as his craggy, stubbled face, and he saunters with ease through the woods. He wears his black-and-yellow bandana in true cowboy fashion, around his neck, ready to be yanked over his mouth and nose should a dust storm arise. He is a thousand miles from his speckled Appaloosa, but riding spurs jut from his leather-bound heels. The spurs are an offering to the camera, given to Rancher by the on-site producer. Upon accepting them, Rancher flicked one to rotation. A dull edge, but an edge nonetheless. Useful, perhaps, he thought. He was also given a striped poncho to wear, but this he refused. 'What's next?' he asked. 'You want me to carry around a stack of corn tortillas and a chili pepper?'

Rancher's ancestors were once categorized as mestizo and largely dismissed by the powers-that-be. His grandfather crossed the border in the night and found work shoveling manure and milking cows at a family-owned ranch. Years later, he married the boss's daughter, who inherited the business. Their light-skinned son married a dark-skinned seamstress from Mexico City. Rancher's skin is the lightly toasted hue that resulted from that union. He is fifty-seven, and his shaggy chin-length hair is as sharply black and white as his beliefs about good and evil.

There are no obstacles between Rancher and the Challenge. Competency — or lack thereof — is not his defining feature. It is his proud, cowboy stride that is on display. His character is established in seconds.

Asian Chick is less easy to peg. She is dressed in khaki work pants and a blue plaid shirt. Her hair is long and straight, bound in a simple tar-black ponytail accented by a neon-yellow bandana, which is tied like a headband with the knot tucked away at the nape of her neck. Asian Chick wears only the makeup that was forced on her: slicks of eyeliner that further elongate her long eyes, and a smear of sparkling pink lipstick.

She scans her surroundings as she breaks the tree line and emerges into an open field. She sees a man waiting at the center of the field.

Beyond the man, across the field, Air Force steps into the sunlight.

For their military selection, the producers wanted a classic, and the man they chose is just that: close-cropped blond hair that glitters in the sun, sharp blue eyes, a strong chin perpetually thrust forth. Air Force is wearing jeans and a long-sleeved tee, but he walks as though in formal dress. Boardlike posture makes him appear taller than his five feet eight inches. His navy-blue bandana — a shade darker than official Air Force blue — is knotted around his belt at his left hip.

Air Force will be touted as a pilot, but his portrayal will include a careful omission. No mention will be made of *what* he pilots. Fighter jets, most viewers will assume — which is what they're meant to assume. Air Force is not a fighter pilot. When he flies, he moves cargo: tanks and ammunition; batteries and metal coils; magazines and candy bars to stock the shelves of the shopping malls the United States is kind enough to erect for her deployed men and women. He's a lean, year-round Santa Claus, bearing care packages from dear Aunt Sally. In an organization where fighter pilots are deities and bomber pilots fly the sun itself, his is a largely thankless job.

Air Force and Asian Chick meet at the center of the field, nod a greeting, and stand before the man waiting for them there. The host. He will not be featured until he speaks, and he will not speak until all twelve contestants have gathered.

Tracker slips from the trees behind the host. Rancher appears to the east, and with him a tall thirtysomething red-haired white man with a lime-green bandana. Soon contestants are appearing from all sides. A white woman in her late twenties with light hair and glasses, a sky-blue bandana around her wrist. A middle-aged black man, a white man barely out of his teens, an Asian man who could pass as a minor but is really twenty-six. A mid-thirties white man, and a Hispanic woman whose age is irrelevant because she's young enough and her breasts are huge and real. Each has a uniquely colored bandana visible on his or her person. Last to appear is Waitress, who is surprised to find so many people already in the field. She bites her bottom lip, and Air Force feels a throb of attraction.

'Welcome,' says the host, a thirty-eight-year-old B-list celebrity who hopes to revive his career – or at least pay off his gambling debt. He's nondescriptly handsome, with brown hair and eyes. His nose has been described in several prominent blogs as 'Roman,' and he pretends to know what this means. The host is dressed in outdoor clothing, and any shot of him speaking will include his upper chest, where a sponsor is proudly declared. 'Welcome,' he says again, in a deeper, excessively masculine voice, and he decides that when they record the real greeting, this is the voice he will use. 'Welcome to The Woods.'

A soft buzzing sound catches the attention of the contestants; Air Force is the first to turn around. 'Holy shit,' he says, an uncommon slip and the first profanity to be censored. The others turn. Behind the group, a five-foot-wide drone with a camera lens at its center hovers at eye level. Cue an additional smattering of awed profanities and a muttered 'Cool' from the light-haired woman.

The drone zips silently up into the sky. After only a few seconds it's far enough, quiet enough, to be nearly invisible.

'Where did it go?' whispers Waitress. By the time she finishes the question Tracker is the only one who can still distinguish the drone from clouds and sky.

'One of the *many* eyes that will be watching you,' the host informs the group. His voice is rich with implication, though the truth is there's only the one drone and since the contestants will be under tree cover most of the time, it's being used primarily for establishing shots.

'Now let's begin,' says the host. 'Over the next weeks, your skills will be tested and your fortitude pushed to the limit. You do have an out, however. If a Challenge is ever too tough, or if you can't stand another night being nettled by mosquitoes, simply say *"Ad tenebras dedi,"* and it's over. Remember this phrase. This is your out.' As he speaks, he hands a notecard to each contestant. 'Your *only* out. We've written it down for each of you to memorize. *Ad tenebras dedi.* I want to make this clear: Once you say this phrase, there's no coming back.'

'What's it mean?' asks Rancher.

'You will learn its meaning,' replies the host.

Black Doctor is shorter and rounder than Tracker, with a goatee. His mustard-yellow bandana covers his head. One of his white-flecked eyebrows perks as he looks at the note-card in his hand. Then a close-up confessional, trees behind him, a hint of scuffed stubble surrounding the goatee. 'It's Latin,' says Black Doctor's future self. ' "To the night, I surrender." Or "darkness," I'm not sure. It's a little pretentious for the circumstances, but I'm glad there's a safety phrase. It's good to know that there's a way out.' He pauses. 'I hope everyone can remember it.'

And then the host, sitting in a canvas camping chair by a day-lit fire, directly addressing the viewers. 'The contestants don't know everything,' he says, his soft tone and downward-tipped chin inviting the viewers to share his secret. His body language reads: We're co-conspirators, now. 'They know no one gets voted off, that this is a race – or, rather, a series of small races during which they accumulate advantages and disadvantages. What they don't know is that this race does not have a finish line.' He leans forward. 'The game will continue until only one person remains, and the only way out is to quit.' No one knows how long the show will last, not the creators, not the contestants. Their contracts said *no less than five weeks and no more than twelve,* though a fine-print footnote actually allows for sixteen weeks in the case of extenuating circumstances. '*Ad tenebras dedi,*' says the host. 'There is no other way. And regarding this, the contestants are truly *In the Dark.*'

A series of confessionals follow, all with generic wilderness backgrounds.

Waitress, who knows her only chance of cashing out is to win Fan Favorite: 'What will I do first if I win the million dollars? Go to the beach. Jamaica, Florida, I don't know, somewhere really nice. I'd take my besties with me and sit on the beach all day, drinking cosmos and anything on the menu that ends in "-tini."'

Rancher, with an honest shrug: 'I'm here for the money. I don't know what they got in store for us, but I don't plan on saying those words. I've got my boys back home taking care of the ranch, but I want them to go to college and there's no way I can pay for that and afford to lose them as workers. That's why I'm here, for my kids.'

The light-haired woman with the brown glasses. She held a spiky yellow lizard in her application video and the editor sees more to her than her hair. 'I know this sounds ridiculous,' she says, 'but I'm not here for the money. I mean, I won't say *no* to a million dollars, but I would have signed up even without a prize. I'm almost thirty, I've been married three years, it's time to take the next step.' Zoo exhales nervously. 'Kids. It's time for kids. Everyone I know with kids says it's never the same, that it changes your life, that you lose all your me time. I'm prepared for that, I'm okay with ceding some of my individuality, and, yeah, my sanity. But before that happens, before I exchange my name for the title of *Mom,* I want one last adventure. That's why I'm here, and that's why I'm not going to quit, no matter what.' She holds up the slip of paper with the safety phrase and tears it in half. The action is symbolic – she has the phrase memorized – but no less sincere for the drama of the gesture. 'So,' she says, looking at the camera with sly intensity, a smile hiding behind her straight face, 'bring it on.'

3.

I lie in my shelter well into the night, but can't sleep for the tightness I feel everywhere – legs, shoulders, back, brow, eyes. The arches of my feet are screaming, as though only the pressure of movement kept them silent throughout the day. My rehydrated body thrums, changed and needing something more.

Finally, I push my backpack out of the front of my shelter and crawl into the night. Leaves crunch beneath my palms and knees, and my loosened bootlaces drag like snakes. Cold air pinches my cheeks. Pausing, I hear crickets and chirping frogs. The brook, the wind. I think I can hear the unseen moon. I stand, leaving my glasses folded through a strap on my pack. Without them, my vision is a pixelated blur of alternating grays. Held at breast height, my palms are pale, their edges nearly crisp. I rub at the base of my left ring finger and relive the uneasy flutter of my heart when I removed the white gold band. I remember slipping it into its velvet-lined box and placing the box into my top dresser drawer. My husband was in the bathroom, trimming his beard into the even stubble I like best. He spoke more than I did on the drive to the airport, a role reversal. 'You're going to be amazing,' he said. 'I can't wait to watch.'

Later, on the short flight to Pittsburgh, I sucked back sobs and pressed my forehead to the window, sharing my anxiety with the sky but not the snoring stranger to my left. It didn't use to be so difficult to leave, but it was different before I met my husband. Before – leaving Stowe for college, that summer hiking hostel to hostel across western Europe, six months in Australia after graduating from Columbia – my fear was always tempered by excitement enough to tip the scales. Leaving was always scary, but it was never hard. But this time I not only left familiarity behind, I left happiness. There's a difference, the magnitude of which I didn't anticipate.

I don't regret New York, or Europe, or Australia. I'm not sure I regret coming here, but I do regret leaving my wedding ring behind, no matter the instructions I was given. Without my ring, the love I left feels too distant, and the plans we've made feel unreal.

At the airport he promised me the retired greyhound we'd been talking about adopting ever since we bought our house. 'We'll find a good one when you get home,' he said. 'Speckled, with some ridiculously long racing name.'

'It has to be okay with kids,' I replied, because that was what I had to say, that was the reason I gave for leaving.

'I know,' he said. 'I'll scout while you're away.'

I wonder if he's scouting right now. Working late but really scrolling through Petfinder or checking the website of the greyhound rescue organization we saw at the farmers' market a few weeks before I left. Or maybe he's finally getting a drink with the new guy, who he keeps saying seems a little lonely.

Maybe he's sitting home in the dark, thinking about me.

Standing alone in the gray night, watching leaves whisk in the wind, I need him. I need to feel his chest beat against my cheek as he laughs. I need to hear him complain of his hunger, a pain in his back, so I can put aside my own discomfort and be strong for us rather than for just myself.

Out here I have nothing of him but memory, and each night he feels less real.

I think of my last Clue. *Home Sweet Home*. Not a destination, because I can't imagine they intend for me to walk the almost two hundred miles home, but a direction. A taunt.

My stomach rumbles – louder than the crickets or the frogs – and suddenly I'm remembering what it is to feel hungry instead of just knowing I should eat. Glad for the distraction, I fish the bag of trail mix from my pack and open it. I pour about a hundred calories' worth of nuts and dried fruit into my palm. A pathetic amount, a toddler's handful. I twist the bag closed and slip it into my jacket pocket. I eat the stale raisins first, pairing them with peanuts, almonds and shattered cashew halves. The four chocolate candies I save for last. I place them on my tongue all together, press them to the roof of my mouth and feel their thin shells crack.

I used to fear that my need for him was weakness. That any concession of independence was a betrayal of my identity, a compromise of the strength I have always used to propel myself away from the familiar and toward the unknown. Out of the sticks and to the city, out of the city into a foreign land. Always pushing – until I met him: an easygoing, athletic electrical engineer raking in six figures while I scrambled for forty grand a year explaining the differences between mammals and reptiles to packs of shrill, ever-squirming schoolkids. It took me two years to recognize that he didn't care, that he would never lord the difference in our incomes over me. By the time I said 'I do,' I understood there's a difference between compromise and cooperation, and that to rely on another takes a distinctive kind of strength.

Or maybe that's just what I needed to tell myself.

A fragment of candy shell jabs my gums, almost painful, then melts away. I taste cheap milk chocolate, more a sense of sweetness than actual flavor. I bend over, stretching my hamstrings. A knotted mass of hair that was a ponytail once upon a time falls over my shoulder, and my fingers stall about twelve inches above my feet. It's been years since I've been able to consistently touch my toes without bending my knees, but I should be able to get closer than this. My inability to reach even my ankles feels like failure, and in a weird way like unfaithfulness. Every night for weeks before I left home, my husband and I held 'strategy sessions,' curled together in bed, brainstorming what I might do to succeed. Stretching was one of the things we discussed – the importance of staying limber. Tapping my shins, I tell myself that I will take the time to stretch each morning and evening from now on. For him.

I wanted to do something big. That's what I told him last winter, the statement that started it all. 'One last adventure before we start trying,' I said.

He understood, or claimed to. He agreed. He was the one who found the link and suggested I apply, because I like wilderness and once said that debris huts were cool. Offering a solution, as always, because the mathematically minded think all problems have solutions. And even if it's growing ever harder for me to feel him, I know he's watching. I know he's proud of me – I've had my moments, but I'm doing my best. I'm trying. And I know that when I get home, the distance I feel now will evaporate. It *will*.

Still, I wish I had my ring.

I crawl back into my shelter. Hours later, as I watch the sky gradually lighten through the opening of my debris hut, I know I didn't sleep – except that I remember a dream, so I must have. There was water in it; I was on a dock or a boat and I dropped him, my squirming, gurgling baby boy who didn't quite fit in my arms, and why did I have him to begin with? He slipped out of my hands and my legs wouldn't move and I watched him drift into the depths, bubbles rising from his mouth as he cried a sound like static and I stood by, helpless and unsure.

Exhausted, I ease out of my shelter and rekindle the fire. While the water heats I eat what's left of the trail mix, stare at the flames, and wait for the dream to fade, as they always do.

I was in college when I first started having nightmares about accidentally killing accidentally conceived children. I was new to sex, and underscoring every experience was my worry that the condom would break. A one-night stand would result in weeks of sporadic dreams in which I forgot my newborn child and left it somewhere like the baking interior of a car, or it rolled off a table onto a concrete floor while I wasn't looking. Once one tumbled out of my sweaty hands on a mountaintop and I watched it fall all the way to the worm-sized road below. It was worst when I was actively dating someone, when it wasn't a one-night stand but an act of love, or at least affection. The nightmares grew less frequent as I entered my mid-twenties and stopped altogether within a year of meeting my husband, the first person with whom I've ever thought I might someday be ready.

They resumed the night after the cabin Challenge. Not every night, not that I remember, but most. Sometimes when I'm awake too. I don't even have to close my eyes, just lose my focus, and I see him. Always *him*. Always a boy.

After I've filled my Nalgenes, I kick apart my shelter and quench the fire. Then I return to the same weather-cracked backcountry thoroughfare I've been following roughly east for days. I hang my compass from my neck and check my direction from time to time.

I've been walking an hour or more when a pain in my shoulder reminds me that I didn't stretch. A few hours of maybe-sleep is all it took for me to forget my promise. *Sorry,* I mouth, looking up. I pull my shoulders down and back, straighten my posture as I walk. Tonight, I think. Tonight I will stretch my every aching muscle.

I round a curve in the road and see a silver sedan ahead, parked askew with all its tires save the left rear beyond the shoulder, resting in dirt. I follow its skid marks uneasily, water bottle thumping against my hip. It's clear that the car has been placed here. There must be supplies inside, or a Clue.

My stomach tightens. I'm trying to keep my face empty of nerves – I can't see the cameras, but I know they're tucked into the branches overhead, and probably in the vehicle itself. They probably have one of those surveillance drones up high, hovering.

You are strong, I tell myself. You are brave. You are not afraid of what might be inside this car.

I look through the driver's-side window. The driver's seat is empty, and the front passenger seat cradles only fast-food detritus: wrappers stained with grease, a bucket-sized foam cup sprouting a gnawed-on straw from a brown-stained lid.

There is a rumpled blanket spread over the backseat, and a small red cooler wedged behind the passenger seat. I try the back door, and the sound of it opening is something I haven't heard in weeks: the click of the handle, the release of the seal, so distinctive and yet so ordinary. I've heard this sound thousands of times, tens of thousands. It's a sound I've come to associate with departure – an association that was unconscious until now, for the moment I open that door, hear that release, I feel my fear fade into relief.

You're leaving. You're getting out of here. You're going home. Not thoughts, but wordless assurances from myself to me. You're done, my body tells me. It's time to go home.

Then the smell hits, and a heartbeat later: realization.

I recoil, stumbling away from their decaying prop. I can see it now, the vaguely human shape beneath the blanket. It's small. Tiny. That's why I didn't see it from the window. The orb of its head was resting directly against the door, and now hangs slightly over the edge of the seat, a slick of dark brown hair slipping from beneath the covering. The nubs meant to approximate feet bulge only halfway across the seat.

This is not the first time they've pretended a child, but this is the first time they've pretended an abandoned child.

'All right,' I whisper. 'This shit is getting old.'

But it's not; each prop is as horrible and startling as the last. That's four now – five, if I count the doll – and I don't know *why*, how they fit, what they mean. I slam the door shut, and this, the sound I associate with triumphant arrival, stirs my anger further. I've hit the child-sized prop's head, caught the brown hair in the door.

Is it real hair? Did a woman somewhere shear her head thinking her keratin threads would bolster the confidence of a child fighting cancer, only to have them end up a part of this sick game? Is the donor watching, and will she recognize the hair as hers? Will she feel the impact of the car door against her own head?

Stop.

I make my way to the other side of the car, take a deep breath, hold it, and open the door on that side. I yank the cooler from the car and slam the door shut. The sound echoes in my skull.

Cooler in hand, I ease myself to the ground in front of the car and lean against the bumper. My teeth feel as though they have fused together, top to bottom, and they tremble with the strength of their connection. I sit with my eyes closed, working to relax my jaw.

The first fake corpse I saw was at the end of a Team

Challenge. The third, I think. Maybe the fourth – it's hard to remember. It was me, Julio and Heather, following the signs: red drips on rocks, a handprint in the mud, a thread caught in some thorns. We got turned around, lost the trail when it crossed a brook. Heather tripped and got wet, then bumbled into a stump or something and started whining about a stubbed toe as though she'd broken her leg. We lost a lot of time and, ultimately, the Challenge. Cooper and Ethan's group got there first, of course. That night, Cooper told me that they found their target with a fake head wound sitting near the top edge of the rock face. I remember the anger in his voice, how surprised I was to hear it. But I understood.

We watched our target tumble over the cliff.

I saw the harness under his jacket; I saw the rope. But still.

At the bottom we found a twisted mess coated in cornstarch blood. It didn't look very real, not that first time, but it was still a shock. The latex-and-plastic construct wore jeans, from which we needed to retrieve a wallet. Heather cried. Julio placed his hat over his heart and murmured a prayer. They left it to me. After I got the wallet my nerves were raw and Heather's hysterics sliced through them. I don't remember exactly what I yelled, but I know I used the word 'bimbo,' because afterward I thought, What an odd word choice, even for me. I remember everyone staring at me, the shock in their eyes. I'd worked so hard to be nice, to be someone to root for – to vote for. But enough was enough.

Walking away from that Challenge, I thought I finally understood what they were capable of. I *thought* I understood just how far they were willing to go. And I knew I had to do better. I apologized to Heather – as sincerely as I could, considering that I'd meant everything I said and only regretted saying it – and I hardened myself until I was ready for anything.

I feel myself getting harder every day. Even when I startle and soften, even when my façade breaks, it seems to me that it always comes back harder, like a muscle strengthening with use. I hate it. I hate being hard and that my hatred hardens me further. I hate that I'm already pushing the child prop from my mind, thinking instead of the cooler.

I press the button, pull the handle so the top tilts away.

A Ziploc bag stuffed with green and white mold. Beneath it, a juice box. Pomegranate blueberry. I fish out the juice box and then close the cooler. I feel as though I should return the cooler to the car, like how I spread out the components of my debris huts each morning, returning everything to its natural place. But this is different, there is nothing natural about the placement of this car, this cooler. I stand and shove the cooler against the front bumper with my foot. A moment later, juice box in hand, I am walking again.

I wonder if I'll make it home without hitting a boundary or finding another Clue – if they'll let me go that far. Have they carved out a corridor for me all the way to the coast? Even this seems possible now. Or maybe – maybe I'm not even going east. Maybe sunrise and sunset have been reduced to parlor tricks. Maybe my compass is rigged, and my magnetic north is really a remote-controlled signal easing me into an oblivious spiral.

Maybe I'll never make it home.

In the Dark – Predictions?

I've never heard of anything like this show! They just started taping yesterday and the first episode airs Monday. Monday! And the production company that did Mt Cyanide is behind it so you know the special effects are going to be INSANE. Their website calls it 'a reality experience of unprecedented scale.' Sure, it's their job to build buzz, but color me excited. What do you all think?

submitted 38 days ago by LongLiveCaptainTightPants

114 comments

top comments
sorted by: **popularity**

[-] CharlieHorse11 38 days ago
My money's on this actually being Mt Cyanide 2. The acid-spewing volcanoes are spreading! Ruuuuuuuuuuuuuuuuun!

> [-] HeftyTurtle 38 days ago
> From what I've read, they've got the budget like it is. We're talking the realm of $100 million here.

>> [-] CharlieHorse11 38 days ago
>> Mt Cyanide was twice that. I don't want half as many acid volcanoes, I want ALL the acid volcanoes.

>> [-] LongLiveCaptainTightPants 38 days ago
>> Source?

>>> [-] HeftyTurtle 38 days ago
>>> Here. Unofficial, but seems legit.

>>>> [-] LongLiveCaptainTightPants 38 days ago
>>>> Whoa. Yeah. Now I'm even more excited!

[-] JT_Orlando 37 days ago

Have you all seen the legal releases that leaked yesterday? 98 pages! Cast had to sign some crazy shit. I couldn't get through it all but of what I did read my favorite was that they had to accept 'All risks arising from engaging in vigorous physical activity in wilderness areas not readily accessible to emergency services, where conditions vary and hazards may not be readily apparent, where weather is unpredictable and where rock falls occur.' Also, 'Risks arising from poisonous flora and fauna, including risks arising from encounters with bears, coyotes, venomous snakes and other indigenous wildlife.' Full text here.

>[-] DispersingSpore 37 days ago
>
>I like 'Severe mental strain arising from solitude, prolonged periods of hunger and fatigue, and other psychologically trying conditions.'
>
>[-] Hodork123 37 days ago
>
>Standard boilerplate waivers resulting from our overly litigious society. Make it sound a lot more dangerous than it is, I bet.
>
>>[-] DispersingSpore 37 days ago
>>
>>Love it or leave it, Commie.

[-] Hodork123 38 days ago

Another wilderness survival reality show? B/c that's just what we need.

>[-] Coriander522 38 days ago
>
>Spoiler alert: It's actually a singing competition.

[-] CoriolisAffect 38 days ago

My buddy's a cameraman on the show. CaptainTight-Pants is right about the timing – it's nuts. And my friend says they've got some seriously f*cked-up shit ahead. Stay tuned.

[-] NoDisneyPrincess 38 days ago
Zombies?

> [-] CoriolisAffect 38 days ago
> As the saying goes, I could tell you but then I'd have to kill you.

>> [-] NoDisneyPrincess 38 days ago
>> ZOMBIEEEEES!!!!

[-] LongLiveCaptainTightPants 38 days ago
Rad! You should get your friend to do an AMA once it's all said and done. I'd love to know what goes on behind the scenes.

> [-] Coriander522 38 days ago
> Seconded!

> [-] CoriolisAffect 38 days ago
> I'll see what I can do.

. . .

4.

'The rules for your first Challenge are simple,' says the host, standing in the field in stark afternoon light. 'You each have a bandana and compass marked with your assigned color, or colors. For the duration of this adventure, anything meant specifically for you will be marked with those colors. Starting with' – he swivels to indicate a series of short painted sticks spaced throughout the field – 'these.'

'Sticks?' whispers Asian Chick to no one in particular. 'What do they do?'

The host shushes her, squares his shoulders, and continues. 'Using your compass, you will need to find your way to a series of control points, and ultimately to a box containing a wrapped package. Do *not* open the package.' He smiles and runs his gaze along the line of contestants, then sticks his thumbs into his front pockets, assuming a laid-back stance that implies he knows something the contestants do not, which, of course, he does. It is his privilege to know many things they do not. 'Find your colors and take your places.'

Waitress already has the compass in her hand, as do two others: Tracker and Zoo. Zoo didn't need to use her compass to reach the gathering point, but she removed it from her pack the moment taping began anyway. She smiled as she did so, and she smiled as she walked with it unnecessarily in her hand, heading a few degrees right of north – following the footpath she was told would take her to the first Challenge. She is still smiling as she looks again to the spot of paint she noticed first thing – baby blue. It is this easy smile that endears her so to her coworkers and students at the wildlife sanctuary and rehabilitation center where she works – not a zoo, but close enough. It is this easy smile that the producers suspect will endear her to viewers.

Zoo sees her stick. Her pace quickens; she's almost skipping. She took an orienteering class a few months ago. She knows to 'put red in the shed,' and to 'plug in' the compass to her chest. She knows to count her first step as 'and' and her second step as 'one.' She thinks it will be fun to put her knowledge to use. For now, this experience is a lark. She hurries to collect her instructions from a plastic bag beside the light blue stick.

A lanky young white man with wavy auburn hair cuts across Zoo's path. 'Excuse me,' says Cheerleader Boy in a snarky tone that betrays his unease. He hates the wilderness, hates that the color of the bandana he has tucked into his shirt like a pocket square is pink. He applied for the show on a dare from his squad's flyer, who, really, should be the one here – she's the bravest person he knows. Cheerleader Boy didn't expect to be selected and accepted the offer for lack of a better way to occupy the summer between his sophomore and junior years of college – and because how could he reject a chance to win one million dollars, even a minuscule chance? By the time he realized taping wouldn't start until mid-August and he would have to take a semester off from school, he was already committed.

The creators of the show all agree that the hostile tone with which Cheerleader Boy spoke to the most upbeat of the contestants is the perfect introduction to the character they've assigned him: the effeminate male so far out of his element he's more caricature than man. Confronted, the off-site producer will argue that they simply followed the story provided by this opening shot. Circular reasoning. They chose the shot, they chose the moment, this flash of one of the many facets of this young man's self. He could have been many things – scared, helpful, inquisitive – but instead he's a jerk.

Settling into place at an orange stick not far from Cheerleader Boy is Biology, who wears her bandana as a headband with the knot above her ear. Biology is gay too – see, it's fair, they'll say: You're allowed to root for her. But Biology, who teaches seventh-grade life science in a small public school, is the least threatening style of lesbian: a shapely, feminine one who holds her sexuality close. Her dark, spiraling hair is long, her light brown skin moisturized. She wears dresses to work as often as not, and tasteful makeup always. If a straight man were to imagine her with another woman, he would likely imagine himself there too.

Air Force steps up to a dark blue marker between Biology and Cheerleader Boy. He looks Biology up and down and then watches as Cheerleader Boy sighs and tries to shake his nerves from his fingertips. It's been years since the repeal of 'Don't ask, don't tell,' and Air Force doesn't assume that Cheerleader Boy will be inexperienced in the skills necessary for the coming weeks. In fact, his first thought is, *I bet he's a ringer.*

The contestants collect their instructions. The host waves to get their attention as cameramen creep into position carefully out of one another's shots. Minutes are reduced to seconds. The host shouts, 'Go!'

Tracker lopes forward, his eyes settled on some distant object. Rancher strides his easy stride. Zoo grins and starts counting to herself as she walks with her compass held perpendicular against her chest. Cheerleader Boy looks around, then studies his map and compass, unsure. Waitress turns in

41

a circle and makes brief eye contact with Biology, who shrugs.

Watching the others is Engineer. He wears his maroon-and-brown-striped bandana around his neck like Rancher's, but it looks very different on this gangly, bespectacled young Chinese American man. Engineer has never rushed into anything in his life, excepting a few nights in college when the liberal application of alcohol led to his breaking character. Once he streaked across campus. It was 4 a.m., and other than the friend who issued the dare, only two people saw him. Engineer prides himself on this memory, on his spontaneity in that moment. He wishes he could be spontaneous more often. That's why he's here – a long-pondered decision to put himself into a situation that will require spontaneity. He wants to learn.

Engineer looks at his instructions: a series of bullet points. 'One hundred and thirty-eight degrees,' he says. 'Forty-two paces.' He twists the compass housing, matches a small tick mark just shy of the 140-degree indicator to a line at the front of the compass. He doesn't know how long a pace is supposed to be, but will experiment until the answer becomes clear, as it quickly will.

The twelve contestants disperse like gas molecules to fill the space of the field.

Tracker stops at the tree line and peers into the branches above, then launches himself into the air – grabbing a stout branch with both hands. He pulls himself up into the tree. All of the contestants who are facing his direction – seven of them – stop to watch, but Zoo and Air Force are the only ones who will be shown to viewers. Zoo widens her eyes, impressed. Air Force raises an eyebrow and shakes his head, less so.

Tracker drops from the tree, landing softly on his feet in the grass below. In his hand there is a red flag. He doesn't want to leave a trail, not even the trail he is intended to follow. He stands straight, tucks the flag into his pocket, consults his instructions and compass, and heads toward his second control point.

Black Doctor struggles to find his first control point. His mistakes are twofold.

His first mistake: after setting his compass to the noted 62 degrees and turning to face that direction, he sets his gaze to the ground and starts walking. He doesn't want to miss his flag if it's hidden in the long grass. A reasonable concern from a reasonable man. But it's a proven if inexplicable fact that people are incapable of walking in a straight line while blindfolded, and Black Doctor is all but blindfolding himself by looking at the grass. With each step he veers slightly to the right, just far enough to take him off course.

His second mistake: he counts each step as a pace, instead of following the and-one-and-two cadence of orienteering. When Black Doctor reaches what he believes is his intended stopping point, he finds nothing but more grass and a low-growing bush. He pauses to observe the others and sees Air Force and Rancher find their flags. He sees Zoo find her flag. He notes that all three did so at the edge of the field, whereas he is only halfway across. He takes his bearing, looks at a tree, and then walks straight toward it.

He will find his mustard-colored marker not in that tree but one tree to the left, and he will double the amount of paces noted on his instructions for each of the following control points.

Biology and Asian Chick will learn similarly, as will Engineer and two white men so far shown only in flashes – the tall one notable for his red hair, the other not notable at all.

Waitress and Cheerleader Boy will not learn. They will

putter about the field, growing increasingly frustrated. Four times, Waitress returns to her violet marker and stalks off in roughly the correct direction, first muttering, then yelling, 'One-two-three-four . . .' stopping at forty-seven, turning circles, and tossing her hands toward the sky. She's worn a crop circle in the grass with all her pacing.

She sits, and Cheerleader Boy, equally at a loss, leaves his path and approaches her. 'I think we're doing it wrong,' he says.

'You *think*?' She waves him away. Cheerleader Boy seems like someone she might like in real life, but here he's clearly a handicap. She knows no one will help her if he's hanging about, needing help too.

The host is conspicuously absent from the shot. He's been told to step aside. He's checking his phone, expecting an email from his agent.

Tracker has reached his fourth flag and is in the lead. Air Force, Rancher and Zoo have each found three. Biology stands beneath her second, looking, looking, and then with a smile seeing.

Successes pass quickly; there's much to cover in the premiere, and successes aren't what viewers want to see.

Engineer stumbles and catches himself against a tree; a branch slaps him in the face. He recoils and rubs at the sting.

After twenty-three minutes – or, depending on one's perspective, eight including a commercial break – Tracker finds his red box. He opens it, sees the red-wrapped package and a slip of paper. He reads the paper only as confirmation. He has deduced the Challenge's finishing point from the path of the control points. Two minutes later, he steps for a second time into the field.

Waitress and Cheerleader Boy see him, and for an instant Tracker is surprised. He cannot believe that these two have beaten him. And then Cheerleader Boy says, 'You're kidding me,' and Tracker realizes they haven't yet left the field at all.

'Well done,' says the host, returned from the off-camera netherworld. He shakes Tracker's hand. 'You will learn your reward when everyone has returned. For now, you have a choice. You can relax, or you can help others in need.' He nods toward Waitress and Cheerleader Boy. Waitress is mired in gloom, and Cheerleader Boy is frustrated to the point of anger.

'Uh,' says Tracker, his first word on camera outside of pre-taping interviews. He doesn't want to help his competitors, but they both look so pathetic he finds it difficult to believe either could ever become a threat. 'Count two steps as one and keep the compass flat,' he tells them, familiar with the mistakes of beginners. 'And look straight ahead, not at your feet.'

Waitress's eyes widen as though her mind has been truly, fully blown; Cheerleader Boy rushes to his pink stick.

Air Force steps into the field. About a hundred feet to his right, only a few seconds behind, so does Zoo. Both hold their colored boxes, dueling shades of blue.

'First one to me!' calls the host. Zoo and Air Force dart toward him.

Air Force takes an easy lead, and then his right foot strikes a depression and he jolts into a hop-skip as pain shimmies through his turned ankle. He slows, favoring the foot. Zoo does not see this; she is in an all-out sprint. She reaches the host well ahead of Air Force.

'I found it!' calls Waitress from the far end of the field. A moment later Cheerleader Boy has found his first flag too.

'Those two are just starting?' asks Zoo, breathing hard and pushing her glasses up her nose. Tracker nods, looking her over. She looks fit enough. A contender, perhaps. He's noted Air Force's sudden limp, and while he hasn't dismissed the man, he's moved him down a notch in his consideration.

Zoo's microphone pack is prodding the small of her back uncomfortably after her run. She fixes it, then turns to Air Force. 'You okay?'

Air Force mutters that he's fine. The host is trying to decide if he should call for an EMT. Air Force is clearly in pain, but he is just as clearly trying to ignore that pain. And he's still on his feet. The host was told to reserve medical assistance for emergencies. This, he decides, is not an emergency. He unnecessarily informs Zoo and Air Force that they are the second and third to finish, then stands his post, waiting for the others while the first three exchange names and make small talk that will not be shown. Zoo does most of the talking.

Rancher is the next to arrive, an oak leaf speared on his right spur. He's followed closely by Biology. Five minutes later, Engineer appears, and then Black Doctor, who blinks at the field in surprise. He hadn't realized his instructions were effectively taking him in a large circle. Asian Chick and the red-haired man race for eighth place.

The red-haired man wins, and he hunches over to catch his breath. He's dressed in plain outdoor clothing with his lime-green bandana tied above his elbow like a tourniquet. But he's wearing Goth-style boots, and a heavy gold cross dangles on a chain next to his compass. The camera zooms on the cross, and then – a pre-taped statement, because the current shot cannot express this man's essence.

He is dressed in what appears to be – what is – a black graduation gown with a hand-stitched white collar. His coppery hair is gelled, and curls upward like flames. 'There are three signs of demonic possession,' Exorcist says. His voice is a grating, self-important tenor. He pokes his index finger toward the ceiling and continues, 'Abnormal strength, like a little girl overturning an SUV, which I've seen.' A second finger flips up to join the first. 'A sudden understanding of languages the individual has no right knowing. Latin, Swahili, what have you.' Three fingers. 'Having knowledge of hidden things . . . like a stranger's name or what's locked in a safe you've got no reason to know about.' He retracts his fingers, reaches down the neck of his robes, and pulls out the golden cross. 'Aversion to the sacred is a given, of course. I've seen flesh smoke at the touch of the cross.' He rubs his thumb tenderly along the charm. 'I'm not an *official* exorcist, just a layman doing the best I can with the tools I got. By my reckoning, I've sent three true demons from this mortal plane, and I've helped some two dozen folks who *thought* they were possessed banish an inner demon of a more metaphorical nature.' He smiles and there's something in his eyes — some will think he doesn't believe himself, that he's playing a part; others will think he's truly delusional; a special few will see their own reality in the one he's projecting.

'It's my calling,' he says.

In the field, Exorcist huffs, rubs some sweat from his brow with his sleeve, and stands. He looks ordinary enough here, but he's been cast as the wild card, the one whose antics will be used for filler as necessary, and to test the patience of the other contestants. He knows this, has embraced this. He is counting on viewers appreciating the brand of crazy he does best. His uniqueness will be revealed to the others in about an hour, and each and every one of the other contestants will have a thought — not an identical thought, but close enough — a thought along the lines of: I have to be in the woods with this nutjob for *how long*?

A few minutes after Exorcist's big finish, Banker comes in, the last of the contestants to receive a close-up. He has dull brown eyes and hair, and a nose like the host's but bigger. His black-and-white bandana is a wide headband, and askew. Banker has been cast as filler; his job alone means most viewers will root against him, thinking he doesn't need the money, doesn't deserve it, that his presence on the show is proof of the endless greed systemic to his profession. He's a swindler, a parasite, as scrupleless as a carpetbagger.

Banker can be crammed into this stereotype, but it doesn't fit him. He grew up the eldest son of middle-class Jews. Many of his childhood peers spent their adolescence in a haze of pot and apathy, but Banker worked hard; he studied; he earned his admission to the Ivy League. The company he's worked for since finishing his MBA thrived through the recession, was not a cause. They match a large portion of Banker's charitable giving, of every employee's charitable giving, and not just for the tax break. Banker is tired of defending his career. He's here on sabbatical, to challenge himself and learn new skills, to escape the anti-elitist ire of those who say they want their kids to get into the best schools and choose rewarding careers but then resent any adult who is the grown outcome of a child who accomplished precisely that.

Twenty-eight real-time minutes after Banker finishes, Waitress finds her way back to the field. The host is napping under an umbrella. Most of the contestants are chatting, bored and hot in the sun. They acknowledge Waitress's arrival tepidly. 'I was expecting this to be more exciting,' says Asian Chick. 'Same here,' agrees Biology. Tracker's eyes are closed, but he's listening. About five minutes later, Cheerleader Boy sulks into the field with his pink box. No one greets him. Even Waitress feels like she's been waiting forever.

The on-site producer rouses the host, who straightens his shirt, runs a hand through his hair, and then stands sternly before the contestants, who are quietly arranged in a line reflecting the order in which they finished. 'Night is approaching,' says the host. A true statement, always, but it strikes Tracker as odd; he has a strong sense of time. He can feel that it's only three o'clock.

The host continues. 'It's time to talk supplies. There are three main concerns in wilderness survival: shelter, water and food. Each of you has a wrapped package marked with the symbol for one of these.' In succession, viewers will be shown etchings of a minimalist tent – like a capital *A*, but without the horizontal bar – a water droplet, and a four-tined fork. 'The rules of the game are simple: You can keep your package or trade it for someone else's – without knowing what's inside.

'Except for our winner,' says the host, indicating Tracker, 'who gets the advantage of opening three items before making his choice. And our loser' – he turns to Cheerleader Boy – 'who will have no choice at all.' A white-elephant gift exchange, more or less, except that a contestant's life could depend on which item he or she chooses – or so the producers would have viewers believe. The irony being that while no one will believe this, it will in at least one case become true.

'Another bonus for our winner is this,' says the host, as he lifts a folded silver-and-red thermal blanket from a table – how did that get there? The unsung intern hustles away – and hands it to Tracker. 'Yours to keep, no stealing allowed. Let's begin.'

Tracker opens the following items: Zoo's iodine pills; Black Doctor's Nalgene-brand water bottles (two, filled); Engineer's emergency fishing kit. He takes the Nalgenes, relinquishing his shelter-stamped package to Black Doctor, who accepts the swap good-naturedly. Black Doctor fears pathogens; he wants the iodine, which would net him far more than two quarts of drinking water.

Zoo is next. She chooses Exorcist's small shelter-marked package. Her flippant tone as she does so makes the choice seem arbitrary, but it's not. She guesses — correctly — that most of the others will focus on food and water. She knows how to purify water and also guesses — again, correctly — that there will be more opportunities to secure sustenance in the future. No one will steal the stolen, still-wrapped fire starter she now holds.

Air Force is confident he can survive with what each contestant already has: a compass, a knife, a one-quart Nalgene, a personal first-aid kit, a bandana in their assigned color, and a jacket of their own choosing. He keeps his fork-marked dark blue box. Rancher steals Waitress's item, marked as water. Asian Chick takes Air Force's food, though her package is about the same size and also marked with a fork — flirtation, plain and simple. Engineer quietly keeps his fishing kit, thinking of what he might build. Black Doctor claims the iodine pills with covetous excitement; no one cares. Exorcist takes Tracker's two bottles, returning Tracker's original, unopened package to him. Tracker now has a blanket and a mystery. Biology keeps her food. Banker trades his triangular water item for the filled bottles. Waitress's turn, and she's thirsty. She too steals the Nalgenes, handing her pocket-sized shelter package to Banker. Cheerleader Boy is left with the item with which he entered the field. It's flat and rectangular, and crinkles when he presses it. He wonders if it's another blanket. If so, it's thinner than the other.

All this compressed into thirty seconds. *Not fair,* think the viewers who bother to think. The contestants who finished earlier actually had a disadvantage, and the second-to-last-place finisher was assured her pick of items.

Don't worry, the twist is coming.

The contestants are ordered to unwrap their items. Zoo

releases an excited 'yes!' upon revealing her fire starter. Asian Chick smiles over a twelve-pack of chocolate bars. Rancher nods noncommittally at a metal cup with foldable handles; it's large enough to double as a small cooking pot. Cheerleader Boy blurts an exhausted expletive at his short stack of black trash bags. Air Force shrugs at a package of freeze-dried cabbage. Biology flips her box of cookie-dough-flavored protein bars and frowns at the long ingredient list. Waitress leans over her shoulder and asks, 'Do those have gluten in them?' Biology's eyebrows lift, but Exorcist forestalls her reply with a cackle like snapping flame. In his hands is a three-pronged dowsing rod. He holds out the rod, steering through the air. He looks directly into the viewers' eyes and says, 'How fitting.' The other eleven contestants recoil, visibly and as one.

The dowsing rod was Banker's initially. He thought it might be a slingshot, but now he understands, though this slight is more subtle than most. He nods toward the dowsing rod, then shakes the box of waterproof matches he just unwrapped. 'These are looking pretty good,' he says.

The host steps up, front and center. 'While you all will ultimately have to build your own camps and survive as individuals,' he says, 'tonight is group camps and tomorrow will be a Team Challenge. To pick our teams – our first three finishers. Captains, your team members each come with whatever supplies they now hold, and while they will retain ownership of their supplies come tomorrow, for tonight they're yours.' He pauses to let meaning settle, then elaborates with a creeping smile, 'Contestants, if your captain wants to use, eat or *drink* your item, you cannot say no.'

'No way,' says Waitress. The shot zooms in on her shocked face – her water, she doesn't want to share.

Tracker, Zoo and Air Force step forward and pick their

groups, one by one. Tracker holds an unwrapped and unwanted flashlight. His first choice confounds: Rancher and his metal cup. A metal cup, when he could have extra water, or matches, or the iodine pills? This needs to be explained. Later, Tracker will be told to sit. He will face a single question, the answer to which will be spliced into the viewers' now: 'I don't like the taste of iodine. I'd rather boil water for drinking.'

Zoo chooses Engineer and his fishing kit. No explanation needed; the river's insides glisten with trout. Air Force chooses Black Doctor because he looks competent, and while he'd love Waitress's clean, clear water, her incompetence seems too steep a price to pay. The selections continue and in the end the teams are presented to viewers with their supplies as subtitles.

Team One: Tracker (thermal blanket, flashlight), Rancher (metal cup), Biology (protein bars) and Banker (matches).

Team Two: Zoo (fire starter), Engineer (fishing kit), Waitress (filled water bottles) and Asian Chick (box of chocolate bars).

Team Three: Air Force (dried cabbage), Black Doctor (iodine pills), Cheerleader Boy (heavy-duty trash bags) and Exorcist (dowsing rod).

It's too much information; few watching will be able to remember who has what. The host doesn't even try. He's tired, anxious for a break. 'Great,' he says. 'Your home base for tonight is this field. You can build your camps here, or in the woods nearby – your choice. I will see you all at first light for your first Team Challenge.' He nods gravely, then intones, 'Make camp.'

As the three groups disperse, the drone buzzes the field. Everyone but Tracker looks up. Exorcist winks and swings his dowsing rod over his shoulder. Tracker leads his team to the north end of the field. Zoo takes the west and Air

Force the east. Black Doctor notices his leader's limp and asks to see his ankle. 'A sprain,' he announces, and he sets off to scavenge a crutch. Of the actual process of building camp, little is shown. Tracker and Air Force know what they're doing, and their teams' camps come together quickly as they assign roles.

Zoo is less accustomed to being a leader. Her first command is a question: 'What do you guys think –' but no one is listening. Waitress is complaining about being cold; Asian Chick berates her, 'You should have worn a shirt.' Engineer is investigating his fishing kit: a kite handle wrapped with line instead of string. Its contours don't fit his hand; it's sized for a child. Three hooks, two weights, two little clips called swivels that Engineer doesn't yet understand. Zoo watches as he unspools a stretch of line and tests its strength. Her question hangs, unfinished and unanswered.

Tracker's team has a fire within TV seconds, which is about twenty real-time minutes. Air Force's team has a shelter moments later, after a commercial break, and Cheerleader Boy is flabbergasted to learn that his garbage bags are key to waterproofing the shallow lean-to.

Zoo tries a new approach. She crouches next to Engineer. 'Why don't you test that out at the river?' she asks. 'See if you can get it to work?' Engineer looks at his leader's entreating smile and sees his own excitement reflected in it. Zoo turns to the others. 'I've got the fire starter,' she says, 'so I'll take care of that. Why don't you two work on a shelter?' Asian Chick waves away Waitress, saying, 'I got this.' Prodded to action, she reveals an expanded identity: Asian Carpenter Chick. Skilled at woodworking, she assembles their shelter with confidence. Though the structure lacks nails and none of its components were measured, it projects sturdiness. More than that, it projects beauty, for the human brain is adapted to see beauty in symmetry. Even the off-site producer, who is so sour his sense of beauty has shriveled like a dehydrated lemon, will recognize that the slender, symmetrical lean-to has a certain bucolic appeal. Identity contracts, sloughing off one defining feature for another, and Carpenter Chick joins the cast.

For dinner, Tracker distributes one of Biology's protein bars to each of his team members. Biology doesn't appear to mind, and in this case appearance reflects reality. The bars are indeed gluten-free, but they contain sucralose, which turns her stomach. She eats one only because a turned stomach is marginally better than an empty one. Tracker leaves Rancher in charge of finishing their shelter and then jogs off, fading into the woods like a specter. A very fast specter; the cameraman cannot keep up. Recording devices mounted on trees every hundred feet catch snippets of his carving and setting a series of small deadfall traps. Tracker hopes to catch breakfast overnight. He too dislikes the protein bars; he thinks they taste of industrialization.

At the river Engineer ties a hook to the line, and baits it with a worm he finds under a rock. The worm is quickly tossed and lost. Engineer takes a sinker and one of the clips out of his pocket, cuts off the hook, ties in the swivel. Attaches both hook and sinker. It doesn't look right to him, the weight and hook together like that, but he tries it.

Well after their shelter is built and the sun beginning to set, Zoo finds him at the riverside, still trying, adjusting. There's several feet of line between the swivel and hook now. 'Wow,' she says. 'You actually turned that into something you can fish with.'

Engineer feels a swell of pride. His knuckles are scraped raw from the too-tight handle. 'I think the next variable to adjust is the bait.'

'Good idea. Tomorrow, though, or we'll never find our way back to camp.'

Their team settles for a child's dream dinner: all the chocolate they can stomach, and then some.

To the east, Air Force rehydrates and shares his cabbage, and then limps into the woods with the help of a walking stick to set some deadfalls, something he hasn't done since basic. Black Doctor follows to learn how it's done. 'If we had the fishing line we could set snares,' Air Force tells him. 'Next time,' Black Doctor answers. Air Force's traps won't work, but their construction is not fruitless; our first alliance is forming.

Night drifts over the campsites. All are exhausted to varying degrees, but Waitress is the most exhausted. She's been shivering for hours, even with her thin Lycra jacket zipped over her sports bra. She curls by the fire, not comfortable enough with her teammates to share body heat. 'It's warmer in here,' says Zoo, wrapped in her fleece jacket. Waitress shakes her head. A cameraman watches her, recording her discomfort and wishing he could lend her his much-warmer coat. When Waitress shifts her back to the fire, he nearly calls out a warning about her hair, but she tugs it over her shoulder without prompting. Waitress is unsettled. She wishes the cameraman would either say something or leave. She knows she should talk, not to him, but to her teammates or at least to herself, but she's too cold, too tired. The night deepens. The cameraman's shift ends. He retreats to the production team's much more elaborate camp at a second field a quarter mile south. There they have tents and grills. Coolers stuffed with meat and milk and beer. Mosquito netting. The cameramen assigned to the other two teams also retire. Mounted cameras are left to watch the contestants.

These cameras don't care that Waitress is cold, or that Air

Force's ankle is throbbing. They record Rancher crawling from his shelter to take a piss, and Waitress's endless shivering, but they miss more than they record. They miss Banker offering Biology his puffy jacket as a pillow, and his face relaxing into relief at her polite refusal. They miss Zoo, Engineer and Carpenter Chick exchanging their backgrounds in bedtime-story whispers. They miss Exorcist's lips framing an honest prayer as he lies tucked into the corner of his team's lean-to.

Mostly, they record dying flames.

5.

The sky trembles. My first thought is that it's a camera drone, crashing, and this is something I want to see. I look up, raising an arm to block out the sun. Instead of a drone come undone, I see an airplane plowing through the high blue to leave a wispy white trail. It takes me a moment to process the sight, the sound, the sensation of having my small human presence overwhelmed so completely. This is the first time I've noticed a plane since taping began. I don't know if this is because I wasn't paying attention or because they weren't around to notice.

Either way, this is important – it means they can't control every aspect of my surroundings. A small assurance, but it inhabits me like a revelation. I feel my insularity retreating. For the first time in too long, I am not *the* but *a*. Just one person among many. I think of the men and women above me. The plane is huge; there must be hundreds of passengers seated up there beneath nubby air vents, napping, reading, watching movies on their iPads. One or two crying, perhaps, frightened by the enormity of the journey they're embarking on.

I stand still, neck craned, until the airplane is out of sight, its contrail dispersing. I hope someone up there is going home. That there is at least one person in that plane who knows unselfish love and is returning to it.

The next few hours are easier than what came before, except that I'm wretched with hunger. I reach a brook a few hours before sunset and decide to make camp early to try to catch some protein. The pieces of the figure-four deadfall I carved during group camp are in my pack, and now that I have something other than pinecones to use as bait it might actually work.

I take the trio of sticks and set them under a tall tree. It takes me a minute to figure out which stick goes where, then I align the notches, balancing and steadying. Once I can keep the trap in its distinctive angular pattern by pinching the top nexus, I smear the end of the bait stick with peanut butter and lean a heavy log over the top to take the place of my hand. It's a precarious piece of work, but it's meant to be, and it holds.

I boil water in batches and build my shelter, glancing regularly toward the trap. The bait lies in the log's shadow, untouched. The woods grow dim and I'm sitting at the fire, waiting, trying not to think the thoughts that come most readily. I hate it. I need to keep busy, so I decide to carve a second trap. I salvage appropriate-sized sticks – each about a half inch thick and a foot long – and start carving. It's only four notches and two sharpened points, but they have to be aligned perfectly. Carving takes me longer than I'd like – the knife I was issued is so dull at this point I wouldn't trust it to slice cold butter. By the time I'm done, my hands are aching, my fingers blistered. I drop the sticks at the base of a tree and head to the brook to collect a long flat stone to use as the trap's weight.

I take off my boots and socks and wade in. Pebbles massage my feet, a small pain. As I pry up the rock, I think that I could never do all this if it wasn't part of the show. This adventure I asked for, it's not what I was expecting, not what I wanted. I thought I would feel empowered, but I'm only exhausted.

I heave the stone upright. It's too heavy to lift, so I drag it out of the water and to the tree. The stone leaves a six-inch-wide trail through my camp. I remember a driveway much wider twisting through the woods, leading from a mailbox choked by blue balloons to a cabin with more balloons by the door. The cabin itself was blue too, maybe, I'm not sure. Maybe it just had blue trim. And there were so many balloons; every time I remember I remember more. The balloons weren't all: a bottle in the sink, a handful of wrapped packages on the table. All blue. Even the bedroom light felt blue when I found him – found it.

I didn't quit then. I didn't quit when I got sick afterward, days of shivering and feeding the fire, boiling water constantly because I was losing fluids and I didn't boil the tap water in the cabin and that must be what made me sick. Vomit and diarrhea, feeling so cold, endlessly cold.

I drop the stone by the tree.

Nothing can be worse than what they've already put me through. I'd never choose this, not again. But I'm here and I'm a woman of my word and I promised myself I wouldn't quit.

I put my boots back on, then kneel to assemble the second trap. As I'm testing the fulcrum stick, there's a soft thud behind me. I turn; the first trap's been triggered. I think I see movement, but by the time I get there the squirrel is dead, its front half compressed into the dirt beneath the log. The thinnest sliver of black is exposed between its fuzzy eyelids. I've never been fond of squirrels; I prefer chipmunks with their racing stripes. When I was six or seven I spent an entire summer prone among the maples and birches behind my parents' house, hoping a chipmunk would mistake me for a log. I wanted so badly to know the feel of his little feet on my skin. That never happened, but once one did scamper close, until we were eye-to-eye. And then he sneezed in my face and disappeared. Like a magic trick, I told my husband on our first date. *Poof.* A story I've told so many times I no longer know if it's true.

Gray squirrels, though – I associate them with cities, with overcrowding and litter. Even so, I feel bad as I pick up the squirrel by its tail. Killing mammals is tough, even when it's a squirrel, even when it's to eat. 'Sorry, little guy,' I say.

Cooper could field-dress a squirrel in less than a minute. We timed him once using Mississippi seconds. I was usually tending the fire. I've cooked squirrel, but I've never skinned one.

It didn't look too hard.

I lay the squirrel belly-down atop a log. Cooper started with a slit under the tail, so that's what I do, forcing my dull knife through the skin. I saw across the base of the tail. And then – this part astonished me every time I saw it, how easy it was – I cover the tail with my foot, stepping hard, and yank the squirrel's back legs up.

Red spritzes through the air as the squirrel rips in half and I stumble backward. Unexpected motion makes my head float; I feel like I'm on a raft, rocking in a ship's wake. Clutching the chunk of the squirrel that came with me, I take a knee and force three slow, deep breaths.

I don't know what I did wrong. When Cooper pulled, the skin of his squirrel always slid right off, like a banana peel.

It doesn't matter what I did wrong, I need to salvage what I can. I look at the carcass dangling from my right hand. A happy surprise – it didn't rip in half. I'm holding everything but the tail. This is correctable, with patience.

I walk back to the log and see the detached tail sitting there, a fluffy gray-and-white lump. Memory brings me an image: Randy, his sweaty red hair puffing up anime-style, his bile-green bandana tight across his brow, a squirrel tail dangling over each ear. I see him dancing wildly around the fire, his tail-ears flapping as he howls a howl that is supposed to sound like a wolf but is purely a showman's call.

I sit on the log and flick the disembodied tail onto the ground, trying to focus. Randy doesn't matter. All that matters right now is skinning this squirrel. Maybe my cut was too deep or I pulled too fast, I don't know, but I think I know what to do next. I creep my fingers along the muscle, separating the skin in tiny increments. It takes forever. I'm probably doing it wrong. But eventually the hide is pulled up to the squirrel's front legs. I place the blade of my knife flat against the midpoint of a front leg, and then I lean over it, pushing. The bone snaps, and the knife digs through into the log; I have to jerk it free. I use less force for the next three legs and the neck. My hands are slick and aching, but I'm almost done. I just have to gut it now. I flip the carcass so it's belly-up, then turn the knife so the blade faces me.

Don't puncture the organs. I know that much, at least.

I ease the tip of my knife through the top of the chest, piercing. Then I bring the blade in tiny jerks toward myself, cutting through the skin from beneath like popping stitches. This time, I don't fuck up. The underside opens and I dig my fingers in. I grab the oesophagus and lungs and everything else I can curl my fingers around, and I pull. The innards come out together, a cohesive system I toss to the ground. The squirrel's nubby spine winks up at me from inside the cavity.

I walk over to the brook and scrub the squirrel blood off my hands and wrists, digging into the dirt at the bottom for abrasion. Afterward I chop up the squirrel and set it to boil in my cup. I wish I had some salt and pepper, some carrots and onion. If I felt stronger, I'd forage for some Queen Anne's lace, but I haven't noticed any and I don't trust myself to identify plants right now, especially not one with poisonous look-alikes.

While the squirrel stews, I gather its inedible parts and

take them away from my camp. Not far, maybe fifty feet. I should bury them, but I don't. I'm tired and they're such a small amount, I leave them in a pile, then wash my hands again. I let the squirrel boil until the meat pulls away from the bone when prodded, then pull the cup from the fire and fish out a piece. It's too hot and I hold it between my teeth until I can chew without blistering my tongue. The meat has little taste that I can discern, but it's not peanut butter. There is, I don't know, half a pound of meat, probably less. I suck down every thread and when the liquid is cool enough, I drink that too. By the time it's dark, all that's left of the squirrel is a pile of skinny bones, which I toss into the woods.

Full, I could sleep for a month. But first I stretch my arms and legs, stand straight and tip side to side, fulfilling my pledge. I pour water over my fire, crawl into my shelter, and hang my glasses on the top loop of my backpack. I drift toward unconsciousness, content.

I awake to a snuffling sound. For a drowsy moment I think it's my husband's breath. I move to nudge him, and something pricks my hand. I jolt to full awareness, remember where I am, see the twig that scratched me.

Something is moving outside the shelter. I focus on the sounds: a powerful, rooting huff, crunching steps. I should have buried the squirrel offal. A black bear found it and now it wants my peanut butter too. The animal sounds too big to be anything other than a bear. It noses the side of the debris hut; leaves rattle, and a skinny ray of moonlight peeps through near the entrance. I hate peanut butter more than ever.

But I'm not scared, not really. As soon as I make it clear that I'm not prey, the bear will retreat. I won't have a problem unless it's habituated to people, and even then it'll most likely back off once I make myself big, holler a bit. Wild animals don't like a ruckus.

I reach for my pack, slowly, quietly, creeping my fingers toward my glasses as my shoulder muscles pinch and ache, resisting.

A rumbling growl; hot, wet breath. A blurred gray-brown muzzle dripping thick white foam three feet from my face. I feel my next heartbeat like a hammer's blow. Even in the dark, even without my glasses, the aggression and frothed saliva of disease are unmistakable. Perched at the only exit from my shelter is not a bear but a rabid wolf.

The only rabid animals I've ever seen before were raccoons and a few emaciated bats, and those in cages – or dead, awaiting necropsy. No danger, not really, not like this: a wolf the size of a bear, the size of a house. A dire wolf brought back from extinction for the sole purpose of ripping out my throat.

I feel terror like a hardening of my veins as the beast growls and ducks its huge head. A glob of slime drops from bared teeth and lands on my backpack.

I grab the pack as the wolf lunges toward me. I'm not a screamer. Roller coasters, haunted houses, a RAV4 running a red light coming straight at me – none of this has ever made me scream, but I scream now. My scream strains my throat and the pressure of the wolf against my pack strains the rest of me. I hear snapping jaws, feel wetness – my sweat, its saliva, not-blood-please-not-blood – and I see the black of my pack, flashes of fur and teeth. I'm compressed behind the pack, tucked into the end of the shelter, shoulders pressing against the roof.

The wolf retreats, only a step or two, and sways side to side, stumbles a step. It growls again.

And though I can hardly breathe, a thought pierces me:

There is no way I can fight off a rabid wolf confined like this. There's no way I can fight off a rabid wolf at all, but especially not like this. But I *have* to; I have to get home. I heave my pack at the wolf and shove myself against the wall of my shelter. With a yell, I push through. The garbage-bag liner resists, then gives, scattering leaves and twigs. As my shoulders break through, the debris hut begins to crumble around me – and I feel a tug, a violent pull on my leg.

The wolf has my foot. I feel the pressure of its bite through my boot, pinching. Like bait on a line, I'm being jolted down, down, down.

All I can see is the back of my tears. Starlight glints in the liquid, a magnification not of detail but of the ethereal splendor of a world I'm not ready to leave.

I kick. I kick and scream and claw at the earth. I fight through the rubble everywhere. My unhindered foot connects against skull; I feel the impact through the heel of my boot like striking concrete, and my other foot is suddenly free too. I scramble toward the expanse of predawn light, the patchy grass and gurgling brook. Behind me, the wolf thrashes as the debris hut collapses on top of it.

I clamber to my feet and grab a thick branch, and as the wolf's sharp muzzle appears from the leaves I bash at the emerging form. I feel the *thunk* of impact, hear the cracking of bone or wood, and I keep swinging. Over and over I swing, until I've lost my breath, until the leaves are dark and heavy. I swing for as long as adrenaline allows, an endless instant, and then my strength abandons me. I stumble backward, my club hanging between my knees. The remains of my shelter are fuzzy stillness and liquid glimmer.

I hurt, everywhere. Not soreness, real pain. Pain like death.

My foot.

I collapse to the ground in my haste to check myself for injury.

My every nerve is screaming so loudly I cannot sense particulars, cannot separate fear from physical wound. Pawing at my leg, I feel prickling growth but don't find any breaks in the skin. The hem of my left trouser leg is tattered and wet, but not bloodied, I don't think.

My boot has been torn from my foot. I run my hands over the wool sock that remains. Twigs and leaves poke my fingers. No holes.

I'm okay.

If I were still in the habit of taking off my boots to sleep — no, don't think about it.

I raise my hands to wipe at my eyes, and see that my fingers and palms are thickly wet with the wolf's saliva, like a mucous membrane.

I launch myself toward the brook.

So many scrapes, so many tiny cuts through which the rabies virus could enter. I rub my hands frantically in the water.

And then I freeze.

Will rubbing my hands push the virus into a cut? Is that possible?

I don't know the answer. I should know the answer; I work with animals, and this is the kind of thing I know. Except that I don't.

I sit in the water, shaking. Sopping wet from the waist down, and cold, I'm not myself. I don't know who I am. I don't know what to do, what to think. All I know is where I am: alone, sitting in a brook.

In time I realize I do know one other thing: Wolves don't live around here. The closest wild wolf would have to be in Canada, or maybe North Carolina. The probability of the animal that attacked me being a wolf is infinitesimal.

Whatever it was, I killed it. Not to eat, not cleanly with a trap. Animal-loving me, who has spent her professional life working with children to inspire in them a respect for – a love of – nature. Not for the kids' sakes. That's what everyone gets wrong. It's not the teaching that I like. I think of Eddie the red-tailed hawk, Penny the fox. I'm not supposed to name the ones slated for release, but I do. I always do.

Eventually, I regain my feet and stumble out of the brook. My legs are numb as I return to the destroyed debris hut. Twilight has given way to dawn; squinting, drawing closer in tiny movements, I'm just able to make out the animal, the front half of which juts from the leaves. Its head looks like a boulder was dropped on it.

Is that what I am now – a boulder careening downhill, driven by inertia instead of will?

I pick up a branch and sweep the crimson leaves off the top of the shelter, then pry up the sticks covering the body. I'm still shaking and my throat is raw.

The animal is smaller than I thought – about the size of a collie – thin-legged, its bushy tail stained with excrement.

Not a wolf, but a coyote. The longer I look at it, the smaller it seems.

I'm sorry.

I'm sorry you got sick.

I'm sorry I killed you.

I dig out my boot and backpack from the rubble. Thick rents run through the toe of the boot. I poke it with a stick, which slips through easily to strike the inner sole. Some of the holes go all the way through the sole; the boot is useless. The front of my backpack is shredded too, and it's several minutes before I find my glasses. The frames are twisted, both earpieces snapped off. Only one lens is intact, the other shattered where a tooth struck it like a bullet.

Fear distinct from the fear I felt during the attack drifts over me. An equal, opposing fear. A slow fear. My vision isn't bad compared to a mole's, but it's bad enough. I haven't gone a day without corrective lenses since fourth grade.

'I can't see,' I say, turning around. I lift my chin, hold up my ruined glasses, and directly address the cameras for the first time since Solo started. 'I can't see.'

Help should be here by now. An EMT should be sitting me down, handing me the ugly backup pair of glasses I entrusted to the producer the day before we started. I look at a bright red scratch that runs across the back of my right hand, dotted with pinpricks of drying blood.

'I need the vaccine,' I say to the trees. My heart is speeding. 'Day zero and day three, post-exposure.'

They required us to get rabies vaccinations before we came. It was one among a plethora of requirements: a full physical, a tetanus booster, proof of a whole host of other shots that I already had for school and work. Rabies was all that I needed to meet their requirements.

'I'm not immune,' I call. My voice cracks. The rabies vaccine is atypical in that instead of creating immunity, receiving it pre-exposure only decreases how many doses one needs after exposure. I hold up my hand and turn in a circle. 'I have a cut, look. I touched its saliva. I need the shots.'

There's no answer. I stare at the blur of leaves, squinting, searching for a camera mounted on a branch, a drone hovering above. It must be there, it *must* be. I think of the boulder, of Heather's taxidermy bear and the first prop splattered at the base of a cliff. I think of the doll, its mechanical cries twisting through the cabin's suffocating air. My fear begins to morph, to sharpen, and even as I wait, I know no one's coming.

Because they planned this.

I don't know how, but they planned this and now my glasses are broken and I can't see.

I feel as though my anger will split my skin, flay me alive from the inside.

I can't fucking see.

6.

The host projects his voice as though onstage. 'For our first Team Challenge you will be working together to find edible plants,' he says. He slept well. The contestants did not, except for Tracker, who sleeps better outdoors than in. 'Whichever team collects the most different types of edible plants in half an hour wins. However, that doesn't mean you can go picking flowers all willy-nilly.' The host wags his finger, and Carpenter Chick's eye roll makes Zoo laugh. Both action and sound will be cut; this is a somber moment. 'For each incorrect identification your team makes, one point will be deducted from your score.' He hands each team leader a brightly colored tri-fold pamphlet. 'You're playing for something very important – lunch.'

Tracker woke before dawn to check his traps, and a rabbit became breakfast for his team. Biology also shared her protein bars, though she was no longer obligated to do so. The eight contestants outside their team are famished, and the host doesn't know about the rabbit.

The next several minutes are compressed to an instant. The teams are ready, and the host shouts, 'Go!'

'I bet Cooper knows all this stuff,' says Carpenter Chick to her teammates. 'One of us should just follow him.'

'I'll do it,' says Waitress, wishing she were on his team.

Zoo doesn't like this idea. All her life she's followed the spirit of the law as well as the letter. 'I know some of these,' she says, looking at the handout. 'And I think I saw Queen Anne's lace yesterday. We can do this on our own.'

'I agree,' says Engineer. Yesterday, he wondered at his

luck, ending up on a team with three women. He didn't know if it was good luck or bad. He's thinking good now. He likes how Zoo's mind works; he thinks they have a chance.

'Whatever,' says Waitress. She's hungry, but this is a sensation she's used to. Her current crankiness stems more from fatigue and a caffeine-craving headache.

Zoo hands her the guide. 'Some of these are easy. We can all look for dandelions and chicory and pine, but how about we each focus on one or two of the others?'

'You're the boss,' says Carpenter Chick.

Tracker's team is off to a strong start; Biology has already collected a handful of mint. She found the patch last night, chewed some this morning after finishing her portion of rabbit. In addition to teaching life science, Biology advises a gardening club. Between her and Tracker, her team has an obvious advantage.

Air Force's ankle hurts more today, and is swollen enough that he can barely fit it in his boot. 'You should rest,' says Black Doctor. 'We can handle this.'

Cheerleader Boy lurks behind them, hair mussed, eyes red and exhausted as they run over the pamphlet. 'What's a basal whorl?' he asks, trying.

'It means coming from the base,' says Black Doctor. 'So all the leaves or petals would be coming from the same spot on the base, not scattered along the . . .' He pinches his thumb and forefinger and runs them up and down in the air, as though drawing a short line.

'Stem?' supplies Exorcist.

'Like a dandelion?' asks Cheerleader Boy.

'Exactly,' says Black Doctor. 'What do we have to find that has a basal whorl?'

'A dandelion.'

Exorcist laughs and slaps Cheerleader Boy on the back.

And now, a montage:

The teams trekking through the trees, searching.

Air Force sitting with his foot in the icy water of a small brook, poor wounded bird.

Banker crouching by some growth at the base of a mossy boulder. 'I think this might be purslane.'

Zoo tearing a leaf, sniffing it. She holds it out to the others and says, 'Smell this.' They pass it around. 'Smells like . . .' Engineer cannot decide. 'Carrot,' chirps Carpenter Chick. 'Bingo,' says Zoo.

In the bottom corner of the screen, a timer races from thirty toward zero. Some believe that time is its own dimension – a sequential continuum – others argue time is an incalculable, untravelable construct of the human mind – a concept, not a thing. The producers and editor care little about physics, or philosophy, and they will travel the half hour, leaping so that minutes disappear in irregular chunks. They will bring the viewers with them.

Cheerleader Boy swats at a needled branch. 'All these plants look the same,' he says. Exorcist grabs the same branch and tells him, 'Pine.'

'Pine,' says Carpenter Chick.

'Pine,' says Biology. Her statement came fifteen minutes earlier but will be presented as a triangle's third side at nine minutes remaining.

Tracker leads in silence, pinching leaves, smelling his fingers, searching.

'You can really eat this?' asks Waitress, holding the bit of root that Zoo handed her. 'I think you're supposed to cook it first,' Zoo replies.

A gong echoes through the woods; everyone stops to listen. Five minutes blinks the timer.

'I guess we should head back?' says Banker.

'We don't have them all,' says Biology.

71

'We have enough,' Rancher answers. Beside him, Tracker nods.

Air Force's team collects him. 'I found mint by the stream,' he says.

Black Doctor helps him up. 'Great. We didn't have that one.' Even though they did.

The teams reassemble in the field. The host is waiting, and he's not alone. At his side stands a large bearded man who needs only an axe to look like a Halloween lumberjack.

The Expert.

He nods his massive head without smiling and looks over the contestants. His flannel shirt and red-tinged beard flutter in a gust of wind. Zoo barely suppresses a laugh – the giant has descended the beanstalk, she thinks, and he looks like he's choosing whom to roast as his next meal.

The host lists the Expert's credentials, which slide over the contestants just as they will slide over viewers, simultaneously impressive and obscure. He's a graduate, an instructor. He advises law enforcement and emergency rescue teams. He has survived for months alone in the Alaskan wilderness, much harsher than here. He has tracked panthers and bears and endangered gray wolves, as well as humans of both the lost and homicidal variety.

In short, he knows his shit.

The team leaders present the Expert with their collections. Zoo is first.

'Dandelion, sure. Mint, pine. You got the easy ones,' says the Expert. His voice is gruff, but not unfriendly. He projects an ultimate confidence that doesn't cross the line into hubris. He has nothing to prove. Tracker feels the simultaneous push and pull of shared characteristics.

'Chicory,' says the Expert, 'very good. Burdock. Hawthorn. Queen Anne's lace. And . . . what did you think this one was?' He holds out a large, glossy leaf.

Zoo looks at her pamphlet. 'Mayapple?'

The Expert *tsk*s lightly. 'This is bloodroot.' He indicates where the rhizome was torn. 'See the red?'

'Toxic?' she asks.

'In large doses. Mayapple leaves are more umbrellalike and glossy in their prime. It's one of the first sprouts to come up in the spring, so this time of year they'll be wilting, and you should be able to find small yellow-green fruit.'

Zoo's team loses a point, for a total score of six, but she has learned something.

Tracker's team earns an easy seven with no incorrect identifications, including a hard yellow orb that proves to be mayapple fruit. The Expert is impressed. Tracker is caught between pride and embarrassment at his pride.

Air Force presents his team's collection without knowing what it includes. The Expert ticks through the plants. 'Pine, mint, burdock, purslane, dandelion, chokecherry.' There's one more. If it's correct, Air Force's team ties for first. If it's wrong, they come in last.

Insert constructed drama: long pauses, a close-up on Black Doctor's eager eyes. Cheerleader Boy shifting, his mouth curled. Exorcist smiling like a mannequin. Air Force standing strong, showing no sign of his discomfort now. The Expert reaching into the bag, huffing a breath that rattles his beard. He extracts a hollow, purple-splotched stalk topped with a cluster of small, papery brown nubs that were once tiny flowers.

And now – a word from our sponsors, and whoever else has paid for a few moments to hawk their goods and services. Some viewers will groan, but they'll be back; others endure only a staccato hint of advertising and the show returns. The viewer too can manipulate time, for a fee.

The Expert holds up the cutting and wrinkles his nose,

letting the viewer in on the plant's rankness. Air Force sucks in his cheeks; he knows something is wrong. 'Queen Anne's lace?' the Expert asks. Air Force doesn't know; behind him, Black Doctor nods.

'No,' says the Expert. 'And if you ate this, it could kill you. Anyone here heard of a man named Socrates?'

Thus is hemlock revealed.

The host steps forward, flourishing his hands to music he will never hear. He doesn't care about the differences between hemlock and Queen Anne's lace. He turns to Tracker's team.

'Congratulations,' he says. 'It's time for your reward.'

7.

I clean and bandage my hand using the small first-aid kit issued to me at the beginning of the show, and then I start walking. I'm missing a shoe and I'm angry. Every branch I brush is a whispered reminder of the coyote's snarls. If I try to focus on something more than a few feet away, I start squinting, which doesn't help much and gives me a head-ache. So I don't focus. I drift, moving through the leaves with creeping steps. And though I feel the stones and branches beneath my shoeless left foot, my vision reduces all texture to fluff. Separate objects coalesce. The forest floor is a great carpet, green here, brown there, a Mother Nature theme.

As I walk, I hold the surviving lens from my glasses in my jacket pocket and rub my thumb along its concavity. The lens has become my worry stone – more than that, my anger stone, my thinking stone, my I-can-do-this stone.

The coyote couldn't have been real. It *couldn't* have been. Now that the heat of the moment has passed, the attack feels distant and dreamlike. It was so dark, so quick. I concentrate, remembering and seeking flaws. I think I remember a mechanical stiltedness to its movement, maybe a flash of metal in the moonlight. I *know* I remember an electronic buzz announcing inauthenticity in the doll's canned cries; maybe that sound was there beneath the coyote's snarls too. I was so scared, I couldn't see, and it happened so quickly, it's hard to be sure.

Ad tenebras dedi. Three words and it's over. All I have to do is admit defeat. If I'd been thinking straight during the attack, I might have done it, but now the moment's passed and my pride won't allow me to quit.

Pride, I think, walking through the abstract blur of my surroundings. I have only a few memories of the catechism classes my mother made me attend throughout elementary school, but I remember learning about the sin of pride. I remember old Mrs Whatshername with her dyed red hair and baggy floral dress sitting the six of us at her kitchen table and pointing at an opal pendant I was wearing.

'Pride,' she said, 'is feeling prettier than other girls. It's wearing too much jewelry and looking in mirrors over and over. It's wearing makeup and short skirts. And it's one of the seven deadly sins.'

I remember sitting there at the table, fuming at her words. I hated being used as an example, and I hated that the example was so grossly inaccurate. The pendant had belonged to my dad's mom, who'd passed away a few months before. Wearing the pendant didn't make me feel prettier than other girls, it reminded me of a woman I loved and missed and mourned. Besides, tomboy that I was, I'd yet to even try putting on makeup.

We had graham crackers as a snack that day, and when I reached for a second I was warned against gluttony. This particular memory sparks a sour laugh in my throat as I shuffle along the pavement.

What else?

I remember kneeling in a church pew as the teacher asked us a single question over and over, my mind spinning – why isn't anyone answering? Tentatively, I offered an idea, only to be shouted back to silence. I don't remember the question I wasn't supposed to answer, or the answer I wasn't supposed to give, but I remember my shame. I learned that day that no matter how demanding a person's tone, no matter how many times she asks something, she might not actually want an answer.

I also remember approaching my mother weeks or months later, asking her to please not make me go back. Not because the classes bored me or scared me, but because even at that young age I knew something wasn't right. Never mind that I didn't yet know the word *hypocritical;* just as with *rhetorical,* I learned the meaning without the word. I could sense the pride of my teacher. I was an imaginative child, happy to declare a house inhabited by ghosts or to see Bigfoot's tracks in the mud, but if I sometimes allowed myself to become lost in a game I still knew I was playing. I knew it wasn't real. Watching a cartoon of Adam and Eve falling for the ridiculous whisperings of a snake and then being thrown out of their home by God was one thing. Acknowledging this cartoon not as fantasy but as an accurate representation of history was another. Even as a ten-year-old, I was repulsed. When I was introduced to the ideas of Charles Darwin and Gregor Mendel in school several years later, I experienced the closest thing I've ever known to a spiritual revelation. I recognized truth.

It is this truth that has shaped my life. I lack the aptitude for higher sciences and mathematics – I figured that out in college – but I understand enough. Enough not to need platitudes. I've heard believers speak of the coldness of science and the warmth of their faith. But my life has been warm too, and I have faith. Faith in love, and faith in the inherent beauty of a world that formed itself. When my foot was caught, my life didn't flash before my eyes; I saw only the world. The majesty of atoms and all that they've become.

This experience might be the horrible construct of some production team, and I might regret some of the choices that led me here, but the choices were *mine* to make. And even if I've made mistakes, that doesn't change the fact that the world itself is beautiful. The scaly spirals of a conifer's cone, the helicoidal flow of a river's curve biting away the bank, the flash of orange upon a butterfly's wings warning predators of bitter taste. This is order from chaos; this is beauty, and it's all the more beautiful for having designed itself.

I step out of the woods; the road stretches before me like smoke.

I couldn't have expected the attack, and yet I should have expected something like it. A farce. The more I think about it, the clearer the truth becomes: The coyote was animatronic. It was too big to be real; it moved too stiffly. It didn't blink and its marble eyes never changed focus. I don't think the mouth even opened and closed, though perhaps the lips moved a little. It didn't bite my foot; they wrapped a snare around my boot as I slept. I was surprised and scared. It was dark and I didn't have my glasses. That's why it seemed alive.

The world in which I now move is a deliberate human perversion of nature's beauty. I cannot forget this. I must accept this. I have accepted this.

With my vision, my missing boot, and my sore, stiff body, I probably make it only a quarter of a mile before I need to rest. It's still early morning, I have time for a short break. I sit with my back against the guardrail and close my eyes. I keep hearing shuffling steps in the woods that I know don't exist. I refuse to open my eyes to check.

My thirst wakes me, an endless stretching dryness in my mouth. I paw for my pack, find a half-full water bottle, and guzzle all that's left.

That's when I notice the sun is on the wrong side of the sky. Panic brushes against me – the world is wrong – and then my rational mind clicks into gear and I understand the sun is setting. I slept for the entire day. I've never done that before. But, I feel better. My head is clear, my chest looser. I feel so much better that I realize just how awful I must have felt before. My bladder is pinching and I'm starving, my stomach rumbling, begging. I'm so hungry I dig out the peanut butter and cram several tablespoons into my mouth, trying to ignore how disgusting it tastes and feels. I climb over the guardrail and squat among the trees. My urine is a deep amber color, too dark. I take out my second bottle and drink a few ounces. As dehydrated as I am, it has to last; night hiking is impossible without my glasses.

While gathering wood for my shelter, I uncover a small red eft. I cup it in my palms, crouching low in case it squirms free. I admire the bright orange skin, the black-rimmed circles dotting the amphibian's slender back. I've always loved red efts. Growing up, I called them fire newts. It wasn't until embarrassingly late in life — well into my first year as a professional wildlife educator — that I realized the red eft wasn't a species, but a life stage of the eastern newt. That these bright juveniles grow into dull green-brown adults.

The eft grows used to my skin and starts creeping forward with a wagging gait, crossing my palm.

I wonder how many calories I'd get from eating it.

Fiery orange skin: bright toxins. I'm not sure how poisonous red efts are to humans, but I can't chance it. I dip my hand to a mossy stone, let the eft saunter off, and finish building my shelter.

That night I dream of earthquakes and animatronic toddlers with fangs. In the morning I break down my camp and creep east along the smoky road. I may not be able to focus my vision, but my thoughts are sharp. I need supplies. A new pack, boots and food — anything other than peanut butter. I'm nervous about my water again; it's like I've gone back in time – how many days, three, four? It feels like weeks – to just after the blue cabin, after I was sick, when I was able to start moving again but before I found the market. I have no food, almost no water, and I'm moving east searching for a Clue part of me fears will never come. It's exactly the same except now I can't see and I'm missing a shoe.

I'm going so slowly, too slowly. But every time I try to move faster I trip or slip or step on something sharp. The sole of my left foot feels like a giant bruise covered in a giant blister.

The morning is chilly and endless. This is worse than the coyote-bot, nearly as bad as the doll, this blurry monotony. If they want to break me, this is what they ought to do, send me walking endlessly with nothing to see, no one to talk to. No Challenges to win or lose. The safety phrase is creeping into my consciousness, teasing. For the first time I wish I weren't quite so stubborn. That I could be like Amy – just shrug and admit I've had enough. That this is too fucked up to be worth it.

What if – what if I were to walk quicker despite my eyesight? Maybe I'd trip for real. Maybe I'd sprain my ankle, worse than Ethan did, a real sprain – maybe even a break. Or what if I weren't so careful with my knife? Maybe it would slip and the blade would cut into my hand, just deep enough that my first-aid kit couldn't close the wound. Circumstances wouldn't allow for continuing. I'd be forced to leave, and everyone would say, 'It wasn't your fault.' My husband would kiss the bandage and bemoan my bad luck, all the while telling me how happy he is for me to be home.

The idea has a certain appeal. Not hurting myself intentionally – never that – but allowing myself the opportunity to slip. With every step the idea seems less ludicrous, and then I notice a blurred structure ahead; a few cautious steps and I make out a gas station with a hand-painted NO GAS sign secured to the pumps, large enough that even without my glasses I can read it from some hundred feet away. My attention snaps fully back to the game and unease clamps my chest. As I get closer to the gas station I see a speckling of buildings down a second road to my left.

Bursts of color litter the intersection. Squinting and approaching, I realize they're lawn signs. I see an ad for little league tryouts and some pro-NRA gibberish. One sign simply says REPENT! At the edge of the cluster, another is covered in bumper stickers – a dozen, at least. Prominent among the stickers: a blue arrow pointing to the left.

The hue is off, darker than the color I was assigned. I'm not sure the arrow's meant for me, I might be reaching, but I need supplies so badly, and Emery said they wouldn't always be obvious to find. What's the risk of following the arrow, just a short distance? If I'm wrong, they won't let me get too far off track, I don't think.

I turn to the north. Walking, I'm tense and watchful, but I don't notice anything out of the ordinary, except for the quiet. The first building I reach is a credit union; it seems closed. Maybe it's Sunday, or maybe the staff is inside, crouching out of sight until I pass. I don't see any blue. A few minutes later, I reach a second building, which is set back from the road. I cross the small, empty parking lot to investigate. I see display windows, figures inside. People? But I don't think they're moving. As I get closer, I realize the figures in the window are mannequins positioned around a tent. I squint to read the sign above the door. TRAILS 'N THINGS. I think of my ruined pack, my missing boot.

The door is locked. This is a first. I stand on the steps, considering. The rules said not to drive, not to hit anyone in the head or genitals, and not to use weapons of any kind.

They didn't say anything about breaking and entering, not that I can recall. In fact, they said any shelter or resources found were fair game.

One of the female mannequins is wearing a blue vest and a fuzzy matching cap. Sky blue, my blue.

I slam my elbow through the lowest pane in the door's window. The glass shatters and the pain I feel is nothing compared to what else I've felt these last few days. I reach through the broken pane and unlock the door from the inside. I take off my backpack and then my jacket, shaking it out in case any glass is lodged in the sleeve. I tie the jacket around my left foot. As I enter the shop, I step carefully to avoid piercing my makeshift slipper. Glass crackles under my right boot heel and I see a piece of paper resting on the floor. I pick it up, thinking it might be a Clue. I unfold the paper and read:

INDIVIDUALS EXPERIENCING SYMPTOMS –
LETHARGY, SORE THROAT, NAUSEA, VOMITING,
LIGHT-HEADEDNESS, COUGHING – REPORT
IMMEDIATELY TO THE OLD MILL COMMUNITY
CENTER FOR MANDATORY QUARANTINE.

I stare at it for a moment, uncomprehending. And then, like dominos falling, I understand. I understand everything. Taking my cameraman away, the cabin, the careful clearing of all human life from my path – they're changing the narrative. I remember Google-mapping the area they told us we'd be filming in before I left home. I remember noticing a patch of green not far away: Worlds End State Park. I remember because I loved the name but cringed at the lack of an apostrophe. But perhaps the name isn't a title, but a statement. Perhaps the park's proximity to our starting location wasn't coincidence. For all I know, it *was* our starting location.

Those clever assholes.

I drop the flyer to the floor. It's a Clue, all right, telling me not where to go but where I am. The story behind their scattered props.

Everything in this store is up for grabs.

The first item I take is the fuzzy blue hat from the window. I slip it off the mannequin's plastic head and over my tangled hair. Then I head toward the register, where I see a standing cooler packed with beverages, sponsored by Coke. A dozen bottles of water, at least. I grab one, suck it down. Fill my Nalgenes, take the rest. I move on to a rotating rack of energy bars. KIND bars and Luna bars, Lärabars and Clif Bars and a half dozen other brands. I stuff my pockets with flavors I know and then I eat one. Lemon. Dessert-sweet, but I don't care; I inhale the whole thing and open a second. I stop after two, though, to allow my stomach to settle. Four hundred calories; it feels like a feast.

Next I walk through the aisles, savoring, dragging my fingers along clothing and flashlights and camp stoves. This, I realize, is my reward for making it through the coyote Challenge. I'd forgotten there would be a reward.

At the wall of footwear I see the ridiculous not-shoes that Cooper wears. Did he also face a coyote for his last Challenge? Maybe each of us got something different, something scaled to our abilities. Cooper got a bear, and he – I don't know how he handled it, except that he was perfect; if he breaks, it won't be because of panic. If Heather's still in the game, she got a bat or a spider. It seems unlikely she's lasted this long, though; she would have quit the second night if we'd made her go it alone. The Asian kid – I can't remember his name – got a raccoon or a fox, something smaller than a coyote, but clever. A squirrel for Randy, of course; or, no, a bunch of squirrels – a whole scurry of squirrels, as a chart I once read and want to believe claims a group should be called.

Whatever their Challenges, I hope they cried for help too. I hope everyone but me remembered the safety phrase and screamed it to the sky.

I hope they're okay.

I find a hiking boot I like – lightweight and waterproof – and take the display tag to what I imagine is the stock room, a door to the left of all the footwear. The room beyond is dark, windowless. Only a trickling of daylight enters from behind me. It doesn't smell.

I return to the aisles, find a flashlight and a pack of AA batteries. My stiff fingers can't open the packaging and my knife isn't much better, so I go to the Swiss Army Knives and Leathermans. I hesitate briefly – no weapons allowed – but as I pick one that feels comfortable in my hand and flip out its longest blade I remind myself that they're called multi-*tools* and are no more dangerous than the blade they gave me. I cut open the pack of batteries. This is beginning to feel like a scavenger hunt. Or a videogame. Find item A to gain access to item B, find item C to open item A. The sense of accomplishment I feel sliding the batteries into the flashlight is oddly intense, and this same sense of accomplishment makes me wary. They're putting me at ease. Something is going to go wrong soon. Something is waiting for me in the stock room.

But when I shine the flashlight inside, I see only inventory. The footwear is stacked on shelves along one wall. I find the boots I like in my size. They fit as though already broken in.

Next I go to the women's clothing section. I've been wearing the same clothing for at least two weeks, and they're thick with filth. When I pinch the fabric of my pants it crinkles and I'm pretty sure there's a little puff of dust. I select wicking undergarments, then a stack of tops and pants. I'm having fun, almost, as I take the goods into a changing room. I'm not sure why I bother with the changing room; they're as likely to have cameras in here as anywhere else and my modesty is long since compromised. By now they not only have me squatting and shitting on camera, they could air an entire episode of just my bodily functions.

I close the door of the dressing room. There's no ceiling; dim light creeps in from above, dusklike. I put my armful of clothing down on a bench, then turn – and gasp, stumbling backward in abject panic. For an instant I'm convinced I'm being attacked by an emaciated drifter.

A mirror. Like I'd forgotten they exist. But they do, and I'm surprised by the changes I see. I step close to the mirror to inspect my face. Below the bright blue hat, my cheeks are sunken. Giant bags hang under my eyes. I've never been this skinny. I've never been this dirty. When I take off my shirts, I see my ribs peeking from beneath my bra line. My stomach is concave. I don't think it's supposed to be. Sucking in my belly, I nearly disappear. Is this why I've been so cold? I step backward and my reflection becomes a smear of grime.

My priorities shift.

Leaving the clothing I've selected in the changing room, I search the store for soap, for cleansing wipes, for whatever I can find to rid myself of the filth that coats my skin. I've bathed a few times, kind of, and I've been rotating my underwear between two pairs. I clean each as best I can between uses, but it's been days since I last switched, and both pairs are stained and sour smelling.

I find the bathroom behind a door that reads EMPLOYEES

ONLY. By the light of a camping lantern, I turn the faucet. Nothing. Unsurprised, I take off the toilet's back lid and fill a collapsible dish with the water. I undress the rest of the way and give myself the most thorough washing I can, decimating a bar of organic hemp soap and turning three travel towels brown. I use the rest of the water from the toilet reservoir to rinse off. Afterward, I still feel a slick layer of soap residue upon the skin of my legs and feet. It's not a bad feeling. My hair is still disgusting, but the rest of me feels nearly clean.

I look at the filthy pants and bra on the floor and notice my mic pack resting in the folds. It's tiny and light, and I'd grown so used to it I forgot it was there. The battery's dead; it's been dead for a while. But surely the store is miked and the coyote was too.

I unclip the microphone just in case – it must be expensive, and I bet there's some clause I can't remember in the contract about keeping it – and carry it as I walk naked to the changing room, the blue hat in my other hand. I dress in clean underwear and a thin sports bra decorated with blue and green stripes. The first shirt I try on is a sack. The pants feel as though they'll slip off as soon as I take a step. I'm no longer a medium. I return to the clothing racks and a few minutes later am fully clothed – everything size S. Each piece is baggy, but it all stays on.

I knew I would lose weight during taping. Secretly, I considered it a bonus to being part of the show. But this degree of weight loss scares me; looking like this, it's difficult to tell myself that I am strong. My last period ended about a week before the show started; I wonder if this frail body is capable of having another.

I select a new jacket, a dark green one with a fleece-lined hood. It has zippers under the armpits, so I won't have to take it off and on so often. I transfer my surviving glasses lens to the jacket pocket. Then a backpack, which I fill with supplies: extra underwear, my second water bottle, a few packs of water purification drops, biodegradable cleansing wipes, a small bottle of Dr Bronner's, the flashlight, extra batteries, a compact poncho, my dull knife and the Leatherman I used to open the batteries, my battered little pot, a new first-aid kit to replace my depleted one, two dozen protein bars of assorted brands and flavors, some granola and beef jerky, trash bags from behind the counter. I find myself drawn toward superfluous gear: a BPA-free plastic spork, binoculars, a pocket trowel, deodorant. Of these luxury items, I allow myself to keep only a collapsible mug and a pack of herbal tea. There's no reason to weigh myself down now. Finally, I tuck the dead microphone into the media pocket at the top of the pack.

I'm ready to move on, but the sun is setting. It seems stupid to leave now.

It's a store, not a house. Maybe it's okay to sleep here. Maybe I'm meant to. I look at the tent in the window. Maybe this is still part of my reward.

I drag the tent through the aisles, setting it between the footwear display and a rack of Darn Tough socks. I stack several camping pads and two sleeping bags inside, then toss in an armful of tiny camping pillows. I illuminate my indoor camp with battery-operated lanterns, then the ultimate luxury: I light a camp stove. I find a rack of just-add-water meals in the corner. All the varieties sound delicious. I take three – chicken cashew curry, beef stew, chicken teriyaki with rice – and place them on the floor. I close my eyes and slide the packets around, then choose one without looking. Chicken cashew curry. I boil water and pour it into the bag. After what feels like the required thirteen minutes, I devour the rehydrated food with the spork I'm still telling myself I won't keep. It's not fully hydrated;

the specks of chicken are chewy and the green bits – celery? – have a serious crunch. But it's delicious – tangy and slightly sweet. Softened by soaking heat, the cashews are an entirely new entity from trail-mix nuts. When I close my eyes I can almost convince myself it's a freshly cooked dish. After I finish eating, I cram five of the meals into my new pack. That's all that will fit.

I crawl into the tent a few minutes later. I'm used to the prickling of pine needles, the crunch of dead leaves, the odd jabs of rocks and pinecones. The tent floor is uniformly soft. It's strange, and I'm not sure I like it. It's also warmer in here than I'm used to. I loosen the laces of my new boots and lie on top of the sleeping bags. As I lie there staring at the nylon sky, my muscles relax. This isn't so bad, I think. I could get used to this.

By morning I know better. I'm anxious to move on. I vaguely remember waking into uneasy semiconsciousness last night. How many times I'm not sure, but more than once. A tightness to my jaw and a lingering sense of fear tell me I had bad dreams, and though I can't remember particulars, I think they involved coyotes. Yes, a sinuous pack of coyotes coalescing like water droplets as they run soundless through the trees.

I shake off the sensation of being surrounded. I've been indoors too long, and I'm sore from sleeping on so much cushioning. I need to keep moving. I rehydrate a Denver omelet for breakfast, and then I go, returning to my road and hiking my way past the gas station, east.

8.

Rancher elbows Tracker and nods toward the picnic table that has appeared beside their fire pit. 'Quite the spread,' he says. Tracker steps away from his arm. Banker and Biology are grinning; the piece of mint leaf stuck in Biology's teeth will be wiped away in editing. There's far more food on the table than these four can eat in a single sitting. Grilled chicken breasts, burgers, rolls, Caesar salad, asparagus, corn on the cob, potato salad, sweet-potato fries piled high in a wicker basket, pitchers of filtered water and lemonade. The feast could feed all twelve contestants, easily. Banker looks at the other teams across the field, walking toward their respective camps.

'We could share,' he says.

Rancher shakes his head. 'Nah, we won, fair and square.'

'It's not like they're starving,' says Biology. 'It's just a game.'

Her last comment will be struck. The on-site producer will approach her later, remind her not to call their situation a game. 'We're trying to maintain a particular *feel,*' he'll say, and his eyes will drift toward her chest.

'Sure, sorry,' she'll reply, too tired to call out his wandering gaze.

As Tracker's team digs in, Zoo and Engineer head to the river, fishing kit in tow. Carpenter Chick and Waitress sit by the ashy remains of their fire, poking still-hot coals with sticks.

'Having a good time?' asks Carpenter Chick.

The day is warm, but Waitress remembers the cold of last night. Smudged mascara accentuates the exhaustion under her eyes. 'The best,' she replies, deadpan.

Carpenter Chick's lipstick has faded, but some of the eyeliner remains, giving her lids a smoky sheen. Her first impression of Waitress was rather contemptuous, but she's beginning to pity the sad, beautiful girl. That's how she thinks of her now – a girl, no matter that only two years separate them and Waitress is nearly a foot taller than she. 'What do you think the next Challenge will be?' she asks.

'I don't know, but I hope it involves caffeine.' Waitress grinds her stick into an orange coal. 'I'd kill for a skinny cappuccino.'

Carpenter Chick gave up caffeine a month earlier; it surprises her that another contestant didn't think to do the same. She wonders if Waitress did *anything* to prepare.

Zoo sits on a rock by the river, above a pool about a dozen yards from where Tracker crossed yesterday. Engineer crouches beside her. Behind his glasses, his eyes shine – he's confusing respect for attraction. Zoo doesn't acknowledge the look, but the editor dwells on it, a swell of music exaggerates it: infatuation. Viewers will notice, and Zoo's husband will too, watching. He won't blame the geeky young man – he understands his wife's appeal – but he will be jealous of him. The simple envy of a man who misses his wife. Of course, by the time this first episode airs, almost a week will have passed since his wife jabbed a hook through a cricket and tossed it into the river. By the time Zoo's husband sees this, the world will be on the cusp of great change.

But for now – Zoo catches a fish! She tugs it from the water, winding the line around the handle. The eight-inch trout flops on land, gasping, while Zoo and Engineer cheer. Engineer moves to hug her. She gives him a high five instead, and then smacks the trout's head against a rock. It takes her three strikes to kill it. For all her love of animals, for all her work with animals, she feels little remorse. She is

90

comfortable in her knowledge that humans are omnivores and that securing reliable sources of protein is what allowed the species to evolve its current intelligence. She will not kill to kill, but she will kill to eat, and she sees little difference between the eyes of a dead fish and a live one.

'Crickets,' she says to Engineer. 'Good call.'

Exorcist and Black Doctor are walking to check Air Force's snares. If any animals are near, Exorcist scares them away with his prattling.

'Last true demon I saw was about a year ago,' he says. 'It was inhabiting this sweet little girl, eight, nine years old. The day I arrived, I waited for her on the front stoop of her house. The girl was at school, where the demon mostly left her alone. Anyway, I was waiting out front of her house with her mom when the girl got off the school bus. She took a few steps and then – BAM!' He smacks his hand against a tree trunk. Black Doctor jumps. 'I saw it enter her,' says Exorcist, 'right there in the driveway. Her whole body shuddered, and then she – she grew. Not so you'd notice if you weren't looking, but I was looking. I took a step toward her' – he crouches slightly and edges forward as he speaks – 'and the demon roars. It takes this girl's body and commands her to exhibit its rage. She stomps' – he stomps – 'to her mom's car, a giant SUV – an Escape, I think, something like that, anyway, a *big* car – and with her tiny little hands she grabs the underside of the vehicle, right under the driver's door, and *wham,* flips it upward.' He throws his hands into the air. 'The SUV somersaults through the air, then lands with a crunch on its roof, right in the same exact spot where it'd been parked.' He holds his index finger and thumb about an inch apart. 'Not this far from where the girl stood. And she didn't move. The demon didn't *let* her move. I'll tell you, that was a humdinger of a job there. Four days to get the demon gone, and more vomit than I care to recall.' Exorcist pauses. 'A scorpion crawled out of her throat, I shit you not. That was the demon, making its escape.' He smashes his boot against the earth, grinding a leaf with his heel. 'I crushed it dead.'

'You killed a demon,' says Black Doctor, flatly. He's having a hard time deciding just how much of his own story Exorcist believes. The fact that he might believe any of it makes Black Doctor uneasy.

'Well, no.' Exorcist laughs. 'I don't have nearly that kind of power. I simply interrupted its manifestation. Demon's back in Hell, probably planning its next trip Earthside.'

Black Doctor doesn't know what to say. Exorcist is used to this reaction and takes comfort in the silence.

They reach the first of Air Force's deadfall traps. It's triggered but empty.

'Maybe the wind set it off,' says Exorcist.

Black Doctor glances at him and replies, 'Or a demon.'

As Tracker's team finishes their lunch, the host approaches. 'In addition to this grand meal,' he says, standing at the head of the picnic table, 'you get an advantage going into the next Challenge.' He pulls four maps from a pack. As soon as he sees the maps, Tracker fills his Nalgene from a water pitcher. The host continues, 'I said it takes place tomorrow, and technically it does. The start time is twelve-oh-one a.m. Your advantage is a head start in daylight, and these — just in case.' He hands each of them a flashlight. Tracker looks at his. It's more cumbersome than the flashlight he won in the first Challenge, and he won't use either — in his experience, with his skills, artificial light only disrupts night vision. He hands it back. The host stares at the flashlight for a second, then jokes, 'Aren't *we* the confident one,' before returning to his script. 'Remember, this is a Solo Challenge. That doesn't mean you *can't* cooperate, but there will be rewards corresponding to the order in which you finish.' With that, he distributes the maps and says, 'Good luck.'

Rancher unfolds his map and addresses Tracker, 'What do you think –'

But Tracker is already moving, wrapping three leftover chicken breasts in a wad of paper napkins.

'We should stick together, at least at first,' says Banker.

Tracker stuffs the chicken and his Nalgene into his backpack, then pulls on the pack and wraps the lanyard of his compass around his left wrist. He opens his map and considers it briefly. He looks at his team and without a word leaves them.

'Wait!' calls Banker. But Tracker's gone. The fittest cameraman scuttles to follow.

What will the rest of the team do? They've gotten on well until now. Banker wants to cooperate. Rancher's torn; he'd assumed they would move on together, but with their leader gone his assumptions are shattered. Biology tops off her water bottle, then declares her independence: 'Good luck, boys.' By the time she disappears into the trees Rancher and Banker are filling their packs, splitting the leftover food between them. They further weigh themselves down with plastic flatware and paper plates. Soon little more than the potato salad remains on the table, and the mayo-based dish is already looking a little off.

Partners for now, Rancher and Banker follow their maps and former teammates toward the waypoint. They're moving east. No one from the other two teams realizes they're on the move. They're busy roasting a fish and some Queen Anne's lace root, dropping iodine into bottles filled with river water. Many viewers will laugh: The chumps don't know what's waiting for them.

Carpenter Chick walks into camp, tightening the knot of her yellow bandana around her hair, no mention made of where she's been, no footage taken: female maintenance. Zoo takes a careful bite of roasted root. She chews, considering, then says, 'Could use a little seasoning, but other than that, not bad.' She offers the root to Engineer to taste.

Exorcist tells his teammates ridiculous tale after ridiculous tale with the air of total belief. He waves his green bandana for effect as he begins the umpteenth, 'I don't specialize in ghosts, but I've met a few. I was in Texas a few years ago –'

'Shut up!' bursts Cheerleader Boy. 'My God, I can't take it. Just shut up.'

'He's my God too,' Exorcist replies, straight-faced. 'More mine than yours, I suspect.'

Is this a gay slur? No one's sure – not Cheerleader Boy, not the producers, not the editor. Cheerleader Boy errs on the side of offense. 'I don't want anything to do with you or your God,' he says. 'Get away from me.'

Exorcist doesn't move; he watches Cheerleader Boy intensely. Without his smile, he's a little frightening. Black Doctor and Air Force both stand. Air Force's ankle gives as Black Doctor moves to intervene, but intervention isn't necessary. Cheerleader Boy sighs, says, 'Whatever,' and moves to the far side of their camp.

The editor will twist the moment. For all viewers will know, Exorcist hasn't spoken since his walk with Black Doctor much earlier in the day. Why did Cheerleader Boy explode like that, out of nowhere? What a huffy, irrational, *hateful* atheist. The spin declares that *this* – not his sexuality – is his fatal flaw. A politician can't win the American presidency without declaring himself a God-fearing man, and a vocal nonbeliever can't be put forth as a viable contender on a program striving for widespread popularity among the citizens of one nation under God. It's just good marketing sense.

Tracker consults his compass, then eyes a pair of boulders indicated by solid triangles on his map. He's on course and making remarkable time. His once-teammates are far behind. Biology stands below the more southerly of a pair of small cliff faces, thinking she's at the northern one. Banker and Rancher have drifted apart; Rancher is ahead. In fact, he's ahead of Biology too, though neither knows it. Viewers will know. They'll be shown a map with funky little symbols: four-legged rakes that have lost their handles stand in for cliffs, and Rancher's bumblebee dot chugs along, passing the northern cliff as Biology's orange dot meanders to the south. Banker's back a ways, about to cross a stream marked by a squiggling line.

Back at the camps, Black Doctor asks, 'How's your ankle?'

'Better,' says Air Force. He doesn't think he'll need the walking stick for much longer. He plans to be back in the game, soon. Cheerleader Boy sulks on the opposite side of the fire.

Zoo has enlisted her teammates in attempting to filter water. She's read about it, watched online how-tos, but never tried it. Carpenter Chick helps her set up a tripod of sticks, from which three bandanas hang like stacked hammocks: maroon with brown stripes, neon yellow and light blue. Nearby, Engineer is grinding charcoal to ash. This could have been Waitress's role, but she objected to getting her hands all black, so Zoo asked her to fill their bottles with water from the river instead. That's where she is now. Kneeling, Waitress swears softly; the rocks hurt her knees. 'Let's see Miss I've-Got-an-Idea carry her own stupid water for her own stupid filter,' she mutters. Her violet bandana holds back her hair.

Zoo drops handfuls of dirt into the yellow bandana, then she and Carpenter Chick join Engineer in grinding charcoal – they need a lot. When Waitress reappears with their bottles hanging heavily from her fingers, the others take handfuls of fine black ash and pile it into Zoo's blue bandana.

'So, how's this work?' asks Waitress, putting down the Nalgenes. Her face glistens with sweat and her bra has darkened between her breasts.

'You pour the water into the top bandana, and it filters down through the layers. Each one gets out more junk,' says Zoo. 'At least, that's the theory.'

'Most of the water filters you can buy are charcoal-based,' Engineer adds.

Zoo pours about a third of a Nalgene into Engineer's empty striped bandana. The water immediately starts dripping through to the middle tier, where it dampens the dirt.

'It's just making it wet,' says Waitress.

'Give it time,' says Engineer, as Zoo pours in more water.

Soon liquid drips through the lowest point of the yellow bandana, plopping into the charcoal below. Carpenter Chick pours a second Nalgene's contents into the top bandana. The drips coalesce into a thin, steady stream.

'What happens once it goes through the charcoal?' asks Waitress.

'We drink it,' says Zoo.

'From what?'

Zoo laughs, a loud, surprised laugh – there's no container under her bandana. 'I forgot,' she says, and she tucks an empty bottle under the bottom tier; there's not enough room for it to fit without impacting the bandana, so she digs a hole. The first few drips of clear water strike dirt, but the editor cuts them away. As far as viewers will know she finishes just in time to catch the first drop.

Three miles away, Tracker reaches a brown log cabin, where the host – having been treated to a journey via four-wheeler on an old logging road – waits.

'That was fast,' says the host, awe unfeigned. Tracker traversed the heavily wooded miles in only sixty-four minutes. Rancher, the nearest contestant, is more than a mile distant. The host sweeps his arm toward the log cabin. 'As the winner, the master bedroom is yours,' he says to Tracker. 'Last door on the left.'

Tracker enters to find a small but lavish bedroom: a queen-size bed thick with quilts and pillows, an en suite bathroom with a standing shower, a bowl of fruit on the nightstand. Two windows, both of which he opens.

Back in the field, eight contestants are preparing for nightfall: busy work and atmosphere.

Rancher breaks the tree line, sees the cabin and the host waiting. He's welcomed and directed to a room across the hall from Tracker's. A pair of twin beds with thin blankets and pillows, more fruit. A shared bathroom in the hall. Banker arrives a few seconds — twenty-two minutes, really — later. He gets the bed across from Rancher's.

'She left before us,' Rancher tells Tracker. 'I don't know where she is.'

Biology knows that she's off track and is trying to determine how far off. She sees a stream and beelines for it. She studies the features nearby: a cluster of boulders, the crumbled remains of a man-made wall. With her finger she searches the map, consulting the key at intervals. She finds the dotted line of the run-down wall, one of only two marked. The symbols match her surroundings. 'Here I am,' she says, exhaling with relief as she glances at the camera. She consults her compass to determine her next move. Northeast, to a marshy area — thin, tightly etched lines — that she should be able to follow to a thicket and boulder cluster. From there, a wooded but relatively flat half mile due east to the finish. She might make it before nightfall.

Carpenter Chick crawls into her corner of her team's

lean-to. 'Good night,' she says. It's more crowded tonight; Waitress has joined them. One by one, Air Force's team also trickles into their shelter. The cameramen chatter over their radios about needing better overnight footage and settle in.

The shadows around Biology are morphing into night. She has the flashlight in her hand. 'It can't be far,' she says. She wants to run, but knows that between the encroaching dark and her weary legs she'd probably hurt herself.

Exorcist snores. Cheerleader Boy lies awake in the dark, his face tight with loathing. In the other camp, Engineer is the one who is still awake. The warmth around him, the softness at his back – he decides his luck is definitely good.

Biology sees light through the trees. Like a moth, she hurries toward it. The host is there to greet her, as though he's been standing at attention for hours instead of reading comment threads on his smartphone.

'You made it,' he says. 'Welcome. You're our fourth-place finisher, which gives you your choice of beds here.' He opens the front door to reveal the log cabin's main room, which the editor will have hidden from viewers until now. The room is crammed tight with bunk beds – no pillows, a sheet each. Six beds total, leaving room for five more finishers, leading to the question: Where are the last three to sleep?

The men emerge to congratulate Biology on her arrival. All three are freshly showered. Banker's chest is bare, his shirt laid out by the fireplace, drying from a recent hand-washing. He clearly makes time for the gym, but Biology is far less impressed by his physique than the average female viewer will be. She collapses onto the bottom bunk nearest the fire. Tracker frowns. Judgmental jerk, bigoted viewers will think, assuming that he is scornful of Biology's relative weakness. Another misinterpretation. Tracker feels bad about Biology's exhaustion, her clear struggle. He is forcefully reminding himself that he's here for the money and that helping these people will only slow him down.

The window behind Tracker shows a setting sun. At the camps the sky is dark and the moon is high. Our narratives are out of sync.

A roaring blare rips through the camps – a sound like fear itself, loud and hard and everywhere. Contestants become a tangle of confused, waking limbs. Waitress yelps; Air Force is on his feet, injury forgotten; Exorcist freezes, tense and waiting.

'Good evening!' comes the host's voice, amplified. 'I need everyone in the center of the field, double time! Bring your gear. You have three minutes.'

Blinking heavily, Zoo shoves on her glasses, then tugs on her boots and shoulders her pack. Carpenter Chick is ready just as quickly. Engineer can't find his glasses; his eyesight is worse than Zoo's. Carpenter Chick is twenty-twenty; she spots his frames on the ground and hands them to him. Waitress is near tears, she's so tired. She doesn't think she can do this, whatever *this* is. Zoo and Engineer disassemble the water-filtration system, quickly. Bandanas are reclaimed. Zoo almost dumps the charcoal ash from hers, then changes her mind and ties the bandana into a little bundle as she walks.

Cheerleader Boy stalks toward the center of the field, alone. Air Force is hard-pressed to make it in time; he's feeling the ankle again. Black Doctor hangs back and offers an arm, which is politely declined – the walking stick is enough. Exorcist drifts along beside them, his pack casually slung over one shoulder. 'When you've dealt with those who dwell in Hell,' he says, 'an early wake-up call isn't so bad.'

The host is waiting. He holds a steaming mug of coffee. Waitress nearly tears it from his hands.

'Where's the other team?' asks Cheerleader Boy.

'Good morning!' says the host. 'And it is indeed morning. Twelve-oh-four a.m., to be precise.' All eight contestants have arrived within the allotted three minutes. A shame – the host was looking forward to penalizing someone. 'It's time for a Solo Challenge. Here are maps.' He indicates a bin to his left. 'And here are flashlights.' A bin to his right. 'First five to the waypoint get to sleep indoors. The quicker you finish, the more sleep you get. And, go!'

Engineer springs toward the maps; Zoo, Carpenter Chick and Waitress for the flashlights. Zoo takes a flashlight for Engineer, and Engineer takes four maps.

Waitress is terrified. She knows she can't make it through the night woods alone. Carpenter Chick catches Zoo's eye and nods a question.

'I'm happy to work this one as a team if you guys are,' says Zoo. If it was daylight, or she wasn't the leader, she'd be less inclined to cooperate, but right now working as a team seems prudent. The others agree; Waitress wants to hug them all.

Air Force and Black Doctor's cooperation is rightfully assumed. The level of mutual trust they've built in a day is remarkable. The producers will share a phone call later, seeking a way to use the allegiance against the allied.

'Maybe we should all stick together?' says Black Doctor to Exorcist and Cheerleader Boy.

Cheerleader Boy is still looking around for Tracker's team, the best team. He doesn't want to be locked into this one. Black Doctor and Air Force are okay, but Exorcist? Any minute spent in his company is a minute too long. Cheerleader Boy allows personal dislike to overwhelm common sense. 'He said it was a Solo Challenge,' he says. 'So I'm going solo.' He flips his former teammates a salute and then walks away – but only a few steps. He needs to consult his map.

'So we're here and we need to get . . . here,' says Zoo. Her finger cuts across a flashlight's beam to cast a thick shadow across the map.

'What are all these symbols?' asks Waitress. Her voice shakes.

'Look at the key,' says Carpenter Chick. 'Each means something different.' She pauses. 'What's a knoll?'

'They live under bridges,' says Waitress.

Her teammates look at her, incredulous.

'That's a *troll*,' says Engineer.

Waitress's embarrassed flush is hidden in the moonlight. She's rattled; her brain isn't working right. Laughter from the producers, laughter from the viewers. Perfect.

Cheerleader Boy is on the move, he's the first to leave. *Northeast,* he thinks. He'll just follow his compass northeast until he finds the stream above the waypoint, and then he'll cut south. Easy as pie.

'Look,' says Engineer, 'there's a road, half mile south. It's out of the way, but it passes right by the waypoint.'

'Genius,' says Zoo. 'That'll be much easier to follow in the dark. Let's do it.' Carpenter Chick agrees, and Waitress is along for the ride.

Air Force watches them go. 'I bet they're making for the service road,' he says.

'Should we do that too?' asks Black Doctor.

'Pah,' says Exorcist. 'Too far out of the way.'

Air Force is torn. He's trying to maximize his decision – what's worth more: shorter distance or easier terrain? If his ankle were healthy, the answer would be easy. Bravado and practicality war within him.

'The road seems like our best option to me,' says Black Doctor. 'I don't want to be tripping over roots and sticks in the dark.'

Exorcist jiggles his flashlight tauntingly, but Air Force

allows his new friend to guide him to the better decision. 'You're right, let's take the road.'

'That's like two extra miles,' says Exorcist. 'I'm out. See you at the finish.' He takes a quick measurement with his compass, then starts walking east. There's a trio of boulders a quarter mile away. He'll find those and then turn north toward a pair of cliff faces, he decides. It seems so easy. That's why they're doing it at night, he thinks – to add an element of actual challenge.

The map, now shown to viewers in a darker shade to indicate night. Dots of color and pattern creeping along: a cluster, a pair, and two singletons.

'What do you think happened to Cooper and the others?' asks Zoo.

'Maybe they left already?' says Engineer.

'Or got a ride,' says Waitress.

'Does it matter?' asks Carpenter Chick.

Their maps are tucked into pockets, and they pick their way through tangled brush. Zoo consults her compass every few minutes.

'They're following us,' says Engineer. The others look back, see two beams of light behind their cameramen, who have multiplied. One per contestant for this Challenge, in case they split up.

'We need to get the Chinese kid on our team next time,' says Air Force. 'Secure the fishing line, get some protein.'

'I'd gladly trade Josh or Randy for him,' says Black Doctor. 'Or both.'

Cheerleader Boy crashes through the trees. His pink dot is wildly off course – he hasn't checked his compass since leaving the field. He rubs at his burning eyes, then keeps walking, flashlight aimed at the ground. His cameraman pauses a moment. To rest, Cheerleader Boy thinks; the cameraman is carrying so much equipment, he must need to rest. He pauses too, and slaps at a late-night mosquito. Though he will not admit as much, the cameraman's presence gave him the courage to head off into the woods alone. It's only pretend alone, he thinks.

But the cameraman didn't pause to rest. He paused for a discreet close-up, which viewers will be treated to now: Cheerleader Boy's pink-dotted compass lying in the leaves. Motion ejected it from his shallow jacket pocket. He should have put it around his neck or wrist. Too late now.

Zoo's team finds the road: a scraggly, unpaved path rich with recent tire tracks. 'So, we follow this east for a couple of miles then turn north,' says Zoo. 'There's a bridge about halfway there, that should be obvious. After that . . .' She's looking at the map, considering.

Engineer steps up. He's never used a map quite like this, but is familiar with schematics. 'It looks like the best place to turn is about equidistant between this tree cluster and the end of this ditch,' he says.

'Perfect,' says Zoo. 'So after we cross the bridge, we'll watch for the . . . third ditch, then halfway between that and' – she laughs lightly – 'some trees, we'll turn north.'

'Some trees,' repeats Waitress.

'We'll figure it out when we get there,' Carpenter Chick assures her.

A couple of miles away, Cheerleader Boy walks through a spiderweb, swats at his face, and drops his flashlight. He wipes away the webbing, muttering curses that will be mostly censored, then bends to retrieve the flashlight. 'This is ridiculous,' he says. 'I've gone like ten miles, I should be at the stream by now.' He's gone less than a mile. He's nowhere near the stream, but he is close to learning just how alone a man can be with only a mute observer at his side.

Exorcist, conversely, is making good time. He's at the

base of the short cliff face Biology visited hours earlier, but he's correctly identified it as the more southerly of two. The northern cliff is his next goal. He checks his compass and proceeds, nimble in the dark.

Air Force and Black Doctor reach the road. They can see Zoo's group ahead. Air Force's ankle is sore but stable. He's still using the walking stick.

Time compresses: Hiking boots clonk over a wooden one-lane bridge, Exorcist whistles a familiar tune, Cheerleader Boy stumbles over a rotting log.

'This must be the ditch,' says Engineer. 'The tree cluster should be about a hundred feet ahead.' Zoo takes Waitress with her to scout. The cluster is easy to identify, a group of seven deciduous trees standing together at the side of the road, an expanse of grass separating them from the larger forest.

'Found it!' Zoo calls. The teammates converge on the midpoint and then strike north. A straight shot. They consult their compasses often, and when an obstacle — brush too thick to cross, the occasional boulder — presents itself, they stagger their advance to maintain the proper direction of travel.

The host is waiting for them on the porch, seated on a swinging bench. He waves.

Black Doctor and Air Force's exit strategy is different. 'If we go north from this ditch, to this wall here, from there it's almost directly northeast to the waypoint,' says Air Force.

Far ahead, Exorcist steps into the clearing before the cabin. He's earned the final bunk. Biology shushes his stomping entrance from her bunk and turns to face the wall.

The host greets Air Force and Black Doctor next, with a pitying 'Hello' as he steps to block the cabin's door. 'I'm afraid our bunks are full,' he says, and he points to a ratty lean-to about thirty feet away. The floor is lined with saw-dust and one corner of the roof has collapsed.

'At least it's not raining,' says Black Doctor.

Air Force asks, 'Who do you think is still out there?'

Cut to Cheerleader Boy, exasperated in light of moon and camera. 'Where's my compass?' he asks, patting at his pockets. He sits on a rock. The beam of his flashlight illu-minates his muddy boots. 'That cretin must have stolen it,' he says, though he knows that's impossible. He hasn't seen Exorcist since he left the group, and he had his compass with him then. He knows he lost it himself. 'The stars,' he says, looking up. 'I can navigate by the stars.' The canopy hides the sky, but even if it didn't, Cheerleader Boy would be unlikely to correctly identify the North Star, much less navigate by it. 'Okay,' he says. 'Okay, okay, okay. I can do this.' He glances imploringly at the cameraman, who stares in turn at his view screen. When Cheerleader Boy looks away, the cameraman turns off his radio, then taps one of the many accessories clipped to his belt.

Cheerleader Boy's flashlight sputters. 'No,' he says, slap-ping it against his palm. 'No no no.' The light dies. The cameraman switches to night vision as Cheerleader Boy stands and throws the dead flashlight to the ground. Cheer-leader Boy's grainy, green face tips from frustration toward fear. For about thirty seconds, he's stuck staring at the flash-light. Then he thinks, *If I leave now, I won't miss this semester.*

'*Ad . . .*' he says. '*Ad tedious . . .* shit.' He addresses the cameraman directly, 'I'm done.' The cameraman adjusts the frame. 'I don't remember the phrase, but I quit.' Cheer-leader Boy jams his hand into his pocket – the notecard! He unfolds it and holds it close to his nose. '*Ad . . . Ad . . .*'

It's too dark to read.

He sits again and cradles his face in his hands. 'Fuuuuuu-uck,' he says. The viewer will hear a long, haunting note.

Morning can't be far, thinks Cheerleader Boy. All he needs is a little light to read the phrase. Hours, that's all. He'll wait it out.

The cameraman taps at his belt again. The trees begin to creak, a wind-borne sound that gradually morphs into a cry and back again. Cheerleader Boy thinks he's hearing things that don't exist, but it's not his mind that's playing tricks. After forty minutes – ten seconds – of this creeping cycle, he begins to shake.

A scream, blood-curdling, from behind him. He leaps up, turns in a circle, sees nothing. The trees around him weep, louder.

Cheerleader Boy turns again to his cameraman. 'Come on,' he says. 'That's enough, I've had enough. I quit.'

Silence as complete as the darkness. Night's unnatural sounds have paused to consider and reject his plea. The sudden absence of sound strikes Cheerleader Boy like a blow.

'Please,' he says, and the first of his tears fall. He gropes toward the cameraman. 'Get me out of here, please.'

He's about to make physical contact.

This cannot be allowed.

A tiny light on the underside of the camera flips on. Cheerleader Boy freezes. The light is dim, but it's bright enough to illuminate a phrase printed sleekly beneath the lens. Cheerleader Boy nearly falls to his knees.

'*Ad tenebras dedi,*' he says, breath shuddering.

The screen goes black.

The host materializes, leaning against an exterior wall with his hands in his pockets. 'One down,' he says, and the first episode of *In the Dark* will end with his smirking face.

9.

I'm passing driveways more frequently now, the occasional farm. I still don't see any people; it's just me and the cameras. They told us this was going to be big – unprecedented – but still, the scope of the production astounds me.

They never said we'd be moving through populated areas, even rural ones.

There's a lot they never said.

Movement in my peripheral vision. I know instantly that it's animal movement. I turn toward a small white house obscured by deciduous trees. A brownish blur disappears into the side yard. I should keep walking. I shouldn't need to see, but something about yesterday's discovery has made me bold, or reckless.

I creep down the driveway and into the house's front lawn, then turn the corner and squint.

Three cats coil away from me, hissing. One calico, one white, and one all or mostly black. I think the white one wears a collar – I see pink on its neck. I step closer. The calico leaps through an open window in the side of the house. The other two scatter into the backyard.

My curiosity leads me to the window and I peer inside. A bedroom painted pistachio green. Bright clothing and a few stuffed animals strewn over milky white carpeting. I can't make out the details of the many posters on the walls, but two look like they're for bands and I recognize the pattern of a third as belonging to a werewolf romance movie that came out last year.

The cat bounds up from behind the bed and pads across

the rumpled comforter. It watches me as I watch it. Then it creeps forward and ducks its head. The head comes back up, then ducks again. It looks like the cat's eating. I blink a few times to refocus. The cat's definitely eating. As I watch, I'm able to make out its meal: a pale, bloated hand with dark fingernails. The cat nips between the thumb and forefinger, tearing away a small fleshy patch that does not bleed.

For a few seconds, I'm stuck, staring.

It's not a hand. It's *not* a hand. Of course it's not a hand, I know it's not a hand, but I'm sick of having to tell myself the obvious. I'm sick of it not feeling obvious.

I close my eyes and breathe, slowly. I need to stop letting them get to me.

I open my eyes and turn away. I start walking. When I notice movement a few minutes later, I don't investigate. All I can see is the puffy road, and I follow it around a curve and into the trees.

Hours later, it's time to make camp. I build my shelter and collect my firewood. I strip some bark for tinder, then reach for my belt loop.

It's empty.

My guts turn cold. My fist clenches.

My fire starter is still clipped to my old pants, discarded on the Trails 'N Things bathroom floor.

The loss makes me woozy. I rock backward to sit; the world rocks with me. I can't go back. I can't go through that town again. I can't lose two more whole days; this is a race and I'm already behind. My throat is so tight I can barely breathe. I cup my mouth and nose with my hands, bracing my jaw with my thumbs. Proximity turns my fingers translucent. The crumbled tinder is soft and sharp against my skin. The worst part is that this loss is wholly my fault – not a failed Challenge, just stupidity.

I had no idea it would be like this. They didn't say

anything about a fake pandemic or props shaped like dead people. About animatronics or feral cats. Empty towns and abandoned children. They didn't say anything about being so alone for so long.

I will not give them the satisfaction of seeing me cry.

Three words and it's over.

I close my eyes and rub my fingertips into the ridges of my eye sockets. My skin shifts with the pressure, skimming along the bone of my brow.

I thought this would be fun.

Ad tenebras dedi. I cannot speak it. I will not speak it. The journey's too hard only if I'm too soft. I don't want to be too soft. I don't want to be hard. I don't know what I want to be. I made it past the night hike. I made it past the cliff. I made it past the blue cabin and the doll. I made it past the coyote. This will not be the moment that breaks me. I will not quit, I *will* not. I can survive one night without fire. I can. And tomorrow? I have the multitool. I can make a spark with one of its attachments. I don't need to resort to the desperate rubbing of sticks. My blunder is not the end. Day-by-day, step-by-step, I will make it home.

I crawl into my shelter without eating and clutch my glasses lens in my palm. My stomach is as knotted as my hair. I sleep fitfully and dream of a baby, our baby, crying endlessly.

The next morning I break into a gas station. It's well stocked and prop-free. I help myself to water, jerky, and trail mix. A few pop-top cans of soup. I take a pack of sanitary napkins; it feels like I should be due soon. Just before exiting, I also grab a box of Junior Mints. As I walk away from the gas station, I shake the box like a maraca. The road bends. I play 'La Cucaracha.'

I'm trying to raise my spirits, but it's not working. My

improvised music only reminds me of all I've left behind. Feeling lighthearted, taking a moment to relax – I miss that. And I miss real food, modifying recipes to suit my tastes. Dicing five cloves of garlic instead of three, pouring in an extra swig of wine, substituting fresh herbs for dried. I miss the smell of sautéing onions and roasting chicken. The delicious wafting steam from a pot of lentil soup. I miss homemade bruschetta. Ripe tomatoes from the farmers' market, a handful each of purple and Thai basil from my herb garden.

'Miss.'

I miss lattes. Driving into town to the good café once a week, the perfect froth a whole-fat treat. Toddlers with iPhones at the next table, Mom and Dad guzzling espresso and pretending muffins are nutritious. Displaced hipsters pushing strollers outside; pocket-sized dogs tied to chairs, yapping and wagging their tails.

'Miss.'

I miss yoga classes. Kickboxing and spinning. Movement that led to strength, not this tightness I feel from brow to toes. I miss the chatty elementary school teacher who always put his mat to my left and the middle-aged lawyer who jabbed and crossed behind me. The lawyer used to tell me how skinny I was getting, nearly every week; now I'm the smallest I've ever been. I wonder if they're watching, if they miss me.

'Miss.'

I miss my husband's dark eyes and light laugh. His black stubble, flecked with white at the chin. Penguin coloring, we call it; inaccurate, but fun. I miss our jokes. I miss him. I miss *us*.

'Hey, Miss!'

The words crash through my thoughts. Actual spoken words and I'm not the one who said them. I stop and hear only my thrashing heart and the gentle slosh of water. Then footsteps from behind. I turn.

A young black man wearing a red sweatshirt and jeans stands only a few feet away. He's shorter than I am, lean, with buzzed hair. The whites of his eyes are huge. Beyond that, I can't discern much other than that his hair is hair, his skin is skin, and the lettering of his sweatshirt pulses lightly with his breath. In living, he is beautiful, as is all he represents: an end to *alone*. For three beats my heart says *yes yes yes*. I want to take this stranger in my arms and say: I've missed you.

My lips crack open. I almost whisper, then I can't. The words are not meant for this man. I blink once, heavily, and remind my heart of the game. I take a step away. He is here for a reason, I tell myself. He might be here to help.

'What do you want?' I ask. My voice crackles with disuse.

'I . . .' He fidgets. His voice is soft, and not very deep. Not deep at all. He can't be more than eighteen, and a late bloomer at that. White letters across his chest read: AUGERS? I squint. No, RUTGERS. He's a college kid – like Josh, who also seemed very young.

'I just haven't seen anyone else in so long,' he says. He's staring at me as though to prove his point.

I cannot trust him.

'Look for someone else,' I say, and I resume walking.

'Where are you going?'

He is walking beside me. When I don't answer him, he asks, 'Can I have something to drink?'

I gather all the generosity I can muster. 'There's a gas station around the bend. Get your own.'

'Will you wait for me?'

I stop and squint at him again. He must have been difficult to cast.

'Sure,' I say. 'I'll wait.'

His eyes widen with exaggerated emotion – I think it's supposed to look like joy. 'Around the bend?' he asks.

'Around the bend.'

'You'll be here?'

I nod.

He begins to jog, shooting glances back at me every few steps. He morphs into a red blur and disappears around the bend. I imagine him sprinting toward sustenance, taking his role seriously.

I wait a few more seconds then slip into the woods. I do my best not to leave a trail, though anyone with a tracker's eye could see where I passed through the tall grass. This kid doesn't seem like he has a tracker's eye, but he might have access to the cameras. A radio and GPS. I move slowly, but it doesn't matter. I'm carrying too much to be quiet and I keep stepping on crisp sticks and crunching leaves that are impossible for me to avoid. A blind man could find me. Maybe I should stop moving at all, but then I wouldn't be getting closer, I'd be stuck here and –

An anguished, wordless howl echoes through the woods.

I pause, momentum banging my water bottle against my hip. I hear another howl and can tell from the intonation that this one contains words, though I can't interpret them. I tell myself not to go back, and then I do. I leave the woods. As soon as I emerge, I see him. The road here is straight and I have not gone far. He runs toward me, sharpening as he nears.

'You said you'd wait,' he cries. His eyes are red and his dirty cheeks are river deltas drawn to scale.

He's a better actor than I figured.

'I'm here,' I say. 'Where's your stuff?'

'I dropped it,' he says. 'When I saw you weren't there.'

I walk with him to collect his provisions. They've spilled

from plastic bags he must have found behind the counter. Bottles and cans and oblong packages lie all over the road, some still rolling.

'You don't have a backpack?'

'I used to, but I lost it.'

I don't like him; his character clearly isn't very bright. While we're packing his supplies — as much soda as water, and mostly candy — he asks my name. For a second I can't remember, and then I lie.

'Mae,' I say. The month of my birth, but I imagine it spelled with an *E*. I've always liked how wise the letters *A* and *E* look, side by side.

He stares at me. Perhaps he knows I'm lying. Perhaps they told him my name. Finally he says, 'I'm Brennan.'

I've never met a Brennan before. I doubt it's his real name. Then again, I don't care. My eyes flick to his sweatshirt.

I begin to walk. The college kid follows, plastic bags in his hands, asking questions. He wants to know about me, where I'm from, how I got here, where I'm going, where I was 'when it happened.' *Why, why, why.* I almost expect him to hand me a second flyer. I play a game and tell him two lies for every truth. I'm from Raleigh, I got separated from a group of friends while white-water rafting and have been alone ever since, I'm going home. Soon I switch to all lies. I'm from a large family, I'm an environmental lawyer, my favorite food is peanut butter. My answers are inconsistent, but he doesn't seem to notice. I think he asks to hear my voice, and to give the editors something to edit other than my walking. I wonder how my lies will be portrayed; if I'll be taken aside to explain myself via confessional. I haven't done that since my fight with Heather.

The kid doesn't comment on my pace and I don't mention my broken glasses or the fog he becomes when more than a dozen feet distant. Around midday he stops asking questions long enough to complain, 'I'm tired, Mae.' He's hungry too; he wants to rest. I realize I haven't eaten since yesterday, and with the realization am light-headed. I sit on an embankment; he sits next to me, too close. I scoot a few inches to the side, drink some water, and pull the beef jerky from my bag. He pulls a Snickers bar and a pack of Skittles from his. He'll crash after the sugar rush, I think. I almost offer him a piece of jerky, then I remember that if he has to stop I can leave him behind. He dumps a handful of Skittles into his hand and pops them into his mouth.

I remember the Junior Mints. What happened to them? I check my pockets, my pack. I can't find them. I don't remember dropping them, or eating them, or anything other than shaking the box. For all I remember, they should still be in my hand. Perhaps I mindlessly tucked them into one of the plastic bags? It bothers me that I don't know, but not enough to ask. I gnaw my jerky, silent.

Despite his questionable diet, the kid keeps pace throughout the afternoon. It seems his youth and my poor vision have negated the difference in our meals. When the sun is a few fists above the horizon, I turn off the road.

'Where are you going, Mae?' he asks.

'I'm calling it a night.'

'There are empty houses all over,' he says. 'Let's find beds.'

I keep walking. I wish I could walk faster without risking a fall.

'Mae, come on. You're not serious?'

'You go find a bed, I'm sleeping here.'

He doesn't let the gap between us grow more than a few feet before following.

I build my shelter, using a low branch as its spine. The kid watches me and after a few minutes begins constructing his own. The branch he uses is too high, nearly shoulder-height. He leaves both ends open and barely layers any leaf litter on top, resulting in a structure that is more wind tunnel than shelter. I don't say anything; I don't care if he's cold.

I vaguely remember reading somewhere that quartz serves well as flint, so as I collect firewood I also collect rocks that glitter. After my tinder is ready, I take the largest stone and rub the dirt from its sharp edge with my shirt.

'What are you doing, Mae? Making a fire?'

I flick out a few of the tools on the Leatherman. I don't know which is best for making a spark, but the fire starter had one sharp edge and one curved, so I decide to try the shaft of the screwdriver. I hold the tool in my left hand and the rock in my right. I'm probably going to hurt myself. I wonder if a warm meal on a warm night is worth the trouble.

'You can really start a fire without matches?'

My stomach drops. Gas stations always have lighters on the counter, or matches behind the counter. I didn't even look. How could I be so stupid – again? Annoyed, I smash the flint and steel together in a downward motion. No spark, but I still have all my fingers. I try again, then again. The dirty bandage on the back of my right hand begins to peel. The rock splinters. I select a new one and switch from the screwdriver to the shortest blade. I should have taken the stupid bow drill they gave us for Solo. I never got a coal, never even got smoke, but I'd have a better chance with that kit than I do with this caveman banging.

'You haven't done this before, have you?'

I can barely see his face in the growing dark. My hands ache.

'Can I try?'

I hand him the Leatherman and a rock. He fails to create a spark for about thirty seconds, then jolts away. 'Ow!' He's dropped the tools and holds his left hand to his mouth, sucking on his pointer finger's knuckle.

On my next strike a lone spark leaps from the blade and floats toward the tinder – I hold my breath, watching. The spark lands, and then flickers out. Too late, I dip my face to the ground and blow.

'Do that again.' This time I can't resist glaring. 'Sorry,' he says.

Four strikes later, another spark lands. This time I'm ready. I breathe; tiny flames appear. The kid cheers and I find I'm smiling too. Within minutes, a full fire crackles before us. This feels like my greatest accomplishment in weeks, perhaps ever. I glance at the kid, who's warming his hands over the flames. I see drying blood on his knuckle. My mood sours instantly. He's not the person with whom I want to be sharing this moment.

I boil some water to rehydrate a packet of beef stew and take out the spork that I kept after all. The kid eyes my meal as he gnaws on a crumbling Butterfinger.

'Did you take anything other than candy?' I ask.

'Chips.' He pulls out a bag of kettle-cooked and his eyes slip again to the stew.

I chose my supplies with care. I cannot give him any.

A few minutes later, he coughs, hand to chest. He takes a sip of water and coughs again. When he sees me watching, he croaks an explanation, 'The peanut butter stuff got caught in my throat.'

Despite everything, I feel sorry for him. 'How about a trade?' I ask. 'I'll give you a beef and broccoli for the chips.' He hurriedly agrees. I don't want the chips and they take up too much space. I open the bag, squeeze out the excess air, and roll it closed. I jam it into my pack.

The kid pours hot water into the beef-and-broccoli pouch and pinches it shut. 'How long?' he asks.

I take another sporkful of my meal. He stares at me as I chew. After a moment I answer, 'Ten minutes.'

He's eyeing my stew again, but I've already given him enough. When he plows into his meal only a few minutes later, I can hear unabsorbed water sloshing in the bag and each bite crunching between his teeth. He pauses to wipe his face with his sleeve. A glitter of firelight reflects off his wrist. A bracelet, I think, and then I narrow my eyes, focusing long enough to make out an oval patch of contrasting color and texture.

It's not a bracelet – it's a watch.

The rules said no electronics allowed. We couldn't bring cellphones, or GPS devices, or wristwatches, or pocket watches, or any other sort of timepiece. My husband and I laughed over the list, and he asked, 'Who owns a pocket watch?'

Not this kid. He has a wristwatch. I stare at the device, stomach churning, and then it hits me – that's why he's here.

He's the cameraman.

There's a camera in his watch, and who knows where else – his belt buckle, hidden in the stitching of his sweatshirt. Mics too. He's the opposite of Wallaby – chatty and obtrusive – which means that he's not only here to record, he's also a Challenge. They've made him seem young and helpless, but he's not. Every action, every word, is part of the world they're creating. Because he's not *just* a cameraman; they've allowed him a name.

After I finish eating I go off to pee. When I return, Brennan's sneakered feet are poking from his worthless shelter. He's snoring and I hate him for it. I step on a twig. It snaps and he doesn't wake. I think about the flashlight in my bag. I could leave him. I wouldn't even have to go far, an hour or two of walking and he would never find me again. But no – this isn't like what Randy did; they would help him. He's a piece, not a player, and it seems they want him with me. Even so, I'm tempted, just to make their jobs harder, to make this kid feel a fraction of what I have felt. In the end, however, I decide sleep is more important than petty vengeance. I slip into my shelter and pull my pack in after me. I'm tired enough to fall asleep despite Brennan's snorts and wheezes.

A scream wakes me, late. A baby, a beast, my fears crash around me. I thrash against them, but after a panicked few seconds realize I'm not being attacked. The sound's gone. Heart thumping, I crawl outside. I see Brennan shivering, his knees pulled against his chest. He cries out, quick and sharp. The scream was his and he's still asleep, or pretending to be.

Solo Challenge obstacle number one thousand and thirty-seven: putting up with a stranger's night terrors. *Great.*

My adrenaline won't allow me to go back to sleep. I sit by the exhausted fire, poking the ashes with a stick as I watch the night. A bat skitters across the sky and I think of my honeymoon. I remember the warmth of my husband's arms around me as we sat on the balcony of a lakeside inn three years ago, watching bats at dusk. I remember him sneaking his hand to my hair and landing it there. I remember play-shrieking, dancing away – *get it off* – and I remember returning to his arms and all that followed. The next day we went swimming in the lake, and when we accidentally stepped on a little girl's sand rampart, my husband stooped immediately to help repair it. My instinct was simply to stand there thinking, *Oh, no.*

The balcony. The bats. My husband's hand in my hair. If he were here with me now, he wouldn't be able to get his fingers through the snarls. I pull my hood over my hair and stare at the ashes, half blind. I'd give anything to be back there, with him. I'd do anything.

Anything but quit.

In the morning Brennan is bright-eyed, nearly cheerful. Yesterday's questions become today's statements. As we walk he tells me about his family, his pet fish — a fighting betta — his school, his basketball team. I don't ask him about his sweatshirt; I don't ask him anything, and still he talks for most of the day, babbling like a toddler who's just discovered speech. He peppers in phrases like 'Before everyone got sick' and 'This one doctor on TV said . . .' When he starts in about weaponized Ebola, I nearly crack, nearly yell at him like I did Heather. This is his job, I remind myself. This is why he's here, to record and to irk. I can't let him get to me. I tune him out as best I can and keep walking.

That night his screams wake me again, and I think that a pack of hostile robo-coyotes would be preferable to this. But I have to put up with it, with all of it, because he's the cameraman.

In the Dark – The twist?

The only way off the show is to speak Latin? That's the twist? Ads had me thinking they'd be cannibals by now. But the maps are kinda cool and the survivalist dude is badass so I'll give it another episode. Plus the gay kid crying in the woods was hilarious.

submitted 33 days ago by Coriander522

242 comments

top comments
sorted by: **oldest**

[-] 3KatRiot 33 days ago

Like most 'reality' television, In the Dark is a totally inaccurate depiction of wilderness survival. That map and compass 'challenge' would barely qualify as an elementary school field trip. Put any of the cast in a real survival situation and they wouldn't last a day. Except for Badass Survival Dude. You're right about him.

[-] Velcro_Is_the_Worst 33 days ago

Meh. I could take it or leave it.

[-] LongLiveCaptainTightPants 33 days ago

You're missing the point: all that JUST happened! They're out there RIGHT NOW! And come on, they're one episode in. Let them find their footing. Friday's the first finale (weekly finales? Rad!), at least give it until then. I am.

> [-] 3KatRiot 33 days ago
>
> Doesn't make it an accurate depiction of wilderness survival. Plus they're shutting down all these public hiking trails and camping grounds to film this joke. This is what's wrong with America.

[-] LongLiveCaptainTightPants 33 days ago
They're not claiming to provide an accurate depiction of wilderness survival. The show's not about getting on in the woods, it's about breaking people – seeing how far each contestant will go before he or she quits. They explicitly said as much after they gave them the safety phrase. And if you want to discuss what's wrong with America, I'm pretty sure there's a thread for that <u>here.</u>

[-] HamMonster420 33 days ago
You can't have a 'weekly finale.' It's not a finale if it happens every week.

[-] Velcro_Is_the_Worst 33 days ago
Show needs more hot chicks.

[-] EarCanalSurfer 33 days ago
I could watch the redhead bend over all day.

[-] Velcro_Is_the_Worst 33 days ago
No way, too skinny. It's remarkable her guts fit inside.

[-] 501_Miles 33 days ago
I like the blonde. She's got moxie! And a great smile.

[-] Velcro_Is_the_Worst 33 days ago
Seriously? I'd choo-choo-choose Boobs over her any day.

[-] CharlieHorse11 33 days ago
Where are the acid volcanoes? I DEMAND ACID VOLCANOES!

. . .

10.

In the morning, the eleven remaining contestants assemble outside the log cabin, murmuring about their missing twelfth. An intern circulates among them, replacing the batteries in their matchbook-sized mic packs. The host steps up. He's holding a black backpack identical to the one worn by each contestant. A large plastic bucket sits on the ground to his right and a tall wooden post juts toward the sky on his left.

'We have our first casualty,' says the host. He reaches into the pack and pulls out Cheerleader Boy's knife and pink bandana. He pins the bandana to the post's midpoint with a violent stabbing motion. A few seconds of shocked silence follow from the contestants, then whispering: 'Did he quit?' 'You think he got hurt?' 'Scared of the dark, I bet.' 'Who cares.'

The host commands their attention with an imperial step forward. 'And now it's time to distribute his supplies.' His voice is light and happy, a startling and intentional contrast to his forceful use of the knife. He pulls Cheerleader Boy's trash bags from the backpack and gives one each to Air Force and Black Doctor. Exorcist steps forward to take the third, but the host turns from him to face the group of contestants who used to be Zoo's team.

He hands the folded trash bag to Waitress. 'He wanted you to have this.'

Waitress accepts the black plastic with a mix of reverence and guilt. Though her head is creaking, she slept on a mattress last night and was able to shower this morning. She feels far better than she did yesterday. But she's not sure what to think about this bequeathal. She wouldn't have given Cheerleader Boy anything.

Next the host pulls a water bottle out of the pack. It's full – though this will go unspoken, any time a contestant quits, his or her Nalgene will be filled with clean water before being given to its next owner. 'As for this, it goes to . . .' The host drags his gaze along the contestants as he paces left to right and back again, drawing out the moment. Waitress is the only one among them who doesn't want the water; she has three bottles already and they're heavy.

Cheerleader Boy's exit interview will be shown now, intercut with footage of his being led out of the woods by an unidentified guide dressed in black. 'Did I think I would be the first to go?' he says. 'No, but who ever does?' He's in the backseat of a car. The windows are tinted. 'I don't regret coming, but enough is enough, I'm ready to go home. I don't really care who gets my stuff.'

The host stops in front of Black Doctor.

'Doc's all right,' says Cheerleader Boy. 'And he's really concerned about having clean water. Give it to him, I guess. Anyone but Randy.' The muscles of his face twitch into hatred, almost too quick to see. He closes his eyes and eases back into the seat. 'I can't wait to be home.'

Black Doctor accepts the bottle solemnly, and the host moves on.

'Our second Team Challenge will take place today,' he says. 'But first, a Solo Challenge to determine teams.' He indicates the bucket with a wave of his hand, and viewers will be treated to a view of what it contains: brown water rich with unidentifiable organic bits. The camera pans out, revealing a table with two more buckets on top. One contains sand, the other chunks of charcoal. Next to the buckets are eleven two-liter soda bottles, labels removed. Zoo's hand is in her pocket, clenching a bundled blue bandana. The host explains what she expects him to explain: Using the items on the table, as well as the supplies already in their possession and whatever they can scavenge, the contestants have to filter water. They have thirty minutes. 'You must have at least one cup filtered by the Challenge's end, or you're disqualified. Whoever's water is the clearest wins.'

The half-hour-long Challenge will be compressed into three minutes. Much of those three minutes is focused on Zoo, who leaps into action, sawing a two-liter bottle in half with her knife then stabbing a series of small holes in its bottom. She dumps in her damp charcoal dust, packing it tight, then layers sand on top, followed by pebbles and blades of grass. Using the top half of the severed bottle, she scoops and pours dirty water into her makeshift filter. She holds the filter above her measuring cup and waits. As Zoo's water dribbles through, Tracker finishes grinding his charcoal to ash and begins constructing his filter. The others are watching these two, emulating them with varying degrees of success.

'Yesterday, I thought she was being noble using her bandana for the ash,' says Carpenter Chick as she puts rock to charcoal. 'I figured that would be the hardest to clean. It sucks that she has it now, but good for her, really. I wouldn't have thought to keep it.'

'Smart,' says Engineer.

'Lucky,' says Waitress. She pokes her two-liter bottle with her knife, tentative.

Zoo's water has filled her measuring cup but retains a yellow-brown tint. 'Ten minutes,' says the host. She scoops the worst of the filtered goop from her top layer and replaces the grass, then dumps the once-filtered water back in.

Banker's filter is a muddy swirl, his measuring cup dry.

'Think they'll notice if I just fill it with this?' asks Black Doctor, holding up the bottle he received from Cheerleader Boy.

Rancher, Air Force and Engineer are doing well. Almost as well as Tracker. If not for Zoo's advantage, this would be a race.

'Time!'

Waitress and Banker have barely any water in their measuring cups. Exorcist is a third of a cup shy. All three are disqualified. Of the remaining eight, there is an obvious winner. Zoo's water is not crystal clear, but it's far less yellow than the rest. Biology's cup looks like she dipped it straight into the dirty bucket.

'Congratulations,' says the host to Zoo. 'As your reward, you get to assign teams for our next Challenge. Partners, but with one team of three due to the . . . oddness of the group.' The producers don't like this; he'll have to re-record the line later, sans pun.

'Do I get to know anything about the Challenge before I choose?' asks Zoo.

'No. Who do you want as your partner?'

Engineer is trying not to smile; it'll be him. It *has* to be him – they caught a fish together.

Zoo doesn't hesitate before naming Tracker. Engineer is quietly devastated. Zoo pairs him with Carpenter Chick, thinking that they will work well together. Her next move splits the young alliance as she pairs Air Force with Biology and Black Doctor with Banker. That leaves Rancher, Waitress and Exorcist as the team of three.

The host motions for everyone to follow him. He leads them west, in the direction of yesterday's field. The trek that follows will be glossed over – they've arrived! They're at the southern cliff, the one visited by both Biology and Exorcist during last night's Challenge. A salmon-colored rope now dangles from the top of the cliff, where it's anchored to two tree trunks and a small sunken boulder.

Banker is smiling. 'Nice,' he says. At Black Doctor's curious look he adds, 'We got this.'

'No way,' says Waitress. The editor decides to make this her catchphrase. 'No way. I hate heights.'

Exorcist gives her a condescending look. 'It's only like thirty feet.'

Rancher considers the cliff face, the rope. 'We have to climb that?' he asks. It's unclear who's more frightened — him or Waitress.

The host steps forward to stand at the base of the cliff. He tugs on the dangling ends of the rope with one hand. 'Rock climbing,' he says. 'It may not be an essential skill for wilderness survival, but it can get you out of a bind. Plus' — he flashes a white-picket smile — 'it's fun. The first part of this Challenge is to get one member of your team to the top as quickly as you can. Your finishing time will determine the order in which you set off on the next phase.' He turns to Zoo. 'Who's first?'

Zoo didn't hear Banker's confident remark to his partner and wonders if anyone here is a climber. She's gone a few times with friends to indoor climbing gyms, but has never climbed outdoors. After a moment, she names Biology and Air Force to start.

'Have you climbed before?' Air Force asks his partner.

Biology shakes her head.

'Who's ascending?' asks the host.

'I am,' says Air Force.

Time skips. Air Force and Biology both wear helmets and harnesses. All the contestants have received an off-camera lesson in how to take up a rope's slack as a climber climbs — Banker scoffs at the equipment, 'Anyone can belay with a grigri,' but he helps Black Doctor when he gets confused – and a guide who will never appear on camera positions himself behind Biology to serve as her backup. Air Force is tied in, and the belay device is clipped to Biology's harness. The leg loops of the harness frame her rump, lifting both cheeks, and the waist is tight only a few inches below her breasts, like an underline. The camera lingers, shameless.

'I've climbed wooden walls, but never a rock wall,' says Air Force. His short hair is oily and his skin shimmers with sweat. There's a smear of dirt down his neck from where he scratched at a mosquito bite. He and Black Doctor are the only two who weren't able to shower since the overnight Challenge. 'We'll see how it goes.' He pauses. 'My ankle? It feels better. It'll be fine.'

'And go!' says the host.

Air Force doesn't have enough experience to race up the cliff face, and he knows this. He considers where to start. Any climbers watching will know what Banker already knows: This route is a 5.5 – an easy 5.6, tops – a slab with juggy holds. This Challenge is more mental than physical.

Air Force touches the rock above his head, then steps onto a knee-high ridge. He's off the ground. Biology yanks the rope's slack through the belay device. She's tense; she truly believes she has another's life in her hands. Behind her, the guide keeps a brake hand on the rope. Air Force begins to move upward, clenching the rock and keeping his body close. He's relying too much on his arms; soon his forearms are pumped and his fingers ache. He's halfway up. He pauses with his cheek pressed to the cool rock face and looks down. The view doesn't affect him; he's out of his comfort zone, but steady. He shakes out his hands, one after the other, then creeps his fingers up to the next hold.

Five minutes and four seconds into the Challenge he swats the white-tape X at the top of the cliff with his gritty palm. Biology yanks out any last inch of slack, then Air Force sits back and lets go of the wall. Biology releases the brake and her partner walks his way back down the cliff face. She doesn't breathe until he reaches the ground.

'Who's next?' the host asks Zoo.

She points at the trio.

'And I will ascend to Heaven,' says Exorcist. He cracks his knuckles, then attacks the wall, scurrying up the rock like a beetle. Waitress is sitting out; Rancher struggles to take up the slack quickly enough. The motion is unfamiliar and he can't quite keep pace.

Exorcist slips, scrabbling with hands and feet as he careens toward the ground. Waitress shrieks. Exorcist jolts to a stop halfway down; Rancher is lifted to his toes and jerked forward, both hands tight about the rope below his waist. His backup holds firm. Exorcist swings left, twirling and bashing his shoulder into the rock. When he finally stills, dangling loosely in his harness, there's blood on his face and hands.

Viewers will now see Exorcist from above, as the camera drone swoops down from invisibility to zoom in on his pale, sweaty face. The blood on his forehead and left cheek is like war paint, smeared from his scraped palm and fingertips. His jaw is tight, his almond-brown eyes wide.

'Can you continue?' the host calls.

Exorcist nods stiffly. His God-given bravado is faltering. For the first time since taping began, he's visibly scared. His fear makes him seem more real, like a person instead of a caricature. The producers are concerned; this isn't why he was cast. But they give the editor the moment. They too are curious where it might go.

A full minute passes – a few seconds for the viewer – as Exorcist collects himself. When he resumes climbing, he moves with unaccustomed care.

'Wow,' says Carpenter Chick. 'He's got guts.'

Engineer nods; he doesn't think he could keep climbing after a fall like that.

On the whole, the respect the contestants have for Exorcist ticks up a notch – from zero to one on a yet-to-be-determined scale.

Exorcist finishes with a time of nine minutes and thirty-two seconds.

Banker and Black Doctor are next. It's clear from Banker's first move that he's an experienced climber. He glides up the wall, moving with smooth efficiency. His ascent will be intercut with a confessional: 'You'll find me in the Gunks most summer weekends, and I climbed El Cap last year. This is a great Challenge for my skill set. I'm pretty confident I'm going to kill it.' He slaps the white X after only one minute and forty-four seconds. He's not even breathing hard. Black Doctor whoops as he lowers his partner. Exorcist's eyes narrow.

'Wow,' says Zoo. 'Nice.' She turns to Engineer and Carpenter Chick. 'You're up. Good luck.'

For the first time, a woman ties in to climb. 'I don't know,' says Carpenter Chick via confessional. 'Heights have never really bothered me. I kind of like them. Some of my favorite days on the job have been on roofs. This looks fun.'

Carpenter Chick is short, which limits her reach, but she is also light and highly flexible – residue of a childhood passion for gymnastics. And though she doesn't make it look as easy as Banker did, there is ease to her movements as she climbs. She taps the X at four minutes and thirteen seconds, placing her and Engineer in second place.

Zoo and Tracker are up. 'Part of me feels like I should've volunteered to climb,' says Zoo, as Tracker ties in. 'Like I should take on anything, no matter how scary or difficult. But you have to take strategy into consideration too, and in this case it's clear that my partner's going to be better at this than me. I mean, did you see him with that tree the other day? He's like a monkey. Or a cat.' She laughs. 'A monkey-cat. Sounds cute, right?' Accusations of racism will pepper the Internet – Zoo would be horrified if she knew. She meant only that he climbs well.

On the cliff face, Tracker lacks Banker's experience, but he knows movement and he knows his body. He moves quickly and sleekly toward the top. The timer ticks. 'One minute down,' says the host. Tracker has just passed the halfway point. He has forty-three seconds left if he wants to beat Banker. He does want to beat him – but he also knows his limits. His fingers are learning the rock, his eyes and brain working together to judge the best holds ahead of time. 'One minute thirty!' He's close to the top, but is he close enough? Black Doctor grips Banker's shoulder.

'One forty-four,' says the host.

Black Doctor and Banker slap a high five.

Fourteen seconds later, Tracker reaches the X. He and Zoo finish in second place.

Between all the delays and transitions, this Challenge has lasted hours. The fruit provided in the log cabin was devoured long ago. Rancher has one burger still tucked in his pack, and Banker a fistful of limp asparagus. Tracker finished the last of his chicken this morning; he prefers calories now to calories later, always. 'I'm starving,' says Engineer. Biology has only a few protein bars left and she's no longer sharing.

The host had eggs and sausage for breakfast. There was no time for lunch, but he ate a Snickers bar and drank a Coke Zero between climbs, turning his back to the contestants as he ate. He's looking forward to sending them off on the next leg of the Challenge so he can have a sandwich. But first, more down time. The contestants mill about, anxious to know what's coming next. After a few minutes, an intern barrels in from the south, shouting, 'Sorry, sorry!' He's chubby and white, in his early twenties. He carries a large duffel bag, which he brings to the host.

'About time,' says the host, as the contestants are ordered to line up in front of him.

The duffel bag contains five rolled-up maps, one for each team. The host flourishes one. 'The next phase of this Team Challenge is tougher than anything you've faced so far. And longer. Inside your map, you will find a printed Clue, which will lead you to a waypoint with another Clue. The third and final Clue will lead you to the Challenge's finish.' He pauses. 'You will *not* finish today.' Several of the contestants grumble, their murmurs an undertone to the host's words as he continues, 'The order in which you leave on this journey will be determined by how you finished your climbs.' He hands one of the rolled maps to Banker. 'You two leave first, followed by the others in ten-minute intervals. Your time starts now.'

Banker and Black Doctor rush to collect their gear, then dart about twenty feet away to unfurl their map. The others mill about; Waitress sits, leaning against a tree and closing her eyes.

The new map is topographical, covering many more square miles than anything the contestants have been shown before. Rounded shapes, never quite concentric, and the *U*'s and *V*'s of running water tell the land's tale. A You-Are-Here dot is settled near the bottom-left corner. Last night's dirt road looks very close at this scale. A curl of paper tucked inside the map reads:

A boulder suns itself at a creek's U-bend. As midday passes, the land's tallest peak casts a blocking shadow. Tucked into the darkest dark, your next Clue waits.

'Okay,' says Black Doctor. 'That's pretty clear, right? We need to find a boulder along a creek to the east of the tallest mountain. Where's that?'

Banker runs his forefinger along the map, scanning contour lines. 'Here,' he says. 'This one's the tallest.'

'And there's a blue line,' says Black Doctor. 'But I don't see the boulder.'

Banker swallows a laugh, not wanting to be rude. Black Doctor doesn't see his smile, but viewers will. 'I don't think they're going to show the boulder on here,' says Banker. 'Not at this scale. We need to look for the bend.'

'Ah, right. So that's . . . this?' Black Doctor jabs the map with his index finger. A comment thread will unexpectedly erupt on this topic – Black Doctor's thick fingers. *How can he use a scaple with fingers like that?* one user will ask; the red line of misspelling obvious beneath as she hits *post,* but she doesn't care. Another, *I don't want those hairy nubs operating on me!* A lone voice of reason will tell people that one can't actually determine an individual's dexterity by looking at his fingers, and besides, they don't even know what kind of doctor he is. And it's true: Black Doctor is not a surgeon. He's a radiologist and his stubby fingers get the job done.

'Looks like the bend to me,' says Banker. 'Now, what's the best way to get there?'

They take turns prodding at the map, exchanging ideas, and after a few minutes settle on a route that mostly involves following water upstream. They check their compasses, then strike out into the woods.

When Zoo and Tracker are given their map four minutes later, they determine the destination almost instantly, and Tracker notes something that Black Doctor and Banker did not: the giant swath of white cutting through the map's abundant green east of the mountain creek. 'I suggest we follow this clearing north, then shoot a bearing to the U-bend from its northern edge,' he says.

'Sounds great,' says Zoo with a laugh. 'But will you tell me what "shoot a bearing" means?'

Tracker doesn't understand why she's laughing. Neither her question nor her ignorance is funny. But they're partners for now and so he answers, 'It's using the compass to determine what direction you should move in, then following your bearing landmark to landmark in an area where it would otherwise be very easy to lose your direction of travel.'

'Oh!' says Zoo. 'We kind of did that last night.'

Tracker blinks at her, then takes out his compass and places it on the ground on top of the map. He shifts the paper slightly so the map's north aligns with his compass's, then twists the compass housing to bring the north needle home. 'Thirty-eight degrees,' he says, mostly to himself. 'That'll get us to the field. Although . . .' He scans the perimeter of the map.

'What are you looking for?' asks Zoo.

'Declination,' says Tracker. There's small print, but not the small print he's looking for. 'Doesn't say. Around here, it has to be at least five degrees. So, forty-three degrees. That's our direction of travel.'

Zoo sets her compass to forty-three, then tucks it perpendicular to her chest. Tracker folds the map to leave their current location exposed.

'That dead tree?' asks Zoo. A decaying, toppled-over birch is as far as she can see along the line.

'Why not,' says Tracker.

They begin walking.

'I've heard of declination,' says Zoo, 'but I have to be honest – I have no idea what it is.'

Tracker doesn't reply. He's already talked more than he'd like.

Zoo allows him a few steps of silence, then insists, 'So, what *is* declination?'

'The difference between true north and magnetic north,' he relents. Zoo's curious look prods him to further explanation. 'Maps are set to true north – the North Pole – and compasses to magnetic north. Factoring in declination corrects for that difference.'

'Ah.' Zoo is trying and failing to move as quietly and smoothly as Tracker. A branch snaps under her foot and she grimaces. The cameraman following them is even louder than she is. He stumbles and nearly falls. Zoo starts to ask if he's all right, then aborts the nicety. He's not here, she reminds herself. And then she laughs again, thinking: *If a cameraman falls in the woods and no one turns to see, did he make a sound?*

Tracker's back and mouth curl ever so slightly.

The next team to receive their map is Carpenter Chick and Engineer. They're on their way within moments, as are Air Force and Biology, once they receive theirs.

But the final group – the trio – struggles. Rancher is so thoroughly flummoxed by the map that he barely registers the Clue as Waitress reads it aloud. He knows his land, but his land is a single rolling vowel. The land here is a series of sharp consonants. Indecipherable lines burrow through his vision. Waitress is also far out of her depth. But the team's biggest problem is Exorcist. His hands, shoulder and pride still ache from his fall. By his reckoning, this Clue belongs to him and him alone – he was the one who climbed, the one who fell. He seethes and struggles not to rip the paper from Waitress's hands. He is full of hateful thoughts – sexist thoughts, racist thoughts. The aftermath of his humanizing crash is the flaring of his most monstrous self.

Exorcist is well aware of this monstrous self, though he would never choose it. He wishes he could banish it. Every time he convinces a spurned mother or belt-whipped boy that their hatred is an outside invader, it helps. Converting another's hatred into a demon and expelling it makes it possible for him to suffer his own. But there is no one here to exorcise. He's taken the lay of the land and it is barren. This leaves Exorcist grasping at past experiences. The Clue echoes through his mind and he says, 'Boulder. I knew a woman from Boulder once. She called on me to help with a certain situation.'

'Now's really not the time,' says Waitress.

Exorcist plows forward. He has to. 'She didn't have a true demon, few of them do. But I could still help. I tell her, "Yes, you're possessed." This woman, she'd been hearing "no" for so long, just hearing "yes" did most of the job. Lord, but did peace settle into her eyes right then.'

'We need to figure this out,' says Waitress.

Exorcist fiddles with the map, crinkling a corner. 'After that, all she needed was a little handholding and prayer. Easy peasy.'

'What's the Clue say?' asks Rancher.

Waitress has already read it aloud twice. 'Here,' she says, handing him the slip of paper.

'They aren't all that easy,' says Exorcist. 'Most take a lot more effort. But there was something sweet about this case. They're always thankful, but she was *thankful*. And I don't mean sexually – I get that sometimes, though usually it's part of the possession.'

'Can you focus, please?' says Waitress. 'Do either of you know how to read one of these maps?'

'A creek's U-bend,' mutters Rancher. 'Well, blue's water,

ain't it? And a creek's a line, so where does a blue line bend?'
He leans over the map. He's holding his hat, and his striated
hair falls forward from either side of his face like curtains
closing.

'Lots of places,' says Waitress. 'How do we find the tallest peak?'

'I think these lines are for elevation,' says Rancher.

Exorcist is quiet. He's thinking more about the thankful
woman. She was one of the few, perhaps the only one, who
understood. She'd held his hand before he left, clenched it
tight, and said, 'I know this wasn't a real exorcism, but
whatever you did it was supremely *real*. It helped. Thank
you.' She was not the kind of woman to use a word like
'supremely,' but that's how he remembers it, though sometimes he thinks that maybe she just held his hand and didn't
speak at all.

'This one's the highest, right?' says Waitress.

'Looks like,' says Rancher. Waitress makes him uncomfortable, crouched there with her midsection exposed. He
thinks women should have a bit more modesty. Yet it's hard
not to sneak a glance every now and then. He's married but
doesn't love his wife. He was head over heels once, though
this no longer feels possible. He does love his children,
however: two boys and a girl, ages fifteen, twelve and
eleven.

'So, a bend near this peak,' says Rancher. It's not hot, but
he's sweating. He can feel the cameras on him.

'A river runs down either side,' says Waitress. 'Both have
bends. How do we know which one?'

'Something about the sunset?' asks Rancher.

'Ah, right!' Waitress claps her hands and smiles. 'Never . . .
eat . . . shredded . . . wheat!' She dabs her finger along the
map's compass points with each word. 'West. The sun sets
in the west, it's the one on this side.' Her confidence flares;

she's enormously proud of herself for figuring this out. Rancher doesn't catch her mistake. Most viewers won't either.

Hours and hours of walking; who has the patience for so much walking? It's unwatchable. Five teams, at least four miles each. Some take unintentional detours, and one is heading toward a point nearly three miles from where they're meant to go. All that walking, all that struggle, condensed into a subtitle: HOURS LATER.

Hours later, Tracker and Zoo skirt a long field of wildflowers, then cut west. Hours later, Banker and Black Doctor totter across stones to cross a creek. Hours later, Carpenter Chick pushes a branch out of her way; it snaps back and smacks Engineer in the chest. Hours later, Air Force is hobbling along, his ankle needing a rest that Biology is willing to give but he's unwilling to take. Hours later, Exorcist has recovered enough to say, 'Let me see the map.'

Waitress hands it to him.

'Where are we heading?'

She shows him. He reads the Clue, looks at the map. His face is twisted with thought. He looks back at the Clue.

'That's wrong,' he says.

'What do you mean, "That's wrong"?' Waitress's posture slips into an offensive stance familiar to fans of reality television; she stands with one hand on a cocked hip, her head pulled back and tucked slightly down, daring, just daring, him to keep talking. Rancher peeks over Exorcist's shoulder.

'As midday passes, the land's tallest peak casts a blocking shadow,' recites Exorcist. He flicks the mountain on the map. 'If it's casting a shadow in the afternoon, that shadow's going to fall to the east.'

'No,' says Waitress. 'The sun sets to the *west*.' She rolls her eyes. Next she'll be accusing someone of throwing her under the bus.

'He's right,' says Rancher, and Waitress spins to face him. 'Look at it this way. If you got a light on the left of an object' – Rancher holds his right arm in front of his face, then pulses the fingers of his left hand to its side – 'the shadow will fall to the opposite side.'

Her mistake is obvious now, to everyone. Waitress's face is flushed. She misses her old team: the scrawny Asians and the bossy blonde.

Exorcist is laughing. 'You ought to have been a teacher,' he says, slapping Rancher's shoulder. He sobers quickly once he looks back to the map. 'We're way off course,' he says. 'We've got to cut east.'

Miles away, Tracker and Zoo are not off course. They are on course, the best possible course.

'There it is!' cries Zoo, pointing at a six-foot-tall boulder resting by a small creek. The water's turn is obvious on the map, subtle in person. Viewers will be shown an aerial shot to confirm that the location matches the Clue.

Zoo jogs ahead of Tracker, who raises an eyebrow at her exuberance. Sunset is only a couple of hours away, and this stretch of land is largely in shadow. 'Tucked into the darkest dark,' says Zoo, as she reaches the boulder. 'Darkest dark.' She's searching the base for a hole. It takes her eight seconds to find it. All eight seconds will be shown, and viewers will feel like she's failing, like she's taking forever, because they're used to scenes like this being shortened. From Zoo and Tracker's perspective she finds the metal box very quickly.

She pulls out the box from its niche and unlatches it. Tracker is at her side now. As Zoo opens the box he cranes his neck to see.

Five rolls of paper, like miniature scrolls.

'We're the first ones here,' says Zoo.

Tracker isn't surprised that they've beaten Banker and Black Doctor. Open ground saves time, always. 'What does it say?' he asks.

Zoo hands him one of the scrolls, then closes the box and tucks it back into its shadow.

Tracker unfurls the Clue and reads it aloud. 'An animal made prey. Pursued, it leaves a trail. Within a mile, it crosses. Follow the trail.'

'Crosses,' says Zoo, and she looks to the stream. She doesn't see a trail. Tracker does. He also sees signs of the human who made the false animal tracks – the Expert wasn't careful; he wants these tracks to be found.

'There,' he says.

Zoo follows his gaze upstream. 'Where?' she asks.

'There,' Tracker says again.

She strains to see, and fails. 'I don't know what you're looking at,' she says. 'Can you please point it out?'

Tracker glances at her, an unspoken statement that Zoo hears.

She pauses. Then, 'I get it. I understand that we're competing against each other. But for now we're a team. I'm not asking for a master class, I just want to know where to look.' All but the last sentence will be cut, and viewers will hear no pause.

Again, it's easier for Tracker to help than to refuse. He walks a few yards upstream, then crouches by the water. 'Here.' With strained patience he shows Zoo where to look, and though she cannot see everything, she sees enough. She sees the snapped flower stem, the tiny tuft of hair on a raspberry thorn, the hoofprint in the mud.

'So it crossed here?' she asks. But before Tracker can respond, she continues, 'Wait, no. It's just walking upstream. It didn't cross yet.'

Tracker nods. Together, they follow the trail. Slowly, watching for more signs.

Banker and Black Doctor approach the boulder. The sun has dipped; Tracker and Zoo have advanced out of sight.

'Someone beat us,' says Banker, startled, when he opens the small lockbox.

'Cooper and the blonde, I'll bet,' says Black Doctor.

'What did they do, run the whole way here?'

'I guess.' Black Doctor takes a Clue and reads it aloud. He's not impressed; he'd expected more of an intellectual challenge, maybe some wordplay or a riddle.

Banker is more intimidated. 'We need to figure out where an animal crossed this stream?' He glances toward the dipping sun, which is tucked behind a cloud. 'We don't have much light left.'

'Then we'd better get started,' says Black Doctor. 'You look upstream, I'll look down?'

They separate.

Several miles away, Exorcist's good humor has faded. A blister has blossomed on his left big toe and each step is agony. 'I never should have followed a woman,' he grumbles.

Waitress's hamstrings are shrieking, part of her body's reaction to having gone several days without caffeine. She was expecting headaches – one of which she also has – but she wasn't expecting these sharp muscle pains. She thinks they are just a reaction to an unprecedented amount of walking. She's frustrated and uncomfortable, and she takes the bait. 'Screw you,' she says to Exorcist. 'You were there, you could have chipped in at any time. But you were yapping about some idiot customer instead. That was *your* choice.'

Exorcist whirls to face her. There is a perfect visual as Waitress steps forward and shoves her face close to his, her

141

profile tipped ever so slightly upward. Our two redheads, face-to-face. Freeze the moment and one could easily think they're about to kiss as anger turns to passion. But no, the passion these two share is strictly hostile.

Rancher places a hand on Exorcist's shoulder. 'Fighting won't accomplish nothing,' he says. 'Come on.'

'You are mistaken,' says Exorcist slowly, leaning in even closer to Waitress, 'if you think I will forget this.' A wisp of wind blows one of Waitress's curls forward to brush his chest. 'Nor will I forgive. I am a godly man, and my God is one of wrath.' He spits onto the ground, the glob landing next to Waitress's sneaker, then pivots and walks away.

'Psycho,' whispers Waitress, but it's clear she's shaken.

At the stream, Banker calls, 'I think I found a track.' Black Doctor hustles over to see. It's the same hoofprint that Tracker showed Zoo, and Zoo's footprint is etched softly in the dirt a few inches away.

Carpenter Chick and Engineer are the next to reach the second Clue, but Air Force and Biology are not far behind – when they spy the boulder, the other team is still standing beside it. It's an awkward moment; the contestants don't know if they should acknowledge one another or not. The editor takes this awkwardness and spins it into mutually disdainful silence.

Air Force sees the first hoofprint and is caught in indecision. He doesn't want to give the direction away to the other team, but every second spent pondering how to gain an advantage over Carpenter Chick and Engineer is an additional second separating him and Biology from the two teams ahead. He decides that is the greater concern and calls to his partner. Carpenter Chick jerks her head toward him like a scent hound.

Soon all four contestants are moving north, Air Force and Biology in the lead by about ten feet.

'It crossed here,' says Tracker, upstream.

Zoo is about to ask how he knows, then decides to try to figure it out for herself. She squats by the grassy bank. She doesn't see any sign of the prey they're following, but notices that the stream is shallower here, that they are at what appears to be a natural crossing.

Then she sees it: fresh scrabble marks in the far bank, the mud there rich and overturned. 'The far bank,' she says.

Tracker feels something he hadn't expected to feel: pride. He's proud of his verbose and jolly teammate, for not asking him for help, for finding the sign — the most obvious sign, at least — for herself. 'There's also this rock here,' he says, pointing to a small round stone that's been kicked up from the streambed and lies atop a bigger rock, breaching the water's surface.

'Oh, yeah,' says Zoo. 'It kind of looks like a cairn.'

A cairn is exactly what the small rock centered on top of the larger rock is meant to be, albeit a shorter, more subtle one than would usually be constructed. The Expert built it to draw the eye.

Zoo and Tracker cross the stream. Zoo leaves several dirty tread marks on stone, which she notices, but Tracker's already moving on and she follows. The trail is obvious from here, matted grass and snapped brush. They follow it toward a copse of birches. A wooden box hangs from the closest tree.

Tracker opens the hanging box. The inside of the lid has HUNGRY? painted across it.

'Yes,' chirps Zoo. 'Yes, I am.' She and Tracker peer inside.

The box contains five circular tokens hanging on pegs. Each token features a different etching: a deer, a rabbit, a squirrel, a duck and a turkey.

'What do you think?' says Zoo. 'Deer?'

'That's what we've supposedly been following,' says

Tracker, which she takes as assent. Zoo extracts the token. It's the size of her palm and made of birch. She flips the token over. On the back is a bearing: nineteen degrees. She sets her compass.

Banker and Black Doctor have nearly passed the crossing when Black Doctor says, 'Hey, are those footprints?' Banker slips and leaves a tear in the far bank. With each crossing, the path becomes more obvious.

The trees around Zoo and Tracker thicken, then thin, and then they see it: a doe, hanging from her hind legs in a tree. Her tongue lolls from her mouth about two feet off the ground. Next to the dead doe is a tarp with a bucket and cast-iron skillet on top of it, as well as a small box with an etching of a deer and a token-sized slot.

Though she's seen many dead animals, Zoo's never seen a deer strung up like this. 'Its eyes look like marbles,' she says as she deposits the token.

'Looks like dinner to me,' says Tracker.

'You know how to dress it?'

Tracker nods. Intellectually, Zoo is interested in learning how to skin and gut an animal, but her stomach churns at the thought of getting all that gore on her hands. She wants to eat the doe; she doesn't want to be the one to butcher it. And despite her good cheer, she's exhausted. All she really wants to do right now is sit with her back against a nice, straight tree and close her eyes. 'I'll collect some wood and start a fire,' she says, tapping the fire starter that hangs from her hip.

'Not here,' says Tracker. He already has his knife out.

'Why not?'

'The blood and offal might draw in predators. Cut back toward the stream and find a site with easy access to water.'

Zoo won the Solo Challenge and she's the one who chose him; shouldn't that make her the leader? And yet she turns away and does exactly as he says. Before viewers see her walk off, they'll see a clip from that night's confessional. 'Cooper is obviously very experienced,' she says, adjusting her glasses. Sweat has plastered a clump of hair to her forehead, and countless flyaways frame her face. 'There's no way I'd be in the lead right now without him. Plus, I think he's just a bit of a stoic. No wasted movement, no wasted words, you know? I admire that, I could stand to be more like that. I've already learned a lot from him. If my choice is between keeping my mouth shut, doing what he says, and learning more, or' – she briefly employs air quotes – ' "standing up for myself," you better believe I'm going to keep my mouth shut.' She laughs. 'Which doesn't come easy.'

Tracker makes his first cut at eye level, approximately an inch away from the doe's anus. He saws a circle, then with his free hand pulls out the rectum, which he ties shut with a piece of string from inside the bucket. Off camera, the Expert has appeared. He was politely rebuffed upon offering advice, and sees now that Tracker indeed does not need his help. He stays and watches, however, since he's being paid to be here and the next team isn't yet close.

Tracker ties off the doe's urethra, then cuts a long line through her hide, end-to-end. Before he digs out the first organ, his cameraman prods him to speak with 'You've got to narrate some of this, buddy.'

Tracker pauses, his knife pressing up on the doe's skin from her insides. 'You need to be careful not to contaminate the meat,' he says, resuming his work. 'That's why I tied off the anus and urethra and that's why I was so careful to avoid piercing the stomach. Now I'm going to sever the animal's windpipe.' Tracker crouches by the doe's head and reaches deep inside. When he withdraws his hands, they're thickly red and holding not only a windpipe, but the deer's heart and lungs. He drops the organs into the bucket and then pauses and turns to the camera. 'Watch this,' he says. He reaches back into the bucket and pulls out the pink lungs, which hang limply from his hands. Then he lifts the severed windpipe to his lips and blows into it. Nearly every one of the millions of viewers who watch this moment will recoil as the lungs inflate, quickly and hugely, like balloons. Balloons that curve into angularity and are netted with tiny blood vessels. Tracker pinches the windpipe closed and holds the inflated lungs away from his body. There is blood on his lips and his torso is eclipsed by the two pink lobes, which looked so small a moment ago. It is immediately clear that deer lungs could never fit inside a human rib cage.

Tracker lets the lungs deflate, then stands still for a moment, thinking about when he first saw someone do what he just did. He was eighteen, taking a three-week wilderness survival course after graduating from high school. His eight-person group had just slaughtered and skinned a ram under the guidance of their instructor, who then took the lead in gutting, narrating her actions as she made them. Then, with utter nonchalance, the tiny, athletic, black-haired white woman lifted the lungs to her mouth and blew. That was the moment when everything changed for Tracker, when he knew: We're all meat. Before that trip, he was on course for a very different life; he had vague thoughts about becoming an accountant or maybe going into IT. But a combination of having consumed fewer than one thousand calories over the previous four days, physical exhaustion, and realizing his own mortality made him determined to change all that. And though it would take him years to obtain proficiency, he fulfilled the ultimate human dream of figuring out exactly who he was meant to be. Unfortunately for Tracker, who he's meant to be isn't paid well and he has a cancer-ridden mother to care for. Staggering hospital bills have brought him here; this is his *because* that will never be shared. He turns back to the hanging carcass and carefully withdraws its bulging stomach.

Black Doctor and Banker reach the box. They choose the duck. 'It's like chicken, but richer,' says Banker.

'I know what duck tastes like,' Black Doctor replies.

They follow the direction indicated on the back of their token and find a mallard hanging from a tree. Black Doctor takes the lead in plucking and gutting the bird; he may not have a surgeon's hands, but he dissected a cadaver in medical school. Between that long-ago experience and the Expert's off-camera guidance, he does just fine.

Tracker walks into Zoo's small camp carrying the bucket and the cast-iron skillet. His hands and wrists are covered in drying blood, which lends his dark skin a matte coating but is otherwise hard to distinguish – until his palms are exposed. Normally a soft peach color, his red-brown palms cry of slaughter. Zoo is tending their fire and is unfazed. But she has a thought: If Tracker were white, would the starker blood-to-skin-color contrast bother her more? She suspects that it might.

'How'd it go?' she asks.

'We have tenderloin for dinner,' Tracker replies.

'Awesome.' Zoo takes the heavy skillet and turns back to the fire. 'I'll start cooking if you want to clean up. I –'

'Thank you,' says Tracker.

A jolt like electricity runs through Zoo. She pauses, skillet in hand, and listens as Tracker walks away.

When he returns from the stream, Tracker's hands are clean and his lips loose. 'There are a couple of things you should know about tracking,' he says. The meat sizzles in the pan, crisping in a thick layer of fat that Zoo melted like butter. 'The first is that you need to start with the big picture. Don't look for a footprint, look for a trail. It's easy to get lost at the micro level when all you need to do is take a step back. An animal or person moving through the woods might not always leave a track, but they'll always leave a trail. Overturned leaves, snapped branches – things like that. Anything recently disturbed will have a different color or texture from what's around it. You need to train your eye to look for these macro differences. For example, scan where I came from. Can you see my path?'

Zoo turns to look. She's squinting.

Tracker admits via confessional, 'I've had many great teachers in my life. I'm honoring them by helping her. Besides, even if she gets better, she'll never match me. Not in time to win.' Zoo's husband will watch this scene and think, She's done it again, eased some crotchety bastard out of his shell. He will marvel, as he has marveled before, at how easily she can win over anybody.

Tracker says to Zoo, 'Don't look, scan. And if you don't see anything, change your perspective – go high or low. Watch for changes in the light.'

Zoo widens her eyes and drifts her gaze along the forest. She stands. She remembers approximately where he walked, but is trying not to rely on memory. 'There?' she says, pointing. 'The leaf litter looks a little different there.'

'Exactly,' says Tracker. 'I walked heavy, to make it clearer. Also, I followed your trail. Most animal trails won't be so pronounced, but this is a good place to start.'

'That was you walking *heavy*?' asks Zoo.

Tracker surprises them both with a laugh. 'The shoes help,' he says, picking up a foot and wiggling his toes. And then – this isn't why he's here – his face falls to neutral. 'We're losing light. I'm going to put this in the water to keep it from spoiling.' He takes the bucket, which still contains several pounds of muscle and fat, and turns away.

'How do you make sure nothing gets it?' asks Zoo.

Tracker pauses. 'I'll cover it with a flat rock. That should be enough to deter most animals.'

After he walks off, Zoo says to the camera, 'I don't know what's gotten into him, but I like it.'

The next two teams to reach the wooden box do so in close succession. Air Force is the first to see it, and at his urging Biology races ahead before Engineer and Carpenter Chick notice. She chooses the rabbit, then jogs back over to her partner.

'Turkey?' asks Carpenter Chick seconds later.

'Yeah,' says Engineer, 'that's got a lot more meat than a squirrel.' The teams separate and find their prey. With guidance, they prepare their meals and shelters. The sun has nearly set.

The trio is still a mile from the boulder. Exorcist is fuming. He feels unappreciated and spiteful. Waitress is glaring hatred at the back of his head, and Rancher is striding along, wary of the both of them. Anger makes Exorcist careless. He trips over a rock and falls to the ground.

'Motherfucker!' he yells. The expletive is easily censored, but his rage cannot be. Waitress and Rancher recoil, and many viewers will do the same.

Exorcist pulls himself up on one knee and waits, head hanging. His shoulders pulse. He can feel his monstrous self trying to break free. He knows he can't let it. If he does, he'll lose control, and he's done terrible things after losing control.

He used to have a wife. Young love: They married at nineteen. Life did not go as planned, and Exorcist's inner monster grew fat on disappointment. One night, his wife complained about money and Exorcist lost control. He struck her, hard, with a closed fist, fracturing his fourth metacarpal and knocking his wife out cold. He remembers watching her head snap back, and how her blond hair whipped like a fan, and then her collapsing to the carpet, where she lay, unmoving, among a month's worth of crumbs and cat hair. Her stillness – he thought she was dead. She came to, and left him that night. The blood vessels in her left eye had burst. The last look she ever gave him haunts him still; it was as though Satan himself was reflected in that bloody eye.

The producers know nothing about this incident. Exorcist's ex-wife didn't press charges, so there was no criminal record for them to find. But at least one person who will watch this moment knows of it; she lived it. The ex-wife will watch Exorcist's explosive crouch and think, *Oh, no.* And when Exorcist leaps to his feet, whirls to face Waitress, and sneers, 'Stupid bitch,' she will feel Waitress's fear as her own. 'Run, honey,' she will plead, but where her own instincts tend toward flight, Waitress's are to fight. Waitress rears to slap Exorcist, but Rancher grabs her in a bear hug and pulls her back.

'Let me go!' Waitress yells, kicking. She's taller than Rancher; he can barely hold her.

'You'll be disqualified,' says Rancher.

'I don't care.' Waitress's face is painted with fury.

But Exorcist has pulled away. Something has happened that he cannot articulate. He does not want to see his anger reflected, does not want to be the cause of this near-stranger's fury. Add to this Rancher trying to restrain her; the nobility in that short, simple man. Exorcist calms. He is sorry for his outburst, and though his apology is plain in his eyes, he is too cowardly to speak it.

Instead he says, 'A woman scorned, indeed. Lesson learned,' and walks away.

His sudden change confuses Waitress, who did not see the apology. She stills, and Rancher lets her go, reddening at the thought of his arms wrapped so tightly around her. He's pretty sure he brushed a nipple.

The sun falls and they reach the boulder. The moon is bright; the trio finds their next Clue easily.

'We can't track in the dark,' says Rancher.

'Then what do you think we should do?' asks Waitress.

'Camp here, start out at first light.'

'But everyone is ahead of us.'

Exorcist folds into a seated position and leans against the boulder. He takes off his boots and prods his blister. 'They'll still be ahead of us if we spend all night running around in the dark,' he says. 'Only then we'll be exhausted and will probably have destroyed the tracks we're supposed to follow.'

'Fine,' says Waitress. She can't look at him, the pale bubble bursting from his hairy toe. 'So, what, we've got to build a shelter?'

Exorcist slaps the rock behind him. 'Bracing a windbreak against this bad boy won't take a minute.' He hauls himself to his feet with a groan and starts collecting long pieces of driftwood, barefoot.

Rancher and Waitress exchange a look. 'What's his deal?' asks Waitress.

'I think he's just crazy.'

'Wonderful,' says Waitress. 'This'll be fun.'

The other groups have all eaten and most of the contestants are asleep, or drifting. Banker's arms are tucked to his chest inside his jacket. Engineer still wears his glasses and with drooping eyelids watches as moonlight bounces off the inky exoskeleton of a passing beetle. Tracker snores, at his most vocal when sleeping. Beside him, Zoo is curled in his thermal blanket, counting sheep and thumbing the space on her finger where her wedding ring should be. She times the leaps so that Tracker's rattling breath becomes nothing more than wind rustling wool.

Only Biology is outside. She sits by a small fire with her arms curled around her legs. She misses her partner and feels very alone. She's thinking about saying the safety phrase, but only vaguely – without intent. She's wondering how she would leave, and if she did how long it would be before she could get a mango smoothie.

'I'd give all the rabbit meat in the world for a mango smoothie,' she says. 'Or a chocolate sundae.' Her body is craving sugar so intensely her head hurts. She takes a sip from her water bottle, wishing that the water had flavor, maybe some bubbles.

Exorcist, Rancher and Waitress build their meager shelter and huddle together inside.

II

'My uncle said it was in the water, so he stopped drinking any that wasn't bottled,' says Brennan. 'Mom thought it was terrorists, like an invisible bomb or something.'

He expects me to respond, but I'm only listening in case there's a Clue hidden in his tale. He's been talking about his mother so much, too much. We're walking. It's midday and the weather is crisp, increasingly autumnlike. By my imperfect calculations, it must be well into September.

He grows impatient with my silence. 'You were probably lucky, being lost out here for the worst of it. From when I started hearing about it and when the president went on TV, it was only like a day. Then we were all told to stay home, and I heard these rumors about some kids down the street being sick. Day after that they moved us all into the church.'

I still haven't had my period. It's overdue, I think.

'Aiden was off at school doing this summer program, and Mom, she said he should come home and he said he'd try, but they wouldn't let him, and then our phones stopped working.'

I wonder if I'm supposed to know who Aiden is, then I remember that he said something about a brother. That must be Aiden, in which case he's inconsequential – filler.

'We were there for a few days,' says Brennan. Plastic bags hang from his hands, filled with soda bottles, candy and other junk food. He had Cheetos and a bottle of Coke for breakfast. 'I was bored, I couldn't really keep track. Then people started getting sick. I mean, there were a few sick from the beginning, but they kept them separated – in the daycare room, I think. And then there were too many, and they were everywhere, and things were starting to smell really bad because people were puking and stuff.'

I know this story. Everyone knows this story. There are no Clues here. 'Was there a food shortage?' I ask. 'Did some guy with a scar on his face hoard the water?'

He shakes his head, for all appearances taking me seriously. 'No, there was always plenty of food – the sick people wouldn't eat. And the faucets ran. Some people didn't want to drink the city water regular like that, but I just kept filling up our bottles at the faucets. I mean, the bathroom sink water's the same as the kitchen sink, right?'

'Right,' I say, emphasizing the word with a swing of my fist.

I remember watching a show with a similar premise on the Discovery Channel, years ago. It was billed as an experiment; people who 'survived' a simulated flu outbreak had to build a little community before finding a way to safety. They got to do cool stuff like wire up solar panels and build cars. All I get to do is walk endlessly and listen to a rambling kid tell a bullshit story. Plus, they knew what they were getting into. They didn't know how hard it would be, maybe, but they knew the premise. But this, *this* was supposed to be about wilderness survival.

I glance at Brennan, who's still blathering about his little made-up church.

The contestants on the Discovery Channel show were contained: X number of city blocks in season one and a section of bayou in season two, if I remember right. I've already covered the equivalent of hundreds of city blocks. Thousands, maybe. And I'm not the only contestant. How do they do it? How do they clear the way?

The answer is as obvious as the question: money. Reality

shows are famously cheap to make, but this one has a block-buster's budget. They made that clear in the application process, called this an opportunity to participate in a 'groundbreaking entertainment experience.' An *opportunity*. They could empty hundreds of homes, repair and reimburse dozens of outdoor gear stores, and it'd be a drop in the bucket for them. It's exorbitant, but it makes sense. The how of it all makes sense.

'When there was no one left but me,' says Brennan, 'I started walking.' This isn't his best performance; there's a matter-of-factness to his tone that is out of sync with the story he's telling. I'm not sure why I find this incongruity irritating, but I do.

There was supposed to be a third season of the pandemic show, but it was canceled before any episodes aired. All that cool stuff the cast got to build? They also had to protect it. One of the season three contestants – experimentees? – was hit in the head by a fake marauder during a fake attack and died, which I suppose means the attack wasn't so fake after all. At least that's the explanation a particular cluster of websites provided for the cancelation. Grain of salt. And yet our contract was very clear about not hitting anyone in the head.

Is that why they're airing our episodes so quickly? In case someone dies?

I doubt that's their primary concern, but it makes sense that they would anticipate the possibility of a production-halting accident. I think of how sick I got. That was close, not to stopping the show, but my role in it. And they've already populated this pretend world with a handful of dead-body props, a screeching baby doll, an interactive cameraman. A marauder isn't such a far next step. In fact, I'm surprised all I've had to fend off so far is a bout of beaver fever and an animatronic coyote.

And this prattling boy, no matter his pretending, is on their side. Their side, not mine. I can't forget that.

'I wanted to get away,' he says, swinging his plastic bags at his side. 'Go somewhere I've never been before. And then I found you.'

Like our meeting was fate. But it wasn't fate, it was casting.

'So,' I say, 'I take it your mother's dead?'

He breathes in sharply and nearly trips.

'I mean, she must be,' I reason. 'The two of you jammed into a church with hundreds of others, everyone coughing and puking and shitting their pants. You're clearly a mama's boy, and you're here and she's not. So that means she's dead, right?'

He doesn't answer. I'd thought to prod him into putting some emotion into his performance, but this is even better. Silence.

As we walk, thoughts of my family slide forward in my consciousness. The family I chose and the family I was born to. My indifference toward the latter. My fear that if I have a child she will someday feel that same indifference toward me.

Odd how my dreams are always about a baby boy, but the possibility of having a girl is what scares me most. A daughter: It seems impossible to raise one well.

'Everyone you know is dead too,' says Brennan.

I turn to him, surprised. His face is so close to mine, his eyes are red, and tears are trickling down his scrunched-up cheeks. Snot runs from his nostrils over his lips. He must be able to taste it.

'Your family,' he says. 'Your rafting friends. They're floating down the river. Fish are probably eating their faces right now.'

'That's . . . excessive,' I say. There's something in his

voice I can't quite define. It's not malice. I don't think he's trying to hurt me. I don't know what he's trying to accomplish.

'Facts are facts,' he mumbles. He shifts his plastic bags to the crooks of his elbows and crosses his arms. The watch face winks at me.

He's sulking, I realize. The thought is laced with amazement. Then again – why not? He's probably homesick. He probably didn't know what he was signing up for either. I feel a little sorry for him, but mostly I'm thankful that he's being quiet again.

What if my mother *were* dead? It's a question I've pondered before; she's only fifty-six but looks much older, mostly because of her skin. Forty miles each way twice a week to maintain her out-of-season hue, puffing on carcinogens all the way. Winter, summer, that deep tan is always out of season in Vermont when it lacks the sharp line of a farmer's sleeve. Factor in her diet – a typical meal being frozen waffles topped with sausage patties doused in syrup and followed by a maple creamie – and she's pretty much guaranteed an early grave.

She *is* dead.

I think the words, to see how they make me feel. They don't have any effect I can discern. They should make me feel bad, I *want* them to, but they don't. I remember when I got into Columbia and she lumbered all over town, bragging: It was her accomplishment, not mine. But anytime I fail – losing that derby when I was eight, not getting the Wildlife Conservation Society job two years ago – she gets this air about her like she knew I wouldn't make it, like it was reckless of me even to try. And still I tried, for years I tried so hard. I remember my wedding day, how joyful I felt. How lucky. I remember my mother leaning in to kiss my cheek at the reception. 'You look beautiful,' she said.

157

'Just like me when I was young.' Her past: my present. Her present: my future. Like a curse. The worst part is I've seen the photos; I know she was happy once too.

My dad, though. That's harder. We're not close – somewhere in my adolescence we lost our ability to communicate, and I don't think he understands why I worked so hard to get away from a place he loves so dearly. But I can't think of him without a buzz of warm nostalgia, without imagining the sweet aroma of baking cinnamon and maple. Always maple.

'Is it possible to have a bad childhood memory about baking?' I wonder.

'What?' says Brennan.

'Never mind,' I say, and I think, These thoughts aren't for you.

My dad and I shared eighteen years, but baking is pretty much all I remember. When I was little, I would help him in his shop before school. My specialty was mushing bananas for the maple banana bread. That, and sprinkling the maple sugar on top of the batter once it'd been poured into the loaf pans. I want to remember something else, something not about food, but all that comes to me is my fourth-grade birthday – whatever age that was. It was a dolphin-themed party, my favorite animal at the time, though I wouldn't see one in person for years yet. My dad baked the cake, of course – dolphin-shaped, slathered in maple buttercream – and there was a piñata. Again, dolphin-shaped. Most of my class was there. David Moreau gave me a kite. We flew it together that weekend. Or was that fifth grade? I'm not sure. I remember my dad presenting the dolphin cake, and my mom gnawing on a thumbnail as she poured orange soda from a can into a clear plastic cup.

And then I have it – my dad cheering in the bleachers. It's high school, a track meet my freshman year, long before I made captain. Was it my first meet? In my memory it has all the intensity of a first. I remember the gurgling nerves in my stomach, the slight pain as I stretched my hamstring. I remember my father yelling my name, waving. The meet wasn't at our home track; it was in another town a half hour's drive from my high school. Dad closed the shop early to come, to see me.

'Mae, I'm sorry.'

I blink. The race is gone; I don't remember how I ran, if I placed.

'It's hard to think about her,' says Brennan. 'I miss her. And . . . and I just miss her.'

It takes me a moment to realize who he's talking about.

'Don't worry,' I say. 'I'm sure she's watching.'

'I know,' he says. He crosses himself; the bag hanging from his arm *thwaps* his chest.

My cheeks immediately begin to sizzle. That's not what I meant. Even if I believed his mother was dead I never would have meant it that way. What's worse – now that he's distorted my words they'll probably air them. The thought of contributing, even mistakenly, to the meaningless spirituality that so pervades American media sickens me.

After a few more steps, Brennan starts rambling about his stupid fish, how he brought it to the church in its bowl, but then a neighbor's cat ate it. He was in the bathroom filling water bottles when it happened.

'It was just a fish,' I blurt. 'They're meant to be eaten.'

'But –'

'Please, just – *please* stop talking for five minutes.'

He looks at me, bug-eyed, but doesn't even last a minute before he starts telling me about his brother and the first time they rode the subway alone together. He yammers about all the rats they saw and how that must be what the entire subway system is now: rats. 'I hate rats,' he says, and with this at least I can't disagree. It's part of my job to hold up rats, talk about how the stigma's wrong — they're actually very clean animals — and I do it. I smile to allay the class's squirmy fears, but inside I'm cringing too; I've never been able to stand how their naked tails feel resting on the inside of my arm. So I just stand there, smiling, and pretend an open-mindedness I've never felt, hoping it will become true.

That night, after Brennan's crawled into his rickety wind tunnel, I don't even try to sleep. I keep the fire bright and sit in its quietly crackling company. My thoughts wind back to the first day of filming, after all the contracts were signed and our final phone calls home made — a slew of I-love-yous and good-lucks, all real but nothing new. I remember walking to the field where the first Challenge started and not being scared, not anymore. I was happy, excited; I know that's how I felt, but the memory is like faded sweetness in the back of my throat — a reminder, not a taste. I want to feel that way again. I want to know I can feel that way again.

A great horned owl calls somewhere off in the dark. I close my eyes to listen. To me, the great horned owl has always sounded mildly aggressive, its call an almost guttural *hur hur-hur hurrrrr hur-hur* as opposed to the inquisitive *hoo* commonly attributed to its kin. I don't think they look wise either. Vexed is more like it, what with their sharply turned-down brows and extended ear tufts.

Cooper was kind of like that at first. Standoffish. I don't know what drew me to him so strongly from the start. No — I do. His air of almost freakish competence. The way he scanned each of us, assessing without looking for allies, because from the moment he leapt into that tree it was clear he didn't need anyone but himself. I bet his entire adult life has been like that: needing no one, being needed by no one – existing without apology and accomplishing wonders. I'd never been around someone so supremely independent before and was fascinated. At first I thought it was odd that they'd cast someone who barely spoke, but his actions were enough, louder than words, as it were. And those of us who lacked his skills filled the silence.

If I could pick any of them to work with again, it'd be Cooper, no question. Heather would be my last choice; I'd even take Randy over her.

Would Cooper pick me?

The owl calls again. Another answers, farther away. A conversation: calls back and forth. It's not mating season, so I don't know what they're communicating, if their calls are cooperative or competitive. I close my eyes. Listening to these familiar sounds, I can almost pretend I'm camping, for just one night. That tomorrow morning I'll toss my supplies into the back of my Outback and drive home, where my husband will be waiting, his signature bacon-and-chive scramble sizzling on the stove while the scent of freshly brewed coffee wafts down the hall to greet me. I can almost smell it.

Almost.

12.

Zoo opens her eyes to find a dark, blurred figure blocking dawn's light at the mouth of her and Tracker's shelter. For a second she forgets where she is, who she slept next to. She reaches for her glasses. Memory and vision resolve. She sees her teammate crouching, facing away from her, the skillet at his side.

'Breakfast in bed?' she asks; before the question's even out, she pales.

Tracker glances at her, then turns to a small box at his feet and takes out their next Clue. 'Go up,' he reads.

Zoo releases a held breath.

Elsewhere, Carpenter Chick and Engineer read their identical Clue, eat cold leftover turkey, and plan their route up the mountain. Air Force and Biology don't have leftovers; they skip breakfast and are the first team to start hiking. Banker and Black Doctor are not far behind.

Tracker and Zoo finish breakfast. As Zoo rinses out the skillet, she asks, 'Do we keep this?'

Tracker is disassembling their shelter. 'No,' he says. 'It's not worth it. Too heavy.'

'What about all the meat we can't eat?'

Tracker tosses an armful of sticks and duff across the ground. 'Production team took it. Promised it wouldn't go to waste.'

No matter the editor's fondness for this pair, this conversation cannot air. There can be no production crew, no cameramen, and non-entities do not eat. The editor cuts from breakfast to Zoo shouldering her pack and following Tracker out of their small clearing.

And then there's the trio, crammed together in their shelter: Rancher closest to the boulder, Exorcist in the warm middle, and Waitress in the tight outer corner. Waitress is the first to wake. She finds Exorcist's pale, red-haired hand resting on her waist. A camera mounted on the mouth of the shelter records her confusion, her quick disgust. She tosses the arm off. Without waking, Exorcist shuffles onto his opposite side. His hand smacks Rancher in the face. Rancher jolts awake, striking his knee against the rock. He bites back a curse. Waitress ignores him and crawls out into the dawn. After a moment, Rancher grabs his hat and follows. Exorcist sleeps through, sprawling to take up the entire shelter.

Waitress and Rancher do not find a box waiting for them. They are a Clue behind the others, and hungry.

Waitress stretches, twisting from side to side. Rancher walks off to urinate, limping slightly as his muscles wake and his knee throbs. Once he returns, Waitress asks, 'Can we leave him?'

'I don't think so.' Rancher nudges Exorcist's shoulder with his foot. 'Rise and shine.'

Exorcist's eyes peep open, then he groans and crawls from the shelter. He walks to the side of the boulder and undoes his fly. Waitress turns quickly away, sneering as she hears urine splash against stone. Exorcist zips up and says, 'We're going to win this. I saw it in a dream.'

'At this rate, we'll be lucky to finish the same day as everyone else,' retorts Waitress.

'Have faith,' Exorcist tells her, reaching out to touch her shoulder.

She pulls away. 'Wash your hands.'

'Piss is sterile.' He waggles his fingers, creeping them

toward her face, then turns abruptly toward the stream. 'Come on, let's find us some tracks.'

They find the crossing quickly; the path is well trod now, plus there's a cameraman on the far bank, munching on a strawberry-flavored fruit-and-nut bar while he waits. Exorcist leaps ahead of his teammates, and Rancher helps Waitress step rock to rock. The two cameramen meticulously avoid each other with their lenses.

The trio continue down the path and find the wooden box hanging from the birch. Exorcist pulls out the only remaining token. Studying the etching, he says, 'Huh.' They follow the bearing and soon see a dead gray squirrel hanging from a tree branch.

'No way,' says Waitress. She thought *preparing your own meals* – one of many purposefully ambiguous statements in the contestants' contract – meant dumping ingredients into a pot. 'No way I'm eating squirrels.'

'*Squirrel,*' says Exorcist. 'There's only one.' He prods the dangling rodent with a finger, sending it swinging on the thin rope. Waitress turns away, grimacing. Rancher steps forward to cut the squirrel down. Off camera he accepts advice on skinning the small animal. Viewers will see close-ups of his worn, golden-brown hands tearing the skin away, the pulse of sleek rodent muscle popping free of its covering.

'We need a fire if we want to eat this,' says Rancher.

'No way,' says Waitress. She's clutching her arms tight to her chest, looking anywhere but at the squirrel. 'No way.'

'What,' says Exorcist, 'you're not hungry?'

She shakes her head, too distraught to feel her hunger. Exorcist laughs. He unzips his pack and tosses his dowsing rod toward her. 'Here, then, see if you can get this to work.' He laughs again, then begins collecting firewood. Waitress kicks the dowsing rod back toward him and leaves her teammates, making her way back to the brook. She crouches over the water and rinses out her mouth.

Her confessional, recorded moments later: 'A squirrel. I'm not eating a squirrel. Who eats squirrel? That's disgusting.'

Cut to the squirrel roasting on a stick, and a caption: TWENTY MINUTES LATER. Exorcist and Rancher are sitting by the fire, watching the meat cook. Waitress hovers in the background. She inches forward, drawn by the smell. Eventually she sits next to Rancher.

'What happened to its head?' she asks.

'Cut it off.'

'What, now that it looks like food you're hungry?' asks Exorcist. 'I'm not sure there's enough to go around.'

There is not enough to go around – it's a squirrel. But all three are salivating. Do they fight, do they share, what happens next? A commercial break will delay the question's answer. Once viewers return, the answer comes quick and boring: They share. Rancher portions the squirrel, placing each pathetic helping on a paper plate, the last of his supply. Waitress lifts a hindquarter to her mouth and takes a dainty bite. The charred flesh tears from the bone. She chews, swallows. 'Not bad.'

Rancher agrees, adding, 'Too bad there ain't more.'

'We could catch some,' says Exorcist. He picks up his dowsing rod and twirls it. 'If I sharpen the ends, we'd have a killer boomerang. Literally.'

It's unclear by his demeanor if he actually thinks he could kill a squirrel by flinging a sharpened dowsing rod at it. He picks his teeth with the squirrel's fibula. After a moment, he tosses the bone aside and jumps to his feet, miming great surprise. 'Hey, what's that?' he asks.

A small box has appeared near the trio, placed there by an intern who implored them not to say anything with a finger to her lips. But now that she's retreated, the box can be acknowledged. Exorcist opens it and reads, *'Go up.'*

As the trio begin their hike toward the summit, viewers will see a map showing the teams' relative positions. Black Doctor and Banker have taken the lead and are heading straight toward the mountain's apex, bushwhacking slowly, with a mile and a half to go. Air Force and Biology are about halfway to the top, following a circuitous trail. Zoo and Tracker are also on the trail, a quarter of a mile behind Air Force and Biology. Carpenter Chick and Engineer are west of the others. They started on the trail, then after an hour decided to strike directly for the summit, through an area where contour lines show a gentle but steady incline. They don't yet regret the decision.

'Hey, look,' says Zoo. They've rounded a corner before a long straight stretch of trail and can see Air Force and Biology ahead. 'How did they get ahead of us?'

'We dithered,' says Tracker.

Zoo enjoys his word choice immensely. 'We dithered, yes, but between us we have four good ankles. Come on!' She takes a few jogging steps, but Tracker whistles sharply and she stops.

'It's better to just keep pace,' says Tracker. 'We'll pass them anyway.'

Zoo falls back beside him. 'I guess I should have figured you for a tortoise.'

He shrugs. 'Depends on the length of the race.'

A short distance ahead, Biology asks, 'Did you hear a whistle?'

Air Force turns and glances down the trail. 'There's another team right behind us.'

'Shoot,' says Biology, her tone thick with expletive intent. 'How far to the top?'

'Too far to make a break for it, but I'll try.' Air Force grimaces and picks up his pace.

His effort only delays the inevitable. Minutes – seconds – later, Zoo calls, 'On your left,' and waves hello as she power-walks by. Tracker moves more naturally. He nods as he passes, but this greeting will be cut in editing.

Zoo pumps her arms and moves quickly until she and Tracker are about fifty feet ahead of the other pair, and then slows to a normal pace.

'I guess I shouldn't be surprised you rushed that,' says Tracker.

Zoo laughs. 'We were so close.'

Soon, the trail becomes a series of tight, steep switch-backs. The viewers' map will show that Tracker and Zoo are nearly head-to-head with Black Doctor and Banker, whose dots – one mustard yellow, one checkered black and white – have barely advanced.

'I wonder what's at the top,' says Zoo. Six and a half minutes later, something rumbles uphill. The editor will slice away those minutes, imply cause and effect where none exists. Zoo and Tracker pause. 'What was that?' she asks, looking to their left.

Tracker hesitates before saying, 'It sounded like –' The sound comes again, cutting him off. Then: scraping, tumbling, sharp rustling, some small *clack clack clack*s. Tracker puts out his arm toward his teammate and turns to scan the woods uphill. Zoo notices that their cameraman has hung back; he's standing about fifty feet away, filming intently. The shot he gets now: her worried glance straight at the lens, Tracker's protective stance, her light skin and hair, his darkness; the editor will love the contrast, the story being told in that moment. This shot will be heavily featured in promos.

'Go,' says Tracker. He urges Zoo ahead of him with a

nudge. She turns, confused, glancing uphill, and then darts up the trail. Tracker follows.

They've gone only a few steps when the first small pebbles tumble down onto the trail. Most of the stones fall behind them, but not all. Zoo leaps over a fist-sized rock that rolls out in front of her — an overhead camera records her quick reflexes, and Tracker's smaller, sleeker movements as he easily avoids tumbling debris. And then — *crash* — a huge sound behind them. Zoo slows and looks back. Tracker tells her, 'Run!' but she sees it: a boulder nearly as tall as she bounding through the trees. It looks strange to her, it's moving too lightly, ricocheting off tree trunks. Seconds later the boulder rolls across the trail behind them and the woods settle back into silence. Zoo pauses to catch her breath.

'That wasn't a real boulder,' she says.

'No,' says Tracker.

'That's messed up.' Viewers will not be given access to Zoo's first comment, but they will hear this one, and then the show will cut to Biology and Air Force listening to the crashing sounds ahead of them.

'What was that?' asks Biology.

'I don't know,' says Air Force. 'Maybe a tree fell?'

At the base of the mountain, Waitress and Rancher outvote Exorcist to take the trail. Exorcist takes ownership of their decision by marching into the lead. Waitress is exhausted, her quads throbbing and weak, and she follows slowly. Rancher takes the rear. Once they find the trailhead he allows the distance between him and his teammates to grow. Looking at the ground as he hikes, he pretends to be alone and thinks about his children. After only a few minutes, the trio's cameraman urges him forward. 'Come on, man. I've gotta keep all three of you in frame.'

Far above and deep in brambles, Black Doctor slips. He catches himself on a rickety tree stump. A toothpick-sized

169

sliver skims in just below the skin on his left pinky and he hisses in pain. Banker squeezes through the brush to help him up.

'It's not deep,' says Black Doctor, inspecting his hand. He pinches the protruding end of the splinter between his fingernails and pulls it out. The wood slides free cleanly and the wound barely bleeds. *Did you see that?* the reasonable man writes on a forum within seconds of this airing. *He's clearly more dexterous than he looks.* Within an hour, this man will be called a racist, a moron, an asswipe and a fag, the last by a twelve-year-old girl who recently heard the derogative for the first time and likes the sense of power she gets from employing it anonymously.

Black Doctor tosses the splinter aside and takes out his first-aid kit. He dabs on some antibiotic cream, then wraps a Band-Aid around his finger. 'Best I can do for now,' he says.

Banker's hair is slicked to his forehead with sweat, and stubble bursts awkwardly from his cheeks and chin. It's not a flattering look, but the day after tomorrow the stubble will hit its prime length and he will for a few days be striking. Hearts will throb; not as many as throb for Air Force, but enough that he will be recognized weeks from now, far out of context.

Banker's not-yet-striking face is pursed with concern for his partner. 'Did that list of plants say what they were good for? If we can find a natural antiseptic —'

'I'm fine,' Black Doctor interrupts. 'It barely pierced the dermis.' He shifts his face into kindliness. 'Besides, even the best plant isn't going to be better than what's in the kit. But thank you.' They resume their climb.

Zoo is still staring after the faux boulder. 'We could have gotten hurt,' she says. 'Really hurt.' She expected challenges and danger, but not like this. She didn't think the creators of the show would roll a five-foot-diameter obstacle down a heavily wooded trail straight at her. Her dismay causes her expectations to shift: a small first step toward inconceivable eventual heights.

'We're okay,' says Tracker. 'And the top's not far.' Zoo turns to follow him. She's no longer smiling.

A quarter of a mile to their west, Carpenter Chick and Engineer push through the woods. Several small twigs are stuck in Carpenter Chick's hair, and Engineer's right sleeve is torn at the cuff and thick with brambles. They pause to consult their map and compasses.

'We're so close,' says Carpenter Chick. 'But all I see are trees.'

'It'll open up any minute,' Engineer replies. 'We have less than a hundred feet of elevation left.' He tucks the map away and leads them forward, then stops and says, 'Whoa.'

'What is it?' asks Carpenter Chick. She ducks beneath a branch to stand beside him. Their cameraman hustles to their side to capture their drawn faces, then pans right to a sheer forty-foot cliff.

Lesson of the day: Contour lines can be deceptive when elevation gain occurs in the form of a cliff at the end of a wooded plateau.

'How do we get up *that*?' asks Carpenter Chick.

'An elaborate system of pulleys?' replies Engineer.

Carpenter Chick is silent for a second, then adds, 'And maybe a lever.'

Suddenly they're both doubled over laughing. Carpenter Chick hiccups and says, 'Next time let's take the trail.'

On the trail, Air Force is grimacing. The incline is agony on his ankle. He is moving by force of will and a drummed-in sense of teamwork – he cannot let his partner down.

'The trail looks different up here,' says Biology.

'You're right,' Air Force replies. They pause, standing

together nine feet before the trigger point. What Biology and Air Force are noticing is subtle: disturbed earth and upturned stones still shaded with the ground's moisture. In their place, many others would have kept walking, oblivious.

'Look at that,' says Biology. She walks a few steps forward, pointing at the Styrofoam boulder that menaced Zoo and Tracker. It's lodged between two pine trees just below the trail.

'You think that's what fell?' asks Air Force. 'A rock that size should have made a lot more noise. And caused more damage.'

Biology glances uphill, then approaches the boulder. 'I guess,' she says. She's uneasy, but experience has taught her to breathe through unease and channel fear into motivation. By any measure she's a remarkable woman, yet other than this moment and a plethora of dehumanizing shots featuring her physique, she won't get much airtime. Too quiet, the editor will say. She was more outgoing in her interviews, where she didn't need to breathe through unease or channel fear. But even she knows she wasn't cast for her personality.

Biology's foot breaks the plane between a stump and a tree with a fake beehive dangling from an upper branch, and their cameraman sends his signal. Biology peers at the boulder. The painted Styrofoam has been chipped and dented in places, revealing white, pebbly patches. 'I don't think it's real,' she says, just as the warning rustle comes. When Biology hears this she has no trouble imagining what's coming. 'Hurry!' she says, taking Air Force's arm. He dashes along as best he can.

The producers don't intend to actually hit anyone with the fake boulders, no matter the waivers signed. There's plenty of warning, warning enough for even slow-moving Air Force and Biology to clear the perilous area. They are almost fifty feet ahead when the boulder careens across the trail; they don't see it, though they hear it. Their cameraman records the boulder's passing. It makes it farther than the first, past the previous curve of the switchback, before getting stuck against the upended roots of a long-fallen tree.

Well out of earshot, their laughing fit concluded, Carpenter Chick and Engineer work together to solve their forty-foot problem. The answer is simple if arduous: They pull themselves up a steep slope littered with leaves, fallen branches, and downed trees. Engineer slips and slides downslope, kicking up a dark trail in the leaf litter. Carpenter Chick helps him and they clamber slowly uphill. They are nearly to the summit.

But they are not the first to finish the final leg of this Challenge. Tracker and Zoo crest a slope and see the host ahead, waiting on an exposed rock slick, green mountains spread behind him. There are signs of civilization in the background: roads, cars turned by perspective into toys zipping soundlessly along, clusters of buildings. The contestants will see these, but the viewer will not – each shot will be either cut to exclude them or blurred to obscure them.

The host welcomes Tracker and Zoo imperiously. 'You are the first to arrive,' he says. 'Congratulations.'

'What now?' asks Zoo. She's looking past the host, admiring the view.

The host's voice turns conversational. 'We wait for the others. You can relax.'

Zoo sits by the host. Tracker gives her a little wave, then disappears into the woods.

'He's not tired?' asks the host.

'I don't think he gets tired,' says Zoo.

Twelve minutes later, Black Doctor and Banker emerge

from the trees to the west of the trail. They have leaves and prickles stuck in their hair. They accept their overbearing greeting, then sit beside Zoo, who is lying in the sun with her eyes closed. Out of sight, Tracker is being shooed away from the production camp. Air Force and Biology appear moments later to accept third place. It's another forty-five minutes before Engineer and Carpenter Chick slink into the mountaintop clearing from the east – they've been wandering the wooded mountaintop for the last half hour, but they ran into Tracker moments earlier and he pointed them in the right direction.

Below, the trio lurches disconnectedly up the trail.

'How much farther is it?' whines Waitress. She feels sick. Despite the dryness of her mouth, she hasn't taken a sip of water in more than an hour. Her calorie-deprived body is too tired for her to want to lift the bottle, and she's shuffling her steps. Instead of leaving footprints on the trail, she leaves scuffs.

Rancher is right behind her, stealing quasi-accidental glances at her rear end. 'Can't be far now. You can do it.'

'I need a break,' she replies, bending over and placing her hands on her knees. Her jacket hem slips up past her waist. Rancher catches himself staring and jerks his gaze out to the trees. Exorcist is ahead, tromping noisily, but staying within sight of his teammates. He notices that they've stopped and doubles back.

'You hurt?' he barks.

'I just need a second,' Waitress replies.

'Drink some water,' suggests Rancher, before taking a sip of his own. Waitress nods and takes one of her bottles from her pack. She holds the water in her mouth for a moment before swallowing, enjoying the sensation of the liquid against her dry tongue and the inside of her mouth. This is a nothing moment, but it will be manipulated into great sensuality as the camera pans up from her slick, pulsing chest to pursed lips and eyes narrowed in pleasure. And then she swallows and the narrative segues clumsily to the future – they're a mile farther up the trail and the sun has passed its peak. They pass the second faux boulder, the one that rolled farther. None of the three notice it, or the first. Their cameraman hangs back. Exorcist is in the midst of a ranting, circuitous monologue that will be played only in snippets: 'His blood was blue – blue! – and tasted kind of metallic,' 'My mother had warned me against girls like her, but I liked the way she smelled, so I married her anyway,' 'And that was the first time I ate lizard meat!'

The cameraman thumbs the trigger.

Neither Exorcist nor his teammates hear the warning rumbles over his chatter, and they're moving slowly. A pebble rolls into Waitress's foot. She glances to the side, but is too worn out to actually process what's happening.

It's Rancher who figures it out first, but he does so far later than the previous teams. There is barely time for him to shout, 'Watch out!' before the Styrofoam boulder bounces down onto the trail between him and Waitress. He jumps backward, out of the boulder's path, and Waitress turns, confused. Exorcist turns too, a safe distance ahead; he is a background figure as the cameraman films the boulder striking a thick trunk and ricocheting up, back onto the trail, where it catches the upper bank and then begins to bounce and roll downward. Rancher turns to run away, and then rational thought strikes and instead of running down the trail, he leaps off it, pulling himself by slender trunks up and out of the boulder's path. The boulder smacks his foot as it passes. Rancher's expectant brain screams that his foot is broken before sensation settles in: the blow barely hurt. He clings to the slope, befuddled.

This leaves the cameraman filming the boulder as it rolls

straight at him. This man is so accustomed to being invisible that he spends several seconds just watching the gray-brown sphere grow larger in his view screen. And then Rancher shouts, 'Move!' and the cameraman finally recognizes the danger. He panics, dropping his camera. Fight and flight fall to a third option: freeze. Scared and dumb, he watches the boulder, and only when it's about to strike does he react, scrambling away. But it's too late. The boulder smashes into him, full on, knocking him to the ground then teetering to the side of the trail to roll to a rest. Rancher pushes past the boulder, coming to help. Waitress is right behind him, her mouth gaping. Exorcist is motionless in the background.

The cameraman is swearing and biting his bottom lip. 'I think I broke my tailbone,' he says. He pinches his eyelids shut as Rancher helps him to his feet. When he reaches for his radio, he notices pain in his wrist too.

'Here, let me,' says Waitress, taking the radio. She presses down the button and speaks, 'Hey, hello? Our cameraman is hurt. He got hit by a rock. We need help.' She pauses, then adds, 'Over.' She takes her thumb off the button.

A moment later, a response comes, 'How badly is he injured?'

'I don't know,' says Waitress. Behind her, Exorcist creeps closer. 'He can stand and talk and he's not really bleeding, but –'

'My tailbone,' says the cameraman. 'Tell him I broke my tailbone and maybe my wrist.'

'He says he broke his tailbone and his wrist.'

'We'll send help. Wait there.'

'Wait here?' asks Exorcist in a contrary tone.

Waitress whirls to face him. 'He's hurt!'

'He's fine,' retorts Exorcist, with a waved dismissal at the cameraman. 'Sorry, friend, but it's not like you're dying.'

'We're already in last place,' says Rancher. 'Waiting isn't going to hurt.'

'How do you know we're in last?' asks Exorcist. 'You two mucked up the first Clue, someone else could have too.'

Rancher still has a supportive arm around the cameraman. Turning to him, he asks, 'Are we in last?'

The cameraman is breathing unsteadily. He glances around. He knows there are mounted cameras here; he knows he's not allowed to tell the contestants anything. But surely, he thinks, this scenario is an exception. 'You're way behind,' he says.

'See!' says Waitress.

'Doesn't matter,' says Exorcist. 'I'm going on. Come with or don't, it's all the same to me.' He starts hiking.

'But we're a team!' Rancher calls after him.

Exorcist yells back, 'See you at the top!'

Above, the other contestants watch an EMT and a cameraman walk swiftly out of the woods, across the small clearing, and then down the trail. The cameraman who was assigned to Zoo and Tracker is doubling back; he's the most physically fit of the crew – a marathon runner.

'I wonder what happened,' says Biology.

'Someone must be hurt,' says Engineer.

They all – save Tracker, who is still off on his own – look to the host, who shrugs. The on-site producer soon comes over and takes the host aside. The contestants watch their conversation, the bobbing heads and thoughtful hand gestures, but are unable to make much sense of it.

'No one seems to be panicking,' says Zoo. 'Whatever happened can't be that bad.'

'I bet it was that rock,' says Biology.

'What rock?' asks Engineer, and they tell him about the Styrofoam boulders. 'Wow,' he says, glancing at Zoo. He's glad she's not hurt. He thinks he will enjoy watching how she reacted to the boulder, later, once he's home – his room-mate promised to DVR the show for him.

Speculation fades to bored silence. Tracker returns and takes a silent seat next to Zoo. Then Exorcist crests the mountaintop, strutting toward the group. The others wait for Rancher and Waitress to appear. When they don't – the EMT, the wait, and now this – assumptions are made.

Air Force stands, ready to take action. The others start talking over one another, asking questions. Tracker listens and watches the woods.

Exorcist basks in the attention. 'It was wild,' he tells them. 'This giant rock came rolling out of nowhere. I jumped out of the way, but it was so fast –' He pauses, shakes his head. Biology puts a kind hand on his shoulder. 'It got our cameraman.'

Gasps. Then, 'How bad is he hurt?' Air Force is the one to ask it, but they all want to know.

'Bad. Real bad.'

The host walks closer, intrigued.

Unease thrums through the contestants.

'I should go help,' says Black Doctor.

'If you go back down you forfeit second place,' the host tells him.

'This man nearly gets killed and you just *leave* him?' says Carpenter Chick to Exorcist. She turns to the host. 'And this is *okay*?'

The host shrugs. 'You get ranked by when the last member of your team finishes, and they were in last, so I don't see that it matters.'

Carpenter Chick stares at him.

And Zoo thinks, It *does* matter. Because if Exorcist could leave them, then Tracker could have left her and now he knows it. She doesn't look at him, doesn't want to see him weighing whether finishing first was worth the burden of her. But Tracker is thinking instead about the injured man, about what injured him.

Below, the EMT reaches the cameraman and checks him over. His coccyx isn't broken, only bruised. He also has a sprained wrist and a few smaller contusions and scrapes; his injuries are light, more the result of his impact with the earth than his impact with the boulder, whose momentum was already largely dissipated by the time they met. The EMT opts to help him to the base of the trailhead; his injuries don't merit an airlift. The two men slink down the trail as the newly arrived cameraman asks Waitress and Rancher to gather around him.

'They don't know how they're going to portray this,' he says. 'If at all. So for now don't talk about it, okay? If they decide to use it, we'll get your reactions later.'

That night the decision will be passed down from on high: Get the cameraman to sign a waiver. His likeness can't be used without this explicit permission, a contractual concession to prove he and his brethren weren't being manipulated. That they were on the in-the-know side of the production. The cameraman won't sign, though. He doesn't want to be known for freezing. The producers will grumble, but there's nothing they can do. In the world of the show, the incident never happens. Nor does its aftermath on the mountaintop. Rancher will be shown scrambling out of the boulder's path, and then footage of the previous boulder rolling to a stop, followed by a commercial break, after which Rancher and Waitress will join the others. Arrivals are stitched together; if Exorcist finished the Challenge before his teammates, it was only by seconds.

The host calls out a last-place welcome and Exorcist bounds over to sling his arms across his teammates' shoulders. 'Couldn't stay away, could you?' he says to Waitress, ruffling her hair.

She recoils. 'Can I *please* be on a different team?' she asks the host.

'Yes.'

Waitress stares. 'Really?'

The host gestures to where the other contestants are seated. 'But first, have a seat.' Waitress, Rancher and Exorcist squeeze in so all eleven contestants are clustered together on the exposed rock face. Several interns and the producer appear, the former rushing about as the latter alternates between conferring and shouting orders. An intern hands the host a mirror. Rancher fields questions, answers them honestly.

'Tailbone?' asks Air Force. 'He made it sound like the guy was dying.'

Waitress wonders about her new team, then notices additional cameramen approaching, covering the group from all angles. 'Another Challenge?' she asks. 'Don't we get to rest?'

'Not when you're last,' the host tells her, checking his teeth.

Waitress is about to protest that their tardiness isn't her fault, that she shouldn't be penalized, but she squelches the instinct as she realizes that though she's not responsible for their cameraman being injured, her team's position *is* in large part her fault. Either Rancher or Exorcist could have caught her mistake, but neither did, and it's still *her* mistake.

I can't depend on them, she thinks, and she looks around at the others. Her eyes lock on Zoo, who is digging dirt out from under her fingernails with a pine needle, and she thinks, *Yes.*

Zoo notices her staring, sees her intent. She keeps her gaze firmly on her own fingernails, willing Waitress to look away. The last thing she wants is a useless someone depending on her.

13.

This time, I break the window with a rock. I throw it as hard as I can from about ten feet away and almost miss.

'In you go,' I say.

'You're not coming?' asks Brennan.

I shake my head and he looks at me like I'm already leaving him behind.

'It's a *boutique*,' I say. 'I can see the back from here.' Which, of course, I can't, but the blurriness beyond the window doesn't feel very deep. We're in a tourist-trap kind of town. All little cafés and kitschy gift shops. This store — its name in loopy cursive I don't have the patience to decipher — has a variety of handbags and satchels hanging in the window. I wonder how much the store owners were paid to be just what we needed.

Brennan slips through the broken window. 'Ow,' he says.

I turn away, rolling my eyes.

'Mae, I think I cut myself.'

'Are you bleeding?' I ask.

'Yes.'

'Well, then, at least you know.'

I hear rustling; he's in. I imagine he's looking back, watching me. Making sure I don't run. As if I have the energy for anything so dramatic.

'Hurry up!' I call. Above me, the gray sky rumbles. I think of the plane, but this is only thunder. 'You should probably get a rain jacket too,' I tell him. 'Or a poncho.' This seems like the kind of place that would stock ponchos.

Not practical, packable ones like the one I have, but something heavy and rainbow-colored, for irony.

A minute later he's out. He doesn't have a coat or a poncho, but he's holding a backpack. It's shiny and striped like a zebra.

'Is that the only one they had?' I ask.

He kneels and starts tucking his supplies into the pack, plastic bags and all. 'I like it,' he says.

'To each his own.' Maybe I shouldn't be belittling a featured product, but it's an *ugly* bag. Brennan zips the backpack closed and swings it over his shoulder. I start walking.

'Mae, look what else I found.' He holds out his hand and I stop to look. Matches. Six or seven booklets, dark blue, with the same indecipherable scrawl on the cover as was on the storefront.

'Good,' I say. 'We won't have to stop again.' I take the matches and put them in my pocket with my glasses lens.

A few steps later he asks, 'Do you have any Band-Aids?'

'How bad is it?' He holds up his arm. His sleeve is pushed back. I can't see any blood on the dark expanse of his arm, it's too far away, the cut too small. I shrug off my backpack and take out my first-aid kit. 'Here,' I say, handing him antibiotic ointment and a pack of bandages. He seems surprised. Maybe he expected me to dress the wound for him. 'Time's a-tickin',' I say. That startles him into action, and he tends to his arm. The sky rumbles again, louder. I predict Brennan will soon regret not taking something waterproof from Loopy Cursive.

I'm right. Hours later he drips and shivers in the rain. 'Mae, can we *please* sleep inside tonight?' he begs. My pants are tucked into my boots, my poncho hood up. My thighs and shins are wet, but otherwise I'm fine.

'No,' I say.

'The owners are gone. They won't care.'

I suck in my top lip to keep from yelling.

'Mae, I'm freezing.'

'I'll help with your shelter,' I say. 'Show you how to keep the wind out.'

He doesn't answer. His sneakers squelch with each step. Lightning cracks the horizon. Seconds later, thunder booms. I feel the ground shake. We've moved out of the tourist-trap town and into the suburbs. This is why they broke my glasses, I think. So they can send me through areas like this and all they have to do is empty the houses for a few hours. I wonder what that costs, a couple of hundred per family? All to fuck with me. And to gain viewers, because I have to admit, if I weren't here, if I weren't a contestant, I'd watch this show. I'd soak in their vision of mangled familiarity, and I'd love it.

Another rumble of thunder. All the houses are taller than we are, so I'm not worried about lightning strikes. Although, there isn't much detritus for building shelters here and we might not reach forest by nightfall. I might have to compromise. A shed, I think. I won't go into another of their staged houses, but I could compromise with a shed or a garage.

'Why can't we just wait until the rain stops,' says Brennan. 'This is stupid.'

You're stupid, I think. He's the one who didn't take a jacket when he had the chance. His contract must prohibit covering his sweatshirt, the cameras hidden there. In which case he's stupid for signing it.

Not that I was any smarter, signing mine.

'You've already slowed me down enough,' I say. 'I'm not losing the afternoon.'

'Slowed you down going *where*?' he asks, stopping. 'The city? It's empty, Mae. Trash and rats, that's probably all that's left by now. We need to find a farm, somewhere we can stay.'

'Is that where you were going before you latched on to me?' I ask. 'To find a farm, milk a cow, and steal eggs from a hen?'

He twitches. 'Maybe.'

'Then go,' I burst. 'Find yourself some farmer's daughter who got left behind and is feeling lonely. Don't worry, if her daddy's still around, you'll either win him over or he'll die. Make sure to find yourself a gun, though, to protect yourself from raiders. Or you can go Medieval retro, use a bow and arrow. I'm sure it's as easy as it looks. Beware anyone calling himself Chief, or the Governor. And protect that little lady of yours, because evil always has rape on its mind.'

He stares at me, rain pouring over his face. 'What are you talking about?'

Every post-apocalypse plot, ever, I think. I turn away. I want to get out of this town, fast. I hear the *squish squish* of Brennan following.

'This isn't a movie, Mae,' he says.

I laugh.

He shoves me from behind, hard. Surprised, I fall forward, landing in a sprawl in a puddle. The heels of my hands shriek as I push myself up. They're shredded from the pavement, dripping red. My right knee pounds.

'Fuck you,' I say, turning to face him. 'Fuck. You.' I want to smash in his cloudy face. I've never punched a person. I need to know how it feels. I need to see him bleed.

No hitting anyone in the face or genitals.

Let them stop me.

He's a kid.

He's old enough.

He's scared.

So am I.

You *have* to follow the rules.

He takes a step backward. 'Mae, I'm sorry,' he says. He's crying, again. 'I didn't mean to . . . I'm sorry.'

My fists are too tight.

'Please,' he says, 'I'll go wherever you want. Just don't leave me.'

I unfurl my hands. 'If you say one more word,' I tell him, 'you're on your own.' He opens his mouth and I raise a finger. 'One more word, Brennan, and I'm gone. And if you touch me again, I don't care what they say, I'll break your fucking face. Understood?'

He nods, terrified.

Good.

For the rest of the day, he's quiet. If not for his soggy footsteps and the occasional sniffle, I could forget he's with me. It's blissful, in a way, and yet, without his prattling, I'm alone again.

I'm cold now, and my wet pants chafe my skin. Brennan must be miserable. It'll be night soon and the storm's only getting worse.

Brennan sneezes.

We're passing a development of crammed-together McMansions. Billboards announce new construction, leases available. Houses, not homes.

If he gets sick, he's only going to slow me down more. No matter my earlier threats, I know they won't let me leave my cameraman behind.

I turn in to the development. The streets are named after trees. Elm, Oak, Poplar. I turn on Birch, because when I was little and a winter storm coated all the trees with ice — half an inch, but it seemed endless — the white birches bent the farthest, rounding their trunks like great humps. When the ice melted, the white birches also sprang most readily back toward the sky. Few were able to straighten entirely — all these years later many are still bowed – but they didn't snap, and I've always liked that about them.

The second house on the left side of Birch Street catches my eye. It looks like all the others, except that there's a sign out front that reads in blue OPEN HOUSE – and I know I am where I'm meant to be. I try the front door. Locked.

'Wait here,' I tell Brennan. I circle to the backyard. My attempts to jimmy open a kitchen window fail. I'll need to break it. There's nothing useful in the back, so I return to the front of the house. The wooden post from which the FOR SALE sign hangs is crooked and loose, like I'm meant to take it. I feel Brennan watching me as I yank the sign out of the ground. When I get back to the window, I smash it with the sign post. The rain's so loud I barely hear the glass break. I drop the sign, clear away the shards, and crawl through into a pristine kitchen. Leaving a dripping trail through a cathedral-ceilinged foyer to the front door, I let in Brennan and set the deadbolt behind him. Off the foyer, two adjacent rooms are staged with copious seating: long plush couches and deep armchairs. In one, the seating is arranged around a dusty flatscreen television, at least sixty inches. In the other, the focal point is a fireplace. There's a stack of Duraflame logs along one wall. A sponsor, probably.

I check the ceiling and see only a smoke detector. They don't need as many mounted cameras now that Brennan's with me.

The logs have instructions printed on their brown paper wrappers. Even Brennan can't mess this up; I toss him a book of matches and go to explore upstairs. I hold my breath every time I open a door, but this house is nothing like the blue cabin. It's huge, anonymous, empty. Stocked but not lived-in. I open a bathroom vanity and pour rubbing alcohol from the top shelf over my palms. The scrapes aren't bad enough to bother bandaging. In the master bedroom, I open closets and drawers until I find a pair of fleece pyjama pants; I shuck my wet pants and pull these on. I find a men's plaid pyjama set for Brennan and then go back downstairs. I toss him the clothing and lay out my pants, boots and socks by the fire.

'Go change,' I say, 'and we'll dry out your clothes.'

'Are we –' A look of horror crosses his face.

'It's all right. You can talk. Just not so much, okay?'

He nods rapidly. 'Are we stopping here?' he asks. 'For the night?'

'Yes.'

It seems the silence has done him good. He pauses for several seconds and then says, 'Thanks, Mae.'

'Go change.'

The pantry is stocked with organic vegetarian canned soups and mac and cheese with animal-shaped noodles. I heat up a can of Tuscan bean and rice soup for myself, and then make the mac and cheese for Brennan, substituting a can of condensed milk for the dairy called for by the box. He polishes off the entire pot's worth and then collapses on a couch with a sigh. Moments later, he's snoring. The sound isn't as annoying as it used to be. In fact, it makes the house feel a little less big.

I toss a quilt over him, then wrap myself in another. The couches are too soft; I sit on the rug, facing the fire and holding a cup of herbal tea. I'm not sure I'm going to be able to sleep here. Although, I checked all the rooms, so it should be okay. I hope it will be okay.

And if it's not, if something happens tonight, it'll be something new. Maybe they'll pump locusts down the chimney or toss some timber rattlesnakes through the broken window. Send in remote-controlled bats with exaggerated fangs. Or maybe my marauders will make their debut.

I know it's useless to try to predict their depravity, but I can't help trying. It makes sitting here, waiting, in this massive, ghostly house a little easier. I'm confident that whatever they do, they won't do it until later. They'll wait until I'm asleep – or nearly asleep – to strike. That's how they do it; they blur the line between reality and nightmare. They give me bad dreams, and then they make them come true.

The worst was the cabin. The too-blue cabin I can't forget, no matter how hard I try.

I found the cabin two days after Wallaby left me. I was following the last Clue given me. *Look for the sign past the next creek,* it said. I'd found a dry creek bed just hours from my camp, but there was no sign, so I kept walking, searching. I was beginning to fear I was off course, lost, and then there it was: a little brook babbling, *You found me, you found me.* Just downstream a culvert, a road, a driveway. And my sign, obvious, if unexpected: a swath of baby-blue balloons tied to a mailbox, dancing, drifting. I followed their driveway to a small single-storey cabin, blue, with a stubby chimney. There were more balloons tied by the front door and a gray welcome mat. I remember bright fish swimming the mat's perimeter, framing the words HOME SWEET HOME and smiling frozen cartoon smiles – though I didn't yet recognize this as my next Clue.

The front door wasn't locked. The cabin was blue and unlocked – they couldn't be more obvious than that. I stepped into a room awash in sky blue. Balloons littered the floor, a tower of blue-wrapped packages stood on the dining table; there was a blue couch, a blue chair. Throw pillows. Everything that was colored was blue. *Everything.* No, an exception – I remember a rug, the contrast of my gray-black handprint on the soft yellow after I opened the flue and built my fire. But everything other than that was blue, I remember.

I kept to the living area, kitchen and bathroom at first, leaving two doors that I assumed led to bedrooms closed. The electricity didn't work, but there was running water – and a blue baby bottle in the sink. I assumed the tap water was safe to drink and filled my bottles without boiling it first, a mistake. There were granola bars and an open bag of cheese curls in the cupboard. I ate my fill, which was also maybe a mistake, but I think it was the water that made me sick. I found some Twinings Lady Grey Tea too and made myself a cup, thinking that was a nice touch.

After finishing my tea, or maybe while I was still drinking it, I started to open the packages on the table. I expected food and a new battery for my mic pack, a Clue telling me where to go next. But the first item I unwrapped was a stack of picture books. One had a giraffe on its cover, another a family of otters. They all had animals on the covers, though on one it was just a teddy bear crushed to a little boy's chest. When I peeled back the paper on the second package – small, soft – I found a row of tiny white and blue socks, six pairs marked NEWBORN.

I remember tossing the socks onto the table and walking to the couch, suppressing – barely – an urge to stomp on one or all of their omnipresent balloons. Even now, I feel the sting of their message. I know I told them my reasons for coming. I told them when I applied and I told them again each round of the selection process. I told them in my first confessional. Again and again, I told them. I shouldn't have been so surprised that they listened.

After that I lay on the couch and failed to sleep for a long time. I was finally dozing when I heard it: a mewling cry. The sound pulled me toward full consciousness and my waking mind struggled to determine the direction of its source. Down the hall, behind a bedroom door.

The only light came from the stars and moon, and was

filtered through windows. I remember creeping down the hall, feeling my way, stepping softly in my socks – this was the last time I took off my boots to sleep. The sound was weak and animal-like. A kitten, I thought, and meant for me. They knew I would take care of it. I'm more of a dog person, but I'd never abandon an orphaned kitten. I'd never abandon any orphaned mammal, except maybe a rat.

When I opened the bedroom door, the mewling stopped, and I stopped with it. A wall of arched windows framed a queen-size bed. Compared to the hallway, the dusky light there was luminous; the bedding reflected the dreamy blue-gray of night. There was a teddy bear on the dresser, one of those nanny-cams. I remember identifying the camera made me feel a little better, a little braver.

But I was still startled when the crying resumed a few seconds later. It was louder, and I was able to identify the source as the mound of blankets on the bed. A hiccupy gulp interrupted the cry. Puzzled, I stepped toward the bed. The oblong shape beneath the blankets made me uncomfortable, but I'd come too far to stop, and they were watching, everyone was watching. I picked up the fabric and pulled it back.

Given the chance, a fraction of a second will gladly feel like forever, and that is the kind of forever I experienced as I lifted and immediately dropped the blanket. The light-haired mother prop lying there with marble eyes, black-brown dripping down her latex face to stain the sheets beneath. And in her puffy, mottled arms, a doll swaddled in pale blue. Its lips puckered and frozen, waiting for the bottle by the sink. I barely saw, but I saw. The blanket drifting so slowly from my hand to cover the prop, the doll.

It shames me to admit that their trick worked, that for the length of that forever I thought the props were real. And then the soundtrack looped back to its beginning and the cry sounded again and this time I heard it: a faint mechanical buzzing within the sound. At the same time they sprayed the smell through the vents, I think, or that's when I noticed it, or maybe in my memory it's just less important than the sound. Either way, this was my first experience of their rotting stench in close quarters and it permeated my being. I stood there, transfixed, a length of time that I know couldn't have been more than a few seconds, but every time I think about it, every time I remember, it feels longer, it feels like hours.

Even though I knew it was fake, even though the doll was ridiculous-sounding, ridiculous-looking, it hit me, hard. I don't know why: exhaustion, the poignancy of what that scene was intended to represent. It was like they knew the secret truth behind my confessionals, that this was their way of telling me that they knew I wasn't really here for a pre-motherhood adventure, but because I don't think I ever will be ready to have a child. I want to be ready, I want to do it — for him — I wish I could, but I can't. I applied, I came, in order to delay not the inevitability of motherhood, but of telling my husband the truth.

Standing in the too-blue cabin, I couldn't stop thinking of myself in the prop's place beneath the covers. The doll's face was — is — seared into my memory, but my guilt grasped the image and warped it. I saw my husband's chin, miniaturized and smoothed. I saw the little pug nose that flares so dramatically in photos of me growing up. I saw the divot on its flaking head pulsing.

The doll's soundtrack reached the cough — a tight, choking sound. I remember my stomach clenching, a visceral reaction.

I panicked. I turned and ran out of the bedroom. I grabbed my pack and jump-shoved my feet into my boots. I stumbled out the front door, sliding on HOME SWEET HOME as balloons entangled my feet. I broke free and took the path of least resistance: the dirt driveway, which spilled onto a crackled asphalt road where my quivering legs poured me to the ground. Just off the side of the road I lay among last year's leaves, mired in exhaustion and hate and dispersing adrenaline. They wanted me to quit, that much was obvious, and I wanted to, I wanted it to be over, but I couldn't give them the satisfaction. I lay there, stewing, for a long time. Eventually, I sat up and took off my glasses. I remember my stomach roiling, caustic fluids riding between my throat and bowels like tides. I pinched my glasses between my fingers and stared at where I knew they were without seeing them, reminding myself over and over that the prop and the doll weren't real, trying to figure out what I was supposed to do next, where I was supposed to go. Then an amorphous bubble of lighter space somewhere beyond my glasses caught my unfocused eye. An iridescent, dancing space that after a breathless moment I realized was the balloons, reflecting moonlight and skipping about the mailbox in the wind.

That's when I understood: The Clue wasn't the picture books or the balloons, it was the welcome mat. *Home Sweet Home.* That's the direction I had to go next. East.

I also knew the creators of the show would love my panicked retreat, and I resolved from that moment on to be as boring as I could be. That would be my revenge. I kept to back roads and avoided houses. It was slow going at first; I got sick – the water, maybe the food but probably the water – and lost a day or two, maybe three but I don't think so, shivering by a fire I was almost too weak to build, even with my fire starter.

I feel the pinch of loss. Just a thing, but such a useful thing. I don't know that I would have made it through those days of illness without the fire starter; they probably would have had to disqualify me, pull me for my own safety. As it was, I came distressingly close to saying the safety phrase; I think it was only the fact that they didn't come for me, that they were confident enough to let me wait it out, that gave me the strength not to quit, that allowed me to believe I would be okay. And I was. I got better, and I knew where I had to go; I started walking and I found peanut butter and trail mix, their next prop, telling me I was still on track.

Beside me, Brennan releases an especially loud snort and shifts on the couch. His arm flops over the side and his fingers twitch briefly into a fist before relaxing to graze the floor. He looks comfortable, at home on the plush cushions. He hasn't screamed tonight.

I stare at his dangling hand. Firelight bounces off the face of his wristwatch. Sleepless curiosity prompts me to check the time. Eight-forty-seven. I've spent so long operating by light, not hours, that I immediately feel as though I've just done something wrong. My face warms, and I realize why as I watch the digital seconds snap toward sixty – I hadn't expected it to be a working watch. Which is stupid; there's no reason for a camera watch not to also tell time.

I put down my cold tea and lean toward Brennan's hand, confronting the watch face unblinkingly. *I know you're there,* I tell the producers with a look. I could steal the watch and smash it, but I won't. I'll let them record me, I'll let them follow and document. That's what I signed on for, after all. What I won't do is let them break me. I won't let them win.

No matter what, I will go on. I will blow through their finish line, wherever it is, and I'll bring this living prop of theirs with me so all can see my victory.

14

The host runs a hand through his hair, ignoring the horizon framing his reflection as he preens into his mirror. An intern deposits a duffel bag at his feet; the host hands off the mirror and at the producer's go-ahead presents himself to the contestants. 'Last night was the last time we'll be supplying you with meat,' he says, 'but the winners of this next Challenge will be rewarded with cooking supplies, so I suggest you all try your best. Everyone ready?'

The contestants stare at him. Zoo gives a halfhearted thumbs-up. Engineer manages a nod. Carpenter Chick wears a deep frown, and Waitress's shoulders slump.

'That's the spirit,' says the host. 'There was a bear here, right here, one hour ago. It's your job to find it. This is a Solo Challenge, but advantages will be allocated based on the order you completed the last Team Challenge.' He picks up the duffel bag. 'For our first- and second-place teams, we have a profile of your target.' He hands Ziploc bags to Tracker, Zoo, Black Doctor and Banker. Each contains a hair sample and a laminated card profiling the black bear, including to-scale depictions of paw prints and scat. 'For our third-place finishers, a less complete profile.' He hands Air Force and Biology a set of cards containing bullet points about black bear behavior. 'And for fourth and fifth, here.' He tosses an orange whistle to each of the remaining contestants. 'Maybe you can scare it out.'

Waitress fumbles and drops her whistle. It clatters across the rock to settle at the host's feet. He waits for her to retrieve it, then says, 'Actually, there are *two* bears. Half of you will be pursuing one, half of you the other. I need the older member of each team to stand north of me, the younger south.'

Some teams are able to split without speaking – Tracker is at least five years older than Zoo, Black Doctor has a decade on Banker, and Rancher is the oldest of them all – but others have to talk it out. Air Force is older than Biology by a matter of weeks, and everyone is surprised to learn Engineer has two years on Carpenter Chick. Waitress doesn't want to say her age, but Exorcist – nearly forty – pretends to be unsure which of them is older. Finally, she says, 'Fine! I'm twenty-two.'

'So am I!' exclaims Exorcist.

'No, you're not,' says Rancher. He's had enough of Exorcist. They all have. 'Go on over,' he says to Waitress.

Exorcist turns to the host. 'It appears I am superfluous.'

The host tells him, 'Choose a group.'

Exorcist considers his options. To the host's left is the northern group, which consists of Tracker, Black Doctor, Rancher, Air Force and Engineer. To the host's right, the southern group, are Zoo, Banker, Waitress, Biology and Carpenter Chick.

'South,' says Exorcist. He's smirking and staring directly at Waitress.

'Great,' says the host. 'You go to the north, then.'

Waitress smiles for the first time today, and a shocked look falls over Exorcist's face. Then he nods – 'Should have seen that coming' – and moves to stand with the northern group.

Chatter to the south:

'I should have saved some of that chocolate,' says Carpenter Chick.

Banker tells her, 'I guess you'll have to make do with bear.'

'You think it'll be a real bear?' asks Zoo.

Carpenter Chick looks at her. 'Why wouldn't it be?'

'He said they're not giving us any more meat. And the deer tracks yesterday were man-made.'

'The deer you ate wasn't,' says Banker.

'True, but . . .' Zoo trails off. She can't believe that the show would have them track a real black bear. The species usually avoids people but can be dangerous if provoked. Besides, there weren't any bears there an hour ago.

'Is everyone ready?' calls the host.

Zoo pulls out the identification card from her Ziploc bag, underwhelmed. It seems to her that winning a two-day-long Challenge should garner a greater prize. She was hoping for a cooking pot, or maybe some gorp. She looks at the bear track – which she already knows how to identify – and then around at the four other people assigned to the south. 'If you find a track, don't step on it,' she says. She doesn't understand how this can work – five people tracking the same animal but not working together.

The host shouts, 'Go!' and the contestants scatter.

Zoo hesitates, watching the mad scramble of her fellows. 'This is going to be a disaster,' she says, and then she too begins to search.

While Tracker was wandering earlier, the producers told him to avoid one area, and it is to that area that he now walks, inferring. Exorcist follows him. The others go their own ways. Tracker sees the trail almost immediately: crushed foliage lined with clumps of brown-black hair. There are two perfect prints in the earth. He knows a bear would never be so obvious, but he also knows they're not tracking a real bear. Exorcist sticks close to him. 'I'm no fool,' says Exorcist. 'If there's a shortcut, I'm going to take it.'

The trail leads to a small cave in which Tracker and

Exorcist find . . . nothing. Just spiders and lichen. The trail was a red herring, specifically placed to draw and delay Tracker. Air Force has found the correct trail, a less obvious one that began very close to the Challenge's point of origin and was created only after Tracker was herded back to the group.

The contestants are too worn out to bicker. 'We should have made this another Team Challenge,' the host whispers to the on-site producer, who replies, 'It's fine, this is just to make sure they're exhausted.' The silent, slogging Challenge is heavily compressed. Viewers will see various contestants pushing through brush, a close-up here and there of bloodshot eyes, slack jaws. In the southern group, the first bear track is quickly destroyed by Banker, who obliviously replaces the print with his own. A cameraman catches this, and the shot will be followed by more bumbling and stumbling. Everyone in that group except for one will be shown falling, slipping, or smacking their head on a branch. The editor likes Zoo the best; he will show her helping Carpenter Chick up from the ground, but will cut when she walks into a neck-height pine branch immediately afterward.

Waitress approaches a patch of blueberries. At the edge of the patch she picks a berry and rolls it around in her open palm. 'I want to eat this,' she says. 'But I don't know if it's poisonous. I mean, it *looks* like a blueberry, but . . . I better not. I better just look for that bear.' She drops the berry and pushes through the dense, waist-high plants. After a few minutes – seconds – she hears a groan and freezes. It's just her and her cameraman here; the nearest other contestant is Biology, about fifty feet away. 'Was that it?' Waitress whispers, and then she sees it: less than ten feet away, on the far side of a log, a rotund mass of black hair three feet tall and six feet long.

Waitress starts shaking, and she mutters quickly and softly, 'No way, no way, no way . . .'

She doesn't notice that the bear isn't moving, not to look at her, not to eat the berries inches from its mouth, not even to breathe. A very long ten seconds pass, then the crunch of Biology coming her way shocks Waitress out of her stupor. She pushes through the blueberry bushes and walks up to the mount – it *is* a real bear, just long dead and expertly preserved – and looks closely at its face, the brownish muzzle, the unblinking glass eyes, the sharp teeth exposed in a mouth that looks ready to roar. And then she notices something around its neck: a single bear claw, dangling on a hide thong. A tiny tab of paper is taped to the thong. It reads: BRING PROOF.

To the north, Air Force finds the second bear and takes its bear claw necklace for himself. But Waitress beats him back to the host, whose face falls into abject shock upon seeing her with the bear claw. He recovers quickly, at least enough to say, 'Well . . . Congratulations.'

'It was the berries,' Waitress says later via confessional. 'I wasn't following any trail. I was just wandering around, then I saw the berries and I thought, *Don't bears eat berries?* And there it was!'

Once Air Force returns, the other contestants are recalled with a series of shouts.

'*She* found it?' Exorcist exclaims. 'No way.'

Waitress flips him off, a gesture that will be featured but blurred, and Exorcist is soothed because he knows that even though she won a Challenge, he can still get under her skin.

'Our winners now get these,' says the host, who is holding two identical duffel bags. He hands one each to Waitress and Air Force. The sun is low on the horizon. The contestants all look exhausted, because they are. It has been a long day. The host looks them over gravely, then says, 'Good night' and walks away.

Murmurs of disbelief run through the contestants. 'What do we do now?' asks Biology. Banker's face is blank. 'I guess we should build a shelter?' says Zoo. She looks at Tracker and is relieved when he meets her eye.

Air Force unzips his duffel bag; Waitress notices and does the same. A cameraman moves in close to her, to record the contents. He coughs as he crouches next to her on the rock slick. The cough sounds like there's sandpaper in his throat. 'Hold on,' he chokes out to Waitress. He hawks and spits and then eases into a seated position, breathing heavily. 'Just a bit of a cold. Sorry, go on.' His hands are shaking, enough that this footage will be useless; the editor will have to use that of the cameraman leaning over Air Force's shoulder instead. The items will pop up as bullet points for viewers as they are revealed: two small metal cook pots with foldable handles – identical to the one Rancher obtained in the first Challenge – a bag of powdered vegetable bouillon, a five-pound sack of brown rice, a plastic salt and pepper shaker set, and a spool of fishing line.

'It'll get cold up here,' says Tracker. He speaks quietly; only Zoo, Carpenter Chick and Black Doctor hear him. 'We should move off the peak.'

'One shelter to share?' asks Carpenter Chick.

Tracker nods, then turns and starts walking away from the rock slick toward a gently sloping wooded area. Zoo and Carpenter Chick follow him.

Black Doctor turns to the others and hollers, 'One shelter tonight, this way!' He waits for Air Force to zip up his bag and stand, then the two walk together into the trees.

Though it takes the contestants some time to get organized, viewers will next see their shelter halfway built. Carpenter Chick has taken the lead in construction, and this shelter is shaping up to be a beautiful lean-to. It's positioned seventy-five feet below the crest of the mountain, in a flat area where the rocks have very little moss. 'Less moss means less water,' explains Tracker. 'So if it rains, we won't be mired in runoff.' Viewers will next see Tracker approaching Air Force. 'I don't know how long we'll be here,' he says. 'I can't catch enough to feed everyone with just deadfalls.'

'You're planning on feeding everyone?' asks Air Force.

'It's the right thing to do.'

'I'll help.'

By nightfall the group shelter is twelve feet long, with a low sloping roof of cut pine branches. Its frame consists of three Y-shaped branches jammed deep into the earth, each with a hefty support log resting in its nook to form consecutive *V*'s. A foot of fallen leaves and needles carpet the inside of the shelter, and a roof of similar material covered with the cut pine completes it. Built in two hours with only wild resources, the lean-to looks remarkably professional and appealing.

Twenty feet from the lean-to there's a second shelter, little more than a pile of leaves against a rock. Exorcist remembers feeling warm last night, but also cramped. He wants to see the stars tonight. He's lying atop the shallow duff, ignoring the others and waiting for the sun to go down.

Waitress sits between the two shelters with her sack of rice, which is lighter now. Two cups of her rice is cooking, along with the same amount from Air Force, split among the five small pots. She was hesitant to share at first, but Air Force's instantaneous generosity squashed her reluctance; tonight the contestants feast on a thick rice porridge flavored with salt, pepper, bouillon, and several cups of stewed dandelion greens that Biology, Black Doctor and

Engineer gathered while Zoo started the fire and the others collected firewood. Everyone has pitched in tonight, and all will share in the bounty.

Everyone except Exorcist, who's been relaxing off on his own for hours. As the others sit around the fire and begin passing around the camping cups, he stands up from his mattress of leaves, stretches, and then comes over and settles between Waitress and Engineer.

'What do you think you're doing?' asks Waitress, who is holding one of her cups and a plastic fork given to her by Rancher.

'I'm starved,' he replies, patting his stomach. 'Pass some of that over here.'

'No way,' says Waitress. Then what viewers will not hear: 'You left us, then went to *sleep*.'

'Don't be ridiculous,' says Exorcist.

'She ain't being ridiculous,' Rancher says from across the fire. He's holding his own cup. 'If you want to eat as a team, you gotta be part of the team.'

Waitress's animosity doesn't surprise Exorcist, but Rancher's agreement does, as do the many nodding heads around the campfire. Briefly, he looks into a camera lens, as though accusing the device of having put the others up to this. Indeed, that's exactly what he's doing; he thinks they're performing – like he is. But the truth is most of the contestants have in this moment forgotten that they're being recorded. An ancient instinct is kicking in, not so much a survival-of-the-fittest mentality as an unwillingness to carry an able but lazy individual. No one else would have actively stopped Exorcist from eating, but now that Waitress has, the others are all solidly on her side. Guilt flashes through almost everyone, but this doesn't convince them they are doing anything wrong.

'I'll starve,' says Exorcist.

'The human body can go a month without eating,' says Tracker. He is the one among them who feels no guilt.

'Go find some grubs,' says Waitress. She takes a bite of rice, then closes her eyes and releases a hum of pleasure.

Exorcist lunges forward and rips the metal cup out of her hands. Waitress's eyes pop open and she launches herself at Exorcist, sending him tumbling and the rice flying through the air. She slaps at him with all her skinny might. Exorcist covers his face and curls into a ball, weathering the blows. Engineer scurries toward the fray: ineffectual intervention. A second later, Banker yanks Waitress up and away as she screeches, 'Let me go!'

And then Biology is with her, rubbing her arms, soothing. Of the many things she says then, the only phrase that will be played for viewers is 'He's not worth it.' Carpenter Chick stands with Waitress too, glaring at Exorcist. Zoo watches this and thinks, That's what I'm expected to do – provide comfort. But she won't allow her gender to define her role. Instead of rushing to soothe Waitress, she pokes a stick into the fire, breaking a glowing mass of wood at the bottom into several distinct orange-and-red-rimmed embers.

Exorcist is fuming and embarrassed, still on the ground. 'She hit me!' he shouts. 'Our contracts said you couldn't hit anyone!'

One of the cameramen is on his radio. The producer at the other end says, 'Jesus, what a day. It's fine as long as it's over. And – tell me you got it?' Later, to his off-site counterpart, he'll add, 'At least we can *use* this. Fucking waivers.'

Back at the fire, Black Doctor points out, 'The contracts only prohibited hitting someone's head, face or genitals.'

Exorcist climbs to his feet and gestures at his own face. 'And what do you call this?'

'Looked to me like she only hit your knees and your arms.'

'It's true,' says Air Force. 'You had a pretty good defensive fetal going on there.'

Zoo laughs; Exorcist glares at her.

'Whatever,' she says. 'You brought it on yourself.' Her dismissive tone surprises Engineer, who had expected her to act as a peacemaker. None of the cameramen catch the slightly disappointed look on his face as he glances her way.

Exorcist throws up his hands and retreats to his meager bedding. The others eat their meal in silence. The segment will end with a series of short confessionals.

Carpenter Chick, heavily edited: 'He deserved it.'

Banker: 'He just took a nap while the rest of us set up camp. I feel a little bad about it, but why should we carry his weight? Besides, it wasn't my call. I didn't win the rice. I was thankful to be getting any myself.'

Waitress: 'He's been needling me for two straight days, and then he steals my food? No f-ing way. I hope he starves.'

Exorcist: 'Every society needs its pariahs; the fact that this is a small society doesn't change that.' He runs a hand through his greasy red hair, stoking the flames. The second episode of *In the Dark* will end here, with his promise: 'They want me to be their villain? Fine. I'll be their villain.'

15

Birch Street was a respite – from external nightmares, if not from those spun by my own subconscious. This means only that my next Challenge is pending. As Brennan and I leave the house, leave the neighborhood lined with streets named after trees, I wonder if they're waiting for some signal from Brennan. Maybe there's a landmark we're supposed to reach.

Mid-morning, we reach it: a neighborhood manipulated in a manner I haven't seen before. It's not abandoned – it's destroyed. Windows are broken, signs bowled over. What I initially think is a very out-of-place boulder resolves into a car smashed against a brick wall. I feel my spine curl and I keep my eyes wide as we pass. What I do see of the car makes me think of high school, when the antidrug club got the local fire department to stage a drunk-driving accident using a wrecked van. Volunteers covered themselves with cornstarch blood and screamed from inside the van as the Jaws of Life gnashed toward them. I remember my friend David crawling from the van's front door, stumbling to his feet, and then weaving toward the firemen. The front-seat passenger, Laura Rankle, 'died.' She was nicer than the average popular girl, and David's screams as she was pulled, limp, from the vehicle were deeply unsettling. Repeatedly I told myself it wasn't real. It didn't help. I did my best to hide my tears from my classmates, only later noticing that most were hiding tears of their own. My dad knew about the stunt; I remember him asking about it at dinner that night. Before I could answer, my mom chimed in with something about how she believed – how she *knew* – that it would save someone's life, and that the van had crashed precisely for this purpose. I had been about to say how powerful the experience was, but after her comment I just shrugged and dubbed it overdramatic.

A few blocks after the smashed car there's a pileup. The color at the center is distinctive; I don't need to know the shape to see it's a school bus. A school bus and a handful of smaller vehicles. As we get close I see a charred prop hanging out the front door of a blackened sedan. For a moment I imagine it has Laura Rankle's face – not the gaunt, defeated face she grew into after she got pregnant and the baby's father abandoned her, but the face she had as a girl.

'Mae?' says Brennan. 'What's wrong?'

It's an absurd question, designed to get me talking. I almost tell him to shut up, and then I think that if I give them a good story, maybe they'll leave me alone. Maybe if I talk the Challenge will end. So I tell him. I tell him all about Laura Rankle and David Moreau. About fake blood and twisted metal, the awful amalgamation of pretend tragedy and the remnants of the real thing. 'Afterward, when one of the firemen helped Laura out of the ambulance and she was smiling this nervous smile and she was fine – it was surreal,' I say. We take a short detour around an overturned shopping cart and I continue, 'It felt real enough to give me this sense of *what if* that was hard to shake.'

I look at Brennan. 'Weird,' he says.

The first fully true thing I've told him, and all he can say is 'Weird.' I suppose that's what I get for treating him like a person instead of the prop that he is. My own fault.

Maybe it's my eyesight, but even though we're getting close to the bus, it still seems very distant. As I walk toward it, I find I don't care about the bus. I don't care about what's inside the bus. Because this isn't my world. This isn't real.

When I was growing up, my teachers and guidance counselor talked about 'the real world' as if it were a distinct existence, something separate from school. Same thing in college, though I was living on my own in a city of eight million people. I never understood that. What is the real world if it's not the world one exists in? How is being a child less real than being an adult? I remember prepping dinner one night of group camp: Amy working the tip of her knife into a rabbit's naked shoulder, separating the limb. The care she took, the time, dividing the meat equally among our cooking pots. 'I thought it would be *different* here,' she said. 'I thought . . .' Her hesitation, I thought it was because her knife struck bone. 'But turns out it's no less fucked up than the real world.' This didn't seem like such a strange thing to say, then. Those Challenges had frames: beginnings and endings that were easy to identify, a man shouting 'Go!' and 'Stop!' I miss that. Now it's like everything is fake and real at the same time. The world in which I move is constructed, manipulated and deceptive, but then there's that plane, and the trees, and squirrels. Rain. My maybe-late period. Things too big and too small to control, contributing and conflicting all at once. This empty world they've made is filled with contradiction.

We've reached the bus. My skin prickles. The bus's yellow front bleeds into the building's gray, but I think there's room to pass behind. There has to be.

'Mae, let's go around,' says Brennan.

'I am going around.'

'Around the *block,* Mae.'

I know that's what he meant. I walk toward the back of the bus.

'Mae, *please* – don't you see them?'

He's talking about the props spilling from the bus's rear

emergency exit. I see five or six, and there are probably more inside. I smell them too, like the others but with charcoal.

I look at Brennan. He's shaking, overdoing it. My high school friends were more convincing.

'Just get it over with,' I say. I cram my hand into my pocket, rub my glasses lens, and walk.

Brennan follows in silence. These props are swollen and bursting, blackened with rot. A pile of newspapers and trash has coalesced like a snowdrift along the bus's rear tire. I step on a paper bag and something mushes beneath my boot. I feel a fleshy pop and something thin, long and hard against my arch.

It's nothing. Don't look.

'Mae, I can't do it.'

I'm past the bus. I don't want to turn around.

'Mae, I can't.' His voice has heightened in pitch. I force myself to turn back. I look directly at Brennan, tunneling my vision. He's a brown and red blur, recognizable as human, but barely. 'Mae, *please.*'

He's just another obstacle, another Challenge. A recording device creating drama.

'Cut it out,' I say.

'But I –' he interrupts himself with a sob. I can't see his face, but I've seen him cry so many times already. I know how his mouth twists, how his nose leaks. I don't need to see it again to know what it looks like.

Leave him.

I can't.

You don't want to.

They won't let me. They want him with me. He needs to be with me.

'You can do it, Brennan,' I say. I force softness into my tone and use his name because names seem to calm him. He calls me Mae with nearly every breath, so much so that I'm almost beginning to feel as though it's my real name. *Real.* There it is again. When the unreal outweighs the real, which is true? I don't want to know. 'They can't hurt you. Just come quick and we'll get out of here.'

He nods. I imagine that he's biting his lip, as he tends to do.

'We're only a few days away,' I say. 'We'll be there in no time.'

I see his arm move toward his face, and then he's getting bigger, clearer, approaching. The black and white stripes of the pack hugging his shoulders. A moment later he's at my side and I can see that yes, he's crying. He's also pinching his nostrils shut with his thumb and forefinger.

'Let's go,' I say.

Within minutes, we clear the worst of the destruction. We've returned to simple desolation. All that work, all that money, and all we had to do was walk by a bus. Not that it was easy, but their wastefulness irks me.

'Mae?' asks Brennan. 'Why don't we take the highway?'

His question rests atop my lingering unease. It's like he's trying to get me to break the rules.

'No driving,' I say.

'Oh.' A beat of silence, then, 'What about to walk on? It's gotta be quicker than this.' Is this a Clue? Have they closed down the highways too? That's big. Too big. I don't believe him. 'There's a sign for it right there,' he says. 'It's close.'

'No.'

'Why not?'

I can't answer; I don't know the answer.

'Mae, why not?'

I keep walking.

'Mae?'

The name burns through me.

'Mae?'

I can feel his fingers crawling through the air, approaching my arm.

'What did I say about touching me?' My voice shudders with all that I'm keeping inside.

He draws back, sputtering an apology. For a moment it seems that he's let his question pass. Then he says, 'So, the highway?'

'No, Brennan.' My frustration is building, turning to anger. 'We're not taking the highway.'

'Why not, Mae?'

'Stop calling me that.'

'Why?'

'And stop saying, "why." '

Agitation speeds my steps. Why is he challenging me like this? Why doesn't he have any regard for the rules of the game?

Why?

You know why.

I grasp my glasses lens, tight. My thumb's callus catches as I rub. I remember all Brennan has said about quarantine and illness. I remember the flyer, a house filled with blue, so much blue, as blue as the summer sky and just as clear. I remember the teddy bear, watching me.

If I allow myself to doubt, I'll be lost. I can't doubt. I don't. It all makes sense. Metal and fur, a drone far above. He's a cog like everything else. Like me. His rules are just different.

I'm walking carelessly, faster than I should be. My foot catches on nothing; I stumble. Brennan reaches out to steady me, but I pull away.

'Mae,' he says.

'I'm fine.' I set my blurred gaze to the ground, start walking again.

'Mae, what's that?'

He's looking ahead. I try to see what he's seeing, but the horizon is a fuzzed mass. I thumb my glasses lens, harder, creating heat. 'What's what?' I ask.

Brennan looks at me. His eyes are huge. He looks terrified. I feel my chest tighten.

Whatever's up there, it's not real.

But even if it's not, it is, and contradictions can be dangerous. Remember the fine print. Remember the coyote. Teeth and gears and blood and fear. The doll's pursed lips crying for Mama.

I pull the lens from my pocket and wipe it on my shirt. I close my left eye, hold the lens up to my right.

Suddenly, the trees have leaves. Crisp, singular leaves. The guardrail to my left has dings and dents and dots of rust. There are lines of white paint edging the road, faint but there, and a squashed frog has dried to jerky not three feet from where I stand. How much subtlety have I missed since my glasses broke? How much roadkill?

I look at Brennan. He has freckles, and a small scab on his cheek.

I look away, look ahead.

A fallen tree blocks the road. A white sheet is tied into the branches so that it falls flat like a sign. There's writing on the sign, but it's too far away to read, even with the lens to my eye. Another Clue, finally. I march forward.

'Mae, wait,' says Brennan.

'Can you see what it says?' I ask.

'No, but –'

'Then come on.' I open my left eye; clarity and ambiguity mingle in my vision, and I weave slightly, adjusting. Within seconds I can begin to make out the letters on the sign, the shapes of the words. There are two lines. The first is two words, maybe three; the second line is longer, giving the overall text a plateau shape. Runs in the paint further confuse the letters, but after a few more steps I can decipher the first word: NO.

I feel as though I've just scored a point. I read a word; I'm winning this Challenge.

'Mae . . .'

I want to figure out the message before I get too close, just to say I did. The second word starts with a *T*. I bet the word is 'trespassing.' A sinuous middle increases my confidence. The second line is harder. A V-word to start. 'Violators,' must be.

Brennan grabs my arm. 'Mae, stop,' he says, frantic.

And then the text clicks into place and I read the full message:

NO TRESPASSING.
VIOLATORS WILL BE GUTTED.

'Gutted?' I say, lowering the lens. 'That's a bit much.' And yet I feel my body constricting, wanting to hide. I can barely remember how it feels to be held by someone I love, but I have no trouble imagining the sensation of a blade ripping into my abdomen. The fire, a moment of frozen time, then spilling outward. I imagine steam rising as my warm guts hit the cool air. Then I imagine myself as the one doing the gutting.

'Let's go,' says Brennan, nodding back the way we came.

The only way out of a Challenge is to say the words, to quit.

'We'll go around, Mae.'

Gutted, I think. The sign is so extreme, so ridiculous. It's like the flyer, meant for the viewing audience, not for me.

With the thought, a sense of extreme unimportance overwhelms me. This show isn't about me. It's not about the other contestants. It's about the world we've entered.

We're bit players, our purpose one of entertainment, not enlightenment. I've been thinking about this whole experience the wrong way – I'm not here because I'm interesting or because I'm scared of having kids, I'm simply an accent on their creation. No one cares if I make it to the end. All they care about is that the viewers watch to the end.

I put the lens back into my pocket and stride forward.

'Mae!'

This is the game I agreed to play.

'Don't!' His hand is on my arm again, but he's not pulling. 'Please.'

Yes, I think. This feels right. I bet Cooper is on the other side of that sign, waiting for me. Maybe one of the others. Probably one of the others. Complication comes in threes: love triangles, third wheels, the trinity.

I'm close enough now that I can read the sign without my lens; knowing what it says helps. Brennan is still with me, so I must be going the right way, no matter what he says. Will Cooper have a shadow too? A pouty white girl? Maybe the Asian kid – what *was* his name? – will be the third; that'd be fitting, a nice TV-friendly diversity. Or Randy, for a dash of drama? I doubt there will be another woman. There's no way Heather's made it this far, and Sofia – well, Sofia's a possibility.

I reach the downed tree. I'm standing next to the banner. Is this a starting line or a finishing line? I don't know, but I know it's something. I reach forward. Touching the tree is going to be a trigger. For what, I don't know. Bells and whistles, maybe, or flashing lights.

My hand slips into the blur, finds a solid branch.

Sirens don't erupt. Signal flares don't shoot into the sky. The earth doesn't shake. The woods are unchanged.

Disappointment thrums through me. I was so certain this moment mattered.

It's not the first time I've been wrong.

I climb over the tree, then take out my lens and scan the road ahead. It's clear. Brennan hops down next to me on the pavement.

'Well,' I say. 'We still have our guts.'

'Shh,' he whispers. He's curled like a thief. 'I heard about this kind of thing.'

I didn't listen closely to his story, but I'm pretty sure this is a contradiction. 'I thought you didn't see anyone after leaving your church.' I speak at a normal volume and he shushes me again. 'Fine,' I whisper.

'I met a few, at first,' he tells me. 'They were always sick.'

That's a fair revision, I think. And I have to admit, his worry is contagious. Are we about to meet my marauders? I creep forward and keep my lens in my palm, ready. As we advance, Brennan's gaze darts from side to side.

I wonder how I'm being portrayed now. I know what my role was when we started. I was the earnest animal lover, always cheerful and up for a Challenge. But now? Will they cast me as off my rocker? Probably not; that's Randy's role, with his stupid gold cross and his tales of possessed toddlers. But whoever I am now, I'm no longer who I was.

I wonder if I can even do it anymore, be that person grinning until her cheeks ache. It was exhausting, as exhausting as this endless trekking, in its own way.

Give it a try.

Well, why not?

I look at Brennan and smile. I summon my most chipper voice and say, 'Some weather we're having, huh?' My stomach turns; being cheerful hurts.

He just looks at me, eyebrows raised. I drop the painful smile and look away. What if I can never be that person again? Not the exaggeration of myself I put on for the show, but the person I really was. The person I worked so hard to become after leaving my mother's sour home. I hate the idea of being this miserable for the rest of my life. But I'll readjust. Once this is over. I have to. My husband will help. As soon as I see him again, all this misery will be banished. This experience will become what it was meant to be – one last adventure. A story to tell. We'll adopt the wacky-looking greyhound of our dreams, toss our condom supply in the trash, make a small family. I'll do it, even if I'm not ready, because you can't be ready for everything and sometimes overthinking a challenge makes overcoming it impossible and I am not my mother. Soon these hardships will be far enough in the past that I'll be able to pretend I had fun here. Or maybe being pregnant will be so awful this will seem like a vacation. I read a book before I left that makes that seem possible, with its talk of grape-sized hemorrhoids and crusty gum growths.

Is that why I haven't had my period yet?

No. I'm not pregnant. I know I'm not pregnant. This is my body's reaction to physical stress – all this hiking, and how long did I go without eating when I was sick?

But. What if?

My last period was a week or so before I left for the show. We had sex after that, but with protection – I've never been on the pill; sex without a condom is nigh inconceivable to me – but maybe something went wrong. Maybe after all these years something finally went wrong.

I remember being so scared that I'd get my period while here, anticipating it, fearing a cameraman would get something incriminating on film. As if menstruation were shameful. As if it were a choice. Now I just want it to happen so I can know, so I can be certain of something.

I think of the doll in the cabin. Its sunken, spotty face. Its mechanical kitten cries.

I'm *not* pregnant.

I want to think about something else. I need to think about something else.

'So, what's with the zebra print?' I ask Brennan.

'Shh!'

I forgot we were whispering. I mouth an apology, just to get him talking.

It works. After a moment he says, so quietly, 'Reminds me of Aiden.'

The brother. I don't remember if he's supposed to be dead or alive. Wait – Brennan said something about calling him, about phones not working. He doesn't know. 'If you survived, he might have too,' I try. 'Immunity could be genetic.'

'My mom didn't survive.'

'What about your dad?'

He shrugs. 'He was in the Army. Died when I was little.'

I'm trying to decide what to say next when a loud *snap* to our left interrupts my thoughts. I pivot toward the sound; Brennan jumps behind me. Hurriedly, I find my lens and hold it to my eye. I close my other eye and scan the woods.

This is it, I think. Everything is about to change.

A flash of white, a curled tan body on stiltlike legs, big dumb eyes. An eastern white-tailed deer frozen in our presence. I take a step toward it and the ice cracks. The deer scrambles over a log, then bounds away, its snowy tail erect.

'What was that?' asks Brennan, voice trembling.

'A deer,' I tell him. I hear anger in my voice, but all I feel is tired.

Soon a driveway sprouts to our right. I take out my lens. The driveway is a semicircle leading past a gas station, a minimart, and a motel, and then back to the road. There's a black pickup truck by the pumps, and the windows of the

216

minimart are boarded. One of the motel room doors is open. There's a vending machine by another.

'I bet this is their base,' says Brennan.

Of course the marauders have a base. I'm anticipating a Challenge, but this place looks abandoned and it's out of the way. There is no blue that I can see.

'Do you think we should check it out?' Brennan asks, suddenly bold.

'You didn't want to cross the tree,' I say, 'but you want to go in there?'

He shrugs.

Something about that open door strikes me as far more menacing than a banner stretched across a fallen tree.

'We don't need anything,' I say. 'There's no reason to.'

'The vending machine's open,' he says. 'I'm going to check.' He dashes toward the motel. I almost call after him.

I keep my lens to my eye and watch as Brennan jogs up to the vending machine. As he said, its front is ajar. He pries it fully open — the metallic screech makes me cringe — and reaches in. He's taking bottles of something, I can't see what. When he's done he creeps toward the open door. I hold my breath as he steps inside. I expect screams, I expect gunshots, I expect silence. I expect everything, nothing. This might be where we part ways, because no matter what happens, I'm not going in there after him.

Brennan steps back outside. He jogs toward me, leaving the door open.

'I got some water,' he says. 'And Fanta.'

'Terrific,' I deadpan, slipping my lens back into my pocket. 'Let's go.'

'Don't you want to know what was in the room?' he asks.

'No.'

'Well, let's just say —'

'No!' I snap. I don't need to be told what's in that room. I already know. More props, more games. A reward if I can hold my breath long enough to cross the room and reach a safe, or a briefcase, or a bag. But there is no blue. If it's a Challenge, it's optional, and I choose not to participate.

Over the next few hours, we pass a handful of houses and see several more deer. When we stop to make camp, I notice Brennan acting squirrely. He keeps looking at me, then looking away. He clearly wants to say something. About halfway through building my shelter I can't take it anymore. 'What?' I ask him.

'That piece of glass in your pocket,' he says.

'I wear glasses,' I tell him. 'They broke shortly before we met and that lens was all I could salvage.'

'Oh,' he says. 'I didn't know.'

Because I didn't tell you, I think.

We finish our shelters, then sit together between them and split a bag of trail mix. As the sun sets I feel heavy and anxious. I don't build a fire and Brennan doesn't ask for one. He chugs a warm soda. I sip my water. I can't stop thinking about the motel, about what was behind the open door. If it was what I thought, then why isn't Brennan upset? Why does he no longer seem to care about the NO TRESPASSING sign? I don't want to ask.

The moon's waning and the sky is clouded. There's very little light. My vision is a checkerboard of grays implying trees, implying a boy. I need to close my eyes. I back into my shallow shelter, snuggle into dry leaves, and pull my hood over my hat.

'Good night, Mae,' says Brennan. I hear rustling as he settles into his own shelter.

That night in my dreams I knock a crying baby off a cliff

and then run to catch it, but I'm too late and my husband's there, watching, and no matter how much I apologize to him it can never be enough.

When I wake up, it's still dark and I'm shivering. I remember my dream too well, variation on a theme. My hood is off and I've squirmed partway out of my shelter. At first I think the cold woke me – ever since the rain, it's as though Mother Nature flipped a switch to turn summer into autumn – but as I push back into my shelter, I realize there's a sound overhead. Another airplane. I look up, but can't see its lights through the canopy, the clouds. It sounds far away, but it's there. That's all that matters.

The next time I open my eyes, it's light out. From the sun's position I know it's later than I usually sleep. I'm still cold – not shivering, but chilly. My fingers are stiff. It might be time to find some warmer clothing. But we should reach the river – if not today, tomorrow. From there it can't be more than another two or three days. I can last that long. Then I'll be able to sleep in my own bed with the covers tucked up to my chin, my husband a furnace at my back. I hope Brennan won't put up too much of a fuss about being cold. That is, if he even feels it. He might not, if he's anything like I was at eighteen. My freshman year at Columbia, I often wouldn't bother putting on a coat while rushing between buildings for class in the winter. My friends would shiver beside me, incredulous, and I would shrug and say, 'Vermont.'

I glance toward Brennan's shelter as I crawl from mine. His zebra pack leans against the exterior. I start pulling apart my debris hut, figuring the noise will wake him, but every time I look in his direction I see only stillness. I toss the last of my framing branches aside. It crashes into leaf litter and strikes a rock. He sleeps through the racket, somehow.

'Hey,' I say, approaching his shelter. 'Time to get up.' I crouch by the opening.

The shelter is empty.

'Brennan!' I shout, standing. 'Brennan!' And then I'm hyperventilating and can't call his name again. I turn in a circle, the forest suddenly ominous. I know he's part of the game and I've been wishing him gone since he first appeared, but I can't do it, I can't be alone. There's not enough of me left to survive being left alone again.

Four words come, like ice down my back: VIOLATORS WILL BE GUTTED.

I turn to the north, where the road waits. He's there, out of sight, I know it with horrendous certainty. He's hanging from a tree, rope around his neck, entrails dribbling from his abdomen. Some psychopath appeared in the night to drag away my only companion. He jabbed a knife into his belly, twisted and sawed with a palm over Brennan's screams. That's what woke me, not the cold, not a plane. I see Brennan kicking and throwing useless elbows. The red of his blood flowing through the red of his sweatshirt. Dead, like everyone, waiting for me who is still here – why? I can't do it, I can't push forward anymore, knowing what's waiting, knowing he's gone, it's too much and I –

'Mae?'

I spin toward the voice and see him, staring at me. For a moment I can't make sense of his appearance or what he said – who's Mae? But as he steps forward and I see the concern written across his face, I remember.

'Where were you?' I ask. I can barely speak. I feel the cool wind on my hot face.

Brennan looks away shyly. 'I had to go to the bathroom,' he says. 'It took a while.'

I bite my bottom lip, readjusting. My body feels cold and tight. I release my lip and say, 'You were off taking a shit.'

He nods, embarrassed. 'Sorry if I scared you.' He walks by me without making eye contact and begins to take apart his shelter.

I feel ridiculous. For a second I thought he was really gone.

It doesn't matter what I thought. He's okay; he's still here. He's still in the game.

And so am I.

In the Dark – Why sign up for this?
Two episodes in and I have to ask – why would anyone
go on this show?
submitted 31 days ago by HeftyTurtle
283 comments

top comments
sorted by: **oldest**

[-] NotFunnyWinger 31 days ago
Million bucks to the winner. $250,000 to second and
$100,000 to third. What other incentive do you need?

> [-] MachOneMama 31 days ago
> Don't forget fan favorite! Another quarter
> million there. I'm voting for the carpenter.
> She's the only woman who's not useless and/or
> annoying.

>> [-] MuffinHoarder99 31 days ago
>> Preach-er! Preach-er! (For the hair
>> alone.)

>>> [-] MachOneMama 31 days ago
>>> Are you kidding? Someone
>>> needs to punch him in the balls,
>>> stat.

>>>> [-] HeftyTurtle 31 days ago
>>>> Agreed. Mactress
>>>> aimed too high.

> [-] BeanCounterQ 31 days ago
> Keep an eye on Albert. I know him
> from college and he'll surprise you.
> Smart guy. Good guy.

> [-] FStokes1207 31 days ago
> What about the pilot? They're ignoring
> his heroism. This show is unpatriotic.

222

[-] LongLiveCaptainTightPants
31 days ago
Wrong thread. Add-a-Flag
Campaign can be found here.

[-] LostPackage04 31 days ago
They're attention whores, every last one of them.
That's the only reason anyone would go on a show like
this.

[-] 501_Miles 31 days ago
Maybe they just want an adventure, or a personal challenge. I think it's brave. Really brave.

[-] LostPackage04 31 days ago
Adventure my ass. If you want an
adventure go cliff diving. Don't prance
about for a prize.

[-] Snark4Hire 31 days ago
I'd do it! Just for that boulder! *Cue Indiana Jones
theme*

[-] NoDisneyPrincess 31 days ago
It's too bad they didn't actually get someone
with one of those. That would have rocked.
Rocked! Get it?

[-] CharlieHorse11 31 days ago
Pretty sure Coop's there just to show how much
everyone else sucks. I mean, holy shit. Did you see him
inflate the lungs?!

[-] Velcro_Is_the_Worst 31 days ago
Because blowing into a severed oesophagus is
a useful life skill.

[-] CharlieHorse11 31 days ago
[content deleted by moderator]

. . .

223

16.

The morning after the bear-tracking Challenge, the cameramen don't reappear, and for the next four days the contestants rarely see anyone except for one another. The host is gone, and gone are the milling producer and busybody interns. Over the course of these four days, the contestants tiptoe toward competence. They are not quite thriving, but they are more than surviving – largely because Tracker has become a mentor to the group as a whole. On the second day, within range of one of the many cameras and microphones mounted around their camp, Black Doctor jokingly refers to him as 'the village elder.'

A cameraman arrives with the third morning, silent and distracting, too close with his lens as he weaves through the group and taps Tracker on the arm. Time for a confessional. He seats Tracker on a log in the sun, in sight but out of hearing of the others. 'Yes, I could just go off and live on my own,' says Tracker. Stubble has grown across his chin and cheeks, and even on his head, shading in a hairline that is not at all receding. 'They'd probably get by. They'd make do. They'd learn, they *are* learning, she – I'm just helping them learn a little faster.' He pauses, glances past the cameraman, to the others laboring in the distance. 'Why? It's *right*. And it's more interesting. I still don't think any of them can beat me in the long run, but this way at least there's an element of challenge. This way, I won't become complacent.'

After this confessional comes a montage, complete with pump-'em-up music. It's kitschy; it's catchy. Air Force's gait becomes increasingly secure under Black Doctor's watchful eye. Waitress struggles to carve a figure-four-deadfall trap; her cuts into the wood are sloppy and often on the wrong side of the sticks – and then: It works. Her cuts aren't quite perfect and her hands are covered in nicks and blisters, but the trap stands, precariously supporting the weight of a long, heavy stick. She's so happy she tears up. Banker builds a snare that actually catches a squirrel. Carpenter Chick and Engineer weave together branches to create a lattice roof for their shelter. Engineer has taken to wearing his maroon-and-brown bandana as a do-rag. Almost everyone is learning to gut and skin small game; Exorcist is a natural. He collects the tail of each squirrel he preps, lets the stub dry, then stuffs it in his pack.

Already the contestants look skinnier, tougher. Faces and hands are perpetually smudged with dirt. Biology's breasts have shrunk and her cheekbones have grown flirtatious in compensation. The group's average skin tone has darkened a shade; the camp is largely in shadow, but they are outdoors, always. Zoo has become the primary fire caretaker, and her jacket is dotted with tiny burn holes from floating, snapping sparks. In one shot Tracker stands beside her, almost smiling as she shows him her perforated sleeve, the fire behind them, flames appearing on either side but not between. Nearly everyone has a rip in the knee of their jeans or the cuff of their shirt. Engineer's green boxers can be glimpsed through a small tear beneath his back pocket.

One negative line runs through the montage: Exorcist. He has been invited back into the group, and though he accepted the invitation with apparent humility, he undermines the efforts of the others. He nudges Waitress's figure-four with his boot to set it off, then winks at the camera. While collecting firewood he stays away just long enough and brings back just little enough that everyone suspects he's slacking, but the only way to prove it would be to quit and watch this episode when it airs. His boldest but quietest move: Late one night he urinates into one of Waitress's water bottles. He dumps it out and fills the bottle with clean water, but in the morning Waitress notices a slightly acidic taste she can't identify.

Montage slides finally into scene: the contestants sitting around the fire following their third full day of group camp. While everyone else chats and bonds, Exorcist carves the ends of his dowsing rod into points. Zoo is stewing the day's catch – a rabbit – with rice and dandelion greens. Carpenter Chick sits close to her and the two joke about joining a commune or kibbutz. 'Maybe they'll make an exception for our not being Jewish,' says Zoo, 'now that we're homesteaders.' Across the fire, Black Doctor is practising tying a square knot with his yellow bandana and Air Force's dark blue. Tracker is reclining, eyes closed, taking a rest all agree is well earned.

Exorcist stands suddenly and chucks his sharpened dowsing rod over Waitress's head into the dark woods. He chases after it, crying, 'Got one!' Waitress is startled, but once Exorcist sprints past her she simply rolls her eyes. 'He *wants* a reaction,' she says. Tracker's lids crack open and he surveys the group. Zoo gives him a thumbs-up and he returns to his rest.

That night, unknown to the contestants, the first episode of *In the Dark* airs. Viewers watch Cheerleader Boy stalk off on his own; they watch him fail.

The next night Exorcist takes two of his collected squirrel tails and ties them in place over his ears with his bandana. 'What now?' asks Rancher, as Exorcist begins to dance a bowing, twirling dance.

'I feel them,' Exorcist cries. He flails his arms and spins.

'I hear them!' One of the squirrel tails flies loose, landing in Banker's lap.

Banker picks it up with two fingers and considers tossing it in the fire. '*Who* exactly are you hearing?' he asks.

Exorcist spins close, grabs the tail from Banker's loose grip. And now he's singing, 'They want us to leave! They bid us to go-oh-oh!' His voice, so irritating when spoken, is surprisingly soothing in song.

'He should talk less and sing more,' says Air Force. Black Doctor nods.

More dancing, and the other tail falls, a gray fluttering at Biology's feet. Exorcist poses, thrusting his arms back and bending his front knee, and howls, flushing an owl from a nearby tree. His howl drifts to a close and Exorcist hops to perfect posture. 'It's okay,' he announces. 'The spirits say we can stay.'

No one is even looking at him.

The next day, Carpenter Chick and Zoo are sitting together on a fallen tree. Carpenter Chick is carving a crude spatula while Zoo hones a figure-four deadfall. 'They should have kicked him off, or at least confiscated his cross,' says Carpenter Chick. 'I know,' says Zoo, in the tone of *you've said this before*. Then Zoo looks up, perplexed. Someone is approaching, crunching heavily through the woods. She knows it's not another one of the contestants. Even the noisiest woods walker among them has adjusted, moving now with steps that are at least careful if not quiet. These steps are proud and destructive. They are alien. Carpenter Chick looks up too, and a moment later the host appears, as clean and arrogant as ever, several cameramen in tow.

'Good morning!' he booms. Zoo and Carpenter Chick exchange a glance, and Zoo mouths, *Morning?* They've been awake since sunrise; ten o'clock feels much later to them than it does to the host, who awoke only two hours ago. 'Gather 'round, it's time for your next Challenge.'

Everyone but Tracker and Air Force, who are out checking traps, quickly assembles around the fallen tree. The on-site producer says into a radio, 'Bring them in.' Fourteen minutes later, Air Force's blond eyebrows jump upon seeing the host. Tracker betrays no surprise; he feels none. When a cameraman appeared and told them, calmly, that they were needed back at camp, he reasoned it was time for another scripted event.

'What you've all accomplished over the last few days is very impressive,' says the host. 'But it's time to leave it all behind for another Team Challenge.' He asks Waitress and Air Force to step forward. 'As the winners of our last Challenge' – surprise flashes across Waitress's face; her victory feels so long ago – 'you each get to pick three teammates. The remaining contestants will form a third team.'

'Ad tenebras dedi,' says Carpenter Chick.

Even the host is for a moment flabbergasted.

Zoo gives a surprised *huh*. The other night while they were cooking together, Carpenter Chick told Zoo she was thinking of leaving, but she'd said it in the same tone with which she had talked about joining a kibbutz. Zoo didn't understand then how much it bothered Carpenter Chick that Exorcist didn't face any repercussions for abandoning his team and an injured man, but she does now.

'What are you doing?' asks Engineer. He liked working on the shelter with Carpenter Chick, teasing each other about pulleys and levers, cracking geeky pop-culture jokes that are all cut by the editor because they reference shows on competing networks.

Biology touches Carpenter Chick's arm. 'You can't give up now,' she says; her teacherly self sees a high-achieving individual refusing to achieve. A few of the others mutter incoherent objections.

'Sorry,' says Carpenter Chick. 'But I'm done.' That's all she is allowed before being whisked away. Her reasons for leaving will be boiled down to a simple statement: 'I knew I wasn't going to win and I wasn't feeling Fan Favorite, so I thought, *Why stay?*' But this isn't precisely true; she thinks she had a shot – not at first, but second or third maybe. When she adds, 'It's not worth it,' she's not referring to the prize money, or her time.

The faces of the ten remaining contestants are a study in surprise – except for Tracker's. He stands at the end of the line, impassive. The host confers briefly with the producer, then announces a change of rules: Waitress and Air Force will now each pick two teammates instead of three, and the remaining contestants will become a team of four.

He stands before Waitress and puts out his hands, fists closed. 'Pick one.' Waitress taps his right hand, which blossoms into an empty palm. The left reveals a mottled pebble. 'You get first pick,' says the host to Air Force.

Air Force is going to pick his best friend. It's obvious, so obvious that even Tracker is surprised when he is chosen instead. It's a gamble. Air Force is noticeably tense until Waitress picks Zoo. Then he chooses Black Doctor, who smiles at him, understanding and approving of his strategy. Waitress rounds out her team with Rancher, whose quiet steadfastness she finds soothing.

'What, no one wants me? *Again?*' Exorcist says, as he moves to stand with Engineer, Biology and Banker. Being divided after working together for so long feels strange to many of the contestants. The last few days lulled them into a false sense of cooperation – which was, of course, the point.

The host gives them the TV version of their instructions:

'Three friends came into these woods yesterday for a day hike. None were seasoned hikers and they were overconfident. They didn't bring water or food or a map. Midday yesterday they reached the peak, where they became separated. They're lost. It's up to you to find them, and it is imperative that you do so before sunset.'

The groups are given clarifying instructions off camera – 'When you find your hiker,' says the host, 'you *must* verify his identity' – as well as a couple of hours to pack their meager belongings and return their camp to a more natural state. But not a fully natural state – they are instructed to leave their shelter. The producers want to make it the focal point of a social media contest, allow a fan to win a weekend stay in the lean-to.

Eventually – and it is mid-afternoon now – the contestants are led back to the clearing where they began their bear-tracking Challenge five days ago. From there, each team is led to the 'last known location' of their specific target and given an envelope containing information about him.

The groups are signaled to begin. Out of one another's sight, Waitress, Air Force and Engineer rip open their respective envelopes.

'Timothy Hamm,' says Waitress. 'Caucasian male, age twenty-six. Five-eleven, one hundred and eighty-two pounds. Brown hair, brown eyes. Last seen wearing jeans and a red fleece jacket.' As she reads, viewers will see an image of an actor fitting that description.

The same occurs as Air Force and Engineer read about their targets, respectively:

'Abbas Farran, Caucasian male, age twenty-five, five-ten, one hundred and sixty-five pounds, black hair, brown eyes. Last seen wearing a yellow sweater and jeans.'

And 'Eli Schuster, Caucasian male, age twenty-six,

five-eight, one hundred and sixty-one pounds, brown hair, hazel eyes. Last seen wearing a blue T-shirt, white vest, and cargo pants.'

At Abbas's picture, many viewers will say things like 'Arab,' 'Islamist,' and 'Terrorist,' with varying intonations. 'No way they're friends' will be the common refrain. But in this case, the show is misrepresenting reality less blatantly than usual. The friendship between the Jewish and Muslim actors is real; it's why they were cast. Though neither had met the man playing Timothy Hamm before this gig.

This Challenge is intended to be the climax of the premiere week, but it starts out slowly. Air Force defers to Tracker and their team sets off after Abbas, whose passage through a tight thicket is marked by snapped branches, scuffed ground cover, and, most tellingly, a duo of yellow threads pulled from his sweater by thorns.

At Waitress's urging, Zoo takes the lead for their team. 'This is going to be fun,' Zoo tells her partners, both of whom look at her dubiously. She quickly finds the boot prints and red threads marking Timothy's passage.

The third group struggles from the start. Exorcist and Banker argue over leadership, while Engineer and Biology begin searching for signs of Eli. They get confused by their own tracks, however, and it's nearly twenty minutes before Biology catches sight of the telltale log with its newly exposed pale wood. Behind the log are scuffed leaves and one clear handprint. Viewers will see a cut scene: a young Jewish man kicking the top of the log in apparent frustration, then jumping over it, slipping and stumbling to hand and knee.

'Come on,' Engineer calls to Exorcist and Banker, who are shooting each other sour looks while ostensibly searching. Unusual behavior for Banker, but he's unsettled by

Carpenter Chick's departure. He is here more for the experience than the money, so the prospect of quitting on the cusp of a new Challenge upsets him, especially because she quit so easily, as though it were nothing. Of everyone, he perhaps fell deepest into the trap of viewing his competitors as teammates, and Carpenter Chick seemed to him an especially useful one.

Engineer and the others follow Biology as she creeps through the trees. After a few minutes, she stops. 'I lost the trail,' she says.

The camera zooms in on a pair of threads — one blue, one white — hanging from a tree branch three feet in front of her. It will be nineteen minutes before Exorcist finds the threads.

Meanwhile, Tracker is leading his team flawlessly through the woods, identifying signs that were left intentionally, as well as those that were not. Then Tracker's eyebrows arch; he's having a surprising day. He kneels before a rock with a dab of red on it.

'What is it?' asks Black Doctor, in awe of the ease with which Tracker follows a trail he can't even see.

'It looks like he fell here,' says Tracker. He points at a deep scuff a few feet from the rock. 'This is from his knee.' Another closer in: 'And this is from his elbow.' Finally he points at the small red smear on the stone. 'It appears he hit his head.'

'Hit his head?' says Black Doctor. He exchanges a concerned look with Air Force.

Tracker stands. 'The trail gets clearer from here. It looks like he's stumbling.'

'Concussion?' asks Air Force.

'Likely,' says Black Doctor. He turns to the cameraman. 'Is this for real?' he asks, his medical training trumping all inclination to play by the rules. The cameraman ignores him. Black Doctor pushes past the camera, gets in the man's true face. 'Is. This. For. Real?' The cameraman is taken aback, uncomfortable. Black Doctor demands eye contact. 'If you don't know, I need you to radio someone who does,' he insists. 'Now.'

The cameraman unclips his radio from his belt. He points its top toward Black Doctor. 'Battery's dead,' he says.

'Like hell it is,' says Air Force, grabbing the radio. He toggles the on-off switch, but the power indicator doesn't light up. He takes the battery out, puts it back in, tries again. Nothing. The producers thought something like this might happen, and the cameramen were all instructed to put depleted batteries in their radios for the duration of this Challenge.

'I think from this point on we need to assume this is for real,' says Black Doctor. At Tracker's incredulously lifted brow he adds, 'Just in case.'

Less than a mile away, Zoo is on her hands and knees.

'What are you doing?' asks Waitress.

'Looking for changes in the coloring, the texture,' says Zoo. 'A shiny path in a dull area, or a dull path in a shiny area. Stuff like that.'

'See anything?' asks Rancher. He crouches down next to her, keeping one hand on his hat.

'I don't know,' says Zoo. 'He obviously came through here.' She points to spot a few feet away to their right. 'But after that . . .'

'After that *what*?' asks Waitress.

'Exactly.'

Rancher stands. 'Do you hear that?' he asks.

Zoo and Waitress both cock their heads to listen. 'Water?' asks Waitress.

'I think so,' says Rancher. 'If I was lost and I heard water, that's where I'd head.'

'Good idea,' says Zoo.

A few minutes later, they find a boot print. Zoo slaps Rancher on the back.

They reach the brook. Waitress points at a red handprint on a rock halfway across the water and asks, 'Is that blood?'

Yes, thinks Zoo, then: No. She almost says, '*Fake* blood,' before thinking better of it. She doesn't know if it's possible to be disqualified for professing disbelief, but she doesn't want to chance it. So instead she says, 'He must have fallen.'

'And then he went that way, look,' says Rancher, pointing downstream, where another rock is smeared with mud and dabbed with more red.

Far behind them, Exorcist finally finds the threads that are intended to lead his team to their blood mark. But the quartet is moving slowly, bickering. Attempting to act as the voice of reason, Biology twirls to the others and claps her hands – *clap, clap, clap-clap-clap* – a trick she uses to get the attention of unruly students. 'Get it together!' she demands. Her teammates are all looking at her, but one's vision is centered noticeably below her face. She stalks up to Exorcist and he meets her eyes, surprised. 'That's better,' she says.

'She's right,' says Banker, stepping between Biology and Exorcist before the latter can respond. 'Let's focus on finding Eli.' His foot lands on their next clue – a scuff – and obliterates it. More subtle clues abound, but no one in this group sees them. Tracker would have; even Zoo or Air Force would likely have caught the general sense of the trail. But this mishmash of a team will from this moment on fail. Engineer's eyes fall on a disturbance: the combination of natural erosion, a deer's passage and imagination. He and his teammates want to see tracks, they need to see tracks, and so they do. Soon they're following a trail that doesn't strictly exist, and they're following it in the wrong direction.

Tracker's group is on course, moving swiftly after their target, who has covered more ground than they anticipated, nearly four miles already. Tracker has two thoughts: first, neither of the other groups will find their target before sundown; second, perhaps they're not meant to.

But Tracker's moving faster than the production team anticipated. When his team is a quarter of a mile away from the endpoint they have to hustle. The actor portraying Abbas Farran is hurried away from coffee and texting and into makeup, and then back to where he ended his trail.

That's where Air Force, Tracker and Black Doctor find him. The actor they think of as Abbas is sitting on a rock toward the top edge of an eroded cliff face. He's moaning and holding his head in his hands. The contestants cannot see the ledge, they do not know how high it is – or even that it *is* a ledge, though the topography beyond the actor suggests at least a steep slope.

'Abbas!' calls Black Doctor. 'Abbas, are you all right?'

The actor moans a little louder and lurches to his feet. 'Who's there?' he asks. He turns toward the group. Red is dripping down his forehead and has been smeared all over his face and hands.

From the cameraman's nonreaction Tracker knows the blood is fake, that there is no true danger. He's disgusted – he has been in real emergencies, has rescued hikers who were truly lost and hurt – and he wants no part of this mockery. But he needs the money. He notices that Black Doctor seems genuinely concerned; this is *his* moment, thinks Tracker, taking a step backward.

The actor playing Abbas stumbles toward the ledge.

'Whoa!' says Air Force. 'Careful, man.'

Black Doctor is walking forward, with purpose but also

caution. Air Force follows his friend. He and Black Doctor reach the actor together. Air Force snags the young man's arm to steady him, and Black Doctor says, 'Have a seat, son.' The actor allows them to lower him onto the rock where he was sitting before, and Black Doctor kneels, looking into his eyes. 'Can you tell me what happened?' he asks.

The actor is moving his head about dizzily. 'I . . . I don't know,' he says. 'I . . . thank you.'

And then the on-site producer strides out of the woods, shouting, 'Nice work! Everyone come this way!' and suddenly the actor portraying injured Abbas is standing, steady, his eyes clear. He wipes at his forehead with his sleeve and then walks toward the producer, asking, 'Can I get a wet wipe?'

Air Force stiffens; Black Doctor stands and looks his way. 'Well,' says Air Force, 'I guess that answers that.'

17

Brennan and I emerge from the woods mid-morning and skirt another town whose residents have been paid to vacate. From what I can see, this area is run-down and has been for a long time; we pass a decaying barn and a years-abandoned gas station with the pumps removed. The kind of place in desperate need of television money, the kind of place easily dressed for the show's needs. As we walk, Brennan yammers about evacuations and bioterrorism, fast-acting transmittable cancer and other inanities, until I shush him.

I'm still days from home, but there are only so many ways to cross the river and we're nearing the bridge my husband and I most often use, a crossing surrounded by woodland and small towns. The Army's premier training ground for kids Brennan's age is just north of here. I wonder briefly what would happen if I continued in that direction instead of crossing the bridge. Brennan would probably find a way to stop me, or there would be another bus blocking the path, this one with no way around. Or maybe they'd finally have to break scene – a producer stepping out from behind a tree, nodding his head east.

I could test them, but I'd rather just go home. I'm beginning to believe that's my true destination, not just a direction, that they've actually done it: cleared a path for me all the way home.

'Let's start looking for a place to spend the night,' I say to Brennan. 'We'll cross the river in the morning.' My announcement energizes him, and he jogs ahead.

Alone, I think about my impending homecoming. I imagine standing in front of the two-storey, three-bedroom house we bought last summer. The half-acre plot has a gentle upward slope; the house will be above me. I'll follow the steps cut into the lawn, which will be overgrown because I was always the one who mowed it – only fair, considering the length of my husband's daily commute, an hour each way. A sacrifice he made for me so I could be close to a much-lower-paying job, the best I could find in my field. But also so we could live somewhere more conducive to raising a family. His commute wasn't meant to be permanent. Kids would be the dividing line, we said. He'd pull in as much money as possible until I got pregnant, then start looking for work closer to home. I agreed to this. I said *later,* because *never* was too hard.

After I cross the overgrown lawn, I will stand on the woven welcome mat – a gift from my mother-in-law. *Home Sweet Home* is the Clue leading me home, but our mat has my husband's surname stitched on it. Not mine. My mother-in-law never accepted that I didn't change my name. We made a joke of it and Sharpied my name on there too – under his, but bigger. She's come to visit only once since then, and she laughed unpleasantly. 'I forgot,' she told me, 'you're *modern.*'

The front door will be closed, of course. It wouldn't be the same if I weren't allowed to open it. I blink, imagining the feel of the cold steel knob in my palm. The knob was our very first purchase as homeowners – or one of our first purchases. We got a cartful of knickknacks and cleaning supplies at Home Depot that day, including a window screen repair kit. That was our first official home repair, covering up a hole in what the realtor referred to as a sunroom but we simply call the porch. It overlooks the backyard, and that's where I sit with my coffee every morning, watching deer and rodents nibble at my failed vegetable garden. Next year I'll fence in the plot.

The front door of the house opens into a small niche, almost a hallway, with the living room to the right and a stairwell to the left. There's a collage from our wedding on the wall. A stack of mail on the table under it. I'll enter, step past those, turn right, and that's where he'll be, in the living room. Waiting. Smiling. The rest of my family will probably be there too, though I'd rather they weren't. They might even drag in my coworkers, or some of the college friends I listed as character references.

There will be a banner strewn across the far wall, my husband centered beneath it. His black hair will be shaggy, needing a cut, because he always waits too long between haircuts – or maybe he'll have just gotten one to greet me. Either way, he'll have run a trimmer through his scruff, so his facial hair will be short, save for the spot on the underside of his jaw that he always misses. Will his penguin coloring be more pronounced, the white thicker? Maybe. His gray always seems to appear in batches. He'll look tired, because he'll have barely slept the night before, knowing I was coming home.

Standing beside him, my parents. My mom looking cranky because she's not allowed to smoke inside the house and who are we to tell her what she cannot do? But once I enter, her frown will flip because she knows she has a role to fill: the Mother, the one who birthed me, raised me, guided me, made me who I am. My father will be maintaining a few inches more distance from her than one would expect a happy husband to. He'll be smiling, though – if not a happy husband, a happy father at least – and I'll be able to smell his maple scent from the doorway, if only in my mind.

For a moment, I'll just stand there, looking. Taking in

the sight of so many familiar faces, the face of the man I love. The person who taught me what it was to be honestly generous, to give without expectation or resentment. Whose steady demeanor and realism helped me to learn that attempting to achieve perfection with every decision is a sure path to unhappiness; that when it comes to choosing a house or a car or a television or a loaf of bread, good enough really is good enough. Whose cereal-slurping helped me learn that being irritated at someone isn't the same as ceasing to love him, a distinction that I know should be obvious but which has always troubled me. Who taught me that together is better than alone, even if it's sometimes harder, even if I sometimes forget.

I don't know if they'll have him in a suit, or if he'll be wearing casual clothes, maybe jeans and the navy half-zip sweater I got him last Christmas. It doesn't matter. All that matters is that he'll be there. That he'll step forward, and then I'll step forward. We'll meet in the center of the room and then I won't be able to see him anymore because my face will be pressed into its remembered niche between his collarbone and chin. Everyone around us will cheer and clap. It'll be like our wedding kiss, ringing support all around. A celebration of a connection both actual and symbolic. I'll whisper some joking apology about how I must smell, but he won't understand because – who am I kidding? – I'll be crying too hard to make sense.

And then there will be some sort of announcement – I won! Or maybe I came in second, or third, or third-to-last. I don't even care, I just want to be home. I just want to be able to say I didn't quit.

We'll celebrate, all of us, whoever is in the house. And then I'll sign any last-minute paperwork, and the cameramen will leave – Brennan will leave, if he came in at all. When evening falls, it'll be just the two of us, alone, together.

I'll have to shower. At some point I will check my email. Within a matter of days I'll be watching television, driving my car, shopping for groceries. Paying bills, using money, being lost in a crowd. Relieving myself in a toilet that refills after being flushed – that one at least is easy to imagine. The thought of never again having to use leaves as toilet paper is a delight. But going back to work? Sitting at a desk, answering email, prepping for an incoming school field trip? I know I will do these things, but I can't quite envision it.

The idea of going back to work feels particularly alien. Before I left, my coworkers and I joked about how I could write about my experiences in our quarterly newsletter, use them to solicit donations. That seems impossible now, but maybe with some distance I'll find the angle I need to manipulate my experiences for the betterment of the center. Rabies awareness, maybe. The shots they must have of my terror in the face of that frothing mouth – that's a brochure cover, for sure.

I wonder if that Challenge has aired yet. I know the production schedule is tight, but I don't know how tight. The scene must look ridiculous. Some lumbering, fur-covered remote-controlled animal bumping into my shelter, sticking its nose inside, cocking a plastic head, and with a press of a button releasing a recorded growl.

I think of my helpless, beseeching pose in the face of such obvious trickery and feel sick.

At least I didn't quit. They scared me, but that's all.

I see Brennan jogging back toward me and I force down the anger I still feel, thinking about their coyote.

'Mae,' he calls, 'there's a supermarket ahead.' He pads to a stop a few feet away. 'It's all locked up, but I found a window.'

The supermarket is less than half a mile ahead, a slightly

243

raggedy-looking building at the far end of an empty parking lot. The front doors and windows are gray, I assume shuttered by pull-down metal. There's a splotch of color on one, graffiti, unintelligible from here. I think of the rewards card dangling from my keychain, which I left hanging on a coat hook at home. Above the mail, next to the collage. 'I wonder what's on special,' I say. Brennan laughs, and as we cross the parking lot he sprints ahead. He's acting so young today, like a real kid. Like he's happy. I used to act like that, but not so much as a kid. It was only after I found happiness as an adult that I was able to relax – to the point that a year into my marriage I was making near-daily fart jokes. I even had a bit where I pretended to be a skunk, cocking my hip and hissing, 'tssssss.'

There's something I'm still not willing to do in front of a camera.

Brennan pauses at the far front corner of the supermarket and waves for me to follow. I wave back and he disappears around the building's edge. Soon I'm walking along the front of the building, and I see the graffiti is a drippy sketch of a mushroom cloud. I round the corner. Brennan is about twenty feet away, balancing on an overturned shopping cart and looking into a high, small window.

'It's an office,' he says.

'Can you fit through?' I ask.

'Think so. Hand me something to break it?'

There's a dumpster nearby, open and fetid. More trash is piled against its side, including a length of rusty pipe. I hand the pipe to Brennan and my hand comes away orange. I wipe the residue on my pants as he smashes the window.

'Clear away the shards,' I tell him.

'I know.' He plucks the teeth from the frame, then crawls inside. 'Come on, Mae!'

I climb onto the shopping cart, bringing my shoulders to

the same height as the broken window. Inside, Brennan stands in a cramped office. He reaches his hand out, but both the window and the room are small. Trying to help, he only gets in the way. Finally I tell him, 'Move,' and lower myself down.

The office door unlocks from our side and opens into a hallway, which is lined with offices and culminates in wide swinging doors. Once as a kid I pushed through a set just like these in search of a restroom and stood aghast at the barren concrete walls that greeted me, then a door to the side opened and a gush of cold air followed a young woman out. She was carrying a case of ice cream, and she ushered me back into the store's retail area kindly. Despite her kindness, I remember being upset that she didn't give me any of the ice cream. I felt as though I'd earned it, finding that secret place.

Brennan kicks open one of the double doors, then scrambles to block its backswing. A ridiculous expenditure of energy. I follow him out the door, emerging into the meat department. To our left I see open shelving that should be refrigerated but isn't. The signs I cannot read but anyone who's ever done the shopping for a household, even a small one, knows: beef, pork, chicken, kosher. A smattering of festering packages, plastic wrap bulging with the gasses of rot. And though I've smelled far worse than this, I pull my shirt over my nose. Perpendicular to the rotting meat is aisle upon aisle of nonperishables, far from fully stocked, but still ample. 'What do you think, canned soups?' I ask.

'What?' replies Brennan.

I repeat myself, articulating carefully through my shirt. 'No,' he says. 'I want Lucky Charms.'

Beneath the fabric, I allow myself a smile as I follow him to the cereal aisle. The supermarket is dim, but not as dark as I'd expected. Light creeps in from ceiling vents and skylights in the produce section's vaulted ceiling. The floor is dusty, and I can see shiny trails winding through the matte covering. The trails are dotted with tiny, dark pellets. At the end of the nearest aisle there are stacks of Rice-A-Roni, ten for ten dollars. Several of the boxes have been chewed through, their contents spilled onto the floor to mingle with more rodent faeces.

I hear Brennan stop, then a sliding sound as he extracts a box of what I assume are his coveted Lucky Charms. The sound of cardboard tearing, then plastic. I leave the endcap display and catch up to him. He's munching on handfuls of oats and marshmallow, a blissful smile laid on top of his chewing mouth.

'I bet we can find some powdered milk if you want an actual bowl,' I tell him. His eyes go wide with possibility and he nods, cheeks bulging. 'But first let's see what I want,' I say. Though several shelves are empty, the aisle still contains a slew of brands. I'm surprised sponsors have allowed this cohabitation upon the shelves. But I suppose they can easily blur whatever brands they want to blur. Lucky Charms is made by General Mills, so I run my eyes along the Kellogg's brands, just because. And then I change my mind – do they have Kashi? A moment later, I find the shelf I want, the brand, and then the product. Two boxes left. I grab one and then we head off in search of powdered milk.

I'm about to dump the milk into my little cooking pot, when I think, *Screw it*. We might as well use what's here. I lead Brennan to the paper-goods aisle and grab a pack of plastic bowls, followed by some spoons. We take our supplies to a display of plastic outdoor furniture surrounded by empty coolers, netted beach toys, and excited signage – SALE SALE SALE! I light a couple of candles and we dine seated under an entirely unnecessary umbrella. The cereal I chose is sweeter than I remember.

After Brennan finishes his third bowl of Lucky Charms, he wipes his face and asks, 'This is a good place to spend the night, isn't it?'

He's clearly seeking my approval. 'Sure is,' I say. And then – why? I don't know, it just comes out – 'Smells pretty bad and I'm concerned about all the mouse faeces, but other than that it's good.' *Bitch,* I think, as I watch Brennan's face fall. I want to apologize, but for what? He's a cameraman, not my friend, and he's not as young as he looks. I can't apologize. Not directly. Instead I say, 'Let's explore some more. Figure out what we want to take with us for the final push.'

'Final push?' he asks.

'Yeah, we're not far. Two or three days.' Miles, I think. So little distance separates us now.

'And when we get there, what happens?'

He probably knows that better than I do. My mood sours. For all my imagining, I know there must be a final Challenge waiting, something more intense than covering distance. Something the audience, the cameras, will find irresistible. At the thought I take out my lens and scan the ceiling. The cameras are easy to find, but I can't tell if they're normal security cameras or if the show has put up more sophisticated ones. Of the two I can see, one is pointed at us and the other toward the inactive cash registers. Because something is going to happen over there or for atmosphere? I'll ready myself for the former. This is the perfect place for a Challenge, after all, because it feels secure.

Brennan and I comb the aisles. At first I don't even consider searching the produce section, because it's all gone to mulch, but then a display of potatoes catches my eye. Root vegetables – they last for ages. With a kind of shy hopefulness, I approach the potatoes. Getting close, it's hard to tell.

I almost draw my lens from my pocket, but then reach out a hand instead, preparing myself for rot.

There's no way they'll allow me this.

My fingers meet firm brown skin. The sensation is so unexpected I don't trust it. I squeeze, lightly, then harder, and still the potato doesn't give.

It's not rotten.

I must have done something right, something incredible, to earn such a prize. The banner, I think. This is my reward for climbing the downed tree, for bypassing the motel. For being both brave and prudent.

I jog to the front of the store and grab a handbasket. I hear Brennan call after me, but I don't answer. Within moments I'm picking through the potatoes, finding the 'best' by some standard I can't name. Really, I just want to touch them all. Then I move to the adjacent stand. Onions. Garlic. Ginger. For all the fabricated decay around me, all I smell is spice. Flavor. The next half hour is a manic blur as I scour the aisles and collect ingredients: lentils, quinoa, cans of sliced carrots and green beans, peas. Olive oil. Diced, stewed tomatoes. I attack the spice aisle – ground black pepper, thyme, rosemary, cumin, turmeric, dried parsley, red pepper flakes. The flavors don't go together, I know that, and yet I want them all.

There are plastic-wrapped packages of firewood at the front of the store, five logs per pack. I clear a space on the floor near where we ate our cereal, then start a fire inside a dinky charcoal grill. 'Isn't that going to set off the sprinklers?' asks Brennan.

'There's no power,' I tell him. I have no idea if sprinkler systems need electricity to work, but they've disabled everything else in this forsaken world. I'll keep the fire small, just in case. I arrange the grill's metal grate atop the flames, then set a pot of lentils to boil.

Next, I place a potato on a cutting board. I pause and lift my knife. I breathe out and slice through the spotty skin. The two halves fall aside, revealing a sheen of moisture on the interior flesh. I sit on a plastic chair, staring at the halved potato on its plastic cutting board beneath this plastic umbrella and feel a stirring like joy. Which is ludicrous; it's just a potato. But there's something about its organic realness amid all the plastic and preservatives that strikes me as extraordinarily beautiful.

It's nice to feel this way – even over a potato – but it also makes me nervous. I'm like a turtle pushing her head into the light while predators still peck at her shell. It's a stupid move, I'm putting myself in danger, and yet – I need to feel this. I need to know that I'm still capable of joy. I brush the halved potato with my hand, and I give in.

First I grin, then I whistle. It's a nothing tune, full of halting trills and looping, lifting patterns. Not a song, an outpouring. I'm not musical; it's the best I can do. I dice the potato, and another, and am about to toss them into the boiling water with the lentils when I think – No, home fries. I hurry back to the cooking-gear aisle and grab a frying pan. I dice an onion, mince four large garlic cloves, green sprouts and all. Digging my hand into an oven mitt, I hold the pan over the grill, heating a swirl of olive oil. Once it's hot, I dump the potatoes, the onion, the garlic all inside the pan at once. The sizzle, the smell; I laugh. I sprinkle a hearty covering of black pepper and a few red pepper flakes, toss it all with a flick of my wrist, then cover the pan and leave the home fries to cook. I chop more onions and garlic, peel some ginger just to smell it, then into the lentil pot it all goes, followed by the canned carrots, beans, and peas once I drain them. The tomatoes I dump in juice and all. At least a tablespoon of dried thyme, more pepper, both red and black, then at first just a dash of rosemary, then another. And – why not? – a single broad bay leaf. I uncover the home fries, give them a stir with a plastic spatula.

Suddenly Brennan is at my side and I'm happy to see him. 'That smells great,' he says.

'Why don't you see if you can find some canned chicken to toss in?'

'On it!' He hurries off.

It's dark in the store now. My cooking area is well lit from the fire, but only a hint of moon and starlight enters from the vents above. I have no concept of how much time has passed since we entered. It simultaneously feels like only a few minutes and many hours.

Brennan returns and dumps half a dozen cans of cooked chicken breast on the table. I peel off the tops of two and scoop the contents into the lentil stew, which is thick now, bubbling and topped with white foam. I give the lentils another few minutes to cook, then pour in half a bag of quinoa. 'It'll be ready in fifteen or twenty minutes,' I say.

'What about those?' Brennan asks, nodding toward the home fries. I give them a stir and poke one with a plastic fork.

'Almost done.' I leave the cover off so they can brown.

'I was thinking,' he says. 'What if we collect all the kitchen towels and stuff, use them to pad the chairs for sleeping?'

An hour or two ago I probably would have dismissed the idea as unnecessary, but now it tickles me. I agree, and Brennan begins hefting armfuls of tiny towels over from their aisle. He tears off the packaging and dumps them onto a pair of beach lounge chairs.

'There might be beach towels somewhere,' I say. 'We can look after we eat.'

He nods, then sits across from me. I scoop a hefty

portion of potatoes onto a paper plate and hand it to him. Remarkably, he waits until I've served myself before eating. Then he's like a vacuum, steadily inhaling. I hesitate, though, relishing the smell.

'How are they?' I ask.

His answer is mangled by his refusal to stop shoveling food into his mouth, but I think he says, 'Awesome.'

I pierce a piece of potato and onion with my plastic fork. I lift the fork and take my first bite, allowing the food to sit between my tongue and the roof of my mouth for a moment. The give of the potato's flesh, the resistance of its browned skin, the tang of lightly charred garlic, the sweetness of caramelized onion. I've tasted this same dish countless times since childhood, and yet I've never appreciated it like this. It's ambrosial. All it needs is – I put down my fork. 'One second,' I say, and I jog off into the darkened store. I can't read the aisle signs, but spot an endcap with pancake mix and turn in. A moment later I have it, a small jug of 'real Vermont maple syrup.' I haven't put maple syrup on home fries since I was a kid; that was how my dad always made them, and as an adult I decided to cut out that extra sweetness.

When I get back to the table, Brennan has finished his potatoes and is eyeing those left in the pan. 'Go ahead,' I say as I crack open the maple syrup's cap. Just a drizzle, that's all I want. The thinnest dribble atop my portion, maybe a teaspoon's worth. I clunk the bottle onto the table and stir my potatoes with my fork. The next bite I take is pure comfort, a composite of every positive moment of my childhood. My parents are reservoirs of love, my life is made of toys, sunshine and maple. It's a sensation of memory rather than memory itself. I know my childhood was never that easy, but for a moment I allow myself to feel like it was.

Brennan is refilling his plate. I reach over and drizzle syrup over his portion too. He looks at me, surprised — about my sharing or the syrup itself, I don't know. 'Trust me,' I say, and then I think: hot chocolate. I want hot chocolate next. I stand, glancing at the lentil stew and giving it a stir. The quinoa hasn't popped yet. I head back to the aisles and return with a box of Swiss Miss, a teakettle, and another gallon jug of water. I tear the packaging off the kettle, fill it, and set it on the grill. I forgot to get cups, though. I turn back toward the aisles.

Bang!

The violent metallic sound rings out from the front of the store. I turn, harried. I don't see anything in the muddled dark where the cash registers rest. *Bang,* again, like thunder, and I'm frozen. Brennan appears beside me. Only when I hear the sound a third time am I able to puzzle out the source. Something — someone — is outside, beating on the metal shutters.

18.

Zoo's group has been walking downstream for half a mile, searching for where their target left the water.

'You think we missed it?' asks Rancher.

'Probably,' says Zoo. 'I mean, why would he stay in the water this long? And we should have seen another sign by now if he did. Right?'

'How much time do we have left?' asks Waitress.

Zoo looks toward the sun. She's been told one can estimate the time by how far the sun is from the horizon, but that's as much as she knows. She hazards a guess. 'An hour?' The correct answer is: seventy-six minutes. They have seventy-six minutes left to find Timothy, and almost two miles to go.

They decide to double back. Approaching from a new angle, Rancher sees it – a snapped branch with a red smear, from where Timothy pulled himself onto a slightly raised bank and reentered the woods. Zoo and Waitress are on the opposite side of the stream from Rancher. They make their way over, balancing on the rocks. Rancher helps Zoo hop the last few steps, then reaches out for Waitress. Before she can take his hand, her left foot slips into the ankle-high water.

'Dammit,' she says. A moment later she's back on land, shaking out her wet foot. She sits on a rock and unties her shoe.

'What are you doing?' asks Zoo.

'I can't walk like this.' Waitress slips off her shoe, then her soaked cotton sock, which is yellowed and ringed with brown. She wriggles her toes; her green nail polish glints in the sun. She wrings out her sock. 'Do we have time to let it dry?' she asks. Zoo and Rancher exchange a look. 'Guess not.' Waitress grimaces as she pulls on the damp sock, followed by her sneaker. She stands and her frown deepens. 'Wet feet are the *worst*.'

'We're probably almost there,' says Zoo. 'You won't have to deal with it for long.' Her tone is consoling, but she's anxious to keep moving. It's harder for her to smile at Waitress than it used to be.

'I bet Cooper's group found their guy hours ago,' says Waitress, following her teammates into the woods.

'Emery didn't say order mattered,' Rancher replies over his shoulder. 'Just that we get there before sunset.'

Zoo calls back to them both, 'Yeah, I think we –'

'Goddammit!' shouts Waitress. Rancher and Zoo turn to find her hopping on her wet foot and muttering additional profanities. Their cameraman catches disdain painted across Zoo's face, but the editor won't use the shot.

'What happened?' asks Zoo.

'I think I broke my toe.' Waitress sits on the ground, tears in her eyes, her top lip pinched tightly between her teeth. She reaches for her dry foot and cradles it in her hands.

'What did you trip over?' Zoo sees twigs and some small rocks, but nothing hard or heavy enough to cause Waitress's ear-splitting pain.

'I don't know, but it hurt.' The camera saw: a root popping up from the earth and obscured by leaves. 'My feet are fucked,' says Waitress.

Rancher kneels by her. 'Take off your shoe, let's have a look.'

An eighth of an inch piece of Waitress's big toenail is cracked, jutting upward. Blood wells from the wound, but

Waitress wiggles the toe just fine. 'That ain't so bad,' says Rancher. 'A Band-Aid ought to do it.'

Waitress is crying now, quietly but openly. She fumbles with her pack and pulls out her first-aid kit. Rancher pinches a piece of gauze around her toe until the bleeding stops, then deftly smears the toenail with antibiotic ointment and wraps it in a Band-Aid. He relaxes as he tends to Waitress, babying her as he would his daughter.

Zoo watches his careful tending and Waitress's wet eyes. 'Stubbed toes suck,' she says, just to say something. Once the toe is bandaged and Waitress makes no move to put her shoe back on, Zoo's limited sympathy fades to nothing.

Waitress is feeling more than the pain of her stubbed toe. She's feeling the frustration of her tired muscles, her body's desperate need for caffeine and sugar, the dampness of her left foot like her spirits themselves have been soaked through. And now that she's crying, she can't seem to stop. 'Sorry.' She sniffles. 'I just need a minute.'

Most viewers will not understand why it is Rancher, not Zoo, comforting her. That Zoo stayed away that night at the campfire was excusable – there were two other women already handling Waitress – but now? Isn't Zoo the one whose chromosomes cry out an unavoidable need to soothe and comfort? Isn't Zoo the one biologically adapted to suckle young? Why isn't she the one holding Waitress's trembling hand?

The explanation most viewers will jump to is as common an assumption as maternal instinct: female jealousy. Waitress is younger, skinnier and prettier, after all. But Zoo doesn't care that Waitress is pretty, or skinny, or young. All she cares about is that she's delaying their team. She would be equally annoyed at a man doing the same.

The minutes tick by as Waitress struggles to stop crying. She's trying, really trying, but her body defies her will, and

Rancher's fatherly hand on her back only makes matters worse. She wants him to ignore her, so she can pull herself together. Thirteen minutes pass between Waitress stubbing her toe and being ready to move. The editor will portray the delay in less than a minute, but will cut in images of the setting sun to make it seem like she sat there for much longer, like she cried for hours.

The rest of the trail is clear; the trio soon emerges from the trees twenty feet from where Tracker's group did earlier. The skyline is deeply flushed. A brown-haired white man wearing a red fleece stands at the edge of the cliff with one hand pressed to his forehead.

'That's him,' says Zoo. 'We made it.'

'Timothy!' calls Rancher.

The man turns toward them. Red runs down his face. His whole body wavers, and then he falls backward, tumbling over the side of the cliff.

Waitress screams and Rancher runs forward. Zoo stares dumbly. She sees the rope that follows the man over the cliff, watches it go taut. She knows that what she's watching is staged, that the man did not fall. She also knows that her team just lost. Her jaw quakes with frustration.

For a long moment, the only sound is Waitress's sniffling, the only movement her wiping her nose with her wrist. Then Rancher says, 'Do we have to . . . verify that it's him?' Zoo and Waitress stare at him, then Zoo says, 'Yes.'

Rancher leads the way down a short switchback. The actor who played Timothy Hamm is long gone. In his place, a gussied-up dummy lies at the base of the cliff, its limbs twisted, a parody of death. The dummy is dressed as the actor was and surrounded by a pool of liquid crimson. It's facedown and wearing a wig, which is split at the side and leaking pink jelly. Latex skin is adorned with gross wounds and a plaster bone juts through the side of one knee.

Waitress's gentle tears explode into wild crying panic. Zoo looks up and thinks, even if the man had fallen for real, the drop isn't far enough to cause this much damage. Rancher turns away from them both, and from the bloody dummy, crouching with hands on knees. Zoo watches him as he removes his hat and says, 'Lord, hear our –'

Zoo's face is drawn, her lip shaking just slightly. Neither of her teammates is doing what needs to be done, so she approaches. She steels herself as best she can, telling herself it doesn't look real, it isn't real. 'It's just a prop,' she whispers, inching closer. Her whole body is shaking now as she reaches toward the artificial corpse. She searches the fleece pockets first – empty. Then she sees the square lump in the dummy's back pocket. She's trying to stay outside the red pool, but she can't reach. She edges her foot closer, into the red. She sneaks her fingers into the pocket and grabs the wallet, then steps quickly away. Waitress is still crying. Zoo opens the wallet and sees a driver's license: Timothy Hamm.

'How could you?' says Waitress. It takes Zoo a moment to realize she's talking to her.

'Excuse me?' she asks, turning.

'How could you get so close?' asks Waitress. Her voice is a mire of fear and awe, but there is something else in it – at least to Zoo's ear. Disappointment. Accusation?

'This happened because of you,' Zoo says. Her voice is tight, angry, and not very loud. 'You and your stubbed toe, whining and delaying like you're the only one who's ever felt pain.'

Waitress is shocked, as are Rancher and the cameraman. The producers will be shocked too, and the editor, who will work so hard to explain away this moment. But there is at least one viewer who won't be shocked: Zoo's husband. He knows this secret competitive side of her, her impatience for wallowing and delay. He also knows how fear can turn her mean.

Waitress knows only that she is being attacked. 'You're crazy,' she says. 'I only stopped for like a minute. This isn't my fault.'

'A minute?' says Zoo, furious and quiet. 'By your reckoning we've been in these woods what, then, an hour? If that was a minute, I'll quit right now. *You* ought to quit; you'll never win, and you'd spare those of us who actually try from being dragged down with you, you fucking bimbo.'

She stares down Waitress, waiting for a retort that isn't coming, then turns and stalks off into the trees. Waitress and Rancher watch her go, wide-eyed. The cameraman is grinning. He's so happy he forgets the discomfort that's been nipping the lining of his belly all day. When Zoo returns a few minutes later, he hopes for more.

'I'm sorry,' says Zoo. 'I didn't mean to . . .'

Waitress won't meet her eyes.

But that night while the second episode of *In the Dark* airs and viewers gasp or laugh as Waitress tackles Exorcist over a pot of rice, Waitress sits with a cameraman and responds to Zoo via confessional: 'There's something messed up about being so nice all the time, all smiles and helpfulness, then exploding like that. I don't really care about what she said, I've been called a lot worse than a bimbo, but I'm not going to be trusting *her* again. I mean, at least Randy's up-front about being ass crazy. You know what you're going to get with him. I'd rather deal with that than someone so fake.'

Zoo's eyes are bloodshot behind her lenses, the sky above her full dark. 'What can I say?' she asks the camera. 'You guys got to me and I took it out on her. Yeah, I do think she's the reason we lost, but I shouldn't have . . . I just shouldn't have.' She sighs and glances toward the stars. 'It's been what, a little over a week? If this is a sign of the direction this whole thing is moving in, I'm . . . well, I'm nervous.' She looks back to the camera. 'But you know what? It's not real. I know I'm not supposed to say that and you'll just edit it out, but that guy jumping off the cliff, and that prop at the bottom? It's all just part of the game. As long as I keep that in mind, I'll be fine, no matter how twisted things get. And if everyone watching this learns that I can be a jerk sometimes, well, I can handle that too.'

She stands. The final shot of the show's third episode will be of her walking away, returning to a fire viewers will not have seen her build. This is Zoo's final confessional.

19.

Brennan whispers, 'Who is it?'

'How should I know?' I say. My fear has thickened to anger. I should have known better than to relax – I *did* know better – and now they have another clip, another moment I will never be able to live down. What's worse, I don't know what to do next.

What do they *want* me to do? Answer the knock. It was a knock, after all.

'Should we leave?' asks Brennan.

'I don't think so,' I say. 'It's dark out. And I don't think they've found the window, otherwise they wouldn't be knocking on the shutter.' I curse myself even as I say this; what better sound bite could I have given them? They'll play it, then immediately cut to someone standing under that window, looking up.

'How do they know we're here, Mae?'

'I don't know, we weren't being quiet. And maybe some smoke got out.' No, they were told. They were in a van playing pinochle as the sun went down, waiting for their moment.

'What do we do?' Brennan asks. All he has are questions.

'Let's pack up,' I tell him, because I'm supposed to play along, aren't I? 'Quietly. Let's wait this out and be ready to move.'

He nods and we both turn back to the fire and our packs. I'm shoving potatoes and onions into mine when the crashing knock sounds again. This time, I think I also hear a voice. I look toward the front of the store, again. I don't see anything, again. Next thing I know, I'm walking toward the registers.

An urgent whisper from behind, 'Mae!'

'Shh,' I tell him. 'I want to hear what they're saying.'

Funny, I keep saying – and thinking – *they*. It seems indisputable that there's more than one person outside. Maybe because the sound is so large, so intrusive.

I creep to the front of the store and through a shadowy checkout aisle. As I reach the bagging area, there's another *bang*. I sense the metal shutters shimmying with contact. A voice, masculine and muddled. The only word I'm certain I hear is 'open.' Whoever they are, they want in.

Maybe I'm wrong. Maybe it's not *they*, but *he*. Someone I know. Cooper in another moment of *enough*. Julio, seeking company after an age alone. The Asian kid, hardened by experience.

Bang.

'Open up!' The words come through clearly this time, and I recognize the voice. It's a showman's tenor, ringing with bravado. *Randy*. I'm amazed. Aggravating others is his oxygen; how did he make it through Solo?

'I know you're inside!' *Bang*. 'Let us in!' *Bang. Bang.*

'Sorry, Randy,' I whisper. I wish there were a peephole, so I could see what he looks like after the last few weeks. I envision him holding a torch, flames lighting his wild hair and glittering off his tacky necklace. He's probably dressed entirely in squirrel tails by now.

Wait.

He said *us*. I was right; it is a they. Randy isn't alone.

A second voice outside, quieter and deeper: 'That's not going to work.'

I know this voice too. Emery said we would know when the Solo Challenge was over and I do; it is. *You can do this,*

262

Cooper's last words to me, unspoken, but I heard, and I thought I *could* do it. But I can't, and now I can tell him *thank you* and *I'm married*. Because I don't know *what* he felt – *if* he felt – but I know what ran through me. I should have told him. The instant it happened I should have told him; instead I – but I didn't *mean* to think it and I was confused, I thought I saw the person I could have been, but no, it's different – we're different – because I never *chose* alone, not until I came here, and this is the biggest mistake of my life. I don't want to be Cooper, I want to be *me,* to be the *us* I left behind – the *us* I chose. And I can, I *will* – because Solo is *over.*

I throw myself at the motion-activated doors. I push and tug, then pound on the glass.

Brennan is at my side. 'Mae, what are you doing?'

'We've got to let them in.' But the doors won't open. I can't figure out how to get them open. 'Help me,' I say.

'Mae, no, it's –'

Then from outside, 'Hello? Who's in there?'

Brennan's head whips toward the doors, and I call, 'Cooper, it's me! I can't get the doors to open.'

A beat of silence, then, 'There's an emergency exit at the other end.'

'Okay!' I rush along the window displays, searching. I fumble for my lens, but my hand is shaking and I'm running and can't quite grasp it.

Brennan catches me by the arm. 'Mae! Stop!'

'It's my friends,' I tell him, pulling away.

'What are you *talking* about?'

His disbelief makes me pause. 'Well, Cooper's my friend. Randy . . . he . . . but if he's made it this long and Cooper's working with him, he's got to –'

'Wait,' whispers Brennan. He leads me to the emergency

exit door, which I suppose he's been able to see the whole time. I'm so amped I'm fluttering, my breath, my eyelids, I feel like I could take flight. 'Hello?' he calls.

'We're here!' says Randy.

'Who are you?' asks Brennan.

'Friends,' Randy replies.

I reach for the door.

'What are your names?' calls Brennan.

The voice I've been identifying as Randy's says, 'I'm Cooper.'

I fall from an unimaginable height.

I'm sinking, shriveling. Fear floods through me, filling me from my toes to my scalp and pulling me under. It's not the presence of these two strangers that scares me, it's that I thought I knew them. That my perception could be so far from reality.

Brennan turns to me, his victory clear on his face. For the first time he feels superior to me – and he's right to.

My fear leaves me, floods out, and I'm empty, washed out and cold.

I can't do this anymore.

Care. Explain. Pretend.

I walk back to the fire and take a seat.

'Mae!' Brennan's eyes are bugged with worry. Outside, the men are yelling, or maybe just the one is.

'What?' I say. I stir the lentils. 'If they're coming in, they'll come in. If not, they won't. It's out of our hands.'

Brennan fidgets. 'I'll pack.'

A few minutes later, the men grow quiet. The stew's bubbling is the loudest sound around, and then the zipping of Brennan's backpack as he finishes.

We eat. The home fries, the stew, it's all tasteless. Brennan looks squirrely. He asks again about leaving. I don't answer. Like the men outside, he soon stops trying. There's more stew than we can eat. 'Breakfast,' I say, putting a lid on the pot and removing it from the dwindling fire. I think of Cooper's first laugh, like a gift. How special I felt as he walked away, bucket in hand.

'You really think it's safe to sleep here?' asks Brennan.

I shrug. I lie on my towel-lined chair. The cloths beneath me bunch uncomfortably. I get up and sweep them all to the floor. I lie down again. Our fire is little more than embers.

'Mae?'

I squeeze my eyelids shut. I'm so tired.

'In the morning, let's find a car. Let's drive the rest of the way.'

'No,' I say.

'Why not?'

'You know why.'

'Oh,' says Brennan.

'Go to sleep,' I tell him.

I open my eyes. The fire's embers are a faint orange blur. *Ad tenebras dedi.* I could say it. I should. I shift in my chair, so that I'm facing the ceiling, the camera somewhere up there, watching me. If I were to say the words, would the electricity flicker on? Would the front doors slide open? Would Emery stride in and pat me on the back, tell me I made a noble effort, but now it's time to hand over the ratty blue bandana I have tied around my Nalgene and go home? Would a car be waiting outside?

Or would nothing happen at all?

The thought pinches. I cannot give up. I cannot fail. As exhausted and frustrated as I am, I must keep going. I've given myself no other choice.

I turn back to the dying fire. I stare at it until my eyelids droop. Mice scuttle down one of the aisles. Their gentle patter helps me fall to sleep.

265

A hand on my shoulder wakes me, I don't know when. Later. It's still dark. I can't see any sign of the fire.

'Mae.' A whisper in my ear. 'I think they're inside.'

'Who?' I ask.

'I heard something in the back. Listen.'

At first I hear nothing, just Brennan's breath by my ear. And then I hear the sound of a door creaking open. Right on time.

Resigned, I say, 'Get our bags.'

We head to the front of the store, then skirt the checkout lanes until we reach the mouth of the produce section. We creep from one stand to another, making our way to the back. Brennan exhales too loudly behind me.

From around the corner I hear, 'Where are they?' Not-Randy's voice. And then the other, louder, 'Hello?' From the nearness of the voices, I guess that the men are standing just outside the swinging doors. We're only about twenty feet to their left, our backs to shelves of salad dressing. This is the home stretch, I tell myself. The home stretch of a game that's lasted far too long.

I hear their footsteps and a rustling sound. The footsteps come our way. I put my arm out to keep Brennan from moving. With my forearm against his chest, I feel his nervous breath.

The two men walk by, moving slowly toward the outer wall of the store. For a few seconds nothing but air separates us, then a rack of bagged walnuts and pecans comes between. Soon, the men are over where I found the potatoes. From their soft footsteps, I can hear that they're moving toward the front of the store, probably planning an aisle-by-aisle search. I gesture for Brennan to follow me and inch around the corner toward the swinging doors.

Crunch. Right under my foot. Whatever I stepped on,

it's loud. Brennan and I both freeze. The footsteps across the store halt, and then suddenly they're pounding toward us.

Fear and flight, instincts stronger than reason. I shout, 'Go!' and shove Brennan through the doors. We run to the office where we entered and I slam the door behind us. Shaking, fumbling, I can't find the lock. Brennan shoves the desk toward the window.

A sudden force against the door pushes me away. Adrenaline courses through me and I push back, slamming the door into its frame. Then Brennan is there, helping.

'The lock!' I say.

He finds it and snaps it closed. 'Will it hold?' he asks. We're both braced against the pounding door.

'I don't know.' I look at the window. I don't think it's possible for us to climb out before they'd break in.

The banging against the door stops. Neither Brennan nor I move.

'We just want to talk,' says Not-Randy.

'Yeah, right!' Brennan shouts back.

'Stop,' I tell him.

Looking out the window, I can see that the sky is lightening. Dawn is close. I don't know why they're here, except that they're meant to be overcome. I don't think they'll hurt us, but they could steal our supplies, or tie us up, or lock us in the walk-in cooler. They could delay us in hundreds of different ways, and I won't stand for any of them.

'Look,' I call out. 'We don't have anything you want. This place is full of food. Just leave us alone.'

'There's food everywhere,' says Not-Randy.

'Then what do you want?' asks Brennan.

'Like I said, to talk. Me and my brother, we've been alone since the shit hit the fan. We live down the road.'

'What do we do?' Brennan whispers to me.

All I can think to do is to keep the man on the other side of the door talking and get out of here. I look around the gray, blurred room.

The desk chair. In movies, they always jam chairs under doorknobs and that holds up the bad guy long enough for the hero to get away. I hold up a finger to Brennan, asking for silence, and for him to wait.

'Where are you from?' asks Not-Randy. 'Are you local?'

As quietly as I can, I step away from the door. The desk chair is on its side, a few feet away. Holding my breath, I pick it up. It scrapes the floor, but Not-Randy is still talking and his voice masks the sound. 'How many of you are there?' he asks. 'Are you family, like us?' I bring the chair back to the door and ease its back under the knob. I have no idea if it'll hold. 'Were you sick? My brother was, but he got better. Me, I never got it, whatever it was. They tried to evacuate us with the others, but we wouldn't have it. This is our place, you know? You must know, you're still here too. Ain't many of us that are.' I nod toward the window, and Brennan moves away from the door. I motion for him to go first, and he climbs onto the metal desk. Not-Randy's still talking. 'Used to be there was this band down the road, these three nutjobs. I knew one of them, and he kept trying to get us to join them. But we didn't. They were real crazy − always talking about trespassers. This group, and my brother and me, I think we were the only ones left in the whole county.' Brennan's standing now, with his hands on the window frame. He pulls himself up and pushes through, feetfirst. I watch him disappear. 'They're gone now, dead or moved on, I don't know,' says Not-Randy. 'Since then, we −'

Banging, bashing, the sounds of a struggle outside the window. Brennan's muffled voice, calling, 'Mae!'

Then a deeper voice, a shout, 'Cliff!'

Motherfucker, I think. That's why Not-Randy wouldn't shut up, so his partner could sneak around outside.

The door behind me crashes open, the useless chair skidding toward the wall. Not-Randy steps inside. He's a hulking, bearded white man. I'm caught between him and the desk; the man outside struggles loudly to hold Brennan.

'There's only one in here!' yells Not-Randy – Cliff. He steps toward me. He's close now, taller than me by about a foot. I can see his face: pudgy and unremarkable. His beard is blondish red.

It goes quiet outside.

'Harry?' calls Cliff.

'I'm okay,' his partner returns. 'It was just a kid.'

It's Brennan who's been silenced.

Cliff reaches out and touches my arm. 'Don't worry,' he says. 'We can take care of you now.'

His arrogance, the laziness of whoever wrote his script. It makes me furious. But what can I do? This guy's twice my size and blocking my path to the door, and his so-called brother is right outside the window.

I say what the script demands. 'I don't need taking care of.'

'It's okay,' says Cliff. Now his hand is on my shoulder. Hitting a man this size in the arm won't accomplish anything except to piss him off, and I know the rules. I can't hit him anywhere that counts. 'We have someplace safe,' he adds. His breath stinks as bad as a prop.

Fuck the rules.

I send a hook straight to the man's jaw. All my strength is behind the strike, years of cardio kickboxing classes. I twist my core with the movement, lift my heel from the floor, smash my knuckles into his face. My fist erupts as the man stumbles away, reeling.

I don't give him a chance to strike back. I run past him, out the door and into the hall, through the swinging doors, and down the nearest aisle. I trip, sprawling forward, scramble to my feet, hear Cliff cursing, pursuing. The swinging doors crash shut behind him.

I sprint toward the emergency exit. I can hear the man behind me, but I'm going to make it. I slam against the exit bar with my shoulder and push through. I'm free, I'm out, I –

The second man stands before me, smiling in dawn's light. He's white, smaller than Cliff, bigger than me. And he's holding a machete.

He lunges toward me, machete at his side. I dodge backward, falling again and landing propped on my side by my pack, then Cliff is there, yanking me to my feet; my head snaps hard enough to tweak my optic nerves.

Furious energy engulfs me. I fight. I kick, I claw. I bite. I mean to kill this man. I can hear shrieking, and I understand distantly that it's my voice, then Cliff steps away, recoiling. I can taste blood, mine, his, I don't know, a coppery drizzle in my mouth. My right hand is throbbing and I can't unclench my fist.

Cliff is hunched over, his nose bleeding. I don't need to see to know there is hate in his eyes. Not-Cooper is watching, swinging his machete idly at his side.

'Fuck you, Harry,' says Cliff to him. 'What are you just standing there for?'

'She's crazy,' says Harry. 'I'm not getting anywhere near her.'

I don't see any red on the blade, but that doesn't mean it's not there. I have to get to Brennan, I have to make sure he's okay. He's somewhere around the corner. Cliff and Harry are between us.

'What did you do to him?' I ask, stalling.

'The kid's fine,' says Harry. The machete continues to swing.

Cliff stands fully and raises a hand to his bleeding nose. I see his hand is bleeding too. The expanded meaning of the metallic taste in my mouth makes my stomach twist. I'm disqualified. I must be. Not only did I strike this man, I *bit* him. Hard enough to draw blood.

Cliff steps toward me. 'Look,' he says. 'I get it. You've been through a lot. We all have.'

Why aren't they stopping him? Stopping me?

I maintain a watchful crouch as Cliff takes another step. I can tell now that much of the blood in my mouth is coming from a cut on the inside of my lip, which I feel swelling and throbbing.

I broke a rule and nothing's changed.

Maybe they're making an exception. A special circumstance, like when Heather hit Randy and the consequences never came? She was provoked and forgiven. I'm being forgiven too. Because conflict makes for good TV and that's all they care about.

Conflict – and the unexpected.

'Okay,' I say. 'I'll go with you.'

Cliff pauses and looks at Harry. It's clear they don't buy my sudden acquiescence. They shouldn't, but I need them to.

'I think my hand's broken,' I say, and I allow myself to feel my pain. I allow all my frustration to surface. As I start shaking, I think of my husband. How badly I need to be home, how far I've come and all that I've seen and done. I think of the blue cabin, the message left for me there. I summon one of the simplest tools available to me – tears. I feel them sliding down my face; I taste their salt.

Cliff immediately relaxes. He puts out his hands in a gesture of appeasement.

'I want to see my friend,' I say.

'This way,' says Harry. He heads toward the corner of the building, toward the broken window. The machete swings casually at his side. Cliff takes my arm. I can see the cut on his face, the already swelling skin at the corner of his mouth, the blood running down his palm and wrist. He's holding me close, but lightly, like I'm not a threat. I'm used to being dismissed as harmless, but that's because I usually don't cause any harm. Does he think my fighting him was some last gasp of feminist fury, now dissipated? Is this what he needs to believe?

I can work with that.

I wipe my face with my sleeve as he leads me around the building's edge.

Brennan is supine upon the pavement, faceup. His zebra-print pack peeks from over his shoulder. I don't see any blood, but between his red sweatshirt and dark skin, my eyesight could easily smooth away a wound. I pull away from Cliff. Kneeling, I place a hand on Brennan's chest, feel that he's still solid, still breathing. Which – of course he is. He's just pretending. I know how this scene works; he's going to open his eyes at the most dramatic moment. All I need to do is create that moment.

I see a glimmer of orange and silver under the window.

Harry prods Brennan in the leg with his foot. 'He wouldn't stop,' he says. 'I didn't know what else to do.'

'I'm not going anywhere without him,' I say.

Cliff nods at Harry, who tucks his machete into a loop on his belt and hefts Brennan over his shoulder.

'He's heavy for such a skinny son of a bitch,' says Harry.

I leap away from Cliff and snatch the rusty pipe under the window. Before either man can react, I smash Harry's left knee. I half expect the pipe to fold like foam, but the contact is solid, rumbling through my arms and shoulders. Harry screams and drops, letting go of Brennan, who against my expectation does nothing to soften his own fall. He's deadweight.

'Shit,' I say.

Harry yanks the machete out of its loop and I swat it with the pipe. The blade clatters across the pavement. I think I hear Brennan groan, but I'm not sure, and then Cliff is barreling toward me. I jump away – too late. His arms catch my waist and pull me down. I lose the pipe as my chin smacks the pavement; my teeth clatter, my vision sparks. Dizzily, I feel myself pulled around so my back's to the ground, my pack lumpy beneath me. My vision's swimming, but I see Cliff above me, scowling. My arms and legs are pinned. His forearm is pressed to my chest, my throat, holding me down.

I could have run, before. Without Brennan. I should have. Why didn't I?

Cliff is snarling meaningless threats. He's going to do this to me, and that. Pain stacked upon indignity. His lips move with fascinating slowness among the bloodied blond hairs of his beard. Everything else happened quickly, but this moment takes its time. I realize that he will kill me. Everyone has a breaking point, and I found this man's. I see this in his too-close eyes. Hazel. A color, a name I circled in a book a lifetime ago, joking about dressing up a daughter for Halloween; baby's first pun. I want to fight, but my muscles are unresponsive. Like half-waking from a dream, I'm aware of my surroundings, I can see, I can understand, but I can't move. Maybe the fall paralysed me. Maybe the best thing is for me to end, here, now.

I shift my line of sight. I don't want this angry stranger to be the last thing I see. I look toward the scraggy trees behind the dumpster where I first found the pipe. My vision makes it easy to pretend the sight is beautiful. I blink, my lids sliding so slowly, so thickly, that they're all I can feel. And then I make a wish. I wish for the producer to come running from those scraggy trees, sprinting toward us. Or

Cooper, or Emery, or Wallaby, or even one of the busy-bee interns. Anyone, as long as he's real and yelling for Cliff to stop. This is my wish, and like all wishes worth making I know it's impossible.

This isn't part of the show.

None of this is part of the show.

Nothing has been part of the show for a long time.

Something within me releases, an almost pleasant untightening; I don't have to explain anymore. I've fought. I've fought and struggled and strived – and I failed. There's peace in this, in doing all I could have possibly done; in failing without being at fault.

At least I didn't quit.

A wet sound, a grunt. My eyes flick unwillingly to Cliff. Twin hazel abysses staring through me. I feel him on top of me, but the weight is different now – gravity is the only force at play. Cliff's mouth is moving, gasping. And then he collapses, his chin smacking my forehead. His bloodied beard covers my eyes. I should probably be screaming, but all I feel is confused. I don't understand how he is dead instead of me.

A ruse, I think. The show, it's all part of –

The distance and pain in Cliff's hazel eyes could never be faked.

But my glasses are broken and I –

You *saw.*

I close my eyes. I feel coarse hair against my lids, I feel him crushing me. I see Brennan falling to the ground, limp. I feel the pipe hitting Harry's knee, the crunch. A vice settles around my heart, my throat, as implication rushes me, and I squeeze my eyes tighter because it's all I can do, but it's not enough, nothing is enough, I know.

I'm alive, and the world is exactly as it seems.

I can't breathe. I don't want to breathe. I have to breathe.

Since *when*? When did it all change?

Above me, Brennan grunts as he tries to drag Cliff off me. He calls what he thinks is my name. The dead man's chin slides off my face and *thunk*s against pavement.

A prop, I think, desperate, but I'm trapped beneath something far heavier than the man on my chest.

'Mae!' I hear. 'Mae, are you okay?'

The boulder was Styrofoam.

The blood was artificial.

The cabin was blue.

Was it?

The cabin was blue, it *was*. So much blue, balloons and blankets and gift wrap. The *light* was blue, everything was blue.

The inside of my eyelids are sparking. I see red light around the edges.

The curtains were red.

An orange vase on the table; I put kindling in it.

My eyes can't close tightly enough. I see brown paint, red trim.

I killed him.

A coughing, crying baby trapped in its dead mother's arms. A house that wasn't as blue as I want to remember. I saw him and I panicked. I ran. I left him to die.

'Mae,' a distant voice right in my ear.

I didn't know. How could I have known?

'Mae, are you okay?'

An endless forever. Mottled pink cheeks, crusty eyes, a divot on the skull pulsing lightly. It wasn't static in the cries, it was *need*. I let the blanket fall and told myself that it was all a lie, but the only lie was mine. I knew.

'Mae!'

I open my eyes. Brennan's face is inches from mine, and I feel his hand touching my shoulder. I look past him and see the machete jutting from Cliff's lower back. My back is cold. I'm lying in a pool of the dead man's rapidly cooling blood.

'I killed him,' I say. My voice is a sob, but I don't feel tears. I feel the cold blood against my back, the dryness of my mouth, the throbbing in my forehead. The warmth and pressure of Brennan's hand. I look back to Brennan's face. It's gaunt, but not long. His cheeks want to be round. Not even the promise of stubble on them yet. This isn't a teenager's face, it's a child's; he's a child. A child who saved my life by plunging a foot-long blade into a grown man's back.

'Can you move?' he asks.

How did I not see how young he was?

'Mae! Can you move?'

I'm nauseated and mired in sorrow and my muscles are stiff and resisting, but I find that I can control them. I nod. Brennan helps me up. My clothes are sticky, drenched in blood. I smell it, fresh death.

I hear a soft cry, a groan so pitiful, and that's when I notice Cliff's fingers are twitching. The man with the machete jutting from his spine isn't dead. A whiff of shit reaches my nose. It's not *death* I'm smelling but *dying*.

Brennan's hand is on my arm. He's shaking; we both are, I think.

A scraping sound from behind us. I pivot unsteadily, taking Brennan with me.

Harry is crawling toward us, dragging the leg I smashed. I feel a coyote's skull caving and I nearly fall, but the boy is there and I keep my feet.

Brennan, softly: 'We've gotta get out of here, Mae.'

Harry's voice is a rumble of threat and grief, and at our feet Cliff's groan is getting louder and his head is moving, rolling back and forth. He's a feral dog, maimed in a misfired trap. He's a coyote and I'm still swinging.

Harry is shouting. I hear his tears for his brother. He inches toward us, a throbbing, uneven blur.

'Mae.' Brennan's arm slips around my waist, and I allow it because I feel enormously unstable.

'Stop!' Harry yells. We pause for this word that used to mean something, mean everything. I wish for Harry to stand with a flourish, to grab Cliff's hand and lift him to his feet, for the two of them to bow and say 'Gotcha.'

How badly I wish.

But neither brother can stand and Harry doesn't seem to know what to say; maybe he didn't think we'd wait. He's just staring at us and thoughts of the show keep pounding my awareness even though I know they're false and a baby's cries echo through my skull.

Harry continues to stare at us – or maybe at his brother, I can't see his eyes – and I hear Cliff's breath, ragged, as his body fights for every last second of existence, despite the pain, despite the inevitable end. Clinging to a useless life, as the human body is wont to do.

Listening to his rasp, understanding strikes like a blade through my heart.

My husband.

If. Then.

The outcome of this logic puzzle is inescapable.

Harry has pushed himself up onto his good knee. He grabs a shopping cart and yanks himself upright. His ascent looks staged, the way the light is rising behind him, and I need it to be. The sky is so bright; I'm searching for a drone. Then understanding reasserts itself, fast and crushing, and Brennan's tugging on my arm with urgency, taking a step. All I can think is maybe I'm wrong again, because I want to be, and I'm confusing myself and I don't know which memories to trust. I'm searching for something concrete and my thoughts settle on a pot of lentil stew. I made it, I *know* I made it, it's sitting inside, and for a moment the existence of that half-full pot is the only thing in my recent memory that I know to be true.

Absurdly, I find myself wanting to offer the lentil stew to Harry and Cliff, as though by sharing this one true thing with them I could undo the world and transport myself home; I'd be there with my husband and he'd be alive and I'd be the me I used to be, and the last month would become less than a dream, less than a thought – it never would have happened. But then Cliff begins to scream and there's liquid in the scream; blood or bile, gurgling beneath. Harry takes a step toward us, then falls back to the ground at his brother's side. My throat is paralysed, I have nothing to offer, and Brennan's leading. We turn our backs on the maimed brothers and hobble together toward the road, in the only direction I know to go.

In the Dark – Week One Down. Reactions?

Why did they make her get the wallet? That was twisted. Admittedly a bit of a slow start, but it's official: I . . . can't . . . stop . . . watching!

submitted 29 days ago by LongLiveCaptainTightPants

301 comments

top comments

sorted by: **oldest**

[-] HeftyTurtle 29 days ago

There's some interesting stuff going on, I'll give them that much. I'd like to see a little more attention paid to the science teacher next week. I think she's the dark horse.

> [-] HandsomeDannyBoy 29 days ago
>
> Agreed. I bet she makes top three. Preacher's going to run off the rest.

[-] MachOneMama 29 days ago

How do they get away with all the killing? I'm surprised PETA hasn't stormed the set.

> [-] BaldingCamel 29 days ago
>
> I'm sure they have all the necessary permits.
>
> [-] CoriolisAffect 29 days ago
>
> Maybe they have. It's not like they're showing us everything. I texted my friend who's on set but he keeps replying 'confidentiality clause.' Lame.

[-] Coriander522 29 days ago

It was fine for staying in on a Friday with the beginnings of a cold. Don't know that I'll go out of my way to keep watching once I feel better.

. . .

20.

Exorcist, Biology, Engineer and Banker trickle into camp long after dark, limp with exhaustion. They failed the last Challenge so badly they had to be picked up in a van and driven back to the others. Their ride will be edited out, their failure will not. If the fourth episode of *In the Dark* were ever to air, it would have opened with a shot of fictitious Eli Schuster limping through the woods, a bloody rag tied around his forehead. A reminder, fading to mystery.

All of the remaining contestants are gathered around a fire.

'I wonder what happened to him,' says Biology.

Zoo feeds a stick to the flames. 'Ours fell off a cliff,' she says.

Biology stares at her and asks, 'Really?'

Zoo's reply is clear: a look that says, no, not really, remember where we are. A look that cannot, will not, be shown, though the editor loves her for it. Loves her despite the exhaustion rolling over him as he watches.

Exorcist is tying a squirrel tail around his wrist. 'We'll find him,' he says. He takes an end of the tail in his teeth and pulls the knot tight. Speaking around the hair, he adds, 'If not in this world, then in the next.'

'Shut up,' Waitress tells him, but her heart's not in it. Exorcist is tired too. He pretends not to hear.

Tracker is sitting off on his own, a shadowy figure far from the fire. As Waitress starts complaining about her aching foot, Zoo stands and walks over to Tracker. She sits next to him so that their knees touch. 'You okay?' she asks.

Tracker slips a hand over his microphone before replying, 'No.'

That night the contestants sleep crowded together in a ramshackle last-minute shelter. In the morning, they gather before the host, wary.

The host greets them from beside the elimination post, then pulls a neon-yellow bandana from his pocket and stabs it in beside Cheerleader Boy's pink. The most surprising thing about the action this time around is the reminder that only one night has passed since Carpenter Chick quit. Banker thinks of the strong, beautiful shelter at their last camp, then glances back at the ugly collection of downed branches they slept under last night.

'Yesterday,' says the host, 'was a tough day for us all.'

Us all? mouths Zoo.

'What do *you* know?' whispers Waitress.

The host continues, 'But as you know, it was too much for one of your companions, who quit before even under-taking your most recent Challenge.' He begins pacing before them, holding Carpenter Chick's backpack. 'Today I have only one item to distribute.' He pulls a full water bottle out of the bag.

Had he ever seen this footage, the editor would have cut now to Carpenter Chick, riding away in the back of a car with tinted windows. 'There's only one other woman I think has a chance of winning anything,' she says. 'So I guess give my water to her. Girl power and whatnot.'

The host hands the water bottle to Zoo.

'Thanks,' she says, not especially surprised. She thought she had about a fifty-fifty chance of getting the bottle, with the other fifty per cent going to Engineer. Engineer had reckoned about the same, though he gave Zoo the edge – sixty-forty, he'd thought.

The host stalks back to his centered position. 'Today promises to be even more challenging than yesterday.'

A cameraman interrupts with a loud, hacking cough. Everyone turns to him. He's to the group's left, the same cameraman who interrupted yesterday. Zoo's silently and secretly given each cameraman a name and she thinks of this one as Bumbles. 'Excuse me,' says Bumbles. 'Sorry.' His voice sounds weak. He coughs again, doubling over. He can't stop coughing. The producer walks up to him and the two speak quietly between loud coughs. The host keeps his distance, openly disgusted. After a moment, the cameraman walks away with the producer, who motions for the host to continue.

'Good thing they have redundancy,' says Engineer to Zoo, motioning toward the half dozen other cameramen currently milling about. In Zoo's internal parlance: Marathon Man, Slim, Wallaby, the Plumber, Goat Face and Coffee Breath, whose breath only smelled like coffee once, but that was enough. A fraction of the crew.

The host coughs a look-at-me cough. 'Today promises to be even more challenging than yesterday,' he says again. 'Come with me.'

As they walk, Air Force says to Black Doctor, 'We never got a reward for finding that guy yesterday.'

'You're right,' says Black Doctor. 'That's strange.'

Zoo overhears and thinks, Your reward was not having to pull a wallet from a blood-soaked pocket. Not having to watch the man jump. Tracker walks beside her, thinking about the vast inappropriateness of receiving rewards for farce.

The group reaches the small clearing atop yesterday's cliff, where the Expert stands in the middle of ten color-coded stations wearing the same flannel shirt he wore in his first appearance. He greets the contestants with a gruff nod. The host steps forward to stand with him and says, 'Until now, you've had modern means at your disposal for starting fires. Now, if you want fire, you will have to learn to make it the way it was made before matches, before' – he looks pointedly at Zoo – 'fire starters. You'll have to use a bow drill.'

'I'm here to show you the technique,' says the Expert. 'Gather 'round and watch closely.' He kneels and picks up the pieces of his bow-drill kit: a curved wooden bow strung with deer tendon, a thin wooden baseboard, a thumb-thick spindle of harder wood, a palm-sized rock, and a tinder bundle made from twisted-together dried grass and threads of inner bark. Within seconds he has the spindle secure in the bowstring and pressed to the baseboard, which he braces against the ground with his foot. The socket rock has disappeared into his palm, which he rests atop the spindle. Bracing his spindle hand, the Expert begins to run the bow horizontal to the ground. The spindle catches, then spins. The Expert bows faster. A thin trail of smoke wafts upward. To the uninitiated: magic. Waitress gasps. Even Tracker is impressed – he couldn't do it better himself.

The Expert pulls the spindle from the baseboard, revealing a charred indent lined with soft black dust. He cuts a pie wedge into the charred hole with his knife. 'The objective here is to make a coal,' he says. He places a piece of bark under the baseboard, reassembles the kit, and bows again. Smoke blooms and he keeps bowing. The smoke thickens. The Expert removes the spindle to reveal a tiny glowing coal, which he tips into the tinder bundle. He cups the bundle in his hands and blows into its center. A speck of warm light expands into flickering orange. With another breath, flames erupt.

The Expert angles the flames away from his face. 'You

know the rest,' he says. He drops the bundle and stomps it out. 'Good luck.'

The host steps up. 'First one to ignite their tinder bundle wins,' he says. 'Go!'

The contestants head toward their respective stations — except for Exorcist, who eschews his lime green for Tracker's red, sprinting. He snatches the red-marked baseboard and flings it over the cliff. 'Now the rest of us —'

Air Force grabs Exorcist's arm and cranks it up behind his back. Exorcist yelps.

'What the fuck?' says Air Force.

'Just leveling the field, friend,' says Exorcist, squirming to relieve the pressure.

Tracker walks to the edge of the cliff and peers down. He's regretting not running to his station. He didn't think he had to hurry to win this Challenge.

Black Doctor touches Air Force's arm. 'Hey, easy,' he says.

Air Force tenses, then relaxes. 'Sorry,' he says. He lets go of Exorcist's arm.

Exorcist punches him in the stomach.

Air Force recoils, more surprised than hurt.

'Wasn't your face!' says Exorcist. 'Wasn't your genitals!' He reaches into his pocket, pulls out a squirrel tail, throws it at Air Force. It flutters down to land near his feet. 'Let's see *your* defensive fetal!' he shouts. Another squirrel tail, this one hits Air Force in the knee. Air Force stares at Exorcist, bewildered.

Black Doctor steps between them. 'Hey, hey, hey,' he says. A squirrel tail *thwaps* him in the chest.

Tracker is walking away from the group; he will make this right on his own.

Exorcist takes off his backpack. Crouching, he pulls out another handful of squirrel tails.

Black Doctor looks at the host for help.

'I'm sure you can settle this on your own,' says the host.

A tail whizzes by Black Doctor's ear.

'Why don't you just take his chunk-of-wood thing?' Biology calls to Tracker from her orange station.

Tracker has collected a piece of deadwood. He takes out his knife.

'He's carving a new one!' cries Exorcist. He flings a tail toward Tracker; it falls about twenty feet short.

'Do you smell smoke?' asks Air Force. Everyone involved in the conflict turns to find Engineer bowing, a thick stream of smoke curling up from his maroon-and-brown-striped baseboard. Engineer is a natural, and far ahead of the others who decided to engage in the Challenge instead of Exorcist's drama. Zoo hasn't even gotten her baby-blue spindle to turn yet; it keeps popping out of the bowstring. Waitress is trying to get her spindle to stand without winding it into the string. Biology can't get hers to turn. Banker's bowing, but instead of smoke his kit produces a high-pitched squeak.

Exorcist springs toward his lime-green kit, and Air Force turns to his navy-blue one. Black Doctor steps toward his mustard-yellow station; his boot strikes a small rock at the wrong angle. He falls, landing heavily on his right hand. He hears the pop of a ligament tearing. He pushes to his knees, holding his wrist tight to his body. The wrist is already swelling, pooling blood pushing angrily at the skin.

Air Force is at his side. 'Doc? You okay?' he asks.

'Need a medic?' asks the host.

'I'm fine,' Black Doctor assures his friend, but then he meets the host's eyes and nods. 'Medic, please.' An intern ushers him away. Air Force watches him dissolve into the tree line, then reluctantly returns to his station. He knows he's lost too much time to have a chance of winning this Challenge.

Engineer finishes carving his notch and winds his spindle

back into the bow. Tracker's new baseboard is almost finished, but it's too late; by the time he starts bowing, Engineer has his coal. A moment of tension as Engineer tips the coal into his tinder bundle and blows, but the bundle ignites and the host cries, 'We have a winner!'

Engineer places his flaming tinder bundle gingerly onto the dirt. He's smiling, shy but proud. 'Do I have to put it out?' he asks.

Tracker drops his kit and stalks up to Exorcist.

Exorcist is sitting cross-legged with his spindle in one hand and his bow in the other. 'Hey, so I –' he starts.

Tracker grabs him by his jacket and hauls him to his feet. Exorcist's spindle and bow clatter to the ground.

'You think you're the scary one,' Tracker says. His face is inches from Exorcist's, his eyes as narrow as Exorcist's are wide. His voice is cold, even. 'But you're wrong. One more stunt like that and I'll make sure you envy those squirrels whose hides you're defiling. Understood?'

'Holy shit,' whispers Waitress, her face flipping between shock and glee as Exorcist nods rapidly and endlessly. Everyone is watching. The host steps forward, uncertain; Tracker has been so steady, he never expected true confrontation. Neither did Exorcist, not even when it was walking straight at him. The only one who understands that this isn't about Exorcist is Zoo. She wants to take Tracker by the arm, take him away, tell him it's okay, it's just a game. Remind him of why he's here. But she fears what it might look like if she steps forward, what it might mean – and she doesn't.

Tracker lets go of Exorcist, maintaining his still stance and iron stare until Exorcist breaks and stumbles back a step. As Exorcist begins sputtering a quiet apology, Tracker turns away and walks back to his station. Awed silence descends on the clearing.

Engineer's tinder bundle has burnt out at his feet. The host attempts to regain control by clapping him on the back. 'Time for your reward!' The contestants trickle over. Exorcist arrives last and stands on the far side of the group from Tracker.

Meanwhile, out of sight, Black Doctor tells the EMT, 'I felt the pop,' and they exchange a knowing look. Black Doctor's next look is for the camera, as he says with only a sliver of bitterness, *'Ad tenebras dedi.'*

The host says to Engineer, 'First, you get to choose one other person to join you in your advantage.'

Engineer names Zoo, quickly and decisively. She steps forward to join him.

The host pulls two plastic bags filled with dry pasta out of the duffel.

Zoo has decided to pretend that nothing unusual has happened, to play the role she was assigned. She takes the one-pound bag of penne and grins until it hurts. 'Pasta!' she says, trying so hard to make up for cracking last night. 'Thank you.' Engineer is as pleased by her reaction as he is by his own bag of penne.

'And,' says the host, 'you each now get to steal one item from any other contestant.' Waitress gasps; Biology grimaces; Air Force doesn't care, he's still thinking about Black Doctor. 'But before you do, know that the next phase of this competition is a long-term Solo Challenge. Starting tonight, each of you is going to be entirely on your own.'

About time, thinks Zoo. Tracker looks to the ground, thinking the same. Most of the others grumble.

Engineer chooses first, stealing Tracker's thermal blanket. 'Sorry, man,' he says. Engineer gets cold easily; he feels chilly even now, despite the warm afternoon air.

'Anything other than the blanket can now be yours,' says the host to Zoo.

Zoo's thinking about her pasta and how to cook it. Her plastic water bottles will melt if put in the fire. Even attempting hot-stone cooking will probably damage them. 'I'll take one of those metal cups,' she says to Waitress. She doesn't feel bad, doesn't apologize. Waitress has two, after all.

An intern bursts out of the woods, lugging a backpack and the post with the pink and yellow bandanas. He sets the post upright near the host and whispers into his ear.

'What happened?' asks Air Force, turning quickly toward the woods. 'Where's Doc?'

'The good doctor didn't make it,' says the host. That's all he knows, but he says it like he's hiding something and Air Force wants to punch him in the face. The host pulls out Black Doctor's mustard-yellow bandana and stabs it into the post.

'What happened?' Air Force demands again.

The host ignores him, stepping away to confer with the on-site producer. When he returns he speaks as though he never left. 'Due to the circumstances of your next Challenge, we will be distributing his supplies now.' He takes two water bottles and the water purification drops out of the backpack. 'I doubt anyone will be surprised by who these go to.' He hands the drops and one bottle to Air Force. 'And this.' He hands the other bottle to Banker, who was kind when Black Doctor hurt his hand. 'But we do have one surprise.' With a flourish he pulls out the wrinkled black trash bag that Black Doctor received from Cheerleader Boy. 'This goes to . . .' He eyes the contestants, and then jerks his head to stare at Zoo. 'You.'

'Huh,' says Zoo. She had a few casual conversations with Black Doctor, but nothing memorable. This gift, as small as it may be, is a mystery to her.

Waitress scowls, watching. If this episode were ever

edited, if it were to air, it would cut now from her sour face to Black Doctor. 'I hope Ethan wins,' he says. He's sitting on a log, his arm in a sling. 'Give him the drops and a water. Elliot can have the other.' He closes his eyes for a moment, clearly in pain. 'The bag? Give it to that woman, the blonde with the green eyes who tries so hard. She's here for the right reasons.' With that, an EMT helps him up and starts leading him down the trail. A moment later, the camera-man turns away, and the EMT drops Black Doctor's arm.

The host hands each contestant a marked orienteering map. 'These will get each of you to your home for the night. You will receive new instructions in the morning. Over the course of this Solo Challenge, new supplies will be made available for each of you, but they will not always be obvious. So, stay aware and remember your color – or starve.'

'How long will this Challenge last?' asks Rancher.

'You'll know when it's over.'

'What are we supposed to eat?' asks Waitress. She's almost out of rice. Her eyes flick toward Air Force, accusing.

'As I said, stay aware – or starve.' The host likes that line. Tonight he will be sleeping in a hotel, and as he gets ready for bed he will repeat it to himself with various intonations and flourishes. 'Good luck,' he says, and then he walks a few steps away, just out of frame.

Tracker orients his map and compass, then turns to the group. He makes eye contact with Zoo and mouths, *You can do this,* then starts off toward the first landmark indi-cated on his map: a small lake about a mile north. He is unfazed by the loss of his thermal blanket; he hasn't used it once.

As Engineer and Zoo pack their new supplies, Rancher, Air Force, Biology and Banker set off on their separate paths. Waitress looks at her map and bites her lip – unconsciously.

She's terrified. Exorcist sees this. He's still a little rattled himself, and for the first time he approaches her with kindness. 'You'll be fine,' he says.

'I know,' she snaps.

Exorcist's anger flares. 'Or maybe you won't be. Maybe you'll starve, or fall down a hole. No loss either way.' He gives her one last sneer, then backtracks down the trail toward where the group spent the night.

Engineer pauses at Waitress's side before following Exorcist. 'Good luck,' he says. Waitress returns his honest smile.

Waitress takes a deep breath. 'You can do this,' she says. Zoo watches her go, then follows her own map into the woods to the east.

The contestants dribble into their campsites – sparse patches of forest or field marked only by a bow-drill kit in each contestant's color – and settle in with varying degrees of comfort. Zoo tosses the bow drill aside, uses her fire starter, and dines on plain pasta. 'It's nice to be alone,' she says. Engineer succeeds in bowing another coal and also eats hot food, though he cooks his in a leaf-lined hole in the ground. 'Whatever works,' he says. He drapes the thermal blanket over his shoulders as he eats. He's soon shivering anyway.

Waitress builds a shallow shelter and distracts herself from her fear by focusing on the swell of nausea in her otherwise empty belly. 'I'm starving,' she says, though she knows that's not right. Exorcist digs up some grubs from a rotting log and swallows them with great showmanship. Biology thinks about her partner back home and chews some mint she found near her campsite. Rancher takes off his boots and flicks a spur as he stretches his toes. Banker runs a hand through his sweaty hair, then builds a small fire. 'Only nine matches left,' he says.

Two of the Solo camps are different. Air Force finds a

dark blue tent at his destination, and Tracker finds a red one. Neither man realizes that this is their reward for reaching their lost hiker in time yesterday. They assume the others are also given shelter. Tracker ducks inside without comment, sprawls across the floor and closes his eyes. Air Force stands outside the tent flap for a moment, fuming silently. He wants to go back for Black Doctor. But this isn't a war zone, or even a training exercise, and leaving men behind is essential to any race. 'What do you think about –' his cameraman starts, but Air Force stalls him with a gruff, 'No.'

Several hundred yards away, an intern disassembles a mustard-colored tent.

21.

He's alive. He must be. I'm alive, Brennan too. The brothers whose cries drift in our wake, they survived. Others must have too. My husband could be among them. He *could*.

'Mae?' whispers Brennan. We're hobbling down the street, moving too fast and not fast enough. 'I had to. Right?'

I see the familiar rivulets running down his cheeks. I think of the machete, jutting.

'You had to,' I whisper back.

But I didn't. I didn't have to apply; I didn't have to leave. None of it was necessary.

'How old are you?' I ask Brennan. My jaw throbs; it hurts to speak, to think, to breathe, to be.

'Thirteen,' he says.

The world rocks, and then he's in my arms and all I can say is 'I'm sorry,' and I'm saying it to him and to my husband and to the child I left to die in a cabin marked with blue. There was blue, I know there was. It wasn't all blue, but there was some. There was.

Pink cheeks. Mottled arms.

'Everything you said about the sickness was true?' I ask.

Brennan nods in my arms and sniffles. His hair rubs against the open wound throbbing on my chin.

I close my eyes and think of my husband, alone through it all. Worrying, wondering, and then maybe a tickle in his throat or a burble in his stomach. Lethargy like lead weighing him down. I'm sorry, I say again, silently, but with all my heart. I'm sorry I implied that life with you wasn't

enough. I'm sorry I wasn't ready. I'm sorry I left. Even if –
even if this was all to come, at least we would have been
together.

If the stories Brennan told are true, then the chances of
any single individual surviving whatever this was are
infinitesimal. For both my husband and me to have been
immune is so statistically improbable as to be impossible. I
know what's waiting for me at home, yet here I am begging: *please* and *maybe*. The smallest maybe ever, and I know
that if I don't go I will wonder for as long as I continue to
exist on this horrid, wiped-clean Earth.

An invasive thought: a cleaning-product commercial
showing a microscope view of before and after – kills
ninety-nine-point-nine-nine per cent of bacteria. Those
few stragglers in the 'after' shown only for legal purposes –
that's us, Brennan and me. Residue. From what he said it was
only a matter of days before everyone inside the church was
dead except for him. At least a hundred people, he said. Extra-
polate from there and it's millions. When did it start, just as
we left for Solo? Sometime between then and when I found
the cabin four or five days later. Such a short window.

I remember the cameraman who left after the lost-hiker
Challenge, too sick to work, and suddenly understand why
Wallaby never showed that Solo morning. And I was
relieved. I was *thankful*.

I called the one who left Bumbles. I *named* him that.

Self-revulsion slams through me.

Did any of them survive? Did Cooper? Heather or Julio?
Randy or Ethan or Sofia or Elliot? The sweet young engineer whose name I can't remember? I need to remember his
name, but I can't.

Brennan shudders in my arms and sorrowful wonder
brushes through me: I thought he was a cameraman. I
thought –

'I'm sorry about your mother,' I say.

I feel the tacky skin of my chin prickle and tear as the boy pulls away from me. 'Why did you act like it wasn't real?' he asks.

Thirteen. I want to tell him the truth. I want to tell him everything, about the show and the cabin and the love I abandoned for adventure, but it hurts too much. I also don't want to lie anymore, so I say, 'Can you blame me?'

He sniffles a laugh and I think, What a remarkable child.

Soon we're walking again, slowed by our respective aches and injuries. My right hand is swollen, useless. I can't move my wrist or fingers. I'm concerned Brennan might have a concussion, but he seems steady and I don't see anything wrong with his pupils, so I think he's okay. Unless there are signs I'm not seeing, signs I don't know to look for.

Eventually he asks, 'Have you ever killed someone, Mae?'

I don't know how to answer because I think the answer is yes but I didn't mean to and I don't want to lie anymore but I can't tell him everything. I can't speak everything. But he needs an answer because he's thirteen and he stabbed a man. A man who was going to kill me and likely him too, but even so. I think of the rabid coyote. I still remember seeing gears, but I also remember seeing flesh, like two versions of that day both exist, equally true. And for a second I think, Well, why not – maybe I'm wrong and that was still part of the show. Maybe it didn't become real until later – but the thought is sour and forced, and I know I'm reaching.

Brennan is waiting for an answer. His puppy eyes watching me.

'Not like that,' I tell him. 'But there was someone I think I could have helped, and I didn't.' My throat is closing; the last word barely escapes.

'Why not?' he asks.

In my memory the mother prop has green eyes I know from mirrors and I don't know if that's real, if her eyes were open or closed.

She wasn't a prop.

'I didn't know,' I croak, but that's not right. 'It was a baby,' I say, 'and I thought . . .' But I *didn't* think, I panicked and ran, and how can I explain something I'm not sure I remember? 'I was confused,' I try. 'I made a mistake.' Not that that excuses it, excuses anything.

'I don't regret it,' says Brennan. 'I feel like I should, but I don't. He was going to kill you.'

The soreness at the base of my throat, where Cliff's arm pressed. Bruising I can feel but not see. Why did he attack me? If this is the world, why would one's instinct upon meeting another be aggression? Why would –

His hand on my shoulder. I remember his hand. His breath. But that's all: a stench.

The first blow, was it *mine*?

'Mae?'

Was he defending himself from *me*?

He was. He touched me, but he didn't strike me. I can't remember his words. I try to clench my fist; a pulse of pain, but my fingers don't move. Brennan's guilt, that's my fault too. But he didn't know and he can't know – that I brought it on myself. That he didn't have to.

'You have nothing to regret,' I tell him.

But I regret everything. All of it.

Their blood, meaningless. Their cries behind us, meaningless. All this death, meaningless. A meaningless observation. There *is* no why, no *because*. All there is is *is*. Systems colliding, wiping out existence, leaving me, an unlucky outlier. Worlds end, and I'm bearing witness.

'Thank you for saving my life,' I tell Brennan. I'm not

thankful for it, but he did; he shouldn't have, but he did. He's been left behind too, and at least he doesn't have to be alone, at least I can carry this burden for him – this burden that I caused.

I'm sorry.

We soon cross the bridge, ducking through an E-ZPass lane, and break into an historic tollhouse to spend the night. I know what dreams will come, so I don't sleep, and I shake Brennan toward wakefulness periodically because I think that's what I'm supposed to do. He seems more annoyed than grateful, and I take that as a positive sign.

After my fourth time waking Brennan I sneak outside and sit, leaning against the tollhouse beside the door. My clothing is heavy with dried blood; the weight of it pins me to the earth.

'I miss you,' I whisper.

Our children would have been born with blue eyes. But would that blue have turned to green or brown, or surprised us both by staying blue? Hair black or brown or blond, maybe even that beautiful auburn shade your mother wears in pictures from when you were young? No way to know. Roll the dice, have a kid. Cross your fingers that the genes are good. What if. Who knows. Questions become statements in this cowardly new world. Our children will never be. But that loss is nothing, nothing compared to the loss of you.

The door beside me creaks open. I look up and feel the sting of my eyes, the pressure in my chest. I feel myself quaking. The physicality of knowing.

Brennan sits down and leans wordlessly against me. I feel him trembling too.

The night passes. The next two days are uneventful, painfully sluggish. I watch Brennan closely and try to identify birdcalls as we walk; anything not to think of my husband, because every time I do I think I might collapse. But it's his impression of a Canada goose I hear in the sky, and when vague movement ahead of us is revealed by song as a cluster of chickadees, all I can see is my husband spilling birdseed as he refills the backyard feeder. In my dreams I'm always walking, and alone. Awake, Brennan's at my side and the desolation all around no longer seems remarkable, not even when we enter streets I know. I leave my lens in my pocket. I don't want to see what's become of my home.

We're less than three miles from my house when the sun sets. I'm so stiff. Everything hurts. My hand isn't any better. Brennan breaks the window of a small house and helps me inside. I whisper an apology as I cross the threshold. This homeowner may be a stranger, and gone, but he or she was also my neighbor.

Between the physical pain and being so close to home, I can't sleep. I stretch out on a rug and watch the speckled blue-gray blur to which my vision has reduced the ceiling. Brennan snores all night. I'd thought his night terrors might return after the supermarket, but he seems fine. Or, better than I expected. Better than me, though maybe it only seems that way because I can hear only my own thoughts, dream my own dreams. I'm holding our blue-eyed baby, shielding him from a storming crowd, and then a blade whose hand I never see pierces me from behind and skewers us both.

In the morning I can barely stand, and it takes about an hour of walking for my muscles to loosen. By then, we're close. We pass what was once my favorite café and a curiosity shop that operated on an unpredictable schedule. An elderly neighbor once told me about a time the store surprised her by being open Christmas Day. She found a china tea set identical to one she remembered her mother owning, but which had been lost in a fire. 'Five dollars,' she said to me. 'A Christmas miracle.' Her mother had never let her use the tea set, and owning it now, she told me, made her almost unbearably happy. I asked her if she used it daily to make up for lost time, and she looked at me like I was the devil. 'I don't *use* it,' she said.

I squint through the store's windows as we pass. There's a dusty display of old cookbooks and vintage kitchenware: a blender, a utensil holder painted with daisies and sprouting a single plastic spatula, a blue cast-iron pot.

Half an hour later, we reach my street. Windblown trash skitters across the asphalt. I pause. Brennan walks a few steps farther before noticing. 'Mae?' he asks, turning.

Four driveways down on the left: my mailbox.

It's there, really there. But I can't see the house. A monstrous Tudor obstructs my view. Inside the Tudor, a tea set isn't being used.

As we walk down the block, I feel my nerves constricting, resisting each step. We pass the Tudor and my house comes into view on its little sloped lawn. Pale yellow siding, front door framed by a pair of leafy shrubs. A gutter that was loose when I left now hangs unabashedly from the roof. The lawn is long and yellowing and dotted with white clover flowers.

'Where are we?' asks Brennan.

I'm shaking as I walk up the stone steps. I peer toward the living room windows, but it's dark inside and I can't see beyond the glass. A plastic-wrapped newspaper rests by the path. Grass has grown around it as though it were a rock. I step over the paper. I'm listening as I walk, but I don't hear anything from inside. Just my breath, my steps, blood pounding through my temples. Brennan behind me, and the autumn breeze teasing the long grass. A distant wind chime, maybe.

Sunlight glints off the doorknob, and I stand still for a moment before finding the courage to wrap my hand around it. The knob is cold, as I envisioned, but also locked. A burst of anger courses through me: After everything else, they're going to make me break into my own house.

But there is no *they*, not anymore.

I take a step back. Something feels off. Something specific. I glance around, and then I see it – the welcome mat is missing. My husband's name and mine, playfully intertwined, gone.

This isn't my house.

I can't breathe, I can't stop trying to suck in air.

'Mae, what's wrong?'

I close my eyes, bend over, and put my hands on my knees.

This is my house.

This *is* my house.

I look up again. I know that chipped paint on the window frame. I know the striped curtains barely visible through the living room window. This is my house. The mat isn't here, but that's just superficial. A legal issue. They didn't want his name in the shot.

If only there were a *they*.

I wave away Brennan's barks of concern and wait for my breath to settle. I refuse to break my own front door, so I walk around to the back. My defeated vegetable garden languishes beside an overgrown flowerbed, and there it is, curled over a bench – the welcome mat. An unraveled hose trails between it and the spigot on the side of the house.

The screen door leading to the back porch isn't latched. I enter, passing a small concrete statue of a meditating frog – one dollar, from the curiosity shop. I hear Brennan following me. A citronella candle sits centered on our glass-top table.

I check the back door. It's also locked, but it has windows, nine stately rectangles. I walk past Brennan and pick up the meditating frog. It's compact and heavy. I use it to smash the glass panel nearest the doorknob. Shattering glass pricks my fingers. I reach through and unlock the door.

The door leads into the kitchen. The first thing I notice as I enter is the smell. Stale, musty. I move slowly through the kitchen, squinting. There are dishes in the sink, a few bowls and a glass. I think the glass has a straw coming out of it. I walk past the refrigerator, toward the hall. My foot catches something, metal clatters, and I hop back, startled.

A dog dish. For a moment, I can't reconcile its presence, and then I realize he must have been preparing for me to come home. A pet for a child. An absurd compromise, no wonder we never acknowledged it as such. I push the bowl back against the fridge with my foot and enter the hall. There's a half bath across from me and the living room is just ahead through an archway to the left.

As I walk toward the living room, my gaze catches on our framed wedding collage, which hangs at the base of the stairs. There we are, eight different freeze-frames of happily-ever-after. My favorite is of just him in his light gray suit and moss-green tie. He's waiting for me to come down the aisle – an outdoor aisle framed with friends and trees and flowers and carpeted with clover. He looks serious. He means business. But the corner of his mouth is pinching toward a grin.

I turn toward the archway. There could still be a banner. He could still be there, waiting.

On our first real date, he compared my eyes to a bottle of Pellegrino. A full bottle, he said – because they sparkle. I laughed and teased him for his cheesiness, belittling the sentiment even as I tucked it away.

The living room slides into view. He's not there. There is no banner. It's just me here in this empty, gently cluttered room. But there are signs of him: a few videogame cases on the floor by the entertainment center, his laptop closed on the coffee table. A pile of laundry on the couch, waiting to be folded. I sit on the couch, recognizing a pair of red boxers decorated with different types of knots. A blue T-shirt from a half marathon we ran together.

Next to the laptop there are several remotes, a PlayStation controller, and the book of baby names we bought before I left. I pick up the book. My knuckles are bloody and my fingers leave bright smudges through dust on the cover. I thumb through dog-eared pages. My mouth tastes sour. Some of the ears are new to me. On one such page *Abigail* is underlined. On another, *Emmitt*.

The first time we slept together, I rolled over the morning after and found him looking at me with those dark cocoa eyes. 'It's a little early for chocolate,' I said, 'but okay, I'll have a bite.' And I crammed my face in close to his and nibbled at his lashes. I felt him tense and regret spiked through me – I went too far, I ruined everything – but then he laughed, a Big Bang of laughter, the start of everything, the start of us.

In the hall, Brennan moves into my line of sight. He's eyeing the wedding collage. I wonder if he can recognize me in the photos, with my hair curled and my face all made up, wearing a clean strapless ivory gown dotted with Swarovski crystals. I flip the book to masculine *B. Brennan*. It's Irish in origin, like I thought, but the meaning is unexpected. *Sorrow*, reads the book. *Sadness. Tear.*

Laughter cracks from my chest, painful.

Brennan looks over.

I close the book and scan the living room, wishing for a Clue. All I see is our life, abandoned. I take the book to the built-in shelves lining the back wall, and slide it into a gap between *Cooking for Two* and *1984*. When we moved in, we unpacked our books first, haphazardly, promising to institute a system once we were settled. The last box was empty within the month, but by then we'd grown accustomed to having to Where's Wally anything we wanted to read. We pretended it was a game we'd chosen to play.

'I'm going upstairs,' I say, and Brennan steps aside.

The third step from the top is going to creak, I think.

The third step from the top creaks.

The first-floor hallway is long and narrow, with two doors on either side. To the right, a bathroom followed by our bedroom. To the left, a guest room and our home gym, which was slated to become the nursery. We planned to move the gym equipment to the basement when it was time. The treadmill and the yoga mats, the mismatched dumbbells we never lifted. The basement is a damp cave, but we'd fix it up. That's what we said.

The bathroom door is open; I glance inside. Our Antarctic-scene shower curtain is scrunched to one side of the tub, but I know which cartoon penguin is which. Fran is posed mid-waddle. Horatio and Elvis are resting on their iceberg in the folds.

Across from the bathroom, the guest room door is closed. The door to the home gym, our nursery-never-to-be, is also closed.

But our bedroom door is open. I've been able to see this since I reached the top of the stairs, and now that I'm only about four feet from the frame, I can see a slice of the room beyond. Our double-wide dresser, the opening of the walk-in closet. I can't see our bed or the master bathroom. Those are to the right of the doorway, hidden by the wall.

My head feels fuzzy and tight.

You shouldn't be here.

There is nowhere else for me to go.

I feel Brennan behind me, close. I brace my left hand against the wall, splaying my blood-dabbled fingers atop ugly yellow floral-print wallpaper – another thing we meant to change but never will. Let me be wrong, I wish. Let him be in there, waiting, holding a bouquet of mixed flowers. He always gets mixed, because he knows that lilies are my favorite, but he forgets which ones are lilies and hates to ask. There's always a lily in a mixed bouquet, at least the good ones, so it works. I think of how sweet that mixed bouquet will smell. Unless he did ask the florist and got only lilies. Lilies with orange pollen bunched along their stamens, looking beautiful but smelling awful and waiting to stain my fingertips.

Maybe that's what I've been able to smell since cresting the stairway. Lily pollen. Maybe the whole room is filled with lilies, and their rotten pollen stench is filling the air, drifting out to the hall to meet me.

'Lilies,' I say aloud. 'It's lilies.'

But this isn't what lily pollen smells like.

'Mae?' says Brennan.

'I can't,' I say. I can't go back, I can't go forward. I can't stand here forever.

'I'll go in,' he says.

I put out my swollen hand to stop him, but he hasn't moved.

It takes all my strength to lift my foot.

I recognize our maroon-and-gold comforter. The bedding is rumpled, mounded on the far side. My side. A patch of fuzzy darkness near the head.

Pressure builds behind my eyes. This is my punishment. For the cliff, for the cabin. For leaving.

I can't look. I can't see you like this.

A baby. Our baby. A little boy with light blue eyes. I left

304

him, crying. I had to have known. His fingers so chubby and grasping, and I left him there and here you are, gone, and I don't even know for how long because I was off playing another game.

We met playing a game, Wits and Wagers, and in the final round you bet it all on my answer: 1866. I was one year over; you lost it all and so did I. Three years later, your best man framed the story of our mutual loss as the story of our mutual gain in a toast that had us laughing tears. Afterward we wondered: How many other weddings have referenced assassination?

My eyes flicker toward the window. Sunlight blinds me. It should be raining.

I feel myself hit the floor without experiencing the fall, without feeling my knees give.

You're gone. Right there, but gone.

Brennan walks past me, toward the bed. I can't watch him; I can't *not* watch him. If I blink my skin will rupture. I stare at the nearest leg of the bed frame. Mahogany, bought from a stranger online; we haggled fifty dollars off the price because of a scratch that later buffed right out. Brennan reaches for the covers, doing what I cannot do because I've done it before, I've seen what lies beneath, and I kneel here willing my heart to stop beating, begging it to – *Please.* A pair of brown slippers, size eleven, at the foot of the bed. A birthday present, from me to you. The practical gift, not the fun, we promised to give at least one of each, always. They're askew, and I can see you there, kicking them off before crawling under the covers. My side.

Maroon and gold rise at the edge of my vision. I hate the boy for it. He shouldn't see you like this. No one should see you like this. You shouldn't *exist* like this. My hands are limp upon my lap, one gruesomely swollen and bruised, the other with shredded skin. I can't feel either. All I can feel is the endless, overwhelming *ba-bump* of my heart, grotesque in its insistence to keep on beating. The comforter, not falling – being placed. You, covered now. My ears are ringing. The boy's looking at me. My forehead strikes the floor, the peeling veneer of what we thought was hardwood.

This isn't what I wanted. This isn't what I meant.

Pressure, Brennan's hands upon my shoulders. The floor retreats; I have no resistance left in me. He's talking – crashing waves, my ears still ringing – and I think: All I'm left with is *you*. Hatred like flame and fear like fuel. This isn't how this was supposed to end, how *we* were supposed to end. The boy's face in mine, imploring, beseeching, needing, trying. One phrase penetrates. 'It's all right.' Over and over: *It's all right*. An automated response; he doesn't know what he's saying. It's not all right, it's all wrong. *I* was wrong. Wrong to leave, wrong to fear, wrong to lie, wrong to think that you couldn't make even raising a child possible. I'm *sorry,* I was *wrong,* I will forever be wrong – but I came back.

It can mean nothing now, but I did.

I came back.

22

Footage from the first full day of the Solo Challenge is sent to the studio, but the editor never sees it, never spins it. Never adjusts the tint of the trees or the saturation of Zoo's eyes. The contestants will search and hike and scratch at mosquito bites in real time, forever. That night the third episode of *In the Dark* airs, the first and only weekly finale. It's widely watched, but few will remember it. Footage from the second day of Solo is never even sent in. A drone lands, never to rise again.

The third day, Exorcist wakes to find his cameraman collapsed outside his shelter with red mucus leaking from his nose. He uses the cameraman's radio to call for help. The voice on the other side is panicked, but assures him help is coming. Exorcist holds the cameraman's sweaty, bloody head on his lap for hours, telling him stories and dribbling water into his mouth. Help does not come, and the cameraman's heart beats its final rhythm. Exorcist tries to carry the body out of the woods, but after a slow half mile falls to the ground, exhausted. He mutters a final blessing, crosses the man's stiffening arms over his chest, and leaves him under a black birch. He soon mistakes a combination of deep thirst and pathogen-caused nausea for hunger, and decides to hunt. Stumbling through the woods, delirium falls over him like mist. A branch sways with the weight of a squirrel; he chucks his sharpened dowsing rod. The rod flies swiftly, hits the trunk of a different tree, and bounces into a bed of leaves. Exorcist searches for the dowsing rod until nightfall. In the dark he begins to sweat, and then his stomach heaves. He can't stop coughing. He feels too warm. He wipes at his runny nose and his sleeve comes back red. He weeps, seeing the bloody eye of his ex-wife. His inner monster is nothing compared to this possession – so quick, so painful, so total. In a moment of semi-lucidity, he wonders why it never occurred to him to try to exorcise the cameraman's sickness. And then the demon grasps his organs with its many claws and rends his innards.

Help does find four of the contestants. Air Force, Biology, Engineer and Banker are brought back to the production camp by their still-well cameramen. And when Tracker's cameraman doesn't show the third morning of Solo, Tracker follows his trail from the previous night and finds him curled in his sleeping bag, feverish. Tracker helps the cameraman back to base camp. These five contestants are evacuated and sent with the remaining production crew into quarantine, where they are caged singularly in plastic cubicles. Here, surrounded by the sounds of crying, dying strangers, they are again recorded.

The quickly mutating and still unidentified pathogen strikes Tracker first, with no preamble. He sweats and weeps and dreams, but he does not bleed and he does not die. A combination of genetics and years of pushing his immune system to the limit spare him. He will live to old age, telling his story to few and never publicly, wondering always if he should have tried harder to find her.

All Banker catches is a cold. He spends his days in quarantine alternating between fear and boredom. When he's later moved to a Californian refugee camp, he will tell his story to anyone who will listen.

By his second day in quarantine, blood leaks from Air Force's eyes and nose to stain his perfect warrior face. He always thought that if he died young it would be in a singular, glorious crash. His last breath is the scream of a falcon missing its prey. Biology slips away with relative quiet, unconscious through the pain, dreaming of her partner. Engineer is conscious until the end. A lifelong optimist, the instant before he dies he will think, *I'm going to get better*.

Rancher is among those left behind in the scramble to evacuate. He finds the production camp, but not for days, not until it is empty of everyone except for the Expert, who insisted on staying behind to search for the others. When Rancher finds him, he is recognizable mostly by his flannel shirt. Flies feast on his leaked and drying blood. Rancher continues to search for the others, and after a week is felled not by the fast-spreading affliction all around him – which he has the genes to survive – but by microbes in ill-chosen standing water. When he dies, he will be delirious, dehydrated, covered in his own filth. But he will be smiling, watching his three children play in the distance. His sons and daughter will never know the details of their father's death. They will grow up wishing they knew more, that he had never gone east. If he'd just stayed home, they'll say.

Waitress does not have the genes to survive. The third morning of the Solo Challenge she wakes feverish, her throat a silent scream. She cannot sit up. Her cameraman stands above her, listening to the panicked callback on the radio, 'Bring them in. Bring them all in!' He sees the trickle of red coming from her left nostril. He drops his camera and runs. Waitress sees him go. Her fever tells her it's a mistake. She clutches the whistle given to her at the start of the bear-tracking Challenge and brings it to her lips, but she doesn't have enough breath left to make a sound. The cameraman will lie and say he could not find her. He will die too quickly and in too much pain to feel remorse.

Zoo wakes that third morning feeling only a little stiff. She waits for her cameraman, but he doesn't show. Unknown to her, he is lying among the fallen leaves of late summer about one hundred yards away, crying senselessly and use-lessly into his radio. Within minutes, the cameraman too will die. Within hours, turkey vultures will find him. Within days, his remains will be scattered by coyotes.

If Zoo were to search for the cameraman now, she might find him. But she doesn't search, she waits. She rests and inef-fectually washes her clothing in a stream she crossed yesterday before making camp and receiving her most recent Clue. As she scrubs the sweat out of her socks, her body prepares for a fight her mind doesn't know is coming. Her second morning truly alone, she concludes that she's supposed to keep mov-ing, to follow the Clue: *You're on track; it's what you seek. Look for the sign past the next creek.* While vultures swirl and land out of sight, Zoo dismantles her shelter, clips a water bottle to her side, and shoulders her pack.

'Well,' she says, speaking to the tiny camera posted above where her shelter used to stand, 'I guess I better find that creek.' She dusts off the seat of her pants and starts walking, walking east because that is the direction they last sent her and the Clue says she's on track. East, past a dry creek bed where an evacuated intern will never place a box. East, toward a brook that runs through a culvert, above which sits a road where driveways sprout like the many tendrils of a single root.

At the base of one of these driveways a new mother now stands, exhausted and slightly queasy – but happy, dismiss-ing her discomfort as a nebulous postpartum affliction. The mother's newborn baby boy gurgles from a carrier at her chest as she ties a trio of blue balloons to her mailbox, pre-paring for a party she will never host in a small brown house with red trim; a house decorated with a touch of blue. A classy amount, the new mother thinks.

Just enough.

23.

Everything has changed; nothing has changed. Brennan and I walk. To where, I don't know. I can't eat, but Brennan hands me a water bottle a few times a day and I drink. Beyond that, I walk through daylight and wait out the night, thinking of you.

I see you sleeping now, your peppered hair, your forehead smoothed of worry. Lids pale and veined, shielding inquisitive eyes, your cocoa eyes. Cold and empty, you lie alone in the bed where all those nights you tried to sleep and there I was, my nose an inch from your nose, just staring, waiting for you to smile or open your eyes. Occasionally I'd augment the stare with a prod, because I could never get over how much you loved me and this seemed an easy way to prove it. Sometimes – often – you complained, but even then you smiled. You felt lucky too.

I could have at least buried you. I could have burned you and carried the ash on my hip. I could have spread you across the garden.

I could have burned the house. I should have.

I didn't even take a picture. I didn't even take my ring. I barely remember leaving, and the only thing I have of us is me.

I couldn't even look. I couldn't look at you not being human. I couldn't see what you'd become.

I'm sorry.

'Mae?'

A stranger. All that's left.

'You were married?' asks Brennan.

Once or twice a day he does this, tries to talk about my home, as if his being there made it a shared experience. As if he knows anything. I shake my head, a thunderous effort. I can't talk about you, I won't.

We're sitting beside a fire it took him nearly all evening to build. He's heating soup or beans, something in a can. It's been two days since he led me out of the bedroom, down the stairs, through the back door. How I moved I still don't know.

Brennan glances my way then back to the dirt. 'My brother liked zebras growing up,' he says. He's been telling a lot of stories about his brother. This I allow – white noise. 'I was a baby, so I don't remember, but Mom always talked about it at birthdays and stuff. Everyone else is playing with cowboys and aliens and robots, and Aiden's drawing stripes on a toy horse he found in the park.'

He pauses to stir whatever's in the can. The smell is atrocious. Every smell is atrocious. Sap and pine and smoke and death: interchangeable.

'That was her favorite story,' he continues. 'I hated it. It made us sound poor, like she couldn't afford to *buy* him a toy. We weren't poor. We weren't rich, but we weren't poor. Mom was a paralegal. Aiden was going to go to law school. Mom told him the lawyers always looked tired, so maybe he should become a doctor instead. I thought that was funny.'

He starts peeling the bark off his stir stick. 'I didn't get sick so maybe *he* didn't get sick,' he says. 'But Mom did, so . . . then, it's like, there's those two guys. So much else that could have happened even if he didn't get sick, you know? But what if he's still out there?'

A memory, triggered: I got sick. After the cabin, I got sick. I thought it was from the water, but it wasn't the water. It was this, whatever *this* is.

I didn't quit because they didn't come; in my delirium, I knew my state couldn't be as dire as it felt because they were leaving me alone. If I were in danger they would help, I told myself. Turns out no one came because they were all dead, or dying, like I was dying, except that I didn't die and they all did.

You did.

I cup my face in my hands, block out the world, a world that keeps insisting on its own existence.

When my grandmother died, my father spoke of Heaven for the first time in my memory. A coping mechanism. I saw how this sudden expression of belief helped him disperse his grief. Me, I had the pendant: an oblong opal that shimmered in my palm and reminded me of her wisdom. I don't remember why I thought my grandmother wise, what she ever said to me. I don't remember her at all, now, though I remember the love I felt for her.

'I hate it,' says Brennan. 'I hate not knowing if Aiden's alive or not.'

My grandmother's not in Heaven and neither are you. The energy that coursed through your brain, that made you *you*, is dispersed now like my father's grief. The cells that housed that energy are dead, and as they decay they will release the atoms that formed your body, that pumped your blood, that *was* your blood. I once read that, the way atoms travel over time, everyone alive today likely contains at least one that was once a part of Shakespeare's body. In this way our ancestors are all one, and one day, your atoms will become everyone. Eventually the atoms that together make my skin, my bones, my marrow, my hair and guts and blood will mingle again with yours. I'll be like you then, nonexistent and everywhere.

We don't need Heaven for this to be true. We don't need God to be together again.

But I wish for it. I wish I could pray, find solace. I wish I could believe that you were still you, more than atoms, watching from above. But I'm done with pretending, with lies and wishful thinking. This leaves me with the truth: You're gone. I can see you in the bed, gone. I close my eyes and see you, gone. I walk through the cloud around me and see you, inert, preserved — gone. I see your face as I remember, but this vision of you exists only in my imagination. I've seen enough to know. Gases, rot, bloating stench. That is what you've become and though the flashes come I cannot bear to think of you that way. I will allow myself this final lie: You're there, like a carving beneath the covers. In this lie I stare until you smile, and then I kiss your forehead good night and turn away to let you sleep.

<u>*In the Dark* – Week one down. Reactions?</u>

. . .

[+] submitted 29 days ago by LongLiveCaptainTightPants
301 comments

top comments
sorted by: **newest**

[-] CoriolisAffect 28 days ago
My cameraman friend is dead. Whatever's happening
it got him. The people on the show are fucked. We're
all fucked.

. . .

24.

When I envision the cabin, alternate visions seem equally true. The house is blue; the house is brown. There are balloons everywhere; there are a handful, scattered. Stacks of blue boxes; a trio of small packages. I want to cut the difference in half, just to stop wondering, but memory shouldn't be a compromise.

The baby would have died anyway.

That's what I tell myself, but it doesn't help and I know it's not true. Not necessarily. I could have saved him, maybe.

And then what, I'd be walking along this curving parkway with a baby strapped to my chest? An infant with no relation to me. That's not survival, that's selflessness, and the only person I've ever wanted to give the better half of anything was you.

Why was the welcome mat in the back? We've never washed it. Why would you wash it?

Why do I think it matters?

I don't. I'm distracting myself. I don't want to distract myself from you. But I have to; my tongue is dry and my stomach empty. You'd tell me to move on and I am. *I am.* I'm walking, I'm moving. But my feet are dragging; I can't lift them, thinking about you. And I see Brennan trying, and I think – I think I can't let him fail.

I came back, Miles. I'm here but you're gone and I have to go on because I don't want to but that's all my body can do. I'm sorry. I'm sorry and I miss you and you're gone.

I blink away asphalt and look up at the yellow-brown

leaves, splashes of clinging green. I used to think autumn was beautiful.

I loved you. You're gone. I'm sorry.

'*Ad tenebras dedi.*'

When I level my blurred gaze, Brennan is staring at me, his thumbs tucked under the straps of his zebra-patterned pack.

'Mae?'

I can feel my body wanting to cry, the tightness of my eyes. I think of his brother, his mother, all that he's lost. He would have saved the baby. He saved me, when all I'd been to him was cruel.

'Where are we going?' I ask.

He's staring at me. After a moment he replies, 'I don't know.'

A careful tone, because my voice still has tones and I have to choose one and he's a *child*. Not accusing, only asking, 'You don't have a plan?'

'Just to get you out of there.' Brennan shifts his pack. 'Where do you think we should go?'

Should. A judgment call I'm not qualified to make. But I do know a place, a place Brennan might like.

'It's far,' I say, 'and it's not a farm, but there's acreage and a well with a hand pump. A little greenhouse and a couple of dozen sugar maples. There were chickens, might still be.' I'm beyond hope, but logic tells me there's a chance, a legitimate chance, because if there *is* a genetic component to resistance, I had to get it from somewhere. One or the other. Though it could be recessive, an invisible, unexpressed connection that couldn't save either of my parents and yet saved me.

'Where is it?' asks Brennan.

'Vermont.'

'Let's go.'

That's it: *Let's go.* Because he trusts me. Despite everything I've done and not done, he trusts me. He keeps trying
to save me. He's trying, so hard.

I can't let him fail.

Five days. I'm eating again, two meals a day, holding my
spork in my clublike fist as a toddler would a crayon. My
jaw still aches and everything tastes like rot. As we walk I
feel my pulse in my swollen hand and wrist, and I wonder
if I'll ever heal.

We're passing a strip mall, I think. Concrete and desolation, chain restaurants and office supply stores. Ubiquitous
logos I know without seeing, that will mean nothing to the
next generation, if there is a next generation.

What a waste, this landscape. Store after store after store;
phones that will never be charged, games never played,
drawers never opened, glasses never –

'Brennan, wait.'

'What?' he asks, pivoting toward me.

'Is that a LensCrafters?'

He looks where I'm pointing across the street, searches,
and finds. 'Yeah,' he says, and with the first hint of affirmation I'm crossing the street. No need to look both ways.

'You think they'll have the glasses you need just sitting
there?' asks Brennan scuttling after.

'No. But they'll have contacts.'

He breaks the glass door and we're in. I beeline for the
back, where I find a wall of sample packs. I scour the selection, taking any within a quarter of a point of my
prescription. Daily, extended wear, anything. I stuff them
into my pack. It's enough to last at least a year, I think.
While I'm filling my backpack, I feel a lump in the media
pocket and pull out the dead mic pack from the show.
Matchbox-sized and useless. I toss it onto the floor and slip

more lenses into the pocket. Afterward I scrub my hands with soap and drinking water in the exam room sink; that's how easy it's been to find bottled water, I can wash my hands with it now. I keep the purification drops I took from the store, though, not knowing what's ahead. I'm almost able to unfurl the fingers of my right hand. I can hold the bottle tight enough to pour, though I have to tip my whole arm.

I think of Tyler gifting me the trash bag. Why me, I'll never know. And I'll probably never know if he's alive or dead, if any of them are. If anyone *should* have made it, it's the doctor, but I bet Heather's the only one who lived. Me and Heather, the most useless of the bunch. Cooper was probably the first to go.

I drop the empty bottle and peer into the mirror above the sink. An empty, wasted face stares back. A crusty scab on her chin, the yellow mottle of old bruising on her neck. Useless, but still here. I peel open a tiny package. I've never put in contacts left-handed before. Even getting the lens out and positioned on my index finger is problematic, and then I keep catching it on my eyelashes. Eventually it sneaks past, makes contact with my eye – and pops out onto my cheek. Another failed attempt, and another, then finally the lens slides in and settles into place, stinging. The second lens takes only marginally less time to get in, then it folds in my eye. I almost puncture my cornea fishing it out. It's like I'm back in sixth grade, struggling with my first pair of contact lenses, running with tears streaming from abused eyes toward the bus –

The bus.

Those were real children.

Those were *real* children and I walked past, blind.

What did I step on?

Who.

I take a seat in the creaky exam chair, bury my head in my hands. It feels like the rest of my life can only be an apology, that with each step forward I have to beg forgiveness for the last.

I rest until I can try again, until I can refocus on something as mundane and concrete as putting in a contact lens. I return to the mirror. Plastic and cornea finally connect. I blink to help the lens settle and suddenly everything is so clear it's startling.

I find Brennan in the front, trying on sunglasses. I see the holes in his red sweatshirt, the frayed cuff of his left sleeve, the fuzzed disarray of his growing hair, his unbroken posture. I see someone who doesn't have to live the rest of his days in regret. He picks up a pair of glasses with huge lenses and bright yellow frames; I think they might be a women's style, but who can tell and what does it matter. I see the pink beneath his fingernails and I think of Cooper's hands covered in blood. A heat in my chest like anger and I know – I would feel it. If it were Brennan's hands turned red, I would feel it. He slides the sunglasses onto his face.

'Those look good,' I tell him, trying.

He moves the sunglasses to the top of his head. 'Thanks.'

We exit the store and follow the road north. The blankness, the bleakness, the rotting litter and stillness all around. It's unmistakably vast. The extent of it overwhelms me. I don't know whether to be thankful that my glasses broke or to resent it. Though, who knows, maybe I would have clung to the lie even if I could see. The brain is a terrifying and wondrous organ, and all it wants is to survive. I doubt I'll ever be able to make perfect sense of those confused and confusing days. I'd rather just forget them.

Brennan and I walk despite the abandoned vehicles all around us. We walk because the world is too quiet for cars and without a word we've agreed to walk and for all I know I'm the last one on Earth who knows how to drive.

By dusk my eyes are itchy and tired, unused to being bound, unused to seeing. These lenses are daily disposables; I toss them into the fire and they disappear.

'Do they make a big difference?' asks Brennan. He's reverted to a blur.

I nod, close my eyes, rub my temples. The fire crackles.

'Brennan,' I say. 'I'm sorry. I didn't know how bad it was. I don't want to talk about . . . before. But I'm sorry.'

'It was because you couldn't see?' he asks.

I nod again. It's not a lie.

'Your eyesight's that bad?' I hear rustling as he feeds the fire. I wait. I know what's coming: a story. About his mom, maybe, but more likely about his brother. Aiden's been walking with us these last few days.

'It didn't seem so bad,' says Brennan. 'I thought it was like – Aiden had glasses, but he only needed them for driving. That's the only time he ever wore them.' He pauses. Did Aiden forget his glasses once and rear-end a traffic cop? Maybe he drove the wrong way down a one-way street. 'Mae' – Brennan's voice lifts – 'at your house –'

'No.' An instinct. I can't, I won't. He's caught me unprepared and my hackles rise.

'But –'

'No! I don't want to talk about it.' Even this is saying too much. My eyelids are tight, but they can't block memory. A shock of dark hair, a blanket falling. I feel the threat to leave him boiling in my throat. I'll speak it if I have to, lie or not.

I can feel him staring at me.

'Brennan. *Please.*'

A long moment passes, and then he says, 'Okay.'

In the Dark – Trying to find my wife

Hello? If anyone is reading this, my wife was a contestant on In the Dark and I've been trying to find her since August. I've tried all the emergency contacts I have for the production but I haven't been able to reach anyone. I know someone on here knew a cameraman, and if you can help me, if anyone can help me, please.

Please.

[-] submitted Just now by 501_Miles

0 comments

25.

The next afternoon as we walk along the road I see a parachute caught in the trees to our left. Brennan darts ahead to get the first look, and it's the third time today he's referred to himself as 'the scout.' I see him pause at the crisp tree line.

'What is it?' I call.

'A box!' he yells back. 'A big one!'

When I get there, he's walking around a huge plastic crate, peering in. It's as tall as he is.

'What do you think it is?' he asks.

'A big box,' I tell him. He laughs, but I'm not there. I might never be.

'But from where?' He's still circling, like a pup investigating a scent.

The box isn't connected to the parachute, which is huge, bigger than I would have guessed from the road, and hangs above us like a great green sky. The cords have snapped, or been cut. *Don't look, scan,* but these tracks are the most obvious I've ever seen. 'It was air-dropped,' I say, remembering a trail in the sky, a sound in the night.

'It's empty,' announces Brennan. He's jittery – excited, I think. 'That means someone emptied it, right? There are other people around here?'

I step forward to touch the plastic box. Cool, smooth, inorganic. I imagine a massive jet stocked with these instead of passengers, arriving home empty. 'Also someone else out there organized enough to pull off a Marshall Plan,' I say.

'What's a Marshall Plan?' asks Brennan, ducking into the crate and examining its ceiling.

It's hard, so hard. Conversation. Is this how Cooper felt at first, talking to me? 'You didn't make it to World War Two in school?' I ask.

'Nazis,' he counters. His voice echoes slightly. 'World War Two was Nazis.'

'Touché.' It slips out and I want it back. More than *I love you,* we said *touché.* Banter followed by a kiss. 'It doesn't matter,' I say. 'I don't think the reference even works.' Because the Marshall Plan was different from the Berlin Airlift, wasn't it? And it was an air*lift* not an air*drop,* and though I've always assumed the supplies drifted in on parachutes, maybe the planes landed.

Are there enough people left for the proper nouns of history to matter?

This crate would suggest so. I'm not sure how that makes me feel, for there to be enough, but for those I loved not to be among them. It's another readjustment, and I don't know how much change I have left in me.

Brennan pops his head out of the crate. 'Should we try to find them?' he asks.

Movement catches my eye and I see it, see them: a trio of strangers standing among the trees, watching. An old black man with bright white hair, a youngish white woman, and another man, also youngish, who looks like he might be Latino, but maybe he just has dark hair and a tan.

'Mae?' asks Brennan.

'I don't think we need to,' I say.

'Why not?' He hops out of the crate. 'Do you –' He notices my gaze, follows my nod. 'Oh,' he says.

'Name?' asks the old man. A different old man. This one is white and bearded, and this farm has been in his family for generations. Or so goes the lore. A little over a month since the plague – that's what they call it, the plague – and this sanctuary tucked away in western Massachusetts already has lore.

This is the first question he's asked us, but he's already taken several notes in his leather-bound ledger. Race and sex, I assume. General impressions. Brennan's bouncy energy, my scowl.

'Brennan Michaels,' says Brennan. He's sitting straight in his chair, too straight. His right leg operates an invisible sewing machine.

'Immune or recovered?' asks the man.

'What?'

'Were you immune to the plague or did you catch it and recover?'

'Oh. Immune.'

The old man makes a note. 'Any skills we should know about? Tasks you'd be especially fit for?'

'I, uh . . .'

'He's thirteen,' I interject.

The bearded man turns to me with lifted brows. I don't like him. 'What about you, what are your skills?'

'I don't die,' I say, 'even when everyone else does.'

The brows lower. 'We've got three hundred and fourteen souls here who can say the same. Any actual skills?'

I dislike him a little less.

'She can build fires!' blurts Brennan. 'And shelters out of branches and stuff. And she's really good at —'

I shoot him a stilling glance. We didn't see much of the farm, walking in with our escort, but it's huge and populated with multiple structures. There were running tractors, noise. Life here is beyond debris huts. 'I'm not a doctor or an engineer,' I say. 'I can't track a deer and I don't know how to build a roof, but I'll do whatever needs to be done. Teach me, or I'll figure it out on my own. Either way it'll get done.'

The man jots a few more notes. 'Well, you don't sound lazy,' he says. 'As long as you're willing to contribute, we can use you. And what are you, immune or recovered?'

'Recovered, I think.'

'What's your name?'

'Mae,' I say. Perhaps I should have hesitated, or given the other, but Mae's the version of me who made it this far.

'Mae what?'

This time I do hesitate, and then I give the only answer that feels true. 'Woods.'

In the Dark – Trying to find my wife

. . .

[+] submitted 1 day ago by 501_Miles
18 comments

top comments
sorted by: **popularity**

[-] LongLiveCaptainTightPants 1 day ago
A friend of a friend of mine met the banker guy from
the show in a camp outside Fresno. He was evacuated
along with a few of the others. Says he thought it was
all scripted at first, took him a bit to realize there was
a real emergency. I'll reach out, see if I can get contact
info.

    [-] 501_Miles 1 day ago
    Thank you. This is the first lead I've had –
    thank you.

        [-] LongLiveCaptainTightPants 4 hours ago
        Got it. PM to follow.

[-] Trina_ABC 1 hour ago
501_Miles – I'm with an ABC affiliate outside of San
Francisco. We heard about your search for your wife
and would love to speak with you. If you're willing to
share your story, please PM me. Maybe I can help.

. . .

26.

'This place is pretty nice, huh, Mae?' asks Brennan. He's sitting on his cot across from mine, tying his shoelaces. We're in a barn that's been converted to a dorm and houses two dozen people. This corner is ours. It was kind of them, to give us a corner.

'Could be worse,' I reply. I'm getting better at putting in my contacts left-handed, but it's still difficult, especially without a mirror.

'About Vermont . . .' says Brennan.

'We're better off here.'

He looks up, hopeful. 'You think we should stay?'

I take my hand away from my eye and blink rapidly. It stings for a second, then the lens settles. 'Yes, I think we should stay.' Because his future is more important than my past.

We've been here four days. It's difficult, being surrounded by people after so long alone, or nearly so. But there's less drama than I expected. Everyone has a role, and seems to fill it with minimal complaint. 'Most of us had it rough, getting here,' the doctor told me when I went to see her about my hand. 'We know how bad it could get, if we let it. So we don't.'

Another bit of lore: There was an attempted rape, early on. They let the assailed choose the punishment and she chose instead to forgive. Something about there being enough grief in this world without adding to it. It's unclear who exactly this woman was – no one ever gives her a name when telling the story – but if this is truly a new world, someone's bound to dedicate a statue to her before too long. Or a church. Soon her memory and eventually her myth will be begged forgiveness for sins beyond count or measure.

There's no one left to forgive me.

I asked the doctor about my period; she said nearly every woman here has missed one. It's the physical stress, like I thought. She had me stand on one of those tall, creaky scales, the type that measures height too. One hundred and four pounds; almost thirty below the weight I think of as mine. She said my body should be getting back to normal soon, now that I'm safe. She actually used those words: 'normal,' 'safe.' I think that's what made me tell her about the coyote. She stared. Turns out I know more about rabies than she does. If I'm still standing a month from now, I'm in the clear.

I haven't told Brennan. I figure it's best not to mention rabies until and unless I develop an irrational fear of water. He's befriended a few kids around his age, but slingshots back to me every meal, every morning, every 'town hall,' and every evening. I'm grateful.

'Mae,' says Brennan as I move on to my right eye. 'When we were at your house –'

A different world, a different life, a different me. 'I told you, Brennan, I don't want to talk about it.'

'But it's different now.'

'No,' I say, firmly. I blink my second lens into place.

'But, Mae . . .'

He looks guilty, maybe a little scared. I wonder if he stole something. Scavenged, in the parlance of our new reality.

'If it's something you need forgiveness for, you have it,' I say. He still looks supremely uncomfortable. I need to give him something. 'Tell me what was in the motel room instead.' Because that's something I still haven't been able to reconcile, and I need to so I can forget it.

'Oh.' His sneakers are tied. He rubs the toes of his right foot into the hay-lined dirt floor, drawing an oval. 'It was stupid. The room was filled with electronics. TVs and laptops, Xboxes, stuff like that.'

'No bodies?'

'No.' A second oval, a slightly rotated twin of the first, making a very slim *X*. 'But things were dusty like no one had been there in a while.'

'So whoever put it there is probably dead,' I say.

'Probably,' he agrees. A third oval. His foot is a slow Spirograph.

I look around the barn. There are a handful of others milling about, preparing for the day. I've heard maybe a dozen different explanations for the plague since arriving, but the majority opinion seems to be it had something to do with fracking. Either the process released a prehistoric pathogen, or it was the dispersal method for a man-made toxin. One of the more outspoken proponents of the unearthed-pathogen theory is an old Indian woman who's currently standing by the barn door. She waves at us, smiling, then takes the hand of the little white girl – four, five years old – who I've never seen more than ten feet from her side. The idea of fracking being behind this doesn't make any sense, and I think the woman knows it. She just needs something to believe; they all do.

'Maybe whoever put that stuff in the motel is here,' I say to Brennan.

'Mae!'

The look in his eyes hurts. 'They could be, Brennan. Or men like those two at the grocery store could show up any day.' Maybe Cliff and Harry *would* be here, if not for me. Maybe they too would have roles to fill. 'This is a good place,' I say, 'but just because someone made it this far doesn't mean they're a good person. So don't get complacent.' He squirms. 'Brennan, promise me.' Because I can't do it, I can't lose him too.

'I promise, Mae.'

'Thank you,' I say. 'I've got to go, I'm on breakfast duty.'

'You're lucky,' says Brennan. 'I'm chopping wood all morning.'

His voice is so forlorn I can't help a little smile, impressed by his resilience, for chopping wood to feel like a burden. 'That's better than scrambling eggs for three hundred strangers,' I tell him. 'I'll be right out there with you as soon as my hand's better.'

'Mae, how long do you think we'll be here?'

'I don't know,' I say. 'Could be another day, could be forever.'

In the Dark – Trying to find my wife

. . .

[+] submitted 5 days ago by 501_Miles
109 comments

top comments
sorted by: **trending**

[-]LongLiveCaptainTightPants 3 days ago
Was Elliot any help?

> [-] 501_Miles 34 minutes ago
> He said she didn't get out when he did. That
> some of them were left behind. She was left
> behind. That's all he knows.
>
>> [-] Velcro_Is_the_Worst 29 minutes ago
>> You know how many bodies there are
>> rotting east of the Mississippi right
>> now? Millions. Your wife is one of
>> them. Dead as a doornail. Accept it and
>> move on.
>>
>>> [-] LongLiveCaptainTightPants
>>> 28 minutes ago
>>> Don't listen to him, Miles.
>>> People survived. There's been
>>> radio contact with pockets of
>>> survivors and there's talk of
>>> sending in recovery teams as
>>> soon as it's safe. As soon as
>>> they can.
>>>
>>>> [-] 501_Miles Just now
>>>> I know. Thank you. If
>>>> anyone could have
>>>> made it, it's my Sam.

. . .

27

Faces swarm the camera. Calmer than expected, cleaner than expected, thinner than they used to be. Most are smiling and many are crying as their breath blurs the air. One by one they accept pamphlets and bottles of water from men and women wearing orange vests. Backs of heads nod and bob as frost crunches beneath boots and shoes and the occasional pair of slippers. As strong a community as was being built here, nearly all want to be saved.

Three thousand miles away a man watches the scene on an old flatscreen. He's lucky, he shares the room with only two others – fellow East Coasters, though he didn't know them before. The man has a four-month-long beard that used to be more black than gray. His chin is tucked into his palm and he gnaws on a thumbnail as he searches the far away faces. An alert to which he will not reply blinks on his iPhone, which lies on the cot beside him. Service was restored locally two months ago, but there weren't any messages, not from her. Her mother left one from the landline back in August; she didn't sound well and no one's answered his attempts to call back. This is the third camp he's watched the rescue teams enter. None have been easy, but this is the hardest yet. It's the largest known cluster, over three hundred people. His best chance.

A news anchor appears in the frame, microphone in hand. She's sleek and polished, her symmetrical face augmented with HD-friendly makeup. She's not the one who's been helping the man search; she knows nothing about him. Looking at her pert grin, one would never know that a mysterious miasmic infection whose origins authorities are only now beginning to trace recently reduced her nation's population by a third and the world's by nearly half. A caption at the bottom of the screen reads: EASTERN US REFUGEES RESCUED.

The caption is a lie. The man searching the screen for his wife's face – he's the refugee. He became one the second he boarded a bus to quarantine instead of taking the last train home. His roommates are refugees, as are the thousands of others like them: the displaced waiting to go home. The people in the camp are not refugees. They are survivors. Each has a story about reaching this thriving community in the hills of Massachusetts. The short Arab man who just accepted a bottle of water was a taxi driver in Washington, D. C. He got sick; so did his wife and children. He was the only one to recover, waking in his apartment dehydrated and surrounded by his deceased family. His will to live was stronger than his sorrow, barely. The elderly Indian woman in the right corner of the screen lost her daughter and grandson days before saving the life of the little white girl who now rides her shoulders; she scooped the girl from her car seat as water rushed in through the window of the Mini Cooper her delirious father had just crashed into a river. The black child in the red sweatshirt held his mother's head as she faded to nothing on a church pew. Alone, started walking south, only to turn east on meeting a stubborn stranger his loneliness wouldn't allow him to leave. The stubborn stranger's story is the strangest of all, riddled with deceit external and internal. Even the man who legally owns the property these many people have begun to think of as home has a story, though he did not have to travel to arrive. His is a story of opening doors, of deciding to give after losing so much.

In time, many of these stories will be celebrated, but for

now the losses are still being counted. For now the mere survival of these people is news enough. All the anchor wants to know is 'How do you feel?'

'Overwhelmed!'

'Exhausted!'

'Blessed!'

Nothing of substance, nothing unexpected. Just tears and platitudes. The man watching hears nothing. A chocolate Lab trots through the shot and his heart pinches. He doesn't know what happened to the greyhound he adopted a week before the world he knew imploded. The dog was supposed to be a surprise for his wife. Speckled and sweet, just like she wanted, and she would have loved the name: Freshly Ground Pepper. He let the dog sleep in their bed, even the night she got into the trash and vomited a foamy pile on the first step of their evening walk.

The anchor spots the black boy in the red sweatshirt. His stranger, a white woman in a stained green fleece and a blue hat, is walking with him, her hand resting lightly on his back. The boy looks delighted and overwhelmed, but the woman's face is stone. The anchor loves the contrast, the connection. She thanks a weepy widow for her time and strikes toward the pair.

The man's eyes and shoulders perk. He thinks his hope and his imagination are working against him. After all this time, all this not knowing, he's not sure. She's bone-skinny and her hair is light and short where it peeps out of the hat, but –

'How do you feel?' asks the anchor. Surrounded by so much ruckus, the boy is at a loss for words. The anchor smiles at him sweetly, thinking him shy, then turns to the stone-faced woman and repeats her question.

Certainty rips through the man, and he stands with a shout, believing – *knowing*. He looks around for someone to tell but is alone. For months he's been seeking, fearing; now he's laughing and pounding the air with his fists.

The camera jolts sidewise; the stone-faced woman is attempting to walk past.

'Miss?' prods the anchor, leaning in.

The woman glances at her, then at the lens. She cannot see the eyes watching her so joyfully. She can no longer imagine these eyes exist, that what she wouldn't let the boy tell her — what the boy didn't know she couldn't see — was this: The body in the bed wasn't human. The woman scans the crowd, the crush, the saviors, the bottled water, and the orange vests. She does not feel blessed. It's over. It's just beginning. She will endure. The cameraman edges closer and the anchor tilts her microphone toward the woman's face. But the woman has no confession and these obstructions, these devices sucking in her breath, her image, these are all things that are no longer real. Her hard green gaze slides past the lens to the man behind it. 'Get the camera out of my face,' she says. 'Now.'

Acknowledgments

I have many thanks to disperse, and my first bundle goes to the smartest man I know, who is just enough of a chump to have legally bound himself to me for life. Andrew, thank you for giving me a second chance at our first date, your loving and logical support during the writing of this novel, and everything in between and yet to come – especially the laughter.

Next up, rapid-fire family thanks: Thank you to my dad for understanding the creative drive and supporting my decision to follow such an uncertain path. Thank you to my mom for my off-kilter upbringing, which I know plays such a huge part in who I am today. Thank you to Jon for answering my Air Force questions and general big brother awesomeness. Thank you to Yvette for her kindness and gentle understanding throughout the years. Thank you to Helen for weathering my teenage ambivalence and for her friendship.

A shout-out to my ninth-floor suities: Purva, Katie, Xining, Shelly, Lynn, Emily and Aditi. Your support and camaraderie over these many and occasionally very long years has meant the world to me, and your outpouring of selfless joy when things finally started to click is the definition of friendship. Extra thanks to Dr He for answering my writing-related medical questions with such speed and thoughtfulness; to Lynn for the photo shoot; and to the Galipeaus for providing dinners, drinks, and much good company while the world shifted beneath my feet.

Alex and Libby: Thank you for your feedback and your

friendship, and for not letting years or miles get in the way of our little writing group. You not only push me to be better, you inspire me to be. I hope I've been half as helpful to you in your own work.

To the incredible BOSS staff: Thank you for a once-in-a-lifetime adventure. Seriously, once was enough. Special thanks to Cat, Jess and Heath; I can't imagine having had better guides through those trying and extraordinary two weeks. Thank you also to the staff (and residents) of the Prospect Park Zoo, for providing sanctuary and inspiration amidst the bustle prior to my escape to the Pacific Northwest.

Thank you to Shelley Jackson for that extra little push toward the weird. Thank you to Lee Martin for the givens, though I later stripped most of them away. Thank you to Julia Glass for her kindness at an airport during an overwhelming time.

Thank you to the Catto Shaw Foundation for a quiet space for the finishing touches. Thank you to the good people of Aspen Words for a community, and for Lucy.

Lucy Carson. To call her a dream agent is an understatement, because I never dreamed I'd have the privilege of working with someone as passionate as she. Lucy, you gave me hope and give me confidence. Knowing you have my back makes all the difference. Thank you. Thank you also to Nichole LeFebvre, for handling the details so deftly and with such kindness.

Thank you to Jessica Leeke for quite possibly the most exciting and surreal morning of my life, and for her continued enthusiasm since. Wider thanks to my entire team at Michael Joseph.

Thank you to Gina Centrello and everyone at Ballantine who's had a hand in bringing this book into the world, including: Libby McGuire, Kara Welsh, Kim Hovey,

Jennifer Hershey, Susan Corcoran, Melanie DeNardo, Quinne Rogers, Kelly Chian, Betsy Wilson, Kara Cesare and – of course and especially – Mark Tavani. Mark, this book could not have become what it is without your insightful questions, on-point suggestions, and good-humored support. I *literally* cannot thank you enough.

Finally, thank you to Andrew, who asked to be mentioned first and last. He may have been joking, but he deserves it.